RICHES

Riches

Una-Mary Parker

HEADLINE

Published by arrangement with New American Library,
New York, New York, USA

First published in paperback in Great Britain in 1988
by HEADLINE BOOK PUBLISHING PLC

All characters in this publication are fictitious and any resemblance to real persons, living or dead, is purely coincidental.

British Library Cataloguing in Publication Data

Parker, Una-Mary
Riches.
I. Title
823'914[F] PR6066.A69/

ISBN 0 7472 3013 7

Typeset by Alacrity Phototypesetters,
Banwell Castle, Weston-super-Mare
Printed and bound in Great Britain by
Collins, Glasgow

HEADLINE BOOK PUBLISHING PLC
Headline House
79 Great Titchfield Street
London W1P 7FN

This is for

Baba and Buffy

with all my love

ACKNOWLEDGEMENT

I feel deep gratitude to these friends for their answers to my questions in the course of research, and for their encouragement throughout: Edward Duke, Dr Trevor Hudson, Howard Levene, James Denker, Francis Butler, Lady Camilla Hipwood, Joanna Drinkwater and especially Pat Loud.

1

Sunlight streamed through the yellow silk drapes, filling Tiffany's bedroom with a warm apricot glow. She opened her eyes languidly and was instantly aware of Hunt stirring beside her. Dark hair ruffled by sleep and a strong suntanned shoulder emerged from the sheets, as he burrowed his face into the downy softness of the pillows. He was all hers. For the moment anyway. Rolling closer to him she wrapped her arms around him as he sleepily nuzzled closer into her warmth. His hand slid up to her breasts and a wave of passion shot through her as his mouth urgently sought hers. With a voluptuous movement of her hips she leaned over him, her long golden hair falling about his face, her soft lips returning his kiss.

'Oh, Honey . . .' he moaned, as she stroked the insides of his thighs, and then silently and gently took him inside her. Flames licked through her loins . . . she was thrusting deeply now, driving both of them wild, surging towards the brink of ecstasy, as her hair swung like silk across his chest, and her breath caught in her throat. Faster. Hotter. Deeper. With a final plunge she brought them both to a shuddering climax and then he held her close, as she lay spent on top of him.

Hunt Kellerman. Her lover. Married man with two sons. A top film and TV director with a string of credits to his name and an Oscar nomination. Sometimes he could stay all night, sometimes he couldn't.

'Coffee, darling?'

'What's the time?' His voice sounded husky.

Tiffany glanced at her gold Cartier watch, a present from Hunt.

'Five past seven.'

He sprang up, all signs of sleep vanishing. 'Christ, I've got a meeting at eight to work out the shooting schedules! I'll grab a quick shower first.' Kissing her lightly he slid from the luxury of the enormous bed.

Everything about Tiffany Kalvin's apartment on Park Avenue was large and luxurious. On her eighteenth birthday her father had settled a more than generous sum of money on her to help her career get off the ground and, if necessary, provide a gilded parachute. When her younger sister, Morgan, reached the same age she had received an equal amount. Morgan had spent a lot of hers on clothes, furs and jewellery, but Tiffany had gone for this apartment. It was more than a real estate asset now. It spelled freedom and independence to her. At twenty-four she was already well known as a costume designer, and she'd proved to her family that *in spite* of her background, and substantial private income, she was capable of having a successful career. Five off-Broadway productions had been followed by two plays and a musical on Broadway – and of course the film, *Fast Traveller*, last year.

Stretching languorously like a cat, she lay a moment longer, savouring the moment, as Hunt sang lustily through the gentle roar of the shower. Then she rushed to the mirror, and seizing a brush did her hair until it floated, cloud-like, round her shoulders. Green eyes of a rare shade of jade, thickly fringed with dark lashes, looked intently back at her from the mirror. Slipping into her navy-blue satin robe, she just knew it was going to be a good day.

Tiffany had met Hunt when she was working on *Fast Traveller*. He was the director and she had been quite nervous when she first saw him. His reputation for being difficult had already reached her and she was sure he'd regard her as a rich amateur amusing herself until the time came for her to get married.

'I like these! They're very imaginative,' he'd said when he first saw her designs. His dark eyes had searched hers for a moment, and then he'd smiled, as if satisfied. By the time the film was rolling they were an Item. Hunt wasn't the first man in her life but he was definitely the best. Wife or no wife.

The coffee hiccupped gently in the percolator as she squeezed fresh orange juice. When she got back to the bedroom with the tray Hunt shot out of the bathroom, a towel slung round his hips.

'Coffee ready? Great.' He gulped down half a cup of the strong black liquid. 'Thanks, Tiff. God, have I got a crappy day coming up. You know I'm really worried about Bob Clarkson being cast in the part of the GI.' He struggled into his trousers and Tiffany looked at his muscular body, a wave of longing filling her loins again. 'If we'd only been able to get Bud Harvey as I wanted –' She wasn't listening. 'And I told that schmuck of a producer that if he really wanted that part to come over strong – Tiff, are you listening?'

She gave a little start. 'Of course, darling, you were saying . . .?'

'Oh, and I won't be able to make it tonight! There's a meeting with the composer – I'm not happy with the score *either* – and Joni's got some people coming over for dinner.' He put his keys and wallet in the pocket of his jacket.

Tiffany smiled wanly. Suddenly it wasn't going to be such a great day after all.

As soon as Hunt left, she showered, and as this was going to be a day of relentless running around, she dressed in a chic white cotton track suit and comfortable pumps, her standard uniform when working. This was when Tiffany Kalvin, society beauty with closets full of original models by Armani, Chloe and Calvin Klein, shed her rich, glamorous image and became the Working Woman. Brushing her hair back into a pony-tail she tied it with a white ribbon; then a touch of blusher on her cheeks, a dab of lip-gloss and she was ready.

Grabbing another cup of coffee, she made her way to the big room at the far end of her apartment she had converted into her studio. This was the nerve centre of her life, an oblong room with a high ceiling, polished floor and sparkling white walls. Under the window stood her work table, and running down one side was a counter under which was stored anything and everything from art materials to samples of fabric. A large mint-green sofa, two high, white stools with mint-green cushions, slanted drawing boards, an easel and a low lucite coffee table completed the furnishings. Scattered around were a profusion of jars holding paint brushes of every size, and books on design, architecture and fashion through the ages, which she used for research purposes. On the walls hung some of her designs, framed in dull aluminium, dating back to when she was still a student, to the most recent from *Fast Traveller*.

By nine o'clock her two assistants, Shirley Hartman and Maria Roth, would be arriving and from then on they would all be working flat out until late evening. But for the moment, this first blessed hour of the day, she could quietly go through her mail, make her calls, sort out her notes and generally psych herself up for the punishing schedule that lay ahead. It was only seven weeks to the opening of *Night Chill*, a strong drama set in the mid-'thirties, with a cast of ten and starring the biggest bitch on Broadway, Janine Bellamy. Tiffany had to design twenty-six separate costumes, plus all the accessories. The actors would be easy. Suits of the period with wide straight trousers with turn-ups, double-breasted jackets with large wide lapels and wing collars to go with their tuxedos. She had already picked out a length of Prince of Wales check tweed that would be perfect for the leading man in act one. It was the actresses' costumes that required more subtlety, catching the last willowy droopy look of the 'twenties, with soft cape sleeves and bias cut skirts, before the crisp squareness that was so popular in the 'forties emerged. Tiffany sucked the end of her pencil thoughtfully and started ticking off the things she'd already set to have made: shoes, with thickish high heels and little button straps over the instep; stockings with seams; fancy purses with brass clasps; wigs, short and neat, with a side parting and deep waves. Today they had to start buying the appropriate material for the gowns. Shirley would come with her to the Lower East Side, where cavernous fabric houses stocked thousands of bolts of cloth from all over the world, and Maria could be sent off in search of ivory and coral necklaces, drop jade earrings and rose quartz rings.

'Hi, Tiff!' Shirley came charging into the studio, beaming with enthusiasm.

Tiffany swung round on her stool and regarded her chief assistant with amused affection. 'Hi. You look happy! What's happened? All your Christmases come at once?'

'Wait until you see!' Small, dumpy and energetic, Shirley ferreted around in her big shoulder bag, cursing as she found hair brushes, spare shoes, an apple and three jotting pads. 'Ah!' A wide smile spread across her freckled features, as she triumphantly whipped out a sample of beige crêpe chiffon, delicately patterned with apple blossom. 'Act two, scene one? Isn't this exactly what you wanted for Janine Bellamy?'

'Shir-lee! You're a genius, where the hell did you find it?' Tiffany examined the fabric, placing it over a piece of cream silk so she could gauge the full effect. 'It's perfect.'

'Nussbaum's have it. I checked and they've got seven metres. I told them to put it all on hold.'

'Go get it today, we'll never find anything as good. Would they have any dark amethyst chiffon, d'you suppose? I need it for that evening dress in the final scene. You know, the one with solid diamanté shoulders, and all those soft frills running across the skirt at an angle.'

'I'll check it out.' Shirley made a note on one of her pads. Disorganized she might look but she was the most efficient assistant Tiffany had ever had.

A few minutes later Maria arrived and they started discussing exactly what fabrics were needed, and in what quantities. Tiffany looked at her watch. It was ten o'clock.

Time to get going.

Down on the Lower East Side of New York, Tiffany and Shirley walked up East Hudson Street until they came to Orchard Street. Here they started searching the fabric houses. It was Tiffany's perpetual fantasy that one day she might just walk in and find exactly what she was looking for, so that two hours later she could catch a cab home, having got everything she needed. Of course it never happened that way. No, they didn't have navy silk with small white spots, nor dove-grey chiffon. There was no chance of finding white piqué, cream shantung or blue crêpe satin. Hot and frustrated, she wondered if she'd have to get what *was* available, then have it dyed to the exact colour she wanted. And this was only the fabrics! What the hell was it going to be like finding the right buttons and braids and belt buckles? And people imagined her career was glamorous, she thought wryly. Here she was, when she might have been lunching at the Pierre, struggling through hot humid streets jammed with angry truck drivers snarling at each other, cab drivers honking furiously and people pushing and shoving.

'What time is it, Shirley?' she asked distractedly.

Shirley straightened her arm with a masculine gesture, before looking at her large watch. 'Nearly one-fifteen.'

Tiffany frowned. At four o'clock she had a meeting with the set designer to discuss further points arising out of his use of colour for the sets, and after that she had to get over to Dianne Giancana who was making up the costumes. 'Christ,' she mouthed quietly. So far they'd hardly found any fabrics that were even remotely right.

By the time she arrived at Dianne's workrooms Tiffany felt drained and vaguely desperate. It would take another week to find everything that was needed.

'Lemon tea, Tiff? You look as if you could use it.' Dianne was an efficient woman in her late thirties who somehow always managed to remain calm and cheerful. Her staff of thirty, all specialists in their own field, be it strict tailoring or fancy bead work, had been with her since she had gone into business on her own account twelve years ago, and Tiffany trusted her totally to interpret her design *and* deliver on time.

'Thanks, it's been one hell of a day! I've been in and out of every fabric house from Orchard Street to the garment district.'

'So what's new, honey!'

Tiffany lowered her aching bones onto the only available chair, half hidden by a forest of costumes hanging on rails.

'How long have we got?'

'Seven weeks' – Tiffany unzipped her portfolio – 'and twenty-six costumes in all. Shirley dropped off what fabric we've got earlier this afternoon, didn't she?'

Dianne nodded. 'We'll get started on those first. So, what are we doing this time?' She leaned forward to look at Tiffany's designs, her eyes sparkling. They worked as a wonderful team and she had great admiration for Tiffany. She was so utterly dedicated, so professional, and her attention to detail made Dianne's job that much easier. She groaned inwardly as she thought of some of the designers she worked for. Most of them hadn't even got a clue about cutting or draping.

'So we've got Janine Bellamy to contend with have we? God, I hate it when she comes for fittings, nothing's ever right.'

'I know, Dianne. She's a pain *everywhere*! These are the designs for her.' Tiffany held up some beautiful water-colour sketches, showing Janine as a tall, slim beauty in a series of soft chiffon dresses, embellished round the neck and shoulders with glittering stones.

'When she sees these she'll be flattered out of her fucking mind!' exclaimed Dianne in admiration. 'Let's hope she's as happy with the reflection in her mirror. You know what happened in her last production, don't you? She screamed and raged and refused to wear any of her costumes. In the end she had her own tacky dressmaker run up some little numbers for her. What will you do if that happens again, Tiff?'

'Tell her to go screw herself,' Tiffany replied pleasantly.

Morgan Kalvin's shimmering white and silver evening dress lay on the bed as she put the finishing touches to her make-up, deftly adding more eye shadow to emphasize the jade green of her eyes.

Two months in England at the height of the summer season did not diminish the thrill she still got from getting dressed to go somewhere! Tonight, it was another ball, this time at Sutton Place, the home of the late Paul Getty. Her long flaxen hair was piled elegantly on top of her head in a profusion of loose curls and waves, and on studying herself in the Regency mirror she realized she felt as excited as when she'd been a little girl, setting off for a children's party back home in New York.

Morgan *loved* parties.

Every day she thanked her lucky stars that her parents' friends, Rosalie and Glen Winwood, had invited her to spend the summer with them in their magnificent Cumberland Terrace house, with its white Corinthian columns and pilasters, that was designed by John Nash in 1821. Overlooking the velvety lawns of Regents Park, where vistas of trees and shrubs and flowerbeds made it seem like summer all the year round, it represented to Morgan the ultimate in town houses. The sweeping curved facade of the terrace, heavy with stucco ornamentation and delicate wrought iron railings along the front, made a perfect backdrop for her entry into High Society.

In fact she couldn't have had a more perfect launching pad.

Mentally she added up all the places she'd been: the private view at the Royal Academy of Arts, the Royal Enclosure at Ascot, centre court seats at Wimbledon to watch John McEnroe win the championship again, and parties every night. Cocktail parties on the terrace of the House of Lords, elegant candlelit dinners at Apsley House, where they dined off the Duke of Wellington's fabulous collection of gold plate; a ball at Hampton Court Palace and a garden party at Buckingham Palace, where she'd even been presented to one or two members of the royal family. Glen, being attached to the American Embassy, had, of course, an entrée everywhere, and he and Rosalie seemed to know everyone. Best of all, Morgan enjoyed visiting some of the magnificent stately homes whose owners could trace their ancestry back hundreds of years.

Slipping into her dress, specially designed for her by Karl Lagerfeld, she added a delicate diamond necklace and drop earrings. And a spray of Joy.

If she couldn't nab a rich titled English aristocrat, looking the way she did, then her name wasn't Morgan Kalvin.

Downstairs, guests were already drinking champagne in the Winwood drawing room, while in the street outside, a line of Rolls Royces and Bentleys waited to take everyone to the ball.

When Morgan made her entrance, everyone stopped talking and turned to stare. She'd perfected that entrance. Sweeping through the double doors, she paused leisurely, scanning the faces of the assembled company until she saw someone she wanted to talk to.

By the carved marble fireplace stood Geoffrey Dent, youngest Member of Parliament and the great white hope of the Conservative Party. He was talking to Captain Alastair Hutchinson, 15th/17th Hussars, looking magnificent in his uniform. He also happened to be wealthy and amusing. Next to them stood Miguel de Carvalhoso, wealthy Brazilian playboy, noted for his skill at polo, skiing and backgammon.

'You look marvellous, my love!'

'Darling, how are you?'

'My sweet angel . . .'

Morgan smiled her most ravishing smile and, offering her cheek to be kissed, returned their greetings with equal warmth.

None of them would do.

When they arrived at the ball she stood with Geoffrey Dent, sipping champagne and watching the crowded dance floor.

Suddenly she spotted what she was looking for. He was tall, elegant, and had the most attractive smile she'd ever seen. He was dancing close to a limpid girl in a Laura Ashley dress who had a single row of pearls round her flushed neck and wilting flowers in her hair.

Morgan turned away from Geoffrey and tapped Rosalie Winwood gently on the shoulder.

'Who are the couple over there?' she asked. 'The tall man and the girl in the flowered dress.'

'Well, my dear, I'm not sure. Wait while I put on my specs.' Rosalie fumbled with the gilt chain of her evening bag and finally extracted a pair of jewelled evening glasses. 'Ah! That's much better. Now let me see, where have they gone?'

'They're in front of the band.'

'Oh, that's Lady Elizabeth Greenly! Her mother is *such* a charming person – she's the Countess of FitzHammond you know. I think Elizabeth came out last year, though they don't call it that any more over here. I can't think why! I believe her mother told me she's learning to type.'

'But who is *he*?' cut in Morgan.

Rosalie shook her head vaguely. 'I've no idea, but they certainly seem to be having a good time, wouldn't you say?' She drifted off to see who else was at the party.

For a few minutes Morgan continued to listen to Geoffrey, pretending to be interested in the details of a debate he'd recently heard in the House of Commons. Then with a charming smile of dismissal she said firmly, 'Will you excuse me? I've just spotted an old friend I want to talk to.' She handed him her empty glass and walked to the bar at the far side of the room. Lady Elizabeth and the young man were standing by it, obviously enjoying a joke.

'Elizabeth! How lovely to see you.' Morgan went up to her with outstretched hands and kissed her lightly on the cheek. 'You're looking so pretty! How are you?'

Elizabeth's smile was polite and blank.

'We met at the Cholmondeleys',' said Morgan hurriedly. 'I'm sure it was there, or it could have been that weekend at the Montgomerys'? Heavens, it's been such a busy season, hasn't it? I'll soon forget where I met my own mother!' She laughed her delicious rippling laugh and even Elizabeth's expression warmed.

'Yes, of course! How are you? Er, do you know Harry Blairmore? And you are ...?' Elizabeth paused in her introductions.

Something computer-like clicked in Morgan's brain. She'd read about him in a feature in *Vogue* entitled 'Britain's Most Eligible Bachelors'. Harry to his friends, otherwise Henry, Marquess of Blairmore, son and heir of the Duke of Lomond.

He would do.

When Morgan got back to the Winwoods' house later that night, she crept into Glen's study as soon as everyone had gone to bed. Taking a heavy scarlet-bound volume entitled *Debrett's Peerage and Titles of Courtesy* down from the bookcase she riffled through the pages until she found the entry she was looking for.

> Lomond, 11th Duke of. Title created 1687. Edgar Robert. Born Aug. 15th 1921. Educated Eton and Christ Church, Oxford. Succeeded his Father, the 10th Duke, 1945. Married, 1956, Lavinia Mary, only daughter of General Sir Stuart Prentiss.
>
> *Son living*
>
> Henry Edgar, Marquess of Blairmore. Born March 3rd 1958. Educated Eton and Christ Church, Oxford.

Seat: Drumnadrochit Castle, Argyll.
Residence: 105, Belgrave Street, London, SW1.
Clubs: White's. Boodle's. Turf. Carlton.

Beside the entry was the magnificent family arms, two rampant lions supporting a shield bearing three fleurs-de-lis and a sunburst, and above it the crest: a wildcat rearing out of a duke's coronet, with its traditional border of eight strawberry leaves. The family motto below read 'Touch Not the Cat Without a Glove'.

There followed a long piece listing the hereditary posts held in Scotland by the dukes of Lomond and how the titles of Duke and Marquess had been granted nearly three hundred years before.

But Morgan had read enough.

It was all a long way from Park Avenue and Bonwit Teller, tea in the Rotunda Room at the Pierre and having money to spend on Lincoln Continentals and twin-engined Cessna Citation jets. This was *real* class, and she could tell the difference.

Harry Blairmore would most definitely do.

Ruth and Joe Kalvin were having their usual formal breakfast in their duplex at Park Avenue and 70th. Behind his copy of the *Wall Street Journal* Joe grunted occasionally while Ruth flipped through the mail, dividing it into precise separate batches: invitations, charity appeals, accounts and personal letters. She would deal with them later in the morning, when she was alone.

Joe read his paper for precisely another three minutes, finished his coffee, exclaiming, 'Ugh! It's gotten cold,' and then wandered absently out of the room with a casual, 'See you tonight, hon.' The door clicked. He was gone. It was the same every morning. By the evening he'd have made another fifty thousand dollars – or maybe half a million – it didn't really matter to Ruth any more.

With a ten-room duplex, plus staff quarters, a house on the ocean's edge at Southampton, a private jet and several cars, there wasn't much else she really wanted. At least nothing Joe or their three children Tiffany, Morgan or Zachary could give her. In her large dressing room hung clothes by Bill Blass, Saint Laurent, Oscar de la Renta, Princess Katalin zu Windisch-Graetz, Bob Mackie and Givenchy. The safe in the study was filled with jewel cases, brimming with priceless pieces by Harry Winston, Van Cleef and Arpels, Mikimoto, Gucci and Eric Bertrand. The large ring she always wore was a forty-carat diamond. What more did she need? Both homes were filled with French and English antique furniture and some very fine Cézannes, Courbets, Dégas and Gauguins. Ruth Kalvin was the woman who had everything, but felt she had nothing, and boredom and inner loneliness hung about her like a sick miasma. If only Joe would talk to her, she reflected. If only her children would let her share their lives – even a bit. But they all thought of her as a vapid fool, and that made her nervous. 'Don't bother telling Mom,' she could hear them say, 'she'll never understand.' And as the years had passed and they had become more and more remote from her, she felt an increasing sense of isolation.

To the outside world she was the beautiful Mrs Joe Kalvin, elegant New York society hostess, but to herself she was a grey insecure figure and she found it very uncomfortable. Rising slowly, she picked her mail off the table and wandered into the drawing room, hoping yet dreading the day would produce some little diversion that would break up the monotony of her life.

Zachary Kalvin lay on the moth-eaten sofa in – what was his name? Oh yeah, Mitch – in Mitch's place and regarded the stained ceiling cautiously. *At least it had stopped moving!* He groped for a vaguely remembered can of beer and took a swig. Instant nausea swept over him and a cold clamminess broke out all over his body. For a moment he thought he was going to throw up but the turmoil in his stomach subsided as quickly as it had begun. Never in his seventeen years had he felt so terrible. *But at least the ceiling wasn't spinning any more!*

Casting his mind back to the previous night, he remembered he'd gone to some hamburger joint, unable to face the boredom of having dinner with his parents again, and had started talking to some lanky kid who, after a few cans of beer, exclaimed, 'Hey, man, how about comin' back to my pad and smoke a stick? I've got some dynamite stuff that'll make you piss a rainbow.'

Later, much later, and after several more cans of beer, Mitch led him to a dingy room in a seedy tenement near Seventh Avenue and 28th. Scrabbling under some old copies of *Penthouse* Mitch triumphantly produced a tiny glass vial. Zachary remembered seeing vials like it in his mother's bedroom, samples of the latest perfume.

Mitch tore up a bit of aluminium foil and, cupping it slightly, poured a few drops of a dark, sticky, varnish-like substance onto it.

'This is boss stuff, man. Hold onto it will ya?' He placed it on Zachary's palm and with swift expertise rolled up a dollar bill, talking in excited jerky sentences, his whole body quivering with anticipation.

'Plenty more where this came from! I've got connections. Here you go! When I light up you inhale – you inhale real deep, now.' He struck a match and held it under the foil with shaking hands.

A little puff of smoke rose and Zachary inhaled.

Suddenly invisible hands tackled him from behind and more invisible hands punched him deeply in the stomach. Panic swept over him. He felt sick and woozy and sweat prickled his armpits.

Mitch was inhaling with exquisite pleasure. 'Beats a fuck any day! This is real, re–eal good. Didn't I tell ya it was good?' He looked up, his dark eyes glazed with pleasure. 'Want another drag?'

Zachary grabbed hold of the battered old table to stop himself from falling and tried to think clearly.

'Mmm – maybe later – it's – like, wow, man! I'm blissed out.' With bravado he flung himself on the stained sofa, wondering how long the strange sensation would last. He wasn't sure where he was and it struck him that if his parents ever found out about this there'd be hell to pay.

All through the night, which he thought was never going to end, he lay on the sofa, spinning along the surface of the sea, over waves, through waves, spinning... And the sky, full of fluffy little clouds, scurried overhead in a frantic attempt to keep up with him. Then the sky turned dark and the clouds turned to millions of stars racing around. He was being propelled at an uncontrollable speed on a journey that was never going to end and he wanted desperately to wake up. But he *was* awake and still he couldn't stop. No matter how hard he thought, 'I'm going to get off this trip and stop somewhere that's quiet and peaceful,' the spinning went on and on.

He looked round the filthy room but Mitch was gone. Gingerly he sat up, running his fingers through his hair, and wondered when he'd feel normal, really normal again. And his parents! God, he'd have some explaining to do. If he went home now there was just a chance they might still be asleep. His father didn't usually get up until seven. He glanced at his watch. It was gone! Shit, it had been a birthday present.

Struggling into his jacket he let himself out of the sordid room and started to walk uptown.

His wallet was missing too.

'This script is garbage!' Hunt flung it down and glared at Flix. 'How on earth can you expect lines like this, and this, and that one there' – he jabbed furiously with his finger – 'to be believable? Christ Almighty! We've got to have a rewrite.' He squashed out his cigarette and immediately reached for another.

Flix Greenberg regarded him impassively. Speaking slowly and patiently, as if addressing a petulant child, he said, 'We're running out of time, Hunt. We've *got* to start shooting in ten days! There's no way we can delay. We're already over budget and if there are any more delays we'll be screwing up Bob Clarkson's schedule. Remember he starts that TV series in seven weeks. Don't sweat it, Hunt, it'll fly as is.' Flix's tone was soothing.

'The hell it will!' Hunt spat.

'There's nothing much wrong with this script that a little careful direction can't handle, and Bob and Jane are big box-office,' said Flix evenly.

'Don't give me that crap!' Hunt's eyes blazed with anger. 'The trouble with you is you just don't see what you don't *want* to see!' He reached over and buzzed his intercom. 'Cal? Get me Milton Schwartz at once, will you? Yup, the guy that wrote the script for *Soul Kids*. Tell him to get his ass over here pronto. I've got a major clean-up job on a script for him to do.'

Flix's jawline hardened and he narrowed his eyes. 'You've no right to go over my head. You seem to forget I *am* the producer.'

Hunt jumped to his feet and made for the door of his office. 'Then you'd better hire yourself another director,' he yelled as the door slammed behind him.

The adrenalin was still pounding round his body as he lay in bed that night, desperate for sleep but unable to stop his mind going over the day's events. He'd won his fight over the wooden script. Flix had eventually agreed to let Milton get to work on it, even though he had been furious. There was still the problem of the theme music for the film. Hunt knew exactly what he wanted, something that conjured up a feeling of patriotism with occasional hints of pathos. A stirring score to go with the shots of the US Army fighting their way across Europe against the Germans. And what had he got? A cross between a funeral dirge and a jingle for a toothpaste commercial. When at last he had got home Joni was drinking vodka with a living room full of LA deadbeats.

'Darling, *there* you are!' She lurched forward, staggering on her high heels and flinging herself at his chest. She miscalculated the distance and Hunt had to catch her before she fell.

'Din-dins is ready, and listen, honey' – she dropped her voice – 'where have you been all day?'

When Hunt didn't reply she gestured in the direction of a jeans-clad young man, shirt open to the fourth button, showing lots of gold chains nestling in matted black chest hair. He was sitting on the sofa casually smoking a joint. 'This is Mose! And what d'ya know? Mose is going to write a one-woman show for me, aren't you, Mose?' Through a long fringe of bushy hair, Mose nodded.

'And listen, honey! Listen! Karen, here, is going to do my costumes, and we'll get in all the critics! I'm gonna be somebody!' Joni hung on to the lapels of Hunt's jacket for support. Then her expression changed as she brought her face close to his.

'So you can stuff your fucking films!' Her voice was raspy. 'Because I'm going to make it on Broadway.'

Life had been different for Joni Kellerman seven years ago. Born in the God-fearing town of Wahoo, Nebraska, the fourth daughter of a builder, she'd run off to Hollywood at the age of fifteen and changed her name from Coote to André – with an accent. No more small-town America for her with their sanctimonious 'We've got a nice little town here and we're going to keep it that way.' It was the razzle and danger of high living that Joni wanted, and if living high meant being paid for getting screwed she wasn't complaining. There were even a few walk-on parts in low-budget movies to be had, and promises of something better if she pleased the director. Joni was convinced her well-stacked figure and strawberry blonde hair would get her the break she needed. One day she'd be recognized as the new Monroe, and *that* would stop them calling her dirty names back in Wahoo. Self-confidence was her middle name. So what the hell if she fucked her way to the top? Plenty of others had got there that way. Hunt Kellerman wasn't exactly a top director when she met him at a promotional party she'd got herself asked to in Bel Air, but he might go places one day and meanwhile he was the sexiest thing she'd ever seen. So pretty little Joni, with her bobbing strawberry blonde curls, had slithered her way into his apartment, and six months later, when she'd discovered she was pregnant, she got him to marry her. Seven years ago. Hunt's career had gone up and up while hers had gone in exactly the opposite direction. The birth of Gus, and two years later Matt, hadn't helped to keep the tits up or the tummy flat, and little lines were forming round her eyes. Why the hell couldn't Hunt give her a part in one of his lousy movies? It was only vodka, straight on the rocks, that gave her any self-confidence these days. And where the fuck had Hunt been last night? As if she didn't know.

Joni slept beside him now, snoring softly. Her body lay slack and motionless. She smelled of a mixture of sweat and liquor. Hunt rolled away, thinking of Tiffany. So cool and clean and sweet. He remembered the taste of her mouth, the hardness of her pink nipples. The warmth of her thighs. He was growing hard.

Whatever happened he must see her again tomorrow. How had he ever got himself into this mess?

2

'Tiffany? Hi! It's Morgan!'

'Morgan! Do you know what time it is?'

'Oh, it's about ten o'clock, I think.'

'Fool! Ten o'clock your time. It's five in the morning here. What the hell's the matter?' Tiffany switched on her bedside light as she plumped up her pillows, now thoroughly awake.

'I forgot! Listen Tiff, I met the most fabulous man last week and I think I'll stay on here a bit longer.'

'What about Rosalie and Glen? Won't they mind?'

'Of course not. Wait till I tell you about him! He's twenty-six, tall, very attractive, and the son and heir of the Duke of Lomond! What do you think of that?' There was a note of triumph in her voice.

A long silence ensued broken only by a faint crackle on the transatlantic line.

'Tiff... are you there?'

'Yes.'

'Good. I thought for a moment we'd been cut off. As I was saying, he's really fantastic and his family have this fifteenth-century castle in Scotland as well as a large house in Belgravia – '

'What about Greg Jackson?'

'What *about* him?' Morgan sounded cross. 'For God's sake, Tiff, I know Greg is sweet and all that but you don't honestly expect me to come back to New York and actually marry him, do you?'

'I thought you and Greg had an understanding that when you got back from this trip you'd announce your engagement? At least that is what Greg thinks.'

Morgan cut in impatiently. 'But I hadn't been to England

then, at least not a trip like this. You can't imagine how wonderful life is here and how I really want to stay.'

'Forever?' Tiffany asked in a small voice.

'Well, I'm not sure. Probably. It will depend on how things go with Harry.'

'Who?'

'Harry Blairmore. I just told you! He's the Marquess of Blairmore and his father is – '

'Yes, you told me.'

'Tiff, what's the matter? I'm just getting ready for a gorgeous lunch party at the Westcliffs' and I thought it would be nice to ring and tell you all my news. Aren't you interested?' Morgan sounded like a rejected little girl.

Tiffany felt herself relenting. Ever since they'd been small it was Tiffany, although only two years older, who had mothered Morgan and made allowances for her.

'Yes,' she replied. 'I'm thrilled to hear from you, darling, and I'm really glad you're having such a good time, I really am. But I don't want you to end up by getting hurt and I am worried about this business with Greg. He's terribly in love with you, you know. I saw him last week and he kept asking when you were going to get back. He'll be heartbroken if you go off with someone else after all this time.'

'But I've changed! When I first knew Greg I was sixteen and a virgin, for God's sake! I want more than he can ever give me, I mean to be *somebody* some day . . . perhaps with Harry, perhaps with someone else. Don't you see? If I were to get married to Harry I'd be a duchess one day! With a castle, being with all the right people, being a society hostess maybe even to the royal family.'

'You've been reading too many Barbara Cartland novels, darling,' laughed Tiffany. 'You'll be talking about coronets next, and attending the opening of Parliament in your crimson and ermine robes!'

'*Exactly!*' Morgan exclaimed with total seriousness. 'You see what I mean! How could I bear to miss a chance like this? I could never settle for Greg now and life in Stockbridge with a bunch of kids and no proper servants.'

'What do you mean by "proper servants"?'

'Well, proper servants! Butlers and footmen and things. Why Mom and Daddy's lot look like a bunch of unskilled refugees compared to people's servants here. Anyway I'd better go, it's getting late.'

'Or early if you're here!' Tiffany could see the first bleak light of dawn seeping through her curtains. 'Take care of yourself, Morgan.'

'I will. I'll write soon – and tell Mom if you see her that I'm staying on for a while.'

'Okay, I will.' Tiffany hung up with an extraordinary feeling of emptiness inside her. She'd miss Morgan very much if she stayed in England permanently. They had different interests, different friends even, and their priorities in life were different. But they looked so alike they could almost be taken for twins, and like twins they shared a great feeling of empathy. Her thoughts turned to Greg. He'd been nineteen when he'd met Morgan at a beach party in the Hamptons. She'd been all long slim limbs, blonde hair that the wind whipped round her exquisite face and large green eyes that twinkled with fun. For Greg it had been love at first sight. Tiffany remembered him looking from Morgan to her and saying, 'Incredible! You sisters sure look a lot alike!' But it had been Morgan he trailed after all the time, passing her the sun oil and fetching her dry towels. They'd been inseparable all that summer and Morgan obviously enjoyed her new-found power over the opposite sex. For the following six years Greg had looked upon her as his girl. He wrote to her every week when he was away at college, saved his allowance to buy her presents, and made a point of finding a job in New York so that he could be near her. He would really have preferred to have stayed near his family in Stockbridge, but his heart was set on marrying her, and Morgan never gave him any cause to doubt that she felt the same. That was like Morgan, reflected Tiffany. She didn't necessarily mean to mislead people, but she did like to be popular, and she'd figured out as a tiny child that the best way to be liked was to agree with everything everyone said.

As she was dropping off to sleep again it suddenly occurred to Tiffany that Morgan hadn't once asked her how she was.

A tepid breeze, bringing with it a wave of refreshingly cool air, lifted Tiffany's hair, which had been sticking to her neck, as she rounded the corner of Park Avenue on her way to visit her parents. Her blue pleated skirt echoed the movement and she paused for a moment to enjoy a respite from the unbearable humidity of the day. New York was shimmering under the blasting heat of a mid-June sun. The pavements were sticky and the grass in Central Park was burnt up. Fumes and gritty dust coalesced in the heavy air and people plunged into shops and stores to catch the instant relief of air conditioning.

For Tiffany it had been a hellish day rummaging through the countless fabric houses in the garment districts. No one, it seemed, had embossed gilt buttons or shot-silk of the exact colour she needed. Stiff shirt fronts were out of stock, and wide black velvet ribbon unobtainable. The costumes for *Night Chill* were becoming a nightmare. To make matters worse, Janine Bellamy, who was playing the lead, was complaining that the costumes didn't become her, and demanding a whole new set of designs. With five weeks to go!

Entering the Kalvins' apartment the temperature, by contrast, was freezing. Goose pimples sprang out on her bare arms and she shivered. What was it about the place that made it so cold? The impersonal grandeur of the decor? The aloofness of her mother? She strode past the Louis XIV table in the hall, on which stood an imposing arrangement of white lilies, past the two Nubian statues on pedestals and went into the blue and white living room. The décor was not to her taste. Ruth's style was a mixture of French and Italian combined with early English and Oriental, ideas culled from her numerous trips abroad. The juxtaposition of rococo mirrors, Venetian chandeliers hung with fruit and flowers in lilac and clear crystal, a Chinese lacquered cabinet where the drinks were kept and a marble Adam fireplace jarred deeply on Tiffany's sense of design, mixed as it was with gilt console tables, Portuguese rugs, Hepplewhite chairs and Victorian gilt candlesticks on tiny Louis XIV tables.

'Hi, Mom! How are you?' Tiffany kissed her mother briefly on the cheek. As always, no matter what time of day or night, Ruth looked every inch the chic New York socialite in a pale yellow linen dress, not a wisp of her fading blonde hair out of place.

'Tiffany, how nice to see you.' She bent her head and went on writing.

Tiffany sank onto the pale-blue sofa. 'How's everything?'

'Your father will be back soon. Would you like a drink?'

Ruth carefully licked an envelope and pressed it down with a fastidious gesture. 'It's so warm today.'

'Thanks. I'd love some iced tea. What are you doing?'

'We're giving a little cocktail party next month, just a few friends and some business contacts of your father's, nothing much.' Her voice trailed off and she gazed vacantly out of the window.

There was silence, then Tiffany spoke.

'I've got a lot of work at the moment. *Night Chill* is driving me mad. I'll be so glad when it's over.'

There was a pause during which Ruth gazed briefly at her and then resumed addressing envelopes.

'Really?' Her tone was polite.

'Isn't that a lot of invitations for a "small" party?'

Ruth shrugged. 'There are so many people your father wants to ask . . .'

'I suppose so.' Tiffany knew she would never manage

small talk with her mother. At that moment Zachary slouched into the room.

'Hi, Sis!' His hands were in his pockets. He looked scruffy and his hair was a mess.

'Hi, Zachary.' Tiffany eyed his dirty jeans and stained sweat-shirt with surprise. Like all of them he'd been brought up to look impeccable at all times, even in casual clothes. She watched as he flopped into a chair and started idly riffling through the pages of a magazine. 'So what gives?' she asked.

'Nothing much.'

'How's school going? History still holding its fascination for you?' she persisted.

'It's okay,' he mumbled.

'I haven't seen you for ages. What have you been doing with yourself?'

Zachary didn't answer. Her mother licked another envelope and added it carefully to the pile.

'For God's sake! What's the matter with everyone round here?' Tiffany exploded. 'I get more conversation from the animals in the zoo!'

At that moment the Javanese servant appeared.

Ruth spoke. 'Iced tea for Miss Tiffany, and I'll have a spritzer.'

'I could use a coke,' added Zachary without looking up.

The servant moved silently from the cool elegance of the room. As if disturbed from a deep reverie, Ruth suddenly turned to Zachary, her eyes snapping wide open.

'Do you *have* to go around looking like that?'

Here we go, thought Tiffany. It will only take Daddy to arrive back from the office for it to be a classic picture of happy family life.

'Have you done *any* work today, Zachary?' Ruth's voice was rising to an angry whine. 'You were told to study during your vacation. Exams are coming up soon and your father will be furious if you don't do well.'

Zachary rose abruptly. 'I'm going out.' His tone was surly.

'You're *always* going out! You sleep until noon every day and then you go off, goodness only knows where!' For the first time since Tiffany had arrived her mother actually looked animated. Perhaps she needed to have a good row with someone, and Joe wasn't the sort of person you could have a good row with. He just walked out of the room while you sat there, filled with a volley of words there was no longer any point in expressing.

'And another thing!' Ruth was really warming to the subject. 'Your room is a boar's nest! I feel ashamed to let the servants see it in the mornings. You never hang up *anything* and the place is cluttered with books and magazines, and goodness only knows what else.'

'Leave me alone, for Christ's sake!' His jade-green eyes, so exactly the colour of his sister's and a younger stronger version of his mother's, blazed with fury. Then he turned and without a backward glance loped from the room.

'Well ... *really*!' Ruth looked after him for a moment, then picked up her gold pen and resumed her writing.

'It's his age,' remarked Tiffany, feeling she had to make some explanation. Secretly she sympathized with Zachary. Life at home had never been much fun. Ruth had spent most of her time straining to keep up with the position and money Joe had thrust on her over the years, and at times, Tiffany reflected, she seemed harassed and drawn. Preoccupied even. Most of the time she'd ignored her children's presence, and then suddenly, like just now, she would snap into life and give them a tough time. The worst part was that it was so unexpected when it happened. Joe had always been tough on them, pushing them to work harder, to achieve more, to be winners, but not their mother. There was no room in Joe's life for losers. He despised failure.

At that moment Joe entered the living room, hot looking, and frowning.

'What's the matter with that boy?' he thundered. 'He nearly knocked me down, tearing out past me like that! You should see to it that he's properly dressed, Ruth! I can't have a son of mine running around town looking like some damned drop-out.'

'But it's awfully hot, Daddy.'

Joe spun round. 'Tiffany! I never saw you there! How's my girl?' He came forward and pecked her on the cheek. 'My, you're sure looking pretty!' He turned back to his wife. 'If *I* can wear a collar and tie and a jacket in this heat, so can he! I've no use for people who slop around. That boy needs taking in hand.'

The servant came in with the drinks on a silver tray.

'Bring me rye on the rocks,' Joe said curtly. 'Are you staying for dinner, Tiffany?' It was more of a challenge than an invitation.

'I'm sorry, Daddy, I can't. Hunt is coming round.' She met his eyes steadily as she sipped her tea. The temperature in the room suddenly fell to below freezing point. Joe pursed his small mouth and regarded her with silent disapproval. Tiffany didn't expect to win a prize for guessing what was going through their minds. *Why can't Tiffany find a nice rich single man to go around with? Why is she stuck on this no-good wacko film director who has a wife and two kids. After all we've done for her why can't she find someone suitable? Suitable. Suitable.*

'I guess I ought to be getting back,' she said lamely. 'I just dropped in to tell you that Morgan rang me at five o'clock this morning.'

'Five this morning?' exclaimed Joe. 'When will that girl remember the time difference?' There was a note of jealousy in his voice. Why didn't Morgan ever ring them?

'She just wanted to tell us that she'll probably be staying in England a bit longer. She's having a ball, I guess, and the Winwoods are being really good to her.'

Joe strutted a few steps across to the marble fireplace and

took a cigar out of a fine wooden cigar box. 'Having a good time, is she? Hum. Is she all right for clothes and things? I hope she's made the right contacts, like dukes and earls and barons with country estates.' He sounded almost wistful. He missed Morgan. She was the only one who had inherited his social ambitions.

'She seemed fine, Daddy, and sent you and Mom all her love,' said Tiffany. Well, it was *almost* true. If Morgan had stopped thinking about herself for a moment she would have remembered to send her love. 'I think she's very happy and meeting lots of interesting people.' Wild horses weren't going to drag from her all the details of Morgan's conversation. For the moment the less they knew the better. If they heard there was a chance that Morgan might wind up a duchess, Joe would be on the next flight, intent on helping his daughter reel in her catch, and in doing so would blow the whole romance to smithereens. Apart from that, knowing Morgan, she'd probably have changed her mind about everything by this time next week.

Zachary pounded down Eighth Avenue, his legs covering the dirty sidewalk with long strides, running shoes kicking aside any garbage that got in his way. With any luck at all he would run into Smokey, who had promised she'd be in Dino's Bar around seven. Last night she'd been too busy to talk much to him but, as she worked the gum energetically round her mouth, she'd agreed to meet him tomorrow at seven. Then they could go round the corner to her place, if he felt like it. *If he felt like it?*

When he'd first set eyes on Smokey O'Mally, burning desire had filled him. Even her cheap perfume was a turn-on. And those scarlet lips – those wide, soft, heavily painted lips ... Her tousled hair, black at the roots and a washed-out shade of wet sand at the tips, excited him deeply. Through her pink crêpe dress, stained round the neck with make-up, her nipples stuck out invitingly.

Zachary had never met a woman like her before. A stirring in his loins made him quicken his pace. Tonight he was going to get laid. He'd cashed two hundred dollars that morning – most of his allowance for the month – because he wasn't sure how much it was going to cost. But he knew one thing for sure! It was going to be worth every penny.

Dino's was packed. A wild mixture of exotic-looking people were jostling each other, drinking and smoking. All were young. All had one search in common. The heat of it was written in the way their eyes searched hungrily and the languorous licking of their lips. Zachary searched round anxiously. No sign of her. He ordered a coke and kept watching the entrance, straining for a glimpse of those red lips and hard nipples. If she were to go down on him . . . Oh Jesus! He was getting another erection.

Suddenly she was there, and she hadn't noticed him! Her street-wise brown eyes glanced round the room, sweeping over each man from head to toe and lingering on his crotch.

'Hi!' Zachary presented himself before her, his smile wobbling and nervous.

'Oh . . .!' She seemed at a loss for a moment. 'Hi.'

'Remember?' A desperate sweat broke out all over him. Supposing she'd forgotten their date? 'We, er, we met here last night. You said, er, that is . . . we arranged to . . .' He flushed a deep red.

Smokey's tone was casual. 'Oh yeah. Get me a drink will ya, hot stuff?'

Zachary felt like melting with relief. He'd scored! She *had* remembered.

'Sure thing. What would you like?' He felt his confidence flowing back.

The drink had only been in her hands a minute when he blurted out, 'Can we go, er, to your place, I mean?' The straining in his trousers was becoming exquisitely agonizing.

'What's the hurry? Your first time?'

His blush deepened. 'Course not! I'm cool. I'd just like to get to know you better.'

Smokey drank thoughtfully. 'Got a smoke?'

'Er, I don't smoke.' Her painted eyebrows shot up. 'But I'll get you some.' Fumbling with his small change Zachary headed for the cigarette machine.

In a daze he found himself walking down the street beside this amazing woman, who exuded raw sex from every pore. Men loitering in groups on the sidewalk gave her the once-over as she teetered by on high heels, her hips swaying as she walked. A tall black man, elegant and confident in his beige cotton suit and Panama hat, murmured sexily, 'Hi, Smokey! How's it goin', girl?' Zachary suddenly felt very proud. In a short time he'd be joining the ranks of real men.

She led him up a narrow flight of sagging stairs, her rounded bottom encased in pink crêpe undulating a few inches in front of him.

'In here.' She led the way into a small square room dominated by a lumpy bed, on which had been flung a stained purple satin cover. 'Put the money on the table.'

Zachary felt suddenly uncomfortable. 'How much?' he asked shyly.

'Like I said' – she flashed him a suspicious glance – 'fifty bucks. You got it or ain't ya?'

'Sure.' He laid the crisp notes on a little table covered with a grimy lace cloth. Trying to look confident he slipped off his sweat-shirt and started unzipping his jeans. It surprised him how quickly she had whipped off her dress and G-string and was now standing naked before him except for her shoes Her body was really something. All curves, her full breasts firm, her nipples large and dark. Her stomach was flat and smooth and her thighs shapely.

'OK?' She reached out long painted nails and ran them across his chest. He tried to grab her and kiss that marvellous mouth but she turned her head away and indicated the bed. His erection was so hard and hot he felt his prick was going to explode. Grabbing her clumsily, he thrust himself forward.

In a flash it was all over. He was lying on top of her and he'd never felt such a deep sense of disappointment in his life.

'Is that it?' he heard himself say. He felt as cheated as if someone had given him an empty gift-wrapped box.

Smokey pushed him off crossly. 'What did ya expect? The whole Kama Sutra in five minutes?' Disgruntled she got off the bed and stepped back into her G-string.

Sulkily Zachary started to reach for his clothes. He felt the roll of bills in his pocket. Taking them out he said slowly, 'Can we do it again?'

Like gimlets, Smokey's eyes bore into the dollar bills, her mind working quickly. 'I have another trick in a few minutes. Tell ya what, for another eighty bucks you can have another fuck and I'll throw in a smoke as well.'

It was better the second time. He didn't come so quickly and he hoped he was satisfying her. Afterwards she climbed onto a rickety chair and ran her hand along the top of a cupboard until she located a small plastic bag.

'Got it! Papers an' all!' she said triumphantly. Sitting on the bed beside him she started to roll a joint. 'Where ya live, baby?'

'Park Avenue,' replied Zachary as he watched her, fascinated.

Her eyes widened and fixed themselves on him.

'No shit? Is that right? What are you, some kind of millionaire or somethin'?' Her tone was joking.

'I suppose my father is. He's president of Quadrant Inc.'

She licked the Rizla paper and reached for a box of matches, watching him all the time. 'No bull!' This nerd was probably loaded!

'Then how come you spend your time hangin' round Dino's? Isn't Doubles more your scene?' Her manner was suddenly belligerent. 'Get a kick out of slumming?'

'It's boring at home,' Zachary explained simply. 'Especially during vacations. It's hopping down here. Things really move.' He took the joint from her and dragged deeply. Immediately his toes started to tingle and his head buzzed pleasantly.

'Oh, so you get bored at home all day?' Smokey mimicked his tone. 'Sitting ass deep in caviar I bet. Here, gimme a toke.'

Zachary leaned back against the pillows as a feeling of well-being crept over him.

'I suppose it could be worse. I get a small allowance now but next year Dad will settle some big bucks on me like he did on my sisters, then I'll be able to do what I want.'

'Now you're talkin', honey!' she crooned. 'Gee, I've never been with a real blue-blood before.' Eyeing the eighty dollars on the table, she suddenly snatched it up and stuffed it into her large pink plastic purse, where she'd already stowed his first fifty. 'When you comin' to see Smokey again? You and me can ring some beautiful bells together.'

'We can?' He sat bolt upright, swaying slightly. Maybe it hadn't been so bad after all. Maybe when he got to know her better it would be the way he'd always imagined. He gazed groggily into her button-bright eyes. 'I can't come tomorrow. Well, not until after eleven. My parents are giving a dinner party and I have to be there.'

Smokey considered this for a moment, then smiled.

'Okay. I'll be at Dino's around eleven. Hey! What's your name?' She scrabbled deeply into her purse again, pulling out lipstick-smeared tissues, a dirty comb and an assortment of cosmetics until with triumph she produced a dog-eared black address book. Laboriously she took down Zachary's name and number, which he gave her with some reluctance. When she had finished writing she closed the book carefully and placed it in an old chocolate box with a picture of a fluffy kitten on the lid.

'Gotta go now . . .' She made for the door, straightening

her dress as she went and running her nails through her hair. Zachary followed, his eyes still drinking in her body.

Outside the air was still and languorous, New York holding its breath for a moment, gathering strength before the non-stop activity of the long night began.

'See ya!' she called over her shoulder, and was gone. Her cheap perfume lingered on the air a moment longer.

Zachary felt for his remaining sixty dollars and wondered what Mitch was doing this evening.

It was past seven when Tiffany got back to her own apartment. Hunt was due at nine. She had time for a shower and rest, while Gloria, her housekeeper, cooked dinner. Thank God for Gloria! Visiting her parents always exhausted her. It was no wonder, she reflected, as she undressed in her beautifully cool bedroom, that when Morgan was at home she actually spent all her time meeting friends and shopping. The atmosphere was claustrophobic, what with Mom tense and strained and remote, as if she knew she could never regain control of the circumstances that whirled around her, and their father terse and demanding, interested only in making money and seeing that his children used it to better themselves in everything. Tiffany sighed. It wouldn't be the same if Morgan stayed permanently in England. She would have no one to giggle with. No one to gossip with. No one to lighten her mood when she was down, or to make her laugh, especially at herself. Greg had nicknamed Morgan 'Glow' when he'd first known her. The name suited her perfectly. She radiated light and vibrancy. Tiffany knew only too well that when Morgan walked into a room the party began.

Rested and refreshed, Tiffany slipped into a pure silk trouser suit, in a shade of green that exactly matched her eyes. Round her neck she hung some simple gold chains, including one that had a shamrock carved in jade. Delicious smells of *boeuf en croute* drifted from the kitchen, and she knew that by now Gloria would have set the table in the intimate alcove of her living room with crisp blue linen, silver and crystal. There would be tall blue candles burning in Georgian silver candlesticks and flowers in the silver rose bowl. In a moment Hunt would arrive and another glorious evening would stretch ahead of them. Tiffany stretched her arms above her head in a gesture of happiness, and let her mind slide into her favourite fantasy. Of Hunt coming home every evening to a romantic dinner with superb food and wine, while they laughed and talked, comparing notes on their work that day, of sitting on the sofa afterwards drinking brandy while they listened to Mahler, their arms around each other. Or planning their vacations together, and what they would do for Thanksgiving and Christmas, or one day, maybe, how many children they would have. Of ending every night in bed together, warm, secure, loving.

The phone rang, startling her from her reverie.

'Hullo?'

'Have you got that mother-fucking son-of-a-bitch with you?' screamed a drunken woman's voice.

Tiffany slammed down the receiver, icy with shock.

So Joni knew!

The band of the Royal Scots Guards paraded in perfect formation as they marched across the manicured polo grounds of the Guards Club at Smith's Lawn, Windsor, moving in perfect precision as they played 'Land of Hope and Glory'. The strains reached the length and breadth of this, the most exclusive polo grounds in Britain, giving a festive air to the atmosphere. On the far side of the grounds, which were set in the lush greenery of Windsor Great Park, the public stands were filling up and in the general car park families were picnicking on the grass. On the near side, exclusive to the élite, the Royal Pavilion stood like a small, white, open-fronted house with a balcony and veranda, banked by immaculate tubs of red geraniums and gentian-blue hydrangeas. Rows of chairs were arranged along the front for the Queen and the Princess of Wales, who would be arriving in a few minutes with their entourage, having lunched at the nearby castle first. Today the matches were being played for the Coronation Cup and the Silver Jubilee Cartier Award and Prince Charles was playing. Later the Queen would be presenting the trophies. Beside the Royal Pavilion the grandstand was packed with members and their families, including film stars, stalwarts of the English nobility, jet-setters, pop stars, the nouveau riche and the nouveau pauvre.

Suddenly a last-minute flutter of activity from the flag-decorated marquees at one end of the grounds signalled the end of luncheon for the special Cartier guests, and they came hurrying across the velvety grass to take their seats.

'We'll have to hurry! The first chukka will be starting in a minute,' cried Harry, as he and Morgan emerged from under the gold canopy over the entrance to the Cartier marquee. He gripped her elbow and propelled her through the crowds. Morgan was aware that she and Harry were attracting a lot of interest. Their picture had already been taken by magazine and newspaper photographers and people were turning their heads as they passed. She could hear a rumble – 'Who is *she* . . .?' and a few audible gasps as the impact of her beauty struck them. She smiled, pleased. She knew she looked good in her perfectly cut white linen suit with dark-blue accessories, her hair swept loosely back under her straw hat.

Richard Young of the *Daily Express* was clicking away now as they took their seats. Tomorrow's newspaper would no doubt carry a story speculating on a romance between the American heiress and the Duke of Lomond's son and heir.

The play was fast and furious as the English team, Les Diables Bleus, in white and dark-blue, with the Prince of Wales among them, challenged Spain. Cheers went up as the captain, John Horswell, thwacked the wooden ball with a brilliant stroke towards Spain's goal, and again as Pedro Domecq galloped up beside him and diverted the ball with a hard shot. After seven minutes' exciting play the first chukka ended. Morgan squeezed Harry's hand. It was the most wonderful display of manhood and horseflesh she had ever seen. He returned her squeeze then gently withdrew his hand. She glanced at his profile. It must be true what they said about Englishmen. They were never demonstrative in public. A peck on the cheek, maybe. A hand on the elbow – yes. But nothing more.

I wonder what he's like in bed, she thought.

The chukka ended. 'Time to tread in the divots,' Harry announced cheerfully, jumping to his feet, as the players galloped off to change their ponies.

'The what?'

'Tread in the divots.' He pointed to the ground, now swarming with people from both the public stands and the members' stand stamping their feet on the grass, to flatten the clods of earth kicked up by the ponies' hoofs.

'In these?' A horrified look crossed Morgan's face as she raised an elegant leg, exposing her high-heeled navy-blue shoes. They'd cost her two hundred pounds at Charles Jourdan the previous day and she was damned if she was going to ruin them.

'Oh! Well, perhaps not.' Harry sat down again, deflated, and watched, almost with childish envy, the crowds cheerfully stamping away.

'Perhaps we could just stroll about,' conceded Morgan reluctantly.

Tea in the marquee was less formal than luncheon. The ladies no longer worried so much about creasing their clothes and some of the younger men had even taken off their jackets, but of course not their ties.

'Oh, there are Ma and Pa ... at the table in the corner. Let's go and see them!' Harry exclaimed as he manoeuvred Morgan in their direction. She tried to guess who they were among the ten people seated at the round table. The pretty plump lady in the flowered dress and pearls? The angular man with the black eyebrows that went in a straight line above hooded eyes? Or the jolly-looking couple who were passing the cucumber sandwiches?

Harry stopped at a thin stiff woman in a grey dress with grey hair and a grey face, stooped to kiss her cheek and then turned to shake hands with a tall man of military bearing whose thick white moustache and laughing eyes Morgan found very reassuring.

'Let me introduce . . .' Harry waved his hand in Morgan's direction.

Eyes cold and colourless, as implacable as steel, turned to Morgan and a mouth that looked like a sliced lemon closed tightly. The Duchess of Lomond gave Morgan a dismissive nod and turned away, addressing a remark to the man sitting next to her.

'How d'you do, my dear?' The Duke was on his feet, a great gentle towering man, pumping her hand warmly. 'Very nice to meet you, m'dear! I'm afraid we're all full up here – ' he glanced round the crowded table '– but get yourselves some tea. Jolly good scones with clotted cream, if you're quick! Having a good day, m'boy?' He clapped Harry on the shoulder as if he were a much-loved dog.

'Fine, Pa. Jolly exciting match, eh? Pity Spain won five goals to our four though.'

Harry and his father chatted amicably while Morgan covertly watched the duchess.

There wasn't one thing she liked about her, from the soles of her low-heeled grey shoes and thick stockings to the tortured bun at the back of her head. Her diamonds were dirty, too.

Greetings over, Morgan and Harry went to a nearby table, joining some old friends of Harry's from his days at Eton College. Their girlfriends were with them and they eyed Morgan with undisguised hostility.

'Too much gloss,' she heard one dowdy girl whisper.

'Terrifying, isn't it,' agreed another under her breath.

Morgan held her head high. If she'd figured out what English men were like by now, she'd also suspected that English women appeared to have a phobia about being overdressed and over made-up. They might disapprove of her *chic* and groomed looks now, but if she were to marry Harry and become the Marchioness of Blairmore, they would be licking her Charles Jourdan boots and inviting her to join their awful charity committees.

Morgan flashed a brilliant smile at the girl next to her. 'Would you like some clotted cream?' she asked.

Polo over, Morgan excused herself from Harry and braved the formidable field cloakroom, which was really a mobile trailer lavatory. She found it full of hot ladies in printed dresses plastering more powder on their sweaty faces and scooping off the lipstick that had spread into little rivers round their mouths. Morgan felt the envy and hostility of their glances as she stood, immaculate and cool. Once outside, she glanced round for Harry. He was nowhere to be seen. The crowds were dispersing, laughing and joking, waving hearty goodbyes, and a group were deciding if they wanted another round of Pimms or not. The fragrance of trodden grass and the sweet aroma of hay from the ponies' enclosure brought back to her sudden nostalgic memories of her childhood, when she and Tiffany had gone to spend long vacations with friends in Maryland. How she'd miss America if she stayed in England permanently! And she'd miss Tiffany too. Tiffany was so wise, and kind, and more like a mother than a sister. Damn it! *Where* could Harry have gone? She walked towards the grandstand, jostled and bumped by the departing crowds, getting angrier every moment. He wasn't in the bar. Could he have got caught up with his parents? Even so, he should have waited where they'd arranged. A ridiculous little jab of fear stabbed her.

Suppose he'd gone back to London without her! She hurried towards the car park, where long lines of Bentleys, Mercedes and Aston Martins were lining up for the exit, and suddenly breathed a little sigh of relief. At least his car was still there, although there was no sign of him. Then suddenly she saw him. He was standing with a group beside an old maroon Rolls Royce, its polished headlights reflecting the evening sun. In the group she saw the Duke and Duchess of Lomond, deep in conversation with a couple they'd been having tea with. Harry was holding the hands of a young woman in a flowered dress and talking earnestly to her, his head at an angle of contrition.

As she turned to look up at Harry, a tremulous smile on her tear-stained face, Morgan instantly recognized her.

It was Lady Elizabeth Greenly.

Morgan was unable to sleep. The hands on her Gucci travel clock pointed to four-thirty, and she was wide awake in the Winwoods' guest room. What had begun as a marvellous day had almost ended in disaster. She and Harry had hardly spoken on the drive back to London. *Damn* Lady Elizabeth. *Damn* and *blast* her limp handshake and those pale innocent-looking eyes that had turned to Morgan with the expression of a kicked dog. Morgan ground her teeth at the memory and kicked some of the little lace pillows onto the floor.

Then the Duchess had said in a loud voice, 'Well, we must be getting back to town before the traffic gets too bad. Come along, Edgar,' to her husband. 'Get into the car. I'll talk to you tomorrow, Cecilia,' she added, addressing herself to the plump lady. 'You and Cedric must come to dinner one night next week and bring Elizabeth too. Harry's not off to Scotland for ten days yet, so we *must* all get together.' With that she climbed briskly into the Rolls and glared at the assembled company. Especially Morgan.

'Did I hear you say you're going to Scotland soon?'

Morgan eventually asked him as they reached the outskirts of London.

'Yes, just a few days. I can't spare any longer unfortunately, but if I don't get out of town from time to time I go quite crazy.'

'I've never been to Scotland. Whereabouts is your castle?'

'On the banks of Loch Ness.' He turned to smile at her for the first time since they had got into the car. 'It's wonderful! Miles and miles of heather and gorse surrounded by mountains thousands of feet high! Oh, I'd give anything to be able to live there all the year round. You've no idea how quiet and peaceful it is.' He changed gear and passed a large truck. 'You should visit Scotland sometime.'

'I'd love to, but I'm not sure what my plans are. I should really be leaving for the States soon ...' Her words hung, invitingly, in the air.

'That's a pity! I thought you were going to be here a bit longer.' He never took his eyes off the road as they spun along.

'I don't think so, Harry. It sort of depends on my family, and things.' She was silent for a moment then turning to look directly at his profile she said lightly, 'Of course I could come up with you if you're going in ten days! I'd love to see your home, and it might be the only chance I'll ever get. Goodness only knows when I'll be over here again.'

To her relief Harry suddenly smiled his attractive, slightly crooked smile.

'What a good idea!' he exclaimed. 'We could fly up on Wednesday week, and then I'll have a chance to show you round before the others arrive.'

'Others?' *Don't tell me*, she thought, panic hitting her like a blow in the face. *Don't tell me!*

Harry's tone was nonchalant. 'Ma and Pa will be there, of course, and someone called David Ridgeley and his wife Davina – I was at Oxford with him – and the FitzHammonds and Elizabeth.'

She knew it.

At least she'd have four days' start on Elizabeth. Morgan decided she'd better make the most of it.

'Joni rang *here*?' Hunt ran his fingers through his hair in a gesture of desperation. 'Darling, I'm so sorry! She was drunk, I suppose?'

Tiffany nodded, trying to fight back her tears.

'What I want to know is how the hell did she find out about you? I don't understand it. I've been so careful not to give anything away. She obviously knew I had someone, but it beats me how she found out it was you. Oh, Tiff, my darling, what an unholy mess.' He shook his head disbelievingly.

'What are we going to do now, Hunt?'

Hunt put his arms round her and held her close to him. After a moment he said, 'What the hell can we do? I can't give you up, you know that. I love you more than I've ever loved anyone.'

Tiffany clung to him, the tears trickling down her face.

'I love you too, darling. I – I don't think I could bear to be without you.' She pressed herself closer, as if by doing so she could imprint herself on him forever. Hunt *was* her life, at least her private life. All of it. Work was great, and stimulating, and she needed it. But you couldn't take work to bed with you at night. What *was* the answer? As if reading her thoughts, Hunt eased her gently away from him, and looked deeply into her eyes.

'I'd like to get a divorce. That is the obvious thing. But you've no idea how much I suffered when my parents split. It screwed me up for years. I don't want to do that to Gus and Matt if I can possibly help it.' Hunt thought back to his childhood and the desolation he'd felt when his father had just packed his bags one day and walked out. He'd gone on asking his mother for years when Dad was coming back.

Gus and Matt were such great kids too, bright, quick, and so far, well adjusted. He let out a great sigh.

Last night he'd got home in time to read them a fairy story before they went to sleep. Gus, clutching a battered teddy bear, his solemn eyes never leaving his father's face, lay silent until Hunt read out the final line, '. . . and so they lived happily ever after.'

'Will you and Mom live happily ever after?' he asked.

'With you guys around, life's a bowl of cherries!' Hunt quipped, the sudden lump in his throat catching him unawares. He rose and went to tuck Gus in. 'Now it's time to go to sleep. Sweet dreams.'

'Good night, Daddy.' Gus snuggled deeper under his Mickey Mouse patterned duvet, dragging his teddy bear with him. A broken sob came from the other bed, disturbing the stillness of the room.

'Matt?' Hunt strode over to his younger son and bent over him. 'What's the matter?'

'You . . . You . . .' Matt's small face puckered, pink and awash with tears. He gave a small hiccup. 'You . . . won't ever leave us, will you?'

Hunt scooped him out of bed and rocked him comfortably on his lap. 'Now what sort of talk is that?' he asked gently. 'I'm your dad, remember? We guys always stick together. Of course I'll never leave you! Whatever gave you such a silly idea?'

'Mom did,' Gus piped up, sticking his head above the duvet. 'Mom said . . .'

'Now you know Mom's a big tease!' Inside Hunt was raging. How dare Joni say things that made the boys feel so insecure. Whatever the parents' problems, Matt and Gus must be protected. In a flash he remembered his mother unburdening herself to him, when his father had walked out. 'Now let me tell you both something,' he continued, making his voice both kind but firm. 'Your Momma's an actress. Now all actresses like to play different roles . . . that is, parts.

Pretend they're someone else. Like you pretend to be cowboys and Indians.'

'That's a silly game,' scoffed Gus.

'All acting is a silly game.' Hunt felt a weariness steal over him. 'Mom has been reading lots of plays. To see if there's a good part in one of them for her. I expect she chose you to be her audience, so she could tell how well she was acting the part.' He prayed they'd swallow it. Briskly he dried Matt's tears and tucked him up in bed. 'Now I can promise you one thing. Momma can act all the parts she likes, but just don't take any notice. I'm never going to leave you and you're both going to stay with me. Always. Okay?'

Still snuffling slightly, Matt nodded his head and Gus gave a relieved little smile.

Outside in the corridor, Hunt had leaned against the wall, filled with deep sadness. Those kids trusted him and he knew he could never let them down. But there was Tiffany. His love. His soulmate. His life.

Now, as if she knew what he was thinking, Tiffany pressed her cheek against his. Suffering his suffering, sharing his despair.

'I'm staying with you tonight, Tiff,' he suddenly said with defiance. 'Whatever happens, I can't completely let you go.' His mouth hungrily found hers, and his hands encircled her breasts stroking her stiffened nipples. 'I need you, Tiff...' His voice was husky, and with a groan he pushed her back onto the sofa. 'Oh God, I need you so much.'

Slowly and with great skill, he undressed her, kissing every part of her body as he did so, his fingertips caressing the soft skin of her neck and shoulders, the inside of her arms and the smoothness of her legs. When she lay naked, her eyes half closed, her lips smiling gently, he buried his face in her, tasting her sweetness, revelling in her swelling wetness, lingering there so that she ran her hands through his dark curling hair, holding his head close. When she cried 'Oh darling, now... Oh please now,' he penetrated her so fiercely that she gasped and clung to him. Moving with a sort of wild desperation, a kind of savage despair, as if this might be their last time together he thrust himself again and again into her, wanting to give the whole of himself to her, wanting her to take from him every last drop of his passion. When they had climaxed, they lay together almost sobbing, spent, drained, wondering if they could ever have enough of each other.

At least he is staying tonight, Tiffany thought later, but how many more nights like this will there be?

3

The high turrets of Drumnadrochit Castle rose with unwelcoming bleakness from the black waters of Loch Ness as they had for the past five hundred years, impervious to man and elements alike.

It was not at all what Morgan had expected.

From a distance the granite walls seemed hewn out of the mighty jagged rock on which the castle stood: the windows were sinister slits, the crenellated battlements and ramparts were a perfect backdrop for a Dracula film.

Who, Morgan asked herself, would want to live in a spooky, bat-infested place like this? She glanced nervously at Harry, who had insisted on driving the Land Rover that had met them at the airport, while Dougal, one of the staff, sat in the back with the dogs. With every mile Harry was looking happier and more relaxed, as he pointed out the mountains, misty with purple and white heather, sweeping down to the banks of golden bracken that grew almost to the water's edge. Dark and mysterious forests with crystal streams and waterfalls and strange-shaped rocks burnished by thousands of years of wind and rain completed the magnificent landscape. Morgan looked at the castle again. Mist was creeping along the edge of the loch, slowly swallowing Drumnadrochit in its swirling clamminess. Suppose the place was haunted?

'Do you have ghosts?' Morgan asked in a small voice.

'Good Lord, yes!' His tone was airy. 'If you hear the skirl of the bagpipes in the dead of night, it will be the headless body of MacVean of the Isle, raising his clan for a blood feud.'

'You're kidding!'

Harry threw back his head, roaring with laughter.

'You should have seen your face! Actually I believe there is a ghost of an old woman who walks through the gun room sometimes, but I've never seen her and I don't know anyone who has. What you should be looking out for is the Loch Ness Monster!'

'I've heard of that! Does it really exist?'

'I believe it does, though I haven't actually seen it myself. I know people who have seen it, but whether it's an actual monster or a physical phenomenon I'm not certain. Our gamekeeper was out in a boat in the loch one evening. The waters became terribly turbulent and he swears he then saw what looked like a horse's head, on a very long neck, about twenty yards away. He was scared shitless, because he said it suddenly got very cold for a few minutes and very eerie.'

'How fascinating!' Morgan was enthralled. What a tale to tell back home. 'When was it first seen?'

'In AD 565, I believe.'

'AD 565!' she repeated, looking at him dazed. 'What, the *same* monster!'

Harry laughed. 'It's either a breeding ground for generations of monsters, or like I said, some sort of phenomenon. About ten thousand sightings have been reported over the years, though.'

'Oh! I hope I get to see it.' She sounded like an excited little girl and Harry smiled indulgently at her.

At last they arrived in the castle's courtyard and Morgan got slowly out of the car and looked up. A shudder, half fear, half excitement, shot through her. Even from here it looked forbidding.

They entered, and in the large square hall the atmosphere was one of comfortable shabbiness. Logs spat in the deep fireplace, and there was a smell of smouldering wood and peat. Above the fireplace the family's armorial bearings and crest, which Morgan remembered seeing in *Debrett's Peerage*, were carved in wood. Originally they had been gilded and painted in rich colours, but years of smoke had almost blackened them. The walls were hung with stuffed animal trophies, and a forest of antlers, interspersed with swords, daggers and ancient shields, filled every space. Jacobean carved chests, tables and chairs were stiffly arranged, and on a large round table in the centre, a pewter jug stood filled with dusty heather. The cold, stone-flagged floor lent a chill to the whole dingy, moth-eaten atmosphere.

Morgan was looking round curiously when, from the length of a dark passage, a figure in a black dress and white apron appeared. It was Mrs Monroe, the housekeeper, a wide smile on her wrinkled face, as she welcomed the son and heir home. Mrs Monroe had been with the family for nearly forty years and Harry swore she knew more about them than they did themselves.

'This is Miss Kalvin,' he said after the initial greetings were over. Mrs Monroe inclined her head solemnly, her clear blue eyes sweeping over Morgan with a critical coldness.

'Good day to you, miss.' She turned back to Harry with a gesture that was both protective and motherly and enquired if he'd like his tea right away.

'Yes please, can we have it by the fire in here? I don't suppose the other fires have been lit yet?' Harry dragged a heavy carved-oak chair near the spluttering logs.

'They'll be lit aye long, for you'll be wanting them this night. We're in for a gale, mark my words! Now sit yourself down, master, and I'll be seeing to your tea.' Her broad Scottish accent made it difficult for Morgan to understand everything she said, but she got the message loud and clear. Mrs Monroe did not approve of her as a companion for the 'young master' as she insisted on calling Harry.

After tea Harry took her on a tour of the main rooms of the castle. First, he led her to the drawing room, and in spite of herself Morgan gasped. The room was sixty feet long and all the walls were hung with sixteenth-century tapestries, woven with a border of fruit and scrolls, with wild animals prowling among giant curling leaves in the centre. The colours had faded to soft muted shades of blue, green and burnt umber and Morgan reckoned they must be priceless. Swiftly her eyes took in the rest of this imposing room, noting the Baccarat chandeliers, their oblong prisms reflecting the fading light, the gilt and brocade sofas flanking the immense marble fireplace, the valuable rugs, the formal chairs and little tables strewn with objets d'art. She let out a long low sigh. It would have been absolutely fantastic were it not for the general air of shabbiness and dustiness.

Harry showed her the library next, where thousands of leather-bound books filled the shelves, and the ballroom, where the county came to practise Highland reels before the round of balls that marked the annual clan gatherings.

Then there was the Duke's study, dominated by a large desk and a collection of fossils, and the gun room, smelling of rubber Wellington boots.

By the time they got back to the hall Mrs Monroe was hovering around, wanting to know if eight o'clock would suit the young master for dinner.

'That would be fine, Mrs Monroe.' Harry turned to Morgan. 'Okay for you?' She nodded, noticing how the housekeeper was pointedly ignoring her.

'Will you show Miss Kalvin to her room, and see that she has everything she wants?'

Mrs Monroe made no comment.

'Then,' continued Harry, not noticing, 'you can have a bath and a rest before dinner, Morgan. I've got a few things to check on around the estate.'

The room had a carved four-poster bed, more heavy Jacobean furniture and massive dusty velvet curtains that, like the armorial bearings, had seen brighter and better days. A peat fire smouldered in the grate. Morgan peered through the window at the dusky melancholy landscape, and shivered with a strange foreboding. The waters of the loch looked black and sinister and those bits of land not shrouded in mist seemed dank and barren. What a difference from Long Island! However, if she did get married to Harry, she'd insist they have a house in London and, as far as she was concerned, come here as little as possible. Harry wouldn't mind living in town once he had a beautiful home of his own. In fact, she'd make life so enticing, so entertaining, that he'd never want to come to Scotland at all! Meanwhile... her thoughts flickered speculatively.

They dined in the panelled dining-room, and to Morgan it was the height of absurdity. Just the two of them, at a polished mahogany table that could seat forty-two people, and frequently did. Round it stood red leather coronation chairs, embossed on the back with ER and the crown in gold. A massive silver centrepiece of a stag at bay flanked by two eight-branch silver candlesticks dominated the table. Besides salt-cellars and pepper and mustard pots of Georgian silver, Morgan noticed, there were silver butter dishes, coasters for the wine, bonbon dishes filled with chocolates and two life-size silver partridges. Everything, including her array of forks and spoons bore the Lomond crest of a rampant wildcat. The crest was also embroidered discreetly on a corner of her damask dinner napkin. *Wouldn't Daddy just freak out if he could see all this!* she thought, trying to keep a straight face at the absurdity of the situation. Wasn't there a cosy little room where they could have had an intimate dinner, especially without McGillivery, the butler, who watched them like a well-trained hawk?

Harry chattered throughout. He talked about Drumnadrochit and the surrounding thousand acres of land that belonged to them, much of it turned over to forestry, but with a home farm nearby. He talked about the history of the family and the part they had played in Scotland's development, and all the while McGillivery kept filling up his wine glass from a heavy crystal decanter, unnoticed by Harry. Morgan sipped her white wine slowly, only half listening. They might have masses of land, with forests and deer, pheasants and streams to catch salmon in, but closer inspection of the castle had shown her it was in a very bad state of repair. Damp was rising up some of the walls, leaving black fungus stains. The stonework was crumbling on the ramparts, and the whole place had a neglected desolate air. An air, she thought with amazement, of poverty. There wasn't any central heating and her bathroom looked as if it had been installed during the Iron Age. The tub was a great deep cast-iron affair, sitting on four iron lions' feet. That she *had* to photograph, or her family would never believe her.

As they went into the study for coffee, she remarked casually, 'An estate like this must take a bundle of money to keep up, doesn't it?'

Harry's head shook almost sadly. 'It certainly does! There's a lot we need to do, repairs to the roof, dry-rot in the cellars . . .'

'Central heating?'

He laughed as he caught her quizzical teasing smile. 'Central heating I suppose! Oh Morgan! Are you cold? I'm so sorry . . .' Concerned, he threw more logs on the fire, and with a long brass-handled poker, raked at the ashes. 'Are you all right now? Can I get you a shawl or something?'

'No thank you!' Morgan would rather have frozen to death than spoil the line of her Saint Laurent! 'But, Harry . . .' She hesitated a moment. 'Why don't you do it up?'

'Lack of funds. Simple as that, I'm afraid. It will be even worse when my father dies. The death duties will be crippling. We shall probably have to sell most of the land, fishing, shooting, the whole lot will go up the spout!' He sighed deeply, and took a gulp of his brandy.

'That's really tough.' Morgan said softly, and thoughtfully.

She had a plan that might just tip the balance in her favour over Lady Elizabeth, by several million dollars.

Morgan listened intently at the open door of her bedroom. Twenty minutes before Harry had bid her a chaste good night as he escorted her as far as her room.

'Sleep well.' His smile was warm and friendly. 'We'll go for a picnic if it's fine tomorrow. I want to show you the ruins of Urquhart Castle, and we'll drive over to Loch Oich.'

'That sounds like fun.' Morgan regarded him with gentle amusement. He so reminded her of Zachary when he'd been a kid, dashing off to see favourite places at the start of vacations as if they were old friends. She watched him walk purposefully away along the corridor, until he entered a room at the far end. The dogs went with him.

Morgan hurried to her bathroom and carefully removed most of her make-up, leaving on just her eye-shadow and mascara. She added a touch of pink lip-gloss, and then slipped into a pale-blue satin negligée edged with a profusion of delicate lace and narrow blue ribbons. A spray of Joy on her neck, between her breasts and behind her knees and she was ready.

The grandfather clock in the hall below ticked sonorously. There was no other sound. It was time to go.

'Harry! Harry!' Morgan banged on his door with clenched fists, and screamed again. 'Help, Harry!'

The door was flung wide and Harry stood there in maroon pyjamas, looking startled.

'What's happened?'

Covering her face with her hands, Morgan let a little sob escape from her lips as she leant against him.

'Oh, I got such a scare! A bat has flown into my room and I'm terrified of bats. It sort of dive-bombed me. Harry, I can't go back until it's gone!'

'Poor little thing.' He put his arms round her comfortingly and laid his cheek against her head. 'What were you doing with the window open anyway? Never mind, I'll go and get rid of it.'

'Oh Harry, don't leave me! I really still feel so scared.' Morgan pressed herself closer and wound her arms round his neck. 'Can't I stay in here with you, just for a while?' She raised her head and a pair of perfect jade-green eyes, mysterious and deep, looked up at him. He noticed her dewy mouth, still trembling, and the way her rounded breasts, half visible through the white lace, rose and fell with her breathing. A fragrance of jasmine, his favourite flower, filled the air, and Harry felt as if his legs and stomach had turned to molten lead.

'Oh, my darling . . .' He strained her to him as tightly as he could, and showered her face with soft kisses. Morgan had fascinated him from the moment he had first met her. Her beauty was extraordinary, and her charm unrivalled. He loved the way she laughed, and her zest for life. He loved her gentleness and the sometimes tender look in her magical eyes. This exquisite creature, he thought, part child, part woman, enthralled him.

They were kissing with ever greater urgency and as he led her gently to his bed, desire shot through him like a hot spear. Never in his life had he wanted anyone as much as he wanted Morgan. Brushing her pink-tipped breasts, he slid down her satin robe, revealing her body, glowing and golden in the soft light of his bedside lamp. Her breasts were full and perfectly rounded, her back a smooth sweep of satiny skin, her legs, long and shapely, tapered into slim ankles and feet, and her toenails were painted a pearly pink. Dropping on his knees beside her, almost in worship, he kissed her feet and then left a trail of burning lingering kisses up her body and across her stomach and breasts, while she undulated sensuously beneath him, her hands stroking his arms and his shoulders until they came to rest on his broad chest, in a gesture of total acceptance. The softness of her pink mouth and the little darting movements of her tongue sent such a thrill through him that, unable to contain himself any longer, he thrust apart her languid golden legs and took her with one swift piercing lunge. Morgan matched her rhythm to his, thrusting her hips upwards. Christ, he never wanted this moment of acute ecstasy to end. He wanted to stay inside her forever. With a sudden cry of exultation he climaxed and then felt her climaxing around him, soft and wet.

'My love ...' Morgan's arms held him with warmth and tenderness. She stroked his hair and kissed his neck. He still held her close, eyes shut, and soon she realized he had fallen into a light sleep.

When he awoke a few minutes later, bright-eyed and refreshed, he turned to her with a smile of wonderment.

'You really are amazing.' His tone was sincere. He eyed her beautiful breasts, just visible above the white sheet she had pulled over herself.

Morgan smiled with contentment. Harry was really very cute. She could even grow to love him in time.

'I'm thirsty!' she suddenly announced, pulling herself up into a sitting position. 'Shall we have a drink?'

'Of course! Why not? Good idea, really. What would you like, a glass of Perrier ... or some coffee or tea?'

She stretched herself seductively, raising her arms above her head and running her fingers through her flowing hair.

'What I'd really like' – she stroked his arm with one of her long red nails '– is some champagne.'

'I'll see what I can do – if that's what you really want.' Harry reached for his tartan robe and made for the door. 'It may mean raiding the cellar and seeing what I can find. Don't go away!'

'Am I likely to, my dear, when I'm so happy here? Don't be long.' Arranging the pillows more comfortably Morgan put her satin negligée round her shoulders, and gave Harry her sweetest smile.

Groping round the dank and cobwebbed cellars of the

castle, as he searched for champagne, Harry felt a mixture of emotions. Of one thing he was certain. He loved her style! She was magnificent, coming to his room in the middle of the night and then commanding champagne after a session of sex that had blown his mind! Wondering vaguely what Elizabeth would be like in bed (pretty boring and unimaginative he suspected), he grabbed a bottle of Bollinger from a rack and blew the dust off it. The way his mother and Elizabeth's mother were putting on the pressure, he supposed he'd find out soon enough. She was a nice little thing, but it was a pity she wasn't more exciting.

Back in bed, Morgan and Harry sipped the wine, already chilled by the cold of the cellar. She looked round his room. The furniture was good and solid but the wallpaper was stained with damp and the curtains were decidedly shabby.

'Harry, how much would it cost to do up this place?'

'God knows! It's a frightening thought. A hundred thousand, maybe two hundred thousand.'

'Pounds?'

''Fraid so. Not dollars, my sweet.'

Morgan carefully placed her goblet of champagne on the bedside table.

'Then you'll just have to marry an heiress, won't you?' she remarked lightly. Then more seriously and with a husky urgency, 'Make love to me again, darling.'

Later, as they lay together, Harry flushed and dozing by her side, Morgan smiled down at him. By her reckoning, when Lady Elizabeth arrived on Saturday the fish would have taken the bait and would be beautifully landed on the banks of Loch Ness.

It was Saturday morning. Harry announced at breakfast, as he tucked into his traditional porridge and Morgan toyed with a slice of toast, that 'they' would be arriving at teatime.

Morgan felt a nervous flutter as she gave him one of her brilliant smiles.

'Great! What shall we do this morning, darling?'

'Whatever you like. How about going over to Glen Douglas? There's a deserted crofter's cottage there, where we used to shelter from the rain when I was a child. I'll ask Mrs Monroe to get us another picnic.'

'With some champagne? Oh Harry, *do* let's have some champagne. After all this is our last picnic together!'

'All right, with champagne!' Her remark caused him to feel a pang, almost a sense of loss. Their last picnic together. What a pity. It had been such a jolly few days, but, he supposed, all good things had to come to an end.

'It has been such a lovely few days,' Morgan remarked, as if she had read his thoughts. 'I can't bear the idea of having to go back to New York.' She sounded genuinely wistful.

'Well, my sweet' – he patted her as if she had been Mackie or Angus, his Labrador dogs – 'you'll just have to come over again one day, won't you?'

There were only seven hours left until Elizabeth and the others arrived.

The courtyard of the castle was full of cars when Harry and Morgan got back. It was late afternoon and the castle was bathed in golden red light from the setting sun. In the hall everyone was seated drinking tea from fine Worcester china. The Duke and Duchess of Lomond, the Earl and Countess of FitzHammond, a couple called David and Davina Ridgeley, whom Morgan remembered meeting at polo, and of course Lady Elizabeth Greenly, curled up on the thick goatskin rug before the dull, smouldering fire. Like a nice little house-broken kitten, thought Morgan, as she and Harry came in, looking the picture of windswept health and vitality. Morgan looked particularly good. In beautifully cut grey flannel trousers and deep jade-green shirt, her cheeks glowed from their long afternoon's love-making in the crofter's cottage. There were still fragments of bracken in her hair from the makeshift bed they'd made.

'Harry!' The Duchess looked up at her son, her parchment skin flushed to produce red spots on each cheek. 'Where have you been? It really is *too* bad! I was expecting you to be here when we arrived.' Her flat grey eyes swept over Morgan who was still hanging onto Harry's arm. 'You didn't tell me you had invited anyone for the weekend.'

Harry had opened his mouth to say something when the Duke rose from the leather chair by the fire and came forward, beaming broadly, and with outstretched hands.

'Why, my dear' – he grasped Morgan's hand and squeezed it – 'it is nice to see you again. Windsor, wasn't it? You're Morgan Kalvin, aren't you? Yes, of course you are, and if I may say so, still as pretty as a picture!' Without waiting for a reply he turned to Harry, chuckling jovially. 'You're a dark horse, 'pon my word, Harry! Not that I blame you . . . Nice to see you, m'boy! Come and sit yourselves down and have a cup of tea!'

Morgan found herself being led to a chair next to the Duke, while he fussed over her. It was good to know she had one friend in the camp.

Harry, having kissed his mother, greeted the others and then stood behind Morgan's chair. She glanced up at him, smiling, and their eyes locked in a moment of intimacy.

'We've had a marvellous time! Harry's been showing me all the sights. I'd no idea Scotland was so beautiful,' Morgan remarked.

In the silence that followed, Morgan was aware of Elizabeth's eyes staring at her with reproach.

'Dinner will be at eight,' announced the Duchess, rising suddenly. 'Come Cecilia, and Elizabeth. I expect you'd like a rest after your journey.' She led them regally up the carved oak staircase.

Not a word had she addressed to Morgan.

Morgan dressed with particular care that night, parting her hair in the centre and coiling up the long thick strands at the back until they formed a loose cascade of knots and loops. She had brought a dress that she knew would have a stunning effect, and she chose her jewellery with equal care.

As the grandfather clock chimed eight, she slowly descended the stairs to the great hall, where everyone was gathered waiting for the gong to be sounded by McGillivery. Dressed in the deepest emerald velvet, with long tight sleeves, a deeply cut square neckline and a skirt that fell in heavy folds to the floor, Morgan looked as if she'd stepped out of one of the Lomond family portraits. Round her neck and from her ears hung glinting emeralds and baroque pearls.

The Duke gave an audible gasp, and the old Earl nearly dropped his sherry glass. Harry's eyes blazed with pride as she glided, smiling, to his side; even David Ridgeley, besotted with his wife of six months, looked riveted.

'She looks like a duchess,' Harry thought as he observed the proud angle of her head and the grace with which she moved. Then he glanced nervously at his mother, sitting hunched up in a dingy black lace dress. The comparison made his mouth twitch. His mother looked more like a housekeeper than a duchess.

There was a deathly silence broken only by the hissing of the fire.

Morgan let her eyes roam with total assurance from woman to woman as she drank her sherry. She hadn't attended dozens of her mother's New York parties without knowing the exact reaction her appearance was having on each of them.

Later that night Harry came to her room for the first time. One look into his eyes told her all she needed to know. They clasped each other joyously, the memory of their love-making that afternoon still fresh in their minds. *We belong*, thought Morgan, feeling for the first time the stirring of love in her. *At last we really belong*.

'My darling one.' Harry covered her face and neck with

kisses, holding her head in his strong hands, as her hair tumbled loose about her shoulders. 'I adore you –'

Harry was never able to finish the sentence.

Standing in the doorway, her eyes flecked with hatred, was the Duchess.

'Just as I thought!' She spat out the words. 'How dare you, Harry! How dare you bring this, this *tart* into my house, and with Elizabeth under the same roof too! I might have guessed this American piece of trash would try and hook you! She will leave first thing in the morning, those are my orders. Kindly see they are carried out. I will get your father to announce your engagement to Elizabeth as soon as possible. She is far more suited for the position of your wife than this ... woman!'

Morgan stood rooted to the spot as the Duchess turned and stalked down the corridor.

'Why didn't you say something?' Morgan cried, aghast, turning on Harry. 'How could you just stand there and let her say those things about me?' She was shaking with shock and rage.

Harry stood looking pink and upset.

'Well, er, it's just that –'

'Haven't you got a mind of your own? Or a tongue?' Morgan's voice rose hysterically. 'She can't make you do something against your will ... or can she, Harry?' She felt desperate. 'Haven't the last few days meant *anything* to you?'

'Of course they have, Morgan.' Harry gave a nervous little cough. 'Only you don't understand ... there's been this sort of understanding for years that Elizabeth and I would get married one day. There are certain considerations too –'

'Like her money?' Morgan shot the question ruthlessly at him. 'Well, let me tell you something. I could afford to do up this crumbling old ruin out of my dress allowance – but if you agree with your mother that I'm a whore there's nothing more to be said.'

She ran from the room and locked herself into the bathroom.

All Harry's whispered entreaties to come out were to no avail.

With infinite care Zachary removed a paperback copy of Harold Robbins's *79 Park Avenue* from his bedroom bookcase and took from between its pages a folded piece of white paper, not more than two inches square. He placed the hand mirror from his chest-of-drawers flat on the table and fetched a razor blade from the bathroom. He'd become quite skilled in the past couple of weeks at chipping away at the tiny lump of cocaine he'd bought, until he had enough fine powder to form a line. There was only one more thing he needed for his trip to Paradise. In another drawer were some plastic straws he'd taken from McDonald's, cut into quarters and angled at one end.

Taking one, he sniffed up the line with deep satisfaction. Suddenly life took on a whole new rosy dimension. Smokey was right! But Smokey and snowstorms were costing him a fortune. At first she had given him a few snorts, to see if he liked it.

'Stay cool, honey! I gotta a friend who lets me have it. Try it! You'll like it.'

At first Zachary found it didn't have much effect, but by the fourth time he realized it gave him such a feeling of euphoria that he felt he could do anything. Once she'd mixed it with speed and the effect had been overpowering. He hadn't been able to sleep for thirty-six hours.

That was when Smokey said she couldn't get him any more unless he produced the cash up front first.

He went to his mother and managed to borrow some money from her, saying it was for books for school. Then he called up a few college friends and asked for a loan until term started. Finally he sold his hi-fi, his camera and a few silver trinkets he'd been given as christening presents. Also the gold cuff-links his grandfather had left him. In a few months' time his father would be settling a huge amount of money on him, so the future could take care of itself. It was the present that mattered, and he couldn't get through a day without something.

It was then that Smokey introduced him to heroin.

'Now we're gonna hit the big time, baby!' She produced the brown powder and gave it to him to sniff. 'Then we'll fuck our heads off, baby! We'll have ourselves a party that's going to blow your mind!' Smokey giggled as she hitched her skirt higher, revealing her nakedness beneath.

Zachary turned towards her, reaching out to stroke her ever-ready pussy, before he sniffed deeply.

Then the rush hit him! He was engulfed by a strange sensation that streamed through his arteries, drowning him ... lifting him ... letting him float into a land of euphoric visions and sounds.

Smokey waited for him at Dino's most evenings. She was giving him priority treatment these days. She had big plans for when her little playmate hit it big.

'Hi, sugar!' she greeted him one night as soon as he came through the door. Business had been good lately and she'd bought herself a scarlet jersey dress that dropped off one shoulder, revealing her breasts even more. Dangling rhine-stones hung from her ears.

'Hi, Smokey.' Zachary returned the greeting with a lazy smile and blank eyes. 'Want a drink?'

When he returned from the bar, Smokey was in animated conversation with another girl. She had long black hair that hung limply down her back, and her eyes were heavily outlined in kohl.

'This is Dinah,' Smokey announced. 'Say, she's just asked us to a party at Sammy's place tonight. Wanna go?'

'What sort of party?'

'Any sort of party you want, honey!' Smokey and Dinah

laughed uproariously, and looked at each other knowingly.

'Okay.' Zachary didn't much care where he spent the evening as long as it was with Smokey.

'Great.' Smokey turned to Dinah. 'We'll be along later. Gotta bit of business to do first, keeping my little friend here happy.' The girls giggled again, and Zachary felt suddenly embarrassed.

Two hours later they arrived at Sammy's place.

The uproar beat against his senses. Pulsating rock music, a pungent smell, the gabble of senseless voices, bodies, dozens of sweating bodies, arms and legs and tongues entwined, on a settee, on the floor, pressed against the wall. Someone was being sick out of the window. Another was slumped in a corner, deathly pale. Zachary looked round and felt a tremor, half shock, half thrill. A naked girl of no more than fourteen was demonstrating a yoga position in the middle of the room to no one in particular and in the doorway two bearded men were locked in a passionate kiss.

Someone handed Zachary a paper cup filled with a vile-tasting liquor, another passed him a joint. Smokey and Dinah disappeared among the writhing mass, with shrill cries of 'Sammy! Hi, Gino! Whatcha doin', dogface?'

Alone and isolated Zachary regarded the throbbing scene. He dragged deeply on the joint but it wasn't the buzz he needed. He wanted to become part of this scene. He wanted to lose himself in the communal embrace of all these erotic bodies, to suck and be sucked, to fuck and be fucked. He wanted to fly.

4

'Tiffany, I feel absolutely *shitty*!' Morgan strode across her sister's studio, flinging her mink bomber jacket and Gucci handbag down on the mint-green sofa. 'How can Harry be so weak? For God's sake, we could have been engaged by now if it hadn't been for that bitch of a mother.' Her tone was deeply aggrieved and bitter.

'Why did you come home then? Why didn't you stay and fight for him? It's really not like you to quit.' Tiffany poured some coffee from the percolator that stood on her worktop, realizing that any hope of work that morning was a wipe-out. Morgan had landed the night before, seething with rage, and had turned up at Tiffany's apartment before breakfast hoping to find sympathy.

'What was the point?' Morgan demanded. 'I was faced with practically a *fait accompli*! His mother had obviously had the whole thing worked out for years! And I know why, too.'

'Why? Because this Lady Elizabeth something will bring money into the family?'

'Crap! Her money would keep us in the style to which we are accustomed for about a week! No, the old Duchess wants Harry to get married to Elizabeth because Elizabeth is the sort of girl she can dominate. Elizabeth will be no threat to her: the silly little bitch will say, "Yes, Duchess", "No Duchess" and that old baggage will be able to rule the roost until she dies.' Morgan stubbed out her cigarette angrily. 'And there was I thinking Harry had some guts! I knew he was easy to get round. That I didn't mind, in fact I quite like a man –'

'You can twist round your little finger?' asked Tiffany.

Morgan glared at her angrily. 'Tiffany, I expect loyalty from you! You know what I mean. All men are a bit weak when it comes to an attractive woman, and if the woman has any sense she will use it to her advantage – and to the man's advantage too, if he can only see it. I would have made Harry a brilliant wife. Think how I could have helped him with money and contacts in the business world, through Daddy! Not to mention entertaining, charming his clients. He owns a gallery you know, dealing in old masters, and exporting paintings to America is the most important part of the business. And I could have brought glamour and style into his life – become a leading hostess – got into royal circles –'

'Okay, okay, you don't have to convince me! I know you'd be good at all that, but how happy would you have been in the long run? It sounds like a pretty dead-end existence to me – not to mention the fact that it's supposed to be a job for life,' Tiffany remarked drily.

'Don't be stupid! You know it's what I've always wanted.' Morgan lit another cigarette. 'What am I supposed to do now? I can't stay at home. As soon as I got back last night Daddy launched into a full-scale interrogation of who have I met, where have I been, and what have I been doing? He'd kill me if he knew I almost hooked a future duke and then blew it!'

'Suppose you get a job? There are so many interesting things you could do.'

'Work!' exploded Morgan. 'Why the hell should I work? I don't need the money and I'd be bored stiff. There's nothing that interests me except making a brilliant marriage. And Harry would have been so perfect. You know, because he wants to move out of his parents' London house, I actually went to look at a Regency house in Knightsbridge with him. There was I planning in my head how I could do it up for when we were married, and now that stupid little cow, who has got about as much dress sense as a dead chicken, is going to be the Marchioness of Blairmore and one day the Duchess of Lomond! What a waste!' Morgan's voice rose to a wail.

Suddenly Tiffany felt sorry for Morgan. She'd been spoiled all her life and simply refused to understand that she couldn't always have her own way. Joe was to blame for that. Joe with his ambitions, his desire for his children to penetrate the class barriers that, even with his self-made millions, he had not been able to cross.

'You need cheering up, darling,' Tiffany said suddenly. 'Why don't we all go out tonight!'

'Who's all?'

'You and I, of course, and Hunt – and we could ask Greg to join us. He's been ringing me constantly to ask when you'd be back.'

'Oh my God, not Greg!' Morgan sank back onto the sofa, running her hands through her hair.

'Why not? You need cheering up and the best consolation in the world is having a man crazy about you. Leave it to me, I'll fix Hunt and Greg and then I'll book a table at Le Club – it always amuses you there doesn't it? – and then we can go on and dance somewhere afterwards.'

Morgan shrugged her elegant shoulders. 'Oh, all right.' Her tone was ungracious, but on the other hand her pride would be partly restored, she figured, if Greg was still in love with her. Not that she wanted him at any price, but it could make an interesting evening's diversion.

By eight o'clock that night Tiffany had got everything organized, thankful that *Night Chill* had opened two weeks before, so that her working life was temporarily quieter. At the moment she was only designing a couple of dresses for a TV show. After Morgan had finally departed, still disgruntled, she finished what work she'd been able to, and now, as she put the final touches to her make-up, she relaxed for the first time that day. Slipping into a clinging white jersey dress by Bill Blass, she added a modern gold necklace and earrings. Then she glanced at her jewelled watch. In a few minutes they would all be arriving for drinks. She just hoped Morgan would be in a better mood. She went to check the living room. It looked wonderful, like a photograph in *House and Garden*. Gloria had arranged great bowls of flowers on the low glass tables. Cleverly concealed spotlights picked out the modern lithographs hanging on the white walls.

Hunt was the first to arrive and one glance told Tiffany he was in a foul mood. That meant one of three things. He had either had a row with the producer, Flix Greenberg, or a row with one of the cast, probably Robert Clarkson, or things were difficult at home.

'What can I get you to drink, darling?' Tiffany kissed him softly and noted the snap in his dark eyes.

'Oh, anything. Do we have to go out tonight? I'm dead beat.' Hunt flung himself into a chair and closed his eyes wearily.

'You'll feel better when you've had a drink, darling, and it *is* Morgan's first night back. She's a bit low too –'

'What's the matter with her now?' Hunt had never had much time for Morgan with her obsession for clothes and parties. And he was certainly in no mood for tragedy queens tonight – he'd had enough of them at the studio all day.

'It's nothing that a nice evening with Greg won't improve,' Tiffany cut in quickly.

'Greg? That moron? Oh, for God's sake, Tiff! I've had an absolutely awful day and all I want is a quiet evening with you and now you've got a whole fucking crowd coming!' He downed his bourbon in one gulp and handed her his glass for a refill.

'I'm sorry Hunt, I ... well, I really thought it might be fun.' Fun! The evening had all the ingredients of becoming a full-scale disaster.

At that moment Gloria showed Greg in, his smile wide with anticipation. Tiffany was always reminded of a big shambling and totally delightful dog when she saw Greg Jackson. His brown hair was always untidy. Even his expensive suits looked as if he'd slept in them. But his face was so amiable, his eyes so kind, and his manner so charming that a kind of warmth spread through one as soon as he entered the room. His greatest asset was his voice. Low, rich and beautifully modulated, it would have carried him far if he'd ever decided to do voice-overs. He also had another great asset, a sense of humour, and he never minded telling jokes against himself. Even the one about the girl who said to him, 'You've got a wonderful voice. If I shut my eyes I could even imagine you were attractive!'

'Hullo, Greg.' Tiffany kissed him in welcome. 'You know Hunt of course.'

Hunt gave him a curt nod, ignoring Greg's large outstretched hand.

'Well . . . this is great!' Greg settled himself on the sofa and took the drink Tiffany handed him. 'I must say, Tiffany, you look fabulous! How are things?'

Greg had known the sisters for six years and marvelled that though they looked so alike they were also so different. Tiffany was all blonde strength, so decisive and capable. And very intelligent too. Morgan was spun-gold candy floss; sweet, fragile, vulnerable. Good enough to eat.

Hunt smoked and drank moodily as Tiffany and Greg chatted.

Greg kept one ear cocked and half an eye on the door, waiting for Morgan's arrival. Tiffany began to feel, as she rattled on, that she was doing a solo performance. Neither man was listening to a word she was saying.

Suddenly, in a whirl of bright pink chiffon, flowing gold hair and twinkling gold high-heeled sandals, Morgan was in their midst. She glowed with high spirits and was smiling as if she hadn't a care in the world. What a different performance, observed Tiffany to herself, from this morning's moodiness.

'Greg . . .!' Morgan swept over to him, her hands outstretched. She twined her arms round his neck and kissed him warmly. It was as if he was the only person in the world she wanted to see. Greg, pink with pleasure, held tightly onto her hand as she turned to greet Tiffany and Hunt.

'What would you like to drink, darling?' asked Tiffany, hoping the party spirit would now get under way.

'Champagne, of course, darling! What else is there?' Morgan sank onto the sofa, pulling Greg down beside her. Her pink dress billowed round her legs in ripples of chiffon. Greg looked at her with wide and eager eyes. He could hardly believe it. At last she was back, and looking more beautiful and exciting than ever.

'Did you have a good time on your trip?' It was Hunt who spoke, more out of curiosity than interest. Morgan didn't look low to him. In fact she looked breathtakingly marvellous – if you liked animated Barbie Dolls. Three whiskies had done their work in restoring a glimmer of his accustomed humour.

'It was fabulous, quite fantastic!' Morgan proceeded to regale them in witty detail about her trip, never omitting the opportunity of dropping a name or a place. As she warmed to her subject she directed her talk more and more towards Tiffany and Hunt. When Greg interjected with a question, it was as if she hadn't heard him. Within twenty minutes of her arrival he might as well not have been there. Not that he seemed to notice her waning interest. Still knocked sideways by her initial greeting, he stared at her as if hypnotized.

Suddenly Hunt jumped to his feet, startling them all.

'If we're going to eat, let's get to it. I'm famished!' He thumped his glass heavily on the table.

Tiffany tried to use her most mollifying tone. 'I've booked a table at Le Club – it's always fun there.'

In uneasy silence they went down in the elevator to the parking lot. As Hunt's car threaded its way slowly across the jewel-spangled city the conversation was awkward, fragmented, disjointed, as if each were making little statements that required no answer.

'What a wonderful show *Cats* is ...'

'It's got quite chilly ...'

'Imagine parking a car *there* ...'

Greg was the only one who didn't say a word. He was too busy looking at Morgan's profile.

'Jesus, this place is bizarre!' observed Hunt as they took their seats at a table.

'What's wrong with it?' Even Tiffany was getting edgy.

Hunt grabbed the large menu. 'It's a fucking tourist attraction, that's what it is,' he retorted. 'What are we going to order?'

'I'm not very hungry,' Morgan said in a small voice.

Hunt and Tiffany glared at her, and Greg tried to take her hand.

'You're probably still jet-lagged, honey,' he sympathized.

'I'm nothing of the sort!' Morgan extricated her hand, suddenly cross.

'... and the excitement of coming home,' Greg was saying.

'Excitement of coming home?' she repeated, looking at him as if he were mentally retarded. 'Who would want to come back to this dump! Everything in New York is so *new* and at the same time shabby and dirty –' The wailing of a passing police siren on the street outside the restaurant, made her pause until it had faded away. 'See what I mean? Those godforsaken sirens going on day and night – it's enough to drive one mad. You know something?' She broke her bread stick and didn't wait for anyone to ask her what. 'In London you only hear them once or twice a *day* and hardly ever at night! Oh, the *peace* of that beautiful city, and the lovely old buildings ...' Her voice gave a slight tremor. Tiffany looked at her searchingly. How many martinis, wondered Tiffany, had Morgan had before she even got to the apartment tonight?

Hunt's tone was one of belligerence, as he swung on his chair to face Morgan.

'Why the hell did you come back then? Why didn't you stay in that rundown smug little country with its aristocracy who think it's still 1900 and believe that Britannia rules the waves? It's self-deceiving stupidity the way the English live in the past, resting on the laurels of a long-gone empire! They're a third-rate country now.'

'Oh, I wouldn't say that,' remarked Greg.

'Well, I would! Tell me one thing, just one thing, the British excel at nowadays?' Hunt demanded.

Morgan looked angry and bewildered and glanced at Greg for support.

'Let's order,' snapped Tiffany, 'or else we'll be here all night.'

They ate dinner in a silence that was only broken when one of them asked a waiter for something. Morgan, like a brilliant firework that bursts into a night sky, entrancing everyone with its cascades of magical sparkles, was spent. Like a burnt-out rocket, she picked at her food and drank a lot of wine. To her New York *did* seem like an ugly menacing maze, in which she felt trapped. Wherever she had looked that day, she saw nothing but bare bold skyscrapers, line after line of them, as soulless as the squares on a chess board, as predictable as a sheet of graph paper. With nostalgia she remembered the regal elegance of Belgravia, the quaintness of Chelsea, the expensive atmosphere of Mayfair, and the splendour of Buckingham Palace and the Houses of Parliament. It was enough to make her cry.

'Let's go.' Hunt rose unceremoniously.

Morgan insisted on being dropped off at her parents' home first, and she refused Greg's request to come up with her for a few minutes.

'Can I call tomorrow?' he asked anxiously.

Morgan shrugged, the curtain of her golden hair hiding her averted profile.

'Have a good night's sleep then, honey,' he said. 'I'll call you around noon. Perhaps we can have lunch?'

For answer she swung away and almost ran to the entrance, leaving Greg standing foolishly on the sidewalk, with Tiffany and Hunt watching from the car.

With a whimsical smile to cover his disappointment, Greg looked at Tiffany. 'I think I'll walk home. It's only a couple of blocks, and I could use some exercise.'

Tiffany nodded, understanding.

'Okay, Greg. Lovely to see you, call me sometime.'

'I will. Thanks, Tiff.' He gave what was meant to be a jaunty wave and set off down the street.

Morgan brushed past the doorman, hardly acknowledging his existence and his polite, 'Good evening, Miss Kalvin.'

Thank God she was home! Thank God she could go to bed and be alone. The strain of the evening had been worse than she imagined. Damn Tiffany with her bright ideas about cheering her up. Now her head ached and a deep cramp of misery clamped her throat, making it painful to swallow. Life was crappy. And why was it all happening to her? Tears of self-pity stung her eyes. Hunt had been an absolute swine and Tiffany no support at all. And as for Greg, with his devoted spaniel eyes and soppy looks! Christ, he hadn't made her laugh once! She stepped quietly into the apartment, trying to restrain the little sobs that were bubbling up in her chest. If only she were still in England. If only Harry had been strong enough to resist his hateful mother. If only . . .! All was quiet in the hall except for the faint sound of the television coming from the study. If she tiptoed down the corridor to her room, she wouldn't be heard. There was no way she could face an interrogation from her father right now. Tomorrow she would feel stronger. Tomorrow she would have collected herself enough to think up some lies about the wonderful time she'd had. Slipping off her gold sandals she began to creep across the Chinese silk rug, past the ornate hall table where she paused at the sight of a cable on the silver tray – and it was addressed to her!

With a bound, she snatched up the envelope, tore down the hall and rushed into her room, shutting the door quietly behind her. Trembling, she opened it and feverishly ripped out the sheet of paper inside.

Her piercing scream penetrated the walls of the apartment, disturbing Ruth and Joe as they sat watching Joan Rivers concluding the *Tonight* show.

Tiffany and Hunt were silent as he headed his car in the direction of her apartment. She slid her hand up his thigh and squeezed gently. There was a pause before he responded by putting his hand over hers.

'Honey ... I'm sorry,' he murmured unhappily. 'I just couldn't take those two tonight. It's been a lousy day and making sweet talk in some noisy hot restaurant was not my idea of fun.'

'I know.' Tiffany sounded regretful. 'I'm sorry too, darling.' Her hand slid higher up his thigh.

'That sister of yours has about as much brain as a chicken on a spit, and Greg's a love-sick ass.' Hunt changed gear violently. 'They sure deserve each other! What was the matter with them tonight anyway? They've been so lovey-dovey in the past, it was enough to make a guy throw up! I thought they were getting engaged once she got back?'

'I think her trip has unsettled her,' Tiffany replied with careful loyalty. 'She had an affair in England that seems to have ended on a sour note. She's also jet-lagged and no doubt worn out answering all Daddy's questions. You know how he likes to live his life through all of us.' Tiffany snuggled closer. 'Let's forget all about them and go home.' Her hand reached out for his crotch – something that usually drove him wild – but he was frowning as he stopped at the traffic lights.

Tiffany withdrew her hand abruptly and in a business-like way took her keys out of her Gucci evening purse. They didn't speak again until he stopped the car at the entrance to her apartment.

'Are you coming up then?' Her tone was casual.

'Do you want me to?' He shot her a questioning look.

Tiffany slid from the car. 'It's up to you.' Quietly she clicked the car door shut and headed straight for the elevator, her head held high.

After a moment Hunt followed slowly.

In her living room he went straight to the bar and poured himself a rye, and without offering her one, went and sat in one of her large armchairs. The gesture isolated him from her. In the past he had always pulled her down on the sofa beside him.

Hunt's expression was serious – for a moment Tiffany thought indifferent – and her stomach contracted and her heart began to pump nervously.

He was the first to speak.

'Tiff – my darling – you know that I love you, don't you?'

Tiffany nodded, her eyes latched to his. Was this the moment she had so long dreaded?

Hunt sipped his drink thoughtfully. 'I had another row with Joni today, in fact she barged onto the set and made one hell of a scene.' He leaned back against the cushions and closed his eyes for a moment, but he found it difficult to obliterate the memory of his drunken wife, screeching like a virago in front of everyone. 'I'd give my soul to split from Joni,' he said slowly, 'but I can't just abandon Gus and Matt. They're already afraid I'm going to leave them. Every morning Matt is in tears, asking if I'll be back before they go to bed. I love those kids, Tiffany, and there's no way I can let them down. Joni would get custody if we divorced, and then I'd only get to see them at weekends; I don't want to be a part-time father. You know, all this reminds me of when my father left us. The pain and the guilt because I thought it was my fault. It wasn't of course, but how do you explain that to a child?'

Silently, Tiffany refilled his glass, her hands trembling. 'Would Joni really get custody?'

'The mother usually does, and in her own way, she loves them, I suppose. Oh, Jesus, Tiff, I feel desperate.' Hunt bent his head, twisting the glass in his hands, so that some of the whisky spilled on the carpet.

'But – but we can go on seeing each other – sometimes – can't we?' Tiffany asked through a blur of tears. 'Even if you don't want to get a divorce?'

Hunt looked at her for a long moment, then suddenly he jumped to his feet, rushed over to her and hugged her close.

'Oh Tiff, I can't live without you.' He buried his face in her hair. 'I love you – really love you, but this is all so unfair to you. We can't get married, yet I want to make you my wife more than anything else. I want us to be together always – but I can't do that to Gus and Matt.' She could tell by his voice that he was on the point of breaking up.

'I understand, honey, I'm glad you talked to me about it.' Tiffany stroked his hair, letting her fingers run through his dark curls. 'But if I can't live with you, I can't live without you either. And if this is the only way to be together, just now and again . . .' She pulled him closer, as if she could not bear to let him go. 'Can't we just go on the way we're going?'

'It's not good enough, Tiffany! For either you or me. You deserve better than this.' The finality in his voice was a spear of ice in her heart.

'We can make it work!' She felt desperate now. She couldn't lose him! He was everything she had ever wanted and more besides. 'To hell with marriage! I'm not interested in getting married; I'm working too hard, for one thing. But there's nothing to stop us seeing each other!' Suddenly she felt strong. Hunt loved her and that was all that mattered. The rest she could cope with. If she had to share him, then half a cake was better than no cake at all. 'Listen, Hunt!' Her tone was fierce, resolute. She gripped him tightly. 'I know the score. In my heart of hearts I've always known it. I never expected you to leave your wife, but if I lose you, I lose everything that makes life worth living. You *are* my life, darling, so don't ever suggest that we stop seeing each other – because I simply couldn't take that.'

Their eyes met, his so dark and penetrating, hers now calm and as green as the Aegean Sea after a storm.

After a moment he leant forward and kissed her lips, reverently at first and then with a surge of desire.

Quickly, as always, he ignited desire in Tiffany, but tonight their love-making was tinged with a gentle sadness, a lingering touching of hands, a softness of kisses, a deep gradual fusing of their bodies and souls, as if they both sensed their time together was nearly over.

Several blocks downtown Zachary was sitting on Smokey's bed, tugging anxiously with his teeth at a hang-nail.

Smokey stood at the window looking down on the grimy poverty of the street below. There was a drugstore opposite and next to it a dingy all-night diner. Lounging in the doorway two swarthy young men chewed gum and watched the young women strutting past.

On the other side of the drugstore stood a second-hand clothes shop. The cotton skirts and cheap blouses had been displayed so long in the window that they were faded from the sun.

Smokey didn't intend to stay in this neighbourhood much longer.

Opposite Zachary, and lounging in the only chair in the room, was a man in his middle forties. He had a flattened, debauched face under a crown of smooth grey hair, combed forward to hide the balding crown. A rubbery nose set between slitted eyes and a wide loose mouth gave the effect of rancid dough.

There was silence in the small cramped room.

'Well, do I get it?' The man spoke at last, manoeuvring a crumpled wet cigar from one side of his mouth to the other.

'I'll get it all right, don't worry, I'll get it.' Zachary gabbled nervously.

'Yeah, but like when? Next Christmas ain't no good! You've had the stuff and now it's pay-up time, see? The boss don't like to be kept waitin'.'

'I tell you it will be okay! No shit! Ask Smokey! She knows I can get the money, it's just that I have to make arrangements – it's tied up, you see.' Zachary was sweating heavily.

'You'll be tied up if you don't deliver by this time tomorrow night.' The man leaned forward, blowing smoke in Zachary's face. 'And like I said, I want the whole fuckin' two thou, no messin', cause it would be a pity if that pretty face of yours got carved up, now wouldn't it?' His bloodshot eyes leered at Zachary, and he gave an ugly smile.

'It'll be okay,' Zachary repeated mechanically, looking at the floor.

'See that it is.' The man rose menacingly. 'Tomorrow night, this time.' He gave Smokey a familiar smack on the bottom and made for the door. They remained silent as they heard him clumping down the narrow stairs.

Zachary felt the cold lump of ice that had been weighing heavily in his stomach explode and splinter through his body. There were goose bumps on his arms and his hands shook.

'Sorry, hon.' Smokey came over and sat on the bed beside him. 'But I'll be the one in big trouble if you don't pay up! I got the stuff for you and Satch will turn real nasty, and I mean *real* nasty, if he don't get the dough. Busted my best friend's face when one of her clients didn't deliver. Jesus, she was in hospital for three weeks! Lost all her front teeth, everything! You wouldn't like that to happen to me would ya, honey!' Smokey gave a shudder at the memory; you didn't cross Satch. Not ever. 'It's only a coupla thou anyway ... you can get it from that smart-assed family of yours, can't you?'

Zachary sat with his head in his hands. He was longing to get high. He was longing to fuck Smokey's wet cunt.

He wasn't sure which he wanted most.

One thing was certain. He'd lose both, and maybe his face as well if he didn't come up with two thousand dollars by this time tomorrow.

Morgan sat on her bed counting on her fingers, working out the time in England. She'd finally got Ruth and Joe off to bed after they'd come rushing into her room. It hadn't been easy. They'd have stayed up talking all night if she hadn't been firm. She also wanted a few minutes alone before she made the call. A few minutes in which to think things through, though there wasn't much to think about really.

At one point she started dialling Tiffany's number but decided against it. Tiff and Hunt were probably in bed and wouldn't want to be disturbed, even if Ronald Reagan had declared nuclear war.

Morgan glanced once again at her diamond watch, then started dialling.

Harry Blairmore put on his tailcoat and gave a final adjustment to his white bow tie and wing collar. One final glance in the mirror – hair smooth, sapphire studs in place, shoes shining like mirrors – assured him he was ready for another boring night of party going. How he hated it! All those ambitious mothers whose teeth stuck out like rabbits', and their vacuous daughters! All those pushy businessmen, who angled for an invitation to shoot at Drumnadrochit. Still, it was good for business; the most unlikely people came to the gallery to buy paintings as a result of his having met them at a party.

Tonight it was drinks at the Ritz first, with Cynthia Beresford, a rich widow and art collector; she was also the chairman of a company she had inherited from her late husband that made secret components for the Ministry of Defence. Then dinner at the Mansion House (that would be long and boring, but also useful) and finally he'd drop in to Claridge's where the Millers were giving a ball to celebrate their son's coming of age and their daughter's reluctant début into society. Winthrop Hart was going to be at the ball, and Mr Hart had shown a great deal of interest in a Rembrandt in Harry's gallery. If he could be persuaded that its presence in his mansion in Dallas wouldn't be only an investment but would raise his social standing by several notches, Harry was in for a nice profit.

Pleased with the thought, Harry swung easily down the sweeping staircase of his parents' Belgravia house, and decided that he just had time for a quick whisky and soda before he left. On a sturdy Victorian table in a corner of the study stood the drinks tray, set with heavy decanters and crystal tumblers. A man of routine, Harry glanced at the clock, decided he had precisely seven minutes in which to enjoy a drink and have a glance at the court circular in *The Times*. His perusal of who had got engaged, married or died was interrupted by the ringing of the telephone.

'Hullo?' He sounded cool and efficient.

'May I speak with Lord Blairmore, please?' For a moment he couldn't place the voice.

'Speaking.'

'Harry! It's Morgan!'

'Morgan... I didn't recognize your voice...' He felt himself tense up, Morgan sounded so far away.

'I got your cable, Harry.' She sounded strange.

'Yes?' Harry's heart was pounding, wondering what she'd say. He'd been too scared to call her up after the way she'd stormed out of Drumnadrochit; he thought a cable would be better.

The pause on the line lengthened.

At last she spoke, softly. 'Harry? Are you there?'

'Yes, Morgan. I'm here.'

'Harry . . . I'd love to marry you.'

'Morgan, darling! . . . God, that's wonderful! I can't believe it . . .' He was babbling incoherently. His brain was dizzy as he realized all that her answer meant.

'Are you sure it's what you want?' He heard her asking as if she were picking her words carefully. 'I mean your family . . .'

'Don't worry about a thing, my darling. I know Pa thinks you're terrific, and my mother will be fine just as soon as she gets to know you.'

'I hope so. I'm so excited. Harry, when can we get married? When can we announce our engagement?' She sounded like a little girl.

Harry smiled as, hitching the phone under his chin, he reached with trembling hands for the whisky decanter. 'Just as soon as you like, darling, only there are a couple of things I have to do first.' Like telling Elizabeth Greenly he wasn't marrying her, for a start. Like asking his parents if they wanted the good or the bad news first. Above all like ringing up *The Times* and the *Telegraph* and telling them not to go ahead and print the announcement of the engagement between the Marquess of Blairmore and the Lady Elizabeth Greenly.

'Why don't you fly over here and meet my family and then we can have an engagement party?' suggested Morgan.

It was a suggestion he liked very much. It could be a beautiful way of avoiding a great deal of friction, especially when the tabloids got hold of the story. His eyes narrowed as he took a swig of whisky and saw the banner headlines staring at him. Duke's Heir Jilts Marquess's Daughter for American Socialite. The tabloids would have a field day and his mother was going to have the shit-fits.

'That's a splendid idea, Morgan, absolutely splendid!

Look, keep the whole thing under your hat for a couple of days. It'll be our secret, darling... and then I'll call you before the weekend and arrange to fly to New York, perhaps on Saturday? How does that grab you?'

It grabbed Morgan perfectly. She knew exactly why he was stalling on the announcement of their engagement, and it didn't worry her a bit. Goodbye, Lady E., and good fucking riddance! She'd known all along she was too dull and mousy for Harry. What Harry needed was a starry wife, a wife who would give him a glamorous image – and God knows these aristocratic English were low on glamour if high on pedigree. Together they would become London's most sought-after couple; Harry for his title, she for her looks and stylishness, and the money to be able to do everything with flair. It was going to be terrific. They were damn well made for each other.

'Come over as soon as you can, darling. I can't wait for you to meet everyone,' Morgan crooned. Ignoring the fact that she had already told her parents the contents of the telegram, plus her plan to rush round to Tiffany's at dawn she added, 'And I won't tell a soul until you say it's all right.'

'Good girl. Take care, my darling, and I'll be in touch.'

'I'm so excited I shall never get to sleep tonight.' It was Morgan, the four-year-old child on Christmas Eve, talking. Harry was enchanted.

'And Morgan' – he cleared his throat nervously – 'I do love you.'

'Glad you realized it – in time.' It was the only reference she was going to make to Lady Elizabeth. 'Good night, darling... and I love you too.'

Harry softly replaced the receiver and finished his drink. Bloody hell, life was amazing. One minute he was engaged to good old Elizabeth, whom he'd known practically all his life, and the next he was engaged to this beautiful American girl, who had seduced him something rotten from the start. There was going to be one hell of a stink from both his parents and

Elizabeth's. His friends would call him an absolute sod and a bounder, but what the hell! Morgan was worth it. Especially in bed. Oh Christ, especially in bed! He wanted her desperately this very moment.

5

Morgan and Zachary arrived at exactly the same time the next morning at Tiffany's apartment. Each came from opposite directions. Neither had slept during the long oppressive night, when the heat had fumed on the sidewalks of Manhattan and the humidity had drenched the city in its torpid grip. Now, at ten o'clock, a heat-haze stilled the air so that New York seemed suspended in a vacuum.

Morgan, fresh and sparkling in spite of everything, stepped from her father's chauffeur-driven Lincoln Continental. Her white linen suit looked as if it had been pressed ten seconds before and her blonde hair, newly washed and gleaming, swung about her shoulders in casual waves.

Zachary, unshaven and red-eyed, shambled uncertainly along the sidewalk, his hands plunged deeply into a pair of dirty jeans. His sweat-shirt was stained and crumpled.

'Zac!' Morgan eyed him with an undisguised repulsion. 'What the hell's the matter with you? You look terrible.'

Zachary stumbled up the steps to his sister's apartment and only just avoided colliding with the security guard.

'Did you come home last night?' demanded Morgan.

'Nope.'

'Where were you then?'

'A party.'

'Some kind of party!' Morgan sniffed delicately as they stepped into the elevator. 'Mom and Dad will freak out if they see you like this.'

'I'll get cleaned up later. Want to talk to Tiff first.'

'What about?'

'Just something.' Zachary stepped out of the elevator in front of her, brushing her pristine skirt with a grubby hand.

'Watch it!' Morgan cried angrily. 'My God, you're really impossible.'

Tiffany had already been hard at work in her studio for several hours, working on some designs for a new TV spectacular. She glanced up, irritated, as they entered. She'd particularly told Gloria she didn't want to be disturbed. There was too much work and too little time to do it in. A glance at Morgan and Zachary as they settled themselves on the sofa, told her one thing. She laid down her paint brush with a quiet sigh. The rest of the morning was going to be a wipe-out.

'So – what gives?' Tiffany asked, looking from one to the other. 'It's a bit early for you to be up and about isn't it, Morgan?'

'You'll never guess,' began Morgan, then jumping from the chair hurled herself into Tiffany's arms. 'The most fabulous news you've ever heard – I'm wild with excitement.'

'You've bought yourself a new dress,' remarked Tiffany, disentangling herself.

'No – no, I haven't actually. Harry and I are going to be married! Have you ever heard anything so romantic? Can you believe it? There was a cable when I got back last night, so I rang him – '

'What did you say?' Tiffany's mouth was wide open with amazement.

'What do you think I said, stupid! I said yes, as quick as a flash in case he changed his mind! Or his mother changed it for him.' Morgan opened her purse and took out a slim gold cigarette case. 'Oh, it was fantastic, Tiff. He was so thrilled, he's coming over – probably on the weekend – then he can meet you all, and we'll announce our engagement and have a fantastic party!' Bubbling with excitement, Morgan lit her cigarette and danced round the room. 'I'm getting married to Harry! I'm getting married to Harry!' she kept repeating, as if she could hardly believe it herself.

Tiffany could feel her sister's happiness as if it were a tangible thing. 'When are you getting married, darling?'

'Harry didn't say, but I tell you what! I want a big wedding in London, somewhere like Westminster Abbey, with a reception at the House of Lords or something. I went to a few big society weddings when I was over there, and they were fabulous, Tiff. So grand and elegant.'

'Well!' Tiffany tried to gather her wits into some sort of order. She was glad that Morgan was so happy. She'd miss her though. Maddening though Morgan could be, there was never a dull moment when she was around.

'Do you realize,' Morgan was saying, as she resumed her perch on the sofa, 'that I will be the Marchioness of Blairmore, then the Duchess of Lomond one day – with Drumnadrochit Castle, and a large house in the best part of London! God, I can't wait!'

'What about the girl he was going to marry?'

Morgan shrugged and made a little grimace. 'That's her bad luck. Drab little thing anyway. Tiff, I'm going to set English society ablaze! I'll give fascinating dinner parties, and *Vogue* will feature me "At Home", and I'll commission Brian Organ, who painted Princess Diana, to do my portrait, and I'll organize shoots at the castle and invite cabinet ministers. Oh, Harry and I will have the most marvellous life. I'll be so good for him.'

Tiffany was silent. None of it was her idea of bliss – all she wanted was her work, with the challenge and rewards it brought. And Hunt. How she wanted Hunt. It made her realize how different she and Morgan were. Their needs and desires were poles apart. Yet they understood each other and recognized that their very differences brought them in many ways closer together. Tiffany smiled. Morgan's ecstatic mood was hard to resist.

'Darling, I'm really thrilled for you.' She went over and kissed her sister warmly. Then she realized that Zachary was slumped in his corner of the sofa, an isolated and dejected figure. A single tear shimmered on his lashes. He hadn't said a word since he'd arrived.

'Honey, what's the matter?' Tiffany put her arm round his shoulders. 'It doesn't mean we won't see Morgan again just because she'll be living in England.'

Miserably, he hung his head. 'It's not that. I'm glad for you, Sis' – he glanced across at Morgan – 'I really am.'

'What's the matter then? You've been behaving strangely ever since we've been here.' Morgan dragged deeply on her cigarette and exhaled a perfect smoke ring.

Zachary turned to Tiffany. His voice shook. 'I – I need money, quite a lot, and I haven't figured out a way of getting it. I've got to have it by tonight, and – and I wondered if you could lend it to me?'

Tiffany looked sympathetic. 'What's it for, Zac? You get a fairly generous allowance from Dad. Why don't you ask him, he'll always help you if it's for books or something. He's reasonable like that.'

'I can't. I mean I already have.' For a moment he looked wildly round the room, as if searching for a means of escape. 'I need two thousand dollars by tonight and if I don't get it . . .' With an impatient gesture he wiped his nose with the back of his hand.

'Two thousand! For Christ's sake, what for?' demanded Morgan shrilly.

'A gambling debt.'

That came out too glibly, thought Tiffany, like he'd been giving it a lot of practice.

'How can you be such a stupid fool!' Morgan was raging. 'Where the hell do you gamble anyway, you're under age?'

Tiffany tried to silence her sister with a chilling look.

'What's really wrong, Zac? You look ill,' she said gently.

'I'm fine.' He made an attempt at tossing his head defiantly. It didn't deceive either of them. 'I'll pay you back, Tiff, promise. As soon as I get my money, I'll pay you back with interest. It's just that I need it quick, and Mom and Dad would never understand – and there'd just be another frigging fight.'

Tiffany was tempted to question him further. Something was very wrong. He was behaving out of character, and he did look ill, but she reached for her handbag and drew out her cheque book.

'Okay, Zac. I'll help you this time. Two thousand dollars is one hell of a lot of money, and I expect you to give it back to me when you are able.' She started writing rapidly. 'There is a condition, though.'

He looked up eagerly, ready to promise anything.

'I'm letting you have this on the condition that you never gamble or whatever again. I don't know what you've been up to or who your friends are, and I'm not asking, but if anything like this happens again I'm going straight to Mom and Dad. Is that clear?' Her gentle expression belied the severity of her words.

'Gee, Sis, thanks. Yes, I promise.' Relief flooded his face, and reminded Tiffany of how he had looked when he'd got out of some scrape as a child.

'Are you mad?' cried Morgan. 'Why should *you* help? He's probably got some girl pregnant! I don't swallow this gambling bit.'

'Like I said,' Tiffany looked coolly at her sister, 'I'm not asking. All I want is that he should stay out of trouble in future.' If only Morgan hadn't been around, I might have been able to talk to Zac, get to the root of the trouble, Tiffany thought. Those two have never gotten along. Many were the times Zachary had taken the brunt of their parents' wrath because Morgan had made it look as if everything was her brother's fault.

Morgan had lost interest in the whole subject. She was flipping through a fashion magazine and saying, 'You'll have to design my wedding dress, you know. Something in heavy white satin, I think, and very dramatic.'

Zachary slipped away, the cheque safely tucked into his

pocket. How long he could survive without a line, he didn't know. He just hoped to hell he could keep his promise to Tiffany.

The atmosphere was elegantly expensive, as Ruth and Joe Kalvin prepared for the party they were giving to celebrate Morgan's engagement. Two hundred guests had been invited, and all day frantic preparations were in progress. Florists arrived and arranged great cascades of exotic flowers wherever they could find a space. Caterers came by the van load, bearing *pâté de foie gras* imported from France, Beluga caviar from Russia, and smoked salmon from Scotland. Dozens of bottles of Dom Pérignon were already on ice, and the bar was fully stocked with a full range of liquor. An army of servants polished silver and rubbed cut crystal until it sparkled, while others smoothed damask cloths over the tables, and got in the way of the florists who were trying to pin garlands of flowers along the front. Cushions were plumped, extra ashtrays were set in position and the housekeeper was fighting a losing battle with the vacuum cleaner as she tried to clean up every speck.

Joe came home from the office in the afternoon to check every detail for himself. Vidal Sassoon's top stylist was working wonders on Ruth's hair in the bedroom, and the dress designed for her by Oscar de la Renta lay waiting on the bed. Joe felt enormously pleased with himself. All his business friends – and a few enemies as well – had been invited, plus a lot of Ruth's friends, most of whom figured largely on her charity committees. Joe was going to show them all! Not one of them could boast of a daughter who was marrying a top-notch English nobleman, and nothing must go wrong tonight. Whatever people said about Joe Kalvin they had to admit he was a winner and a lavish host. Since the wedding was going to take place in England he planned to fly out at least a hundred and fifty friends, put them up at the Savoy and take over Annabel's for a party on the night of the wedding. When Joe did anything, he did it with style. Pursing his small mouth with pleasure, he rubbed his chubby hands together. All he had to do now was check that Ruth had got it together.

Morgan had set off at eleven o'clock that morning to meet Harry at JFK. Looking exquisite in a beige silk suit with pale crocodile shoes and purse, she sank into the back of her father's car and felt a deep thrill of satisfaction.

At last Harry was arriving. The past two weeks had seemed like the longest she'd ever lived, and it was in fact nearly three weeks since she'd last seen him. She tried to recall his face, but it kept eluding her, the features dissolving in her mind's eye as she tried to picture him. But his voice was wonderful – they'd talked daily on the phone since she'd agreed to marry him. It was rich and warm, not overripe like some English accents.

Most exciting of all was the fact that he was bringing the one thing she longed for most, the engagement ring. The outward symbol of their relationship. He'd refused to tell her what it was like, as he wanted to surprise her, but he'd said it was 'rather nice' and a family heirloom.

At least, thank God, she'd have it to wear for the party tonight and if it was a coloured stone, she just hoped it would go with her new dress.

Tiffany, nearing the deadline for completing her designs for the TV spectacular, worked furiously in her studio all day. Propped all round her were sketches, drawn and painted to show every detail of the costumes. Clipped to each design were samples of relevant fabric, bead, sequin and feather. The results were pleasing. Having had endless conferences with the set designer, Russ Habe, and Tony Setter, who was doing the lighting, she felt the final impact would be sensational. Colour would pile on colour in some scenes; in others, starkness and style would predominate. Dianne

Giancana was making the costumes again, and Tiffany felt happy in the knowledge that her designs would be carried out to perfection. It was five past five now, and she'd started working with Shirley and Maria at eight that morning. God, did she feel weary.

'Gloria,' she called through to the kitchen, 'could you fix me some lemon tea, please?'

'Sure thing, Mizz Tiffany, and would you like some cookies?'

'No thanks.'

Tiffany stood up and stretched. Her neck and shoulders were aching and her head hurt slightly. She'd done enough for today. Her objective eye was going and she felt absolutely drained. After tea she'd lie down for a while, and then have an invigorating shower before changing for the party. She hadn't decided what to wear.

Ruth Kalvin was worried about the guest list. She was also worried about which of her many sets of jewellery looked best with her new dress. Would the emeralds and pearls really look better than the diamonds and sapphires? She fiddled with the back of her newly styled hair and hoped it didn't look too fluffy. Ruth knew she was being silly fussing over these small details, but she simply couldn't help it. If anything went wrong, Joe would blame her.

The news of Morgan's engagement had appeared in all the papers several days ago; Suzy had done a large piece on Harry, describing him as 'the future English Duke of Lomond, who lives in an ancient castle in Scotland, surrounded by 100,000 acres of prime land'. Other columnists had followed the line and now the press were coming in force. At this rate the party would be featured in every tabloid the next day, and Joe would feel it had all been worth it. But supposing the hired waiters arrived late? Or the most important guests failed to turn up? Supposing someone got drunk, or the champagne ran out?

Clasping her manicured and bejewelled hands, Ruth reached for her bottle of Valium.

The first dozen or so guests arrived, the exquisitely dressed women eyeing each other ruthlessly while they gushed and kissed air. Ruth and Joe stood in the hall receiving, with Morgan and Harry beside them. On the third finger of Morgan's left hand she proudly displayed a large dark ruby set in beautifully fashioned gold and surrounded by diamonds. Harry told her it had once belonged to Mary Queen of Scots, who had given it to an ancestor of his after she had visited Drumnadrochit Castle. In a second, sighing with relief, Morgan realized her crimson lace and chiffon dress had been an inspired guess. It might have been designed to go with the ring! And to think she'd nearly chosen royal blue! The press were lapping it all up, scribbling the details furiously, while flash bulbs popped all around them. Harry kept his arm proudly round Morgan's waist as he was introduced to all their friends. Charming and smiling, he admitted that yes, he was a very lucky man, and yes, he knew they were going to be very happy.

When Tiffany arrived the photographers pressed closer; a shot of the sisters together would be great. Tiffany was becoming mildly famous in her own right, and the cameras caught them just as Morgan was extending her left hand to show Tiffany her ring. That would make a nice shot.

Sipping champagne, Tiffany went into the living room to see who was there. No sign of Hunt yet. She just hoped he was going to make it. White-jacketed waiters moved smoothly among the guests with silver trays of drinks and exquisite platters of Beluga caviar, grapes wrapped in slivers of smoked salmon, gulls' eggs and tiny lobster patties. Everyone seemed to be having a good time. Tiffany wandered back into the hall.

Ruth's smile was becoming more fixed by the minute as she greeted new arrivals, her heart skipping a beat every time a group came through the door. Almost all the VIPs had arrived, but there were still a few missing. She bit her lip while Joe became more jovial and relaxed as he greeted his friends, slapping the men on the back, flattering the ladies, and urging everyone to have a drink.

'Everything okay, Mom?' Tiffany asked quietly as she slid to her mother's side.

'So far, so good, I think. Do you think the party's going all right?'

'Of course it is! Stop worrying. If you like I'll go and see if anyone looks lost or thirsty, though they seem all right to me.'

'Oh do, Tiffany! Make sure everyone has everything.' Looking strained, Ruth turned to greet her husband's partner, Sig Hoffman, and his wife. Tiffany, seeing who it was, moved quickly back into the living room before Sig could say anything to her. Having to be civil to that man was one thing she couldn't face.

Wandering in a large circle round the living room, making sure that glasses were filled and everyone seemed to have someone to talk to, Tiffany decided there was no one she wanted to get engaged in conversation with. None of them were show-biz and worse, none were interested or understood what it was all about. Her work was so important to her that she found it infuriating that these people thought of her only as the Kalvins' pretty eldest daughter, who had plenty of money amusing herself with a nice little hobby until she got married.

'You're looking very lovely, my dear.'

Tiffany turned and saw it was an elderly congressman whom her father had been trying to befriend for years.

'Thank you. How are you?' He was probably the most intelligent man there and Tiffany was pleased to see him.

'Doing all right. This is a very happy occasion, isn't it?' He glanced round the room with a mellow smile.

'Yes, it's wonderful,' agreed Tiffany, looking at Morgan

and Harry, who, hand-in-hand, were now mingling with the guests. 'I'm so happy for Morgan, although I shall miss her when she goes to live in England.'

'Her young man looks like a really nice guy.' He patted Tiffany's shoulder in a fatherly way. 'And when is a pretty girl like you going to get married?'

For an almost uncontrollable second Tiffany felt her eyes smart.

Hunt was the only man she'd ever loved – the only man she'd ever wanted to marry, and he wasn't even here. She shrugged, gained instant control and replied lightly, 'One of these days, I suppose! I'm too busy at the moment to even think about it. I'm doing the costume designs for a television show, which is the biggest thing I've done so far . . .' and she launched into a description of her work. It was the one part of her life over which she had complete control and it always made her feel better to talk about it. A slightly glazed look crept over the senator's eyes, and Tiffany realized he was no more interested in her work than any of her parents' other friends. 'If you'll excuse me,' she said with an apologetic tone in her voice, 'I'll just check to see if my parents want any help.' She sidled away but he was gone before she had even finished her sentence.

Ruth was beginning to breathe more easily, although her head was splitting. She and Joe had stopped receiving twenty minutes before. Everyone seemed to be having a good time, so why did she still feel so apprehensive?

Joe was murmuring in her ear, 'I think it's time I proposed their health. Tell the waiters to make sure everyone has full glasses.'

He strode off to find Morgan and Harry.

Ruth nodded. Soon it would all be over. She could hardly wait.

'Daddy, this is the most fabulous party.' Morgan grabbed his arm and squeezed it.

'Yes, it's going very well.' Joe reached to kiss her on the cheek. 'Well, it sure is a memorable occasion. You doing all right, Harry?'

Harry beamed. He'd drunk quantities of Dom Pérignon and felt very good indeed.

'Yes, thank you, sir! It really is most awfully good of you to lay on all this for us you know.'

Joe smiled. Polite boy. Real class, too. He just wished he'd drop the 'sir' bit.

'Okay. Okay. You both hang in right there. I'm going to make a little speech in a minute.'

'Oh Daddy! Do you have –' Morgan stopped. Her father's speeches at Thanksgiving were bad enough – but tonight! On the other hand it would be really mean to deprive him of this moment of glory, for sure as eggs hatch into little chickens he wouldn't be allowed to make a speech at the wedding. 'All right, Daddy.' She smiled swiftly. 'What do you want us to do?'

'Just wait over there in front of the fireplace. Now where has your mother gone? I don't know what the hell's the matter with her tonight.' Frowning, Joe went off in search of his wife and caught sight of Tiffany rushing to the door to fling her arms round a tall good-looking man. Joe's small mouth tightened. He didn't know Hunt Kellerman had been invited. For God's sake, when was Tiffany going to get herself a regular guy?

Ruth and Joe stood side by side, in front of one of the vast flower arrangements that all but obliterated the fireplace. Beside them Morgan and Harry held hands and giggled quietly.

'My friends,' Joe began. No one paid the slightest bit of notice. A waiter tapped loudly with a silver spoon on the bar and the conversation quietly died away as Joe waited, poised on his toes like a fat little bird ready to take flight. He wanted everyone's attention.

'We are here tonight,' he began, 'to drink the health and happiness of my beautiful daughter Morgan, and her fiancé, the Marquess of Blairmore. Both Ruth and I are delighted to welcome this fine upstanding young man into our midst, into our family in fact, and I know, from the bottom of my heart, that he is going to take good care of our little girl. When they get married in England in the fall, with all the traditional pomp of a stately British occasion, with all the noble heritage attached to the Marquess's family, it is my dearest wish, and the wish of my wife also, that you will all be able to join us again so that we can witness the joining of this fine young couple...'

'Oh shit!' Tiffany breathed in Hunt's ear, as they stood in a far corner of the living room. 'This is awful! How can we get him to stop?' Hunt gave her a knowing wink.

'... So I ask you now, my dear friends,' Joe droned on, well into his stride, 'to raise your glasses and drink a toast of wealth, health, happiness and great prosperity to –'

A figure burst through the doorway and Ruth's heart gave a great lurch. Wild-eyed and dishevelled, it hurled itself through the startled guests and charged right up to Joe, glaring viciously into his confused face.

'Quit that crap, you mother-fucking son of a bitch. You're – you're nothing but a fucking shit-head!'

Flash bulbs exploded in every direction. Zachary was going for his father's throat.

6

Doctor Louis Herwitz's face was grave as he came out of Zachary's room.

'Can I talk to you and your family for a moment, Mr Kalvin?' He glanced round the room where a few remaining guests lingered, talking and drinking quietly, determined not to leave until they had picked up every last shred of gossip they could glean. It was a story they intended to dine out on for weeks. 'Is there another room we can go to?'

'Sure, this way.' Joe led the doctor to his study, followed by Tiffany with Hunt holding her hand tightly, and Morgan and Harry.

'My wife's gone to her room. She's too upset to take any more tonight,' Joe snapped.

'Oh I'm sorry, I'll give her something to calm her down in a minute.' The doctor was the essence of compassion and kindness.

'Well?' Joe's eyes were cold chips of fury. He would like to kill that no-good son-of-a-bitch for lousing up the party.

Morgan frowned, lit a cigarette and glanced anxiously at Harry. What was he going to think of her family?

Tiffany sank suddenly into a chair, her legs weak because she felt she knew exactly what the doctor was going to say.

Herwitz spoke in a low voice. 'I'm sorry to have to tell you, Mr Kalvin – if you weren't already aware of it – but your son is on drugs.'

'Drugs!' thundered Joe, after rushing to slam the door so that the remaining guests wouldn't hear.

'He's on heroin, and maybe more besides. From what I can gather, though he's in a bad way and isn't about to talk, I believe he's been taking drugs for several months, including cocaine, heroin, Mandrax, amphetamines. Tell me, weren't you aware of a change in his behaviour?'

Joe's eyes suddenly bulged with fury and his face turned a dull red. 'What d'you mean? Do you think I'd *let* a son of mine do that to himself, and me in my position?'

'The damn fool, where could he get them from?' Morgan turned angrily on the doctor, as if he were to blame.

'I'm afraid they're very easily available.' Herwitz's voice remained quiet and level.

'Oh Christ!' A sob broke from Tiffany's throat and Hunt put his arm round her shoulders.

'So what do we do now?' demanded Joe. 'I don't want another scene like we just had.'

'Quite.' The doctor's tone became as crisp as a new dollar bill. 'I'll arrange for him to be admitted to the Moyes Clinic. It's in the Peekskills, in the lower Hudson Valley, so it's not too far away. It's the best clinic in the country for treating this type of case, and unless Zachary is given professional help, my bet is he'll be dead within a couple of years.' He picked up his black bag and made for the door. 'I'll ring you later this evening to give you the details. Someone must go with him though . . .' he glanced round the room.

'I'll take him in.' Tiffany rose as she spoke. There was silence in the room. As far as the rest of her family were concerned she was welcome.

Tiffany blinked furiously, trying to disperse the tears that kept welling up in her eyes. She leaned back in the hired limousine. Her father hadn't let her take his car in case the chauffeur found out the truth about Zachary. It had to be the worst day of her life. The nightmare had started when she'd arrived at her parents' duplex before breakfast to collect Zachary. A distracted and angry Morgan rushed at her, hissing, 'Get him out of here, for God's sake!' Clutching her blue satin and lace robe round her with one hand, she grabbed Tiffany's arm with the other.

'We've none of us had a wink of sleep – just listen to that!' She jerked her head in the direction of Zachary's room. Tormented animal sounds and occasional banging could be heard. 'Harry and I have been up practically all night. Zac's been yelling his head off since four o'clock this morning, and it's getting on my nerves.'

'Poor Zac, he's going cold turkey.' Tiffany rushed into her brother's room, where he lay on the floor, clawing at his stomach as the pain tore through him.

'Help me...!' His face was contorted and running with sweat and his arms started flailing helplessly.

Tiffany dropped onto her knees beside him and tried to cradle his head, but his body twisted away from her in an involuntary movement and he started screaming, 'You're killing me... don't kill me.'

'Morgan!' yelled Tiffany, over her shoulder.

'Shall I call the doctor again?' asked a quiet voice.

Tiffany looked up. It was Harry, still in his robe. His face showed sympathetic concern, as he bent over Zachary's writhing body.

'Yes, and tell him to get a private ambulance. The car can follow and bring me back, but I can't take him in a car in this state.'

It was when Zachary started retching in the ambulance, and messing himself, that Tiffany became really scared. The nurse was calm and efficient, but even the injection she gave him only quieted him for a short while.

'It's going to be all right, darling,' Tiffany said gently as he thrashed about on his cot. But he didn't seem to hear her and continued to scream hoarsely with pain.

A feeling of utter helplessness engulfed Tiffany, as she watched his torment. Was this demented creature really her kid brother, who'd been such a happy little boy, so full of sparkling life, and with such a sense of fun? He seemed like a stranger now, a sick, paranoid stranger, who'd been taken over by some evil force.

'Zachary,' she whispered. 'Hang in there, kid. You're gonna be all right.'

The limousine was entering the outskirts of New York, sweeping over the 59th Street Bridge on its way into Manhattan.

Tiffany opened her eyes, and looked at the Manhattan skyline, as it stretched across the horizon. Nothing was ever going to blot out the final parting scene when she had tried to say goodbye to Zachary at the clinic. As long as she lived, she felt she'd never forget the look in his eyes, a look of hostility and accusation, mingled with fear.

Watching the familiar landmarks of the World Trade Center, the Pan Am Building and the Empire State Building, as they glinted in the afternoon sun, Tiffany felt as if she had been away for a long time. Was it only this morning that she had glanced, uncaring, at the trees in Central Park? She suddenly felt a melancholy pang for the city she had known all her life, because now it seemed different, changed. And she wondered if she would ever see it again through the eyes of a carefree young woman. She decided, as Hunt had flown to Los Angeles that morning to discuss a new film, she would have a long soak in the tub, get Gloria to give her supper on a tray and perhaps watch something on television. Then she would turn in early. A quiet evening at home was exactly what she needed.

Morgan grabbed the morning papers, and poured herself a cup of strong coffee. They'd finally got Zachary into the ambulance, and now at last they could settle down to a quiet breakfast.

'Shit!' she gasped with annoyance. The papers carried nothing but pictures of her brother and an account of his disgraceful outburst the night before. A small line at the bottom of all the accounts merely said that the party had been intended as an engagement celebration for Harry and herself.

'Look what they say!' Morgan thrust the paper at Harry. Joe stomped into the breakfast room at that moment, looked over Harry's shoulder and let forth a stream of expletives. He'd spent twenty thousand dollars on the party of the season, only to be exposed to this public embarrassment.

'The sooner that boy's locked up where he can't do any more harm, the better!' he shouted, as he sat down heavily at the head of the table.

'But he's very sick, sir,' Harry interjected. 'He could easily end up dead unless he's treated. Taking drugs is an addiction...'

'You don't have to tell me what it is,' snarled Joe. 'If he'd been any sort of a strong character, like me, he'd have damn well never started in the first place!'

'The trouble is it's so easily available. I've known young chaps who just tried it for a lark, and before they knew what had happened, they were hooked. Someone at my college was sent down because of taking heroin. Tragedy of it was, it eventually killed him,' said Harry.

Joe looked at him stonily. Reminiscences of Harry's youth were something he could do without right now.

'Perhaps that's why...' Morgan exclaimed and then looked doubtfully at her father.

'Why what?'

She shrugged her pretty shoulders, still encased in blue satin and lace. She decided there was no harm in telling him what had happened at Tiffany's.

'And you let Tiffany give him that sort of dough without demanding a proper explanation, or better still, coming to me?' Joe's eyes bulged and his mouth became invisible.

'I thought, well, we thought,' Morgan stammered, 'that is, we really thought he'd only got some little bit of fluff pregnant and wanted money for an abortion, or something.'

She looked down uncomfortably. Harry was giving her strange looks. She raised her head defiantly. He was beginning to show signs of becoming a bore and a prig. Perhaps once they were married she'd be able to make him a bit more sophisticated. After all what were drugs? And what was so shocking about some girl getting an abortion?

Joe sighed with deep irritation, and folded his *Wall Street Journal* carefully.

'Where's Mother?' Morgan enquired brightly, to change the conversation.

'She's not well. Can you wonder? I told her to stay in bed.'

Joe rose, pausing by Harry's chair as he crossed the breakfast room.

'I'd just like to apologize to you, Harry. Last night was spoiled by my son's behaviour, and I'm very sorry. I hope it won't reach the ears of the Duke and Duchess.'

'Please don't apologize, sir.' Harry sprang to his feet. 'I just feel so sorry for Zachary, sir.'

Joe stalked out. Zachary could stew in his own juice for all he cared.

'Millionaire Joe Kalvin's Son in Furore at Party', ran the headlines. Smokey put a dime in the vending machine and grabbed a newspaper. In a nearby café she read the account of the top society party that had ended in chaos. Her eyes widened as she pored over the description of some of the guests: Mrs Wyngard Schuster in half a million dollars' worth of emeralds; Lady Stanhope, from England, wearing the famous Stanhope diamonds; the presidents of several oil and real estate corporations each worth in excess of ten million; a sprinkling of congressmen and their mink-draped wives; and Morgan, with her fiancé, the future Duke of Lomond. It was reported that the party had cost over fifty thousand dollars, with French champagne and food imported from all over the world. Joe Kalvin was quoted as saying of Zachary's 'outburst', 'Nothing we can't handle...

after all it was an engagement party... he just got a bit overexcited.'

Nothing more. No mention of drugs. Just a picture of Zachary, his mouth wide and distorted, struggling with two men who were gripping him as he tried to attack his father.

Smokey smiled to herself. Zachary hadn't been kidding when he said his father was rich. She checked the paper once again, as she drained the last of her coffee. 'The host,' she read, 'is President of Quadrant Finance Inc. on Wall Street.'

'Bingo!'

Back in her little room, which looked even dirtier by daylight, she carefully selected a short tight skirt made of fake leather, a see-through lace top, cut low at the front, and a pair of high-heeled white sandals. Adding scarlet lipstick and a pair of gilt hoop earrings, she went out once again and walked as far as 14th Street. She could easily pick up a yellow cab that would take her to exactly where she wanted to go.

Tiffany dumped her handbag on the hall table of her apartment, and slipped off her shoes. The apartment was beautifully quiet, and obviously Shirley and Maria had finished work and left. Was she glad to be home!

'Gloria, I'm back,' she called, 'any urgent messages?'

'There sure is!'

Tiffany spun round.

In the archway that led into her living room stood a short dumpy figure in a pink dress that strained tightly over melon-like breasts. Pink ribbons held back strawberry blonde curls and small eyes looked at Tiffany from a puffy face. She held a drink in one hand and a cigarette in the other, and as she tottered forward on high spiky heels, she rasped again, 'There sure is.'

It was Hunt's wife.

'What do you want?'

'My husband.'

'Isn't that something you should discuss with him?' Tiffany slipped on her shoes again. She towered over Joni.

'I'm warning you...!' A tremor shot through Joni as anger overtook her. 'You keep away from him! He's just been amusing himself with you. It means nothing! Nothing!' She headed back into the living room. Tiffany followed slowly.

'Don't think you're anything special,' Joni cried, 'it's me and the kids he loves, and it's me and the kids he's going to stay with! You can fucking lay off him, you bitch, you with your grand airs and money. Buying him! That's what you're trying to do.'

Staggering slightly she made her way to the bar. Seizing a bottle of vodka, she slopped some more into her glass and knocked it back fast.

'This is a pointless conversation,' said Tiffany, perching herself on the arm of one of her easy chairs. 'Hunt and I are in love. We didn't plan for it to happen this way, he was just someone I happened to be working with and then – '

'Crap!' Joni poured herself another vodka. 'You're just hanging on to him because you think it will help your lousy career.'

'That's not true!' Tiffany's cheeks flushed with anger. 'I've got where I have on my own merits. I had a good career before I even met Hunt. Now will you please leave.'

'I'm not going.' Joni stood aggressively, swaying slightly, feet planted wide. 'I'll stay just as long as I like! Who do you think you are? Just some crummy designer. I've heard Hunt say so. No real talent, that's what he said. Now I'm an actress –'

'Your performance tonight certainly deserves an Oscar,' Tiffany flared back.

'You mother-fucking cow!' screamed Joni, throwing the contents of her glass in Tiffany's face. 'I'll teach you to go off with my husband, I'll kill you, you fucking cunt.'

Blinded by the vodka, Tiffany tried to get to her feet, but

lost her balance and fell sideways onto the chair.

'Do you hear me?' Joni was yelling, as she picked up a bronze statuette from a side table.

There was a shout from Gloria, as she burst into the room. The last thing Tiffany remembered was Joni rushing at her, the bronze clenched in her raised hand.

Zachary lay on his side in his narrow cot at the Moyes Clinic. He'd been in two days now and in spite of the injections they'd given him, he was still in his own private hell. He shifted his position, trying to get more comfortable, but rats were gnawing at his stomach, and he was shaking violently. Sweat seeped through his hospital pyjamas and made his hair stick to his neck. Last night had been sheer hell. Half the time he couldn't make out whether he was awake, or asleep and having nightmares. He'd been lying in a big tin container and it was full of black spiders. They crawled all over him, up his legs, and round his shoulder blades. Then they linked legs and wove themselves into a chain round his neck. A nurse had appeared carrying a large pile of packages that she'd put before him. They were wrapped up in thin white muslin. He opened the first package and it was a human leg. The second contained a beautifully butchered shoulder. Then came the hand of his father, severed at the wrist. He knew it was his father's hand, because he recognized the heavy gold ring. Compulsively he had to open all the packages, although with each he dreaded finding the one object he most feared, his father's head, its cold grey eyes glaring at him over the small pursed mouth. Another nurse had then appeared and had led him into another room, a larger one, where he immediately saw his record player, and beside it a stack of records, all shiny and smooth and black. But as he walked towards them they started to bubble and twist and squirm. By the time he reached the table they were a mass of distorted plastic globules dripping slime onto the floor.

Why were these things happening to him? Perhaps Tiffany had brought him here so that they could torture him until he went crazy. Perhaps he'd already gone crazy? He opened his eyes cautiously. Through a narrow crack in the white painted wall, a large purple snake was undulating its way into the room towards him, two feet above his head.

With a strangled sob of terror, Zachary buried his head under the pillow and squeezed his eyes tightly shut.

For the third time, Hunt put a call through to Tiffany. There was still no answer. Looking at his watch he cursed softly. In Los Angeles it was five in the morning. It would be 8 a.m. in New York. Where the hell could she be? And where was Gloria? And why weren't Shirley and Maria answering the phone? He'd rung Tiffany as soon as he'd checked into the Beverly Wilshire yesterday and again at nine in the evening, but still there'd been no reply. Perhaps she'd stayed overnight at the Moyes Clinic to settle Zachary. He reached for his pack of cigarettes and shifted restlessly. For some reason he felt uneasy. It wasn't like Tiffany to change her plans and not tell him.

Worried now, he decided to call the Kalvins. Perhaps she'd stayed over to discuss Zachary with her family. He picked up the phone again and asked for the number. There was a long pause.

'Sorry, Mr Kellerman,' the switchboard girl informed him brightly, after an interval, 'the line's busy. Shall I keep trying?'

'Yes,' Hunt replied tersely, 'and put me through to room service, please.'

Ordering fresh orange juice, coffee and French toast he thought about the day that lay ahead of him. He had to be at the studio for a script conference, and then there were shooting schedules to work out. He only hoped he'd be able to concentrate. Perhaps a cold shower would help put Tiffany out of his mind.

A sharp burst of knocking on the door stopped him in his tracks as he padded naked across the room. Frowning, and shrugging on his dark-blue terry cloth robe, he checked the security chain, opened the door a couple of inches, and peered cautiously through the crack. In a crazy city like this you couldn't be too careful.

'What the – !'

'Hunt – oh Hunt!'

He unlocked the door quickly and Joni came tumbling into the room, her make-up streaked down her face and her pink dress crumpled and torn.

'I had to come... Look! Look!' Sobbing loudly, she stepped back to reveal heavy bruises on her chest and upper arms and along one jaw-line. The skin was ugly shades of purple, and lacerated in places.

Hunt stared, appalled.

'Look what your fucking girl friend's done to me?' screamed Joni. 'She tried to kill me. I've just flown from New York to be with you and to escape from her!'

'What are you talking about?' He felt ice-cold.

'She attacked me, that's what happened! She said you belonged to her and she'd never let you go. She said – she said –' Joni fell onto his chest, clinging to his bath robe, the tears streaming down her face.

'Where did this happen?'

Joni jerked away impatiently. 'Where do you think? The North Pole? She's mad, Hunt. Crazy mad.' She started sobbing again. 'You've got to look after me, gotta protect me!'

'Where is Tiffany now?' His voice had an impersonal, matter-of-fact tone.

Her head shot up. 'What the fuck does it matter where she is? Sitting on her ass in that flashy apartment of hers, for all I know. What difference does it make?'

'What about Gus and Matt?' He moved swiftly to the phone by the side of the bed.

'What's *with* you, Buster? I'm your wife! Remember? The kids are okay! Why shouldn't I be here? What's all this interest in everyone else?'

As he was about to pick up the phone, it suddenly rang.

'Yes, Morgan, it's me,' she heard him say.

'So now it's Morgan, is it?' Hunt heard her sneer in the background, as she kicked off her shoes and flung herself on the bed. 'Another of your frigging screws, I suppose?'

He was listening intently, refusing to let Joni distract him.

Then she heard his gasp, 'Oh my God... How is she?... And Gloria saw it happen? Christ! ... Look, Morgan, I'm flying back right now. Yes.' He slammed down the receiver.

'Aren't you going to order me a drink?' Joni was whining. 'Or do I have to get it for myself?'

'For all I care you can get everything for yourself in future!' Hunt yelled as he struggled into his clothes.

Everything was unnaturally quiet. Tiffany opened her eyes slowly and gazed up at a strange cream ceiling and wondered where she was.

'Tiff. How are you feeling?' It was Morgan's voice, and it sounded anxious.

Tiffany tried to turn her head, but it hurt horribly. When she tried to speak her voice sounded hoarse and gravelly.

'What happened?' she croaked.

'It's all right, honey, you're going to be fine. You're in Doctor's Hospital. You were brought in last night.'

Alarmed, Tiffany strained to find her sister's face. She couldn't remember a thing.

'Was I in an accident?'

'Not exactly.' Morgan bent over her. She'd decided to play this one as lightly as possible. 'It seems a certain lady – if you can call her that – took an exception to your sleeping with her husband, so she came round to your apartment and bonked you on the head with one of your bronze figurines. However, don't worry, the bronze hasn't even got a dent!'

'What?' Tiffany tried to sit up but fell back on the pillows with a groan of pain.

'Don't move,' warned Morgan. 'You've got a concussion and you're in no state to take on Mrs fucking Kellerman right now.'

'Hunt's wife.' Tiffany felt dazed. If only she could remember what had happened.

Morgan perched herself on the edge of the cot and nodded. 'Yup. She turned up at your place just before you got back from taking Zachary to the clinic, and Gloria let her in because she said she was an actress and she had an appointment with you over some costume designs. Apparently Gloria heard her yelling at you, and when she rushed in to see what was happening, there was this drunk woman attacking you! Thank God she had the sense to ring for an ambulance and call us, but she couldn't stop Hunt's wife. She just ran off.'

It was coming back to Tiffany. That small volatile bundle in a pink dress, who'd exploded like a tornado as soon as she'd set eyes on her. And where was Hunt? Had he been there too? She felt woozy and confused. And where was Hunt now?

As if reading her thoughts, Morgan said, 'I got hold of Hunt this morning. He'd been trying to call you from LA since yesterday. He's flying right back. He'll be here any time now.'

Tiffany shut her eyes and the tears ran down the sides of her cheeks and trickled into her ears.

Morgan squeezed her hand. 'Don't cry, Tiff. Everything will be all right, he's bound to leave her after this. He sounded distraught when I told him what had happened.'

'It's not that simple. She is his wife, and there are the two boys. It's because of them that he stays, he doesn't want them to have a broken home.'

'Well, try and get some rest now, I'm sure it will all sort itself out. I'll be back this evening with Harry.' Kissing her sister, Morgan crept quietly out of the hospital room.

Gingerly Tiffany felt the lump on her head. The pain was searing through her skull. If only Hunt hadn't been away. Joni would never have dared come round to her place if Hunt had been in town.

Hunt landed at JFK and took a cab straight to his apartment. Florence, the housekeeper, greeted him with relief.

'Mr Kellerman! Am I glad to see you! The boys . . .'

'How are they, Florence?' Hunt slammed down his travelling bag and strode towards the living room.

'They're watching television but they've been very upset. First you go away and then Mrs Kellerman disappears! I had an awful night with them and I'm glad you called this morning to let me know what was going on. They've been very frightened, Mr Kellerman.'

'Daddy! Oh, Daddy!' Gus and Matt came hurtling through the living-room door and flung themselves at Hunt, who gathered them up in his arms.

'Hey . . . hey there,' he said soothingly.

'We . . . we thought you'd left us,' Matt cried, 'and then Mom went away too . . .' He buried his face in Hunt's shoulder and sobbed loudly.

'Where have you been? And where's Mom?' Gus demanded, his relief at seeing his father again expressing itself in a burst of anger.

Hunt looked at Gus's pinched white face and saw the little boy struggling not to cry also.

'Now listen, you guys. Didn't I promise I'd never leave you?'

Matt gave a loud sniff and they both nodded solemnly.

'Momma flew down to Los Angeles to see me, as a surprise,' Hunt continued, 'and now she's staying with some friends there, for a few days. Okay?'

The boys nodded again. Hunt hugged them tightly. 'Now

I want you to be good for just a little while longer. Daddy has a couple of things to do and then I'll be right back and we'll have supper together and play games and I'll read you a story.'

'Great!' The colour had returned to Gus's face. 'What do you have to do?'

Hunt straightened his back. First he wanted to talk to Gloria and then he wanted to go to Doctor's Hospital to make sure Tiffany was all right.

'Just check up on the new film I'm making,' he replied reassuringly, hating himself for having to lie, 'and then I promise I'll be right back.'

'And you'll play with us?' asked Matt, snuggling closer and planting a wet kiss on Hunt's cheek.

'Sure thing, boys.' He lowered them gently to the ground and settled them in front of the television again.

Whatever happened, he knew now that he could never let them down. They were his sons, and he was going to have to be doubly responsible for their happiness in future.

Tiffany awoke as Hunt came into her room, his arms full of orchids. Without a word he went to her, and putting his arms gently round her, kissed her tenderly. He could never forgive Joni for this. Not only for nearly killing Tiffany but for inflicting those wounds on herself. Gloria had told him everything, and Hunt had listened with growing horror. Joni was sick.

'Don't worry, my darling,' he whispered, tracing the line of Tiffany's cheek with his fingers. 'Everything's going to be all right. Just leave it to me.'

Joe Kalvin was pissed off. He paced up and down his lavishly decorated office on the 49th floor of Quadrant House, like a peacock whose tail feathers had been damaged. What in God's name, he asked himself for the umpteenth time that morning, had he done to deserve a family that brought him nothing but acute embarrassment? With the exception of Morgan, of course. She'd taken after him. Coolly ambitious she was, with a keen eye for opportunity. One trip to England and she was all set to become a duchess. Now that trip had been money well spent. Of course his contacts had helped. The invitation to stay with the Winwoods, whom he'd been cultivating for years, had been the launching pad.

Joe had been making 'contacts' ever since he could remember. He believed in them. You never knew when a contact could produce exactly the right thing at the right moment. The most useful contact he'd ever made had undoubtedly been Sig Hoffman. He'd met him at CCNY when they'd both been struggling to get good grades and make something of themselves.

Joe had decided at fifteen that he didn't intend to ride on the subway all his life. His family had no money, but Sig's did, and when Sig's father, who was a coat and suit manufacturer, died, Sig decided to sell out and go into partnership with Joe. Investments was to be the name of the game. Thirty-four years later Joe was President and Sig was Vice-President of Quadrant Inc. The deals had gotten bigger and better as the years passed. Making dough was what mattered, and then buying respectability with it was what counted. Sig was the financial genius. It was Joe who got the clients in the first place, did the big selling spiel, assured people that Quadrant was the only finance company they could trust. But it was Sig who worked out the terms for lending money, the percentages, the repayments, like he had some damn computer in his head.

Yes, of all the people Joe had taken up with over the years, Sig had been the most valuable. Now Joe and Quadrant couldn't do without him.

Joe's pleasant reminiscences took a downward plunge as his thoughts turned to his son. Zachary was a real pain in the ass. Then Tiffany getting herself involved with a married man, who had a crazy alcoholic wife! For two days running now – he ran his palm over his sweating bald head – for *two days running*, there had been stories in the press about the activities of his family, and it wasn't *Wall Street Journal* stuff either.

Giving a growl of anger he went to the antique mahogany cabinet in the corner, poured himself a bourbon and drank it in one gulp. Fuck the ulcer. The hat-trick to make his fury complete had been the arrival in his office yesterday of a hooker who had called herself Smokey O'Mally. He hadn't been in close quarters with a whore like that since his youth. His flush deepened as he remembered the dose he'd caught then.

How could Zachary have been such a goddamn schmuck as to have got involved with a girl like that! Scared that one of his colleagues would find Smokey in his office and get the wrong impression, he'd given the whore two thousand dollars in cash from his private safe, so that she could get an abortion, and to shut her trap as well. Morgan had been right. Zachary was a fool.

Joe got up and poured himself another bourbon. He felt he'd handled Smokey very well. It was easy, really, to get rid of a small-time hooker like that. Bet she'd been impressed by him. It was obvious she knew nothing about Zachary taking drugs or she'd have said. Yes, he'd handled that one very well. Then he pressed the intercom buzzer on his desk and, speaking rapidly, asked for the Company PR Director to be sent up right away. The press had to be silenced. He'd worked hard to buy the right image, and by God, his family wasn't going to destroy it.

At least Ruth gave him no trouble. She'd been a nice clean girl from Shaker Heights when he'd married her. With a bit of money of her own too. Thank God she'd had a strict father. Never been allowed to mess around before she married. Pity she wasn't just a bit more intelligent though. But you couldn't have everything.

At least Zachary was out of the way for the time being. He'd send him to Europe when he got cured, an extended absence till the whole mess blew over.

Tiffany would have to stop seeing this bastard movie producer too. Joe had never trusted anyone in show-biz. Once again how right he'd been.

Feeling better, he picked up a file on the financing of a new computer company that was opening out west. No one was going to jeopardize the position Joe Kalvin had built for himself.

Harry was due to return to England in three days' time.

Morgan would join him a month later, staying with Rosalie and Glen Winwood until the wedding. Although Harry felt a certain sadness at leaving her, he had found his two weeks in New York exhausting. The Kalvins took him everywhere, introducing him to all their friends who, in turn, invited them to their parties. The city was coming alive again after a summer of stifling humidity, and as the air began to crisp, the lassitude of the long sticky days was forgotten. Suddenly everyone wanted to socialize.

Joe insisted on showing Harry the length of Wall Street before taking him to the United Nations and luncheon at La Bibliotec. On another day he took him to lunch at Windows on the World on the one hundred and seventh floor of the World Trade Center so he could see the stunning view of the city. Morgan showed him the treasures of the Metropolitan Museum and the Museum of Modern Art, the galleries in Soho and the new Graffiti Art galleries on the Lower East Side. They lunched at the Russian Tea Room or the fashionable Positano and they dined at Le Cirque, Lutece and even Caramba. He was taken to see *La Cage aux Folles*, *Cats*, *Nine* and *My One and Only* and he was dragged up and down Madison Avenue and Fifth Avenue looking at famous shops like Tiffany's, Henri Bendel, Bergdorf Goodman and Saks. At night they danced at the Palladium before taking a midnight stroll up Columbus Avenue. But Harry found the heart of the city lay in its streets, in the flotsam and jetsam of lost souls, and the ant-like rushing of its workers, and not in the false glitz of smart restaurants or benefit balls. Morgan found this hard to understand.

Weekends were no less arduous. Joe's private jet flew them to 'Four Winds', their white-wood slatted house by the beach at Southampton. Here he proceeded to show off his future son-in-law to the residents of Long Island.

Each morning they drove along Gin Lane to the exclusive tennis club, where Harry and Morgan played a singles match while Joe engaged the other members in conversation. Then there was a lunch party by the pool, back at the house, where they were joined by neighbours. Every night they were invited to a party.

And through the whole of the two weeks of Harry's visit the only real topic of conversation had been the forthcoming marriage.

Joe wanted the wedding to be in the autumn but Morgan agreed with Harry that with so many preparations to be made, there simply wasn't time. Especially as Ruth firmly stated she would not go to London to help with the arrangements unless Joe could go too. Joe could not get away, so Morgan, with the help of Rosalie, was going to have to cope on her own. She didn't mind. In fact she knew exactly what she wanted, and it would be easier for her to get things organized without a nervous and distraught Ruth by her side.

Finally, after much argument, the date was fixed for 20 February. Exactly four months hence. Joe and Ruth would fly over together two weeks before. Morgan was delighted. This was her wedding and she didn't want some sort of rushed job. It was going to take her weeks, as it was, to get her trousseau together.

They decided that Harry would buy the London house he and Morgan had been so enchanted with. It dated from 1820 and had a white stucco facade that went up to the level of the first-floor balcony, and was near Hyde Park, in quite elegant Montpelier Square. The beautiful large reception rooms opening onto a lovely terrace would, Morgan felt, make a perfect backdrop for entertaining. There were five bedrooms, each with a bathroom *en suite*, and a staff apartment next to the kitchen. Her first mission when she arrived in London would be to get a leading interior decorator to do the place over.

As far as Harry was concerned, the busier Morgan was when she arrived, the better. Somehow he had to keep her and his mother apart as much as possible, because the Duchess's fury at the engagement distressed Harry very much, and he feared that when Morgan became aware of it she would change her mind and catch the first flight home.

Tiffany, discharged from Doctor's Hospital, was better although she still suffered from headaches and bouts of depression.

She had, however, little time to brood. A twenty million dollar musical, *Glitz*, was opening on Broadway in four months' time at the St James Theater and she had been asked to design the costumes. This was her big chance. The greatest break she'd ever had and she just wished it had come at a better time. The story line was set in Paris, a symbolic fantasy centring round the Folies Bergère, and there was going to be a chorus of thirty, plus eight leading roles. The opportunity to create fantastic and outrageous costumes was terrific, but the responsibility was so great that already she was waking up in the middle of the night with her heart pounding. The more she thought about the one hundred and seventy costumes she had to design, the greater grew the excitement and terror. She spent days researching in the theatrical section of the library at the Lincoln Center, for the wide variety of costumes she had to produce was formidable. They varied from space suits, which she decided she would cover with tiny squares of mirror, to headdresses of weaving snakes and bodystockings to look like snakeskins. These she would have stitched with mother-of-pearl sequins to look like scales. There were of course also the feather and rhinestone costumes of the chorus, and here she pored over the designs of Erté. But more tricky was the transformation scene when the chorus girls changed into the Angels of Truth, flying high over the orchestra pit. How the hell was that going to be done if they weren't to look as if they'd been draped in sheeting? The show was going to require every bit of ingenuity she could muster, especially the section in the script that described 'a fifteen-foot silver platter on which are posed ten chorus girls, all dressed as cakes; a chocolate éclair, a cream-filled meringue, etc'. It was all very Parisienne and exotic, and Tiffany knew only too well that if the costumes weren't well designed and well made, they would look ridiculous. And so would she.

On top of all this, Morgan had persuaded her to design *the* wedding dress. 'It will do you a lot of good, it will help your career, you know,' she had added naively. Morgan was obsessed with how she was going to look on the great day.

'I'll get the family tiara out of the bank,' offered Harry, just before he departed back to England. 'That is, if you don't think it will be too much.'

Morgan didn't think it would be too much at all. The previous week he'd promised her a whole load of jewellery his grandmother had left him and her eyes shone as he vaguely described necklaces of pearls and emeralds, diamonds and sapphires, rubies and aquamarines. He said there were some rings too, and a few bracelets and brooches. She looked so pleased he glowed at how easy it was to make her happy.

'Oh Harry . . .' Her soft and beautiful mouth bent to his as she pressed her body against him. She always smelled wonderful, like flowering jasmine on a summer's evening.

'You're spoiling me, darling,' she whispered, looking deeply into his eyes.

'But I love you, my sweet, with all my heart! You can have anything you want.'

She found his earnestness very touching.

He kissed her neck and shuddered at the thrill that went through him. 'You're the most wonderful, beautiful, amazing thing that has ever happened to me,' he murmured. Electric sparks seemed to fly whenever he held her close, and his groin was on fire. He could never have enough of her. He wondered if she felt the same. Sometimes she seemed preoccupied with material details. His thoughts dissolved instantly as her hands slid round his waist and then dropped to hold him.

'Let's go to my room.' Her voice was husky.

Hardly able to wait, he slid open the zipper down the back of her dress as they walked along the corridor. Her hand was still working stealthily.

'Darling, my darling.' Harry pulled her down on the bed, tugging at his clothes with one hand. Then her tongue was flicking over him, leaving a fiery trail. In a moment he would burst and drown them both. She moved away and was licking him just behind the ear. God, she knew how to prolong the ecstasy. The way she brought him up to a pitch, then let him subside for a few seconds, only to bring him to a higher pitch. He could stand it no longer. Seizing her, he plunged himself deeply into her. They moved in frantic unison for a few seconds, then their cries mingled as their bodies exploded in orgasm.

7

Tiffany hadn't seen Hunt for nearly a week.

A week in which she'd thrown herself into her work, getting up at six every morning. A week in which she'd had recurring headaches and a sick cold feeling of despair in her stomach, feeble echoes of the worse pain in her heart. A week in which she'd avoided everyone, including Morgan. At night she fell into bed, too tired to eat, too weary to read.

Hunt had gone back to his wife.

Tiffany went through their last meeting again and again as if she were replaying the scene on video tape. Hunt had come round to see her one evening when she thought he was working late at the studios.

'I've just got to give Joni a chance to straighten out,' he'd announced without preamble. His face was grim and his eyes had a strained and haunted look. 'If only for Gus's and Matt's sake.'

Tiffany remained silent as he reached out and took her hand.

'I told you she'd collapsed in the bar of the Beverly Wilshire after I flew back to see you, didn't I?'

Tiffany nodded. He was making it sound as if it were her fault.

'The doctor who examined her told me she'd be dead in a year if she didn't quit drinking. I've got her into a clinic. She's in a terrible mess, so you see I've got to give her a chance, haven't I?'

'Her chances are better than Zachary's,' Tiffany observed in a small voice.

'Maybe, but he's got youth on his side – what is he, seventeen? I can't help feeling that I'm partly to blame for what's happened to Joni. I've been living my own life for years now – wound up with work – and lately you. In the end I was only going home to see Gus and Matt. Do you understand what I'm saying?'

'I do understand, Hunt. I understand you love your sons very much, and you feel guilty about your wife. But once she's had treatment, do you intend to stay with her for the rest of your life?'

'The rest of one's life is a very long time. I don't know, that's the honest answer. Gus and Matt are still so young. I just know that right now I've got to give her support, give her something to strive for. If I walk out now, she's a goner. This is all bad for Gus and Matt too. They keep asking about their mother, and why she has left them, and worse, am I going to leave them too? Maybe she'll never get cured, maybe there's more wrong with her than just booze. I don't know, but I've got to give her a chance, even if it's only for the boys' sake.'

Tiffany sat silent, her eyes brimming. Of course Hunt was right. He was doing the right thing to protect his sons. If only it didn't hurt so much.

'Believe me, I love you, Tiff. There is nothing I would like more than to ask you to marry me, but you can see, can't you, that this is not the moment to walk away from Joni?'

'Let's not kid ourselves, there never will be a moment,' Tiffany replied, clenching and unclenching her jaw as she struggled for composure. 'We both know, that whatever happens, she'll do everything in her power to hang on to you, and she'll use your sons as her reason.'

Tiffany rose from the sofa and went over to the bar.

'Can I get you anything?' Her hands were shaking.

'No thanks. I can't stay. I promised the boys I'd be back to read them a story and I – I –' His voice broke as he looked across at her.

'Oh Tiff.' He came towards her. She stopped him with a quickly raised hand and her smile quivered.

'It's all right, Hunt. I do understand how you feel and what you have to do. That's what makes you such a wonderful person. That's the very reason why I love you so much.'

His eyes burned into hers for a long second, and there was utter stillness in the room. She turned hurriedly back to the bar. If she'd held his gaze a second longer she would have been finished.

When she looked back he was gone.

The days that followed were the worst she'd ever known. There wasn't a thing that didn't remind her of Hunt. Music was the worst. In the end she put away all her tapes and records, vowing never to play them again. And she flung herself into her work with an obsessive passion she had never felt before. The costumes for *Glitz* were going to be the most sensational seen on Broadway for a decade, even if the effort and dedication killed her.

But Gloria looked anxious as she cooked Tiffany's favourite dishes. Everything came back untouched.

'I'm sorry, Gloria,' Tiffany said each time, with an apologetic little smile. 'That bump on the head has really affected my appetite.'

'Bump on the head, my ass!' Gloria snorted to herself as she bustled angrily round the kitchen. 'I'd like to lay my own two hands on that fancy director guy, and then we'd really be talking about bumps on the head.'

Around six one evening the telephone rang. Shirley and Marie had already left, exhausted by the gruelling schedule. If she was alone in the apartment Tiffany had instructed Gloria to take all calls and find out who it was before she said Tiffany was in.

'Who is it?'

'It's a Mister Greg Jackson, Mizz Tiffany.'

Greg. She hadn't seen him since that disastrous dinner at Le Club on the night of Morgan's homecoming. Poor Greg.

It must have been awful for him when Morgan had announced her engagement.

'I'll take it.'

'Tiffany, hi!'

'Hi, Greg. Lovely to hear from you. How are you?' She made an effort to sound bright.

'I'm okay, and you?' He sounded just the same, his voice deep and warm as ever.

'Fine, thanks.'

'What are you doing with yourself these days? Busy with work?'

'Frantically.' On an impulse she added, 'Say, why don't you come round, if you're not doing anything. It's ages since I've seen you, and Gloria's getting bored just cooking for me. Why not come round for supper tonight?'

'What, er, well, thanks ... but I thought ...' He paused, obviously confused.

'Hunt and I have split.' There, she'd said it. It was no longer a painful illness that she'd kept secret. It was like lancing a boil and letting all the poison flow out. Suddenly she felt better.

'Hey, I'm sorry, Tiff. I had no idea ... but I know how you feel. Shall I come about eight?' His voice was sympathetic, but not so sympathetic that it wanted to make her start crying again.

'Great. See you then, Greg.'

As she hung up she reflected that if she was going to start talking about it there was probably no one better than Greg. He was an old and trusted friend from way back – and he'd recently been there too.

8

Joe wanted to make sure that every detail of Morgan's wedding was nothing short of perfect. He wanted a high-profile spectacle and, with the dollar being so strong against the pound, he reckoned that a couple of million dollars should give everyone a good time. And an impressive one.

With Ruth at his side, he flew into England ahead of the arrival of his two hundred guests, for all of whom he'd taken suites at the Savoy. He himself was staying at Claridge's. He'd read somewhere it was 'the hotel for Kings and Queens' and as soon as he saw the floor of suites he had booked, furnished with antiques and Chinese silk rugs, he told Ruth they'd definitely come to the right place. He arrived in the wake of a stream of telexes and phone calls demanding that all his instructions be carried out to the letter by his advance guard, Dwight Blettner, Director of Public Relations for Quadrant Inc. He'd also brought a personal assistant, three secretaries, and a famous and costly New York professional party organizer.

From his suite he headed a major campaign to attract the media. If he was spending two million dollars he wanted everyone to know about it.

'Who the hell does he think he is?' grumbled Ginny, one of the secretaries, as she carefully applied Silver Frost nail-polish. On her desk lay a long list of acceptances that had to be typed out in alphabetical order, then duplicated three hundred times.

'Ronald Reagan, running for the White House?' suggested Candia, another secretary. 'I've been given a press release to type that reads like the outline for a De Mille production. He wants it circulated to all the British TV companies.'

'Thank your lucky stars there aren't as many channels over here as there are back home. Do you think Morgan likes all this crap?'

Ginny, having finished her nails, started to apply Silver Frost lipstick.

Candia shrugged. 'I'd say she was as ambitious as her father. Why would she be marrying this duke, or whatever, otherwise? She was engaged to a great guy called Greg before she went to London.'

'Spoiled bitch,' agreed Ginny, 'and I'll bet she's spent a fortune on her trousseau. Wanna take a bet on how long the marriage will last?'

'Oh, it'll last! After all this, her Daddy wouldn't let her get a divorce! What with everything that's gone down already, he won't stand for any more scandal.'

Giggling, the girls reluctantly tackled their respective piles of typing.

'I want every newspaper, journal and magazine invited,' snapped Joe from his suite, which was along the corridor from where the girls were working. Dwight Blettner smiled assuringly.

'They've all had an invitation, and they'll be getting a press release and a guest list first thing tomorrow.'

'Yes, but are they covering it?'

Dwight hesitated for a second then swiftly said, 'They've all accepted, but you know as well as I do that we can't guarantee they will write anything, or that the pictures will hit the front page. I mean, if Mrs Thatcher decides to make an important announcement or Princess Diana changes her hair style again –'

'Crap!' spat Joe. 'I've flown you four thousand miles to do a job any dumb schmuck could handle, so quit making excuses. After all Morgan's marrying a future duke and half the aristocracy of Britain is coming. If that don't make news,

I don't know what will! Tell 'em it's going to be as big a shindig as the royal wedding, and tell 'em how much it's costing me. They'll go for that.'

Quietly, Dwight slid out of the room. At least Joe hadn't ordered him to contact 10 Downing Street or Buckingham Palace to tell them to hold off anything of interest until after the wedding.

Alone, Joe continued to plan. He was flying over a dozen journalists on Concorde. Rooms had been booked for them at the Savoy and they were to order anything they wanted during their stay. On a junket like this, he reflected, he was bound to get good coverage back home. He could practically smell the sweet success of shares in Quadrant rising on the stock market as a result of the publicity.

Pouring himself a bourbon, he just wished Morgan wasn't quite so twitchy about there being press coverage. It was all Harry's fault of course. And those dumb parents of his. Harry thought having Norman Parkinson or Patrick Lichfield to take the formal group shots was enough. Formal groups my ass, thought Joe, downing his drink at one gulp. If Harry went on like this, Morgan would end up losing her *chutzpa*.

With only four days to go, Joe still had a lot to do and he found the reaction to his activities both baffling and frustrating. He was nearly arrested when he barged into the House of Lords, accompanied by Sig Hoffman and his personal bodyguard, demanding to see the catering manager. When he stormed into Annabel's to check the dinner menu for the party on the night of the wedding, and proceeded to ask the head chef if he was used to doing parties on this scale, his frosty stare amazed Joe. Florists were interrogated, the choice of music questioned, and he wanted the church choir to audition. He only stopped short at telling the bishop who was to perform the ceremony what his lines should be because Sig said the guy probably knew his job anyway.

Ruth stayed in their suite most of the time, going through agonies of indecision about her wedding outfit. Mistakenly, she reflected, she'd brought over several choices in different colours and fabrics, one trimmed with silver mink, another with aquamarine ostrich feathers, and a third in deep-red velvet, heavily encrusted with gold embroidery and beads, rather like a maharaja's coat. It made the final decision more difficult, especially as she wasn't sure what the English weather would be like on the day, and Joe didn't much like any of them anyway. It also made her choice of jewellery impossible. Her best bits looked awful with the red and gold, or were swallowed up and disappeared under mounds of fur or feather with the other outfits.

There was nothing for it, she would have to ask Tiffany's advice, and if that didn't work, she'd just go right out and see what Norman Hartnell had in stock.

At last the day they had all been waiting for arrived. Morgan was up early and spent the morning surrounded by make-up artists, manicurists and hairdressers. For luncheon she toyed with a little smoked salmon and a glass of champagne.

In the hotel restaurant downstairs, Joe and Ruth entertained ten of their closest friends at luncheon, Joe noting with satisfaction that there were several very famous people also lunching in the stately dining room, including King Constantine of Greece. For a moment he felt tempted to go over and invite the good-looking King to the wedding, then decided reluctantly that it might look a bit pushy.

Tiffany, in a stunning white suit, with black mink collar and cuffs, and a huge white cartwheel hat with a black mink crown, stayed upstairs with Morgan, helping to get her ready. She had designed the wedding dress on Tudor lines, with a deep square neckline, flowing sleeves, and a skirt that fell into heavy folds, forming a train. She had researched the period thoroughly and had chosen silky white velvet, with white watered silk front panniers and large revers on the sleeves, embroidered with a stardust of tiny diamonds. Standing back, looking at Morgan objectively, she had to admit it was one of her best designs.

When the moment came for the hairdresser to place the magnificent Lomond tiara on her head, Morgan trembled with excitement. Her gold hair had been coiled into a heavy chignon, and the silk-tulle veil floated softly from the glittering diamonds.

Picking up her bouquet of white orchids, she looked at herself in the long mirror. The whole effect was spectacular. She looked like a picture out of one of the fairy-tale books she used to pore over as a child.

Even Joe was going to be satisfied.

The area surrounding St Margaret's Church, as it stood in the shadows of the great Westminster Abbey, was thronged with crowds of well-wishers and gawping passers-by, all eager to catch a glimpse of a glamorous wedding. The police, many of them mounted on fine black horses, controlled the jostling sightseers with goodhumoured patience, and tried to keep the heavy traffic flowing smoothly past Big Ben and the Houses of Parliament and round the grassy lawns of Parliament Square. A long line of gleaming Rolls Royces and Bentleys dispensed the exquisitely dressed guests at the wrought-iron gates that led to the church, as press photographers and two television crews fought for the best positions. The occasion was generating the sort of excitement associated with a royal wedding.

Inside the church, guests were squeezed into every available pew by tall handsome ushers in pale grey morning suits. White flowers almost obliterated the pillars and the altar had all but vanished under great banks of white lilies. By contrast the fashionable hats and clothes of the women guests brought a kaleidoscope of colour into the old grey church. As the organ thundered to announce the arrival of Morgan and her father and the congregation rose and turned to look, it was as if a breeze had swept through a herbaceous border. Harry, standing nervously by the altar rails with his cousin and best man, Andrew Flanders, could only think how glad he would be when it was all over.

'We are gathered here together . . .' intoned the bishop in a voice of deep richness, but only Harry was listening.

Morgan, deeply dazed by the excitement, was only aware that everyone was looking at her and marvelling at her beauty. She was really and truly the Bride of the Season and had captured one of England's most eligible bachelors. Harry was so sweet too. She was very lucky. He'd always let her do whatever she wanted.

Joe, standing by her side, sweated profusely, and for no particular reason thought of his childhood in the Bronx and how poor he and his family had been then. He suddenly wished his parents were alive to see him today. Feeling very emotional, he wished he'd had another bourbon before leaving Claridge's.

Ruth, having decided on the royal blue edged with silver mink, with a silver mink hat, inspected the Duchess of Lomond out of the corner of her eye. How typical of her to be wearing a drab shade of beige, with beige ostrich feathers on her large hat. It looked like a dusty lampshade. Ramrod stiff and unsmiling, the Duchess was staring straight ahead, having completely ignored Ruth's ingratiating smile when she arrived at the church. Fuck the old bitch, thought Ruth with unusual annoyance.

Tiffany, standing by her mother, wondered what Morgan's future really held for her. Her sister was happy and thrilled today, but how much did she really love Harry? Wouldn't she get bored in time with all the social trivialities that would be expected of her? Presiding over charity committees, opening Conservative fêtes, going grouse shooting in the winter and attending race meets in the summer. It wasn't the life Morgan was used to – formal dinners instead of fancy discos, fishing for salmon instead of fashion shows, Badminton instead of Broadway. Tiffany said a little private prayer to herself. Please may Morgan be happy – always.

'For richer, for poorer,' the bishop was saying in sepulchral tones.

Morgan's eyes widened as she looked at Harry. He was giving his responses in a clear firm voice. 'Till death us do part.'

A sudden chill shot down her spine and she shuddered involuntarily. Till death us do part. There was nothing more final than that. Then Harry was slipping the narrow platinum band on her finger, and she felt the strong warmth of his hands. Looking up she saw the tenderness of his smile. Probably all brides felt as if someone was walking over their grave at a moment like this. She returned his smile confidently.

As they came down the aisle to the music of Widor's Toccata, Morgan felt a resurgence of excitement. Hundreds of people were beaming benevolently at them and through the open portals of the church she glimpsed photographers, cameras at the ready. When they appeared on the steps, a great roar of approval went up from the waiting crowds and flash-bulbs popped in all directions. Holding Harry's hand, she smiled this way and that, feeling like a royal princess. But at least she was now a marchioness.

Behind came a retinue of small bridesmaids and pages, the little girls in white, the boys wearing kilts of the Lomond plaid, with white shirts. Then came the Duke of Lomond, chatting amiably to Ruth, a fixed smile on her face that Tiffany always called her Nancy Reagan expression. After them came Joe, clutching the Duchess's bony elbow in a vice-like grip. He was thinking, I hope the special car I ordered for Morgan has arrived. Smiling for the photographers, he assumed the pose of a relaxed father while inwardly panicking.

'Do you see the cars, Tiff?' he muttered out of the corner

of his mouth as she joined the group on the steps of St Margaret's.

'Yes, over there.' She nodded in the direction of a line of Rolls Royces, half hidden by the swarming crowds. 'Daddy, what on earth have they done to the front one? It looks like a funeral wagon.'

Joe glanced at the special car he had ordered for Morgan and Harry, its bonnet and radiator smothered with white flowers. 'What's the matter with it?' he snapped. 'That's what I asked for.'

Joe and Ruth stood receiving the guests in the great oak-panelled receptions rooms of the House of Lords, with the Duke and Duchess of Lomond. Whenever friends from back home were announced by the red-coated toastmaster, they greeted them as if they were welcoming them back from outer space. It was so nice to be among one's own sort of people, thought Joe, who wasn't sure he liked the charming condescension of the English guests. There were so many bewildering titles and ranks to cope with that it was a real relief to see the Steins and the Schwartzes and the Bergdoffs again. Joe wished he could relax and enjoy himself, but when he tried to introduce anyone to the Duchess, giving her elbow a friendly squeeze, it brought no response but a chilling frigidity. Really that woman was a pain in the ass. He felt glad that Morgan was strong enough to cope with her.

Suddenly it was time for Morgan and Harry to cut the cake, a five-tiered construction of white icing and miniature Corinthian pillars, with the Lomond coat of arms delicately traced on the top of each tier, garlanded by sugared thistles of Scotland.

Tiffany edged forward so that she could see better. She too shared Joe's feeling of depression, and she wasn't sure if it was because she so wished Zachary could have been there, or whether seeing Morgan so happy with Harry made her ache for Hunt.

'Morgan sure looks swell, doesn't she?' murmured a voice in her ear. Tiffany went stiff. She knew that voice only too well. It was Sig Hoffman, pale and beady-eyed, his breath smelling of whisky. He slid his hand round her waist and dropped it to caress her bottom.

'Take your filthy hands off me!' Tiffany hissed through clenched teeth, and turning swiftly away, walked over to where Ruth was standing. Sig's eyes followed her as a dull flush crept up his bony cheeks.

'What was that about?' demanded Joe, coming up to join them. 'How dare you be so rude to Sig.'

'I have nothing to say to Sig, Daddy. Not now, not at any time,' replied Tiffany evenly, and walked away.

Joe turned bewildered eyes to Ruth. 'What the hell's got into her now? Sig's been part of the family since before she was born.'

'Hush, dear, the First Lord of the Admiralty or something like that is going to propose their health,' whispered Ruth.

'But Sig's my oldest friend!' Joe looked round in agitation. 'I don't want him upset, he's far too valuable to Quadrant.'

'I don't suppose she meant anything by it, she's been a bit on edge all day. Here' – as a waiter passed bearing a tray of champagne – 'have some more champagne, we're going to need it to drink their health.'

Scowling, Joe helped himself to a glass. Children! Who needed them! – except for Morgan. She was the only one with any sense. Zachary was a disgrace to the whole family, and now Tiffany was insulting Sig. Sig of all people! Come to think of it, she'd been fairly cool to him on the rare occasions they'd met during the past few years. Perhaps, Joe tried to reason, Sig had laughed at her ambitions to be a designer when she'd been a kid, and she was still holding a grudge against him.

'Will you drink to the health of the bride and bridegroom,' boomed a voice, interrupting his thoughts. Everyone raised their glasses and a battery of flash-bulbs popped. Morgan and Harry cut the cake with a ceremonial sword that had been flown down from Drumnadrochit Castle, then held hands and smiled for the photographers.

Joe looked round the room. Morgan would be going off to change in a minute, then there'd be the last flurry of goodbyes and the guests would start to drift away home. A feeling of anticlimax would soon hit them all. He had a sudden pang of feeling very alone. Perhaps he'd invite a few of their best friends back to Claridge's for drinks before the party at Annabel's. He'd start with Sig and his wife, Pearl.

In a flurry of pink rose petals and cheering crowds, Morgan and Harry came through the ancient stone archway of the House of Lords, out into the inner cobbled courtyard, where their Rolls Royce awaited to whisk them to Heathrow. Morgan, in a burgundy velvet suit edged with black braid, and a confection of burgundy ostrich feathers framing her exquisite face, laughingly threw her wedding bouquet, and a roar of approval went up as it was neatly caught by one of the child bridesmaids. A moment later everyone was waving, Morgan was kissing her parents and Tiffany, and Harry was shaking hands with the Duke and kissing the Duchess.

They got into the car. The doors shut with an expensive clunk, the car began to move slowly forward, and Morgan gave a backward glance to smile at her family. Then she turned her head sharply away. She had just seen the Duchess, and she was looking directly at Morgan, her eyes filled with undisguised hatred.

9

Morgan quietly slid open the dressing-table drawer and groped for the flat packet that lay hidden under her make-up. With a swift movement she flicked one of the pills out of its plastic bubble and popped it into her mouth. When Harry came out of the bathroom he found her lying on the bed reading.

It was the second week of their honeymoon at the St Geraint Hotel in Mauritius, the most beautiful hotel in the world, Morgan had assured him, and he had to admit she was right. Anyway, she had insisted on paying – part of her wedding present to him – and for that he was grateful, if slightly emasculated, but buying the Knightsbridge house had cost him a fortune and necessitated getting a mortgage. It also had to be redecorated to Morgan's specifications, and she had insisted that they buy new beds, sofas and carpets because she said the ones he had in storage, left to him by his grandmother, were probably damp. However, her father's enormous cheque, which he referred to as Morgan's 'dowry', was going to pay for doing up Drumnadrochit. The thought cheered Harry a lot. He wandered to the sliding glass door of their suite and stepped out onto the still warm sand of the beach. Above, the night sky was like a jewel-studded canopy hung over his head. The sea washed softly across the tips of the coral reef, and in the distance frogs croaked in the artificial lake of the hotel. It was wonderful here, but he was beginning to feel bored. It wasn't Morgan. She was as fascinating and wonderful as ever. It was having nothing much to do during the days that troubled him. He suddenly wished he could take a bracing walk with Mackie and Angus across the hills.

'What shall we do tomorrow?' he asked, as he turned back into the bedroom.

Morgan looked up lazily. 'Do? What do you mean, do? I need a rest after the past few weeks, you know. It was exhausting organizing all the wedding preparations, not to mention getting the house ready. As it is, I've still got to collect over a hundred presents from Rosalie's house and get them over to ours. I'm only just beginning to feel human . . . and isn't my tan getting a good colour!' She stretched her long slim brown legs in the air and looked at Harry with a wicked smile.

'Your tan is wonderful, darling,' he smiled back, feeling himself weakening.

'Brown tits too!' She pulled open her negligée and revealed perfect breasts, deep golden in colour.

Harry could feel an erection starting. Christ, she was sexy.

'You're right, my darling. Let's just go on being lazy.' He kissed her smooth shoulder. 'After all, this is probably the last time we can have a holiday abroad for years and years, certainly on our own.'

Morgan looked at him, silently and reproachfully.

'Well . . . I mean it is, isn't it!' He sounded defiant. 'Once we have a baby, it won't be so easy to get away, not while the children are small anyway.'

Morgan shifted and turned to look out of the window at the starry night. Her eyes hardened. A week ago he'd been talking about their having a baby – a son and heir – as soon as possible. Now it was *children*. The line of her mouth tightened. *Not yet, my love*, she thought. *Not until I'm good and ready. Not until I've established myself as the Marchioness of Blairmore on both sides of the Atlantic – and not while I can go on secretly taking the Pill.*

She turned back to Harry with a warm and loving smile. 'You're right of course, honey.' Gently she nibbled his ear. 'Once we have babies it will be much more difficult.'

Harry was lost in an abyss of warm, soft valleys and

hungry wet deepness. He submerged himself to the hilt and thanked God for her love.

Fragrant blue smoke drifted from the Duke of Lomond's cigar as he settled back thankfully into the depths of the very comfortable armchair. Morgan had just taken him on a tour of their new Montpelier Square house and his arthritic hip was aching.

They were sitting in the drawing room, which Morgan had decorated in a symphony of spring-like shades of green. The white walls were tinged with the faintest hint of green, and the silks and taffeta of the chair covers, cushions and swagged curtains were a clever blend of white, eau de nil, lime, apple and sea-green. A pale aquamarine carpet covered the floor. White rococo-framed mirrors, white marble-topped gilt gables and a white fireplace, on which were arranged Meissen figurines, gave the room an incredibly delicate air; one of gilt on glass, mirror on crystal, the whole theme bound together by vases filled with armfuls of green leaves and white lilies.

'Good job you've made of it, m'dear,' he observed as she handed him his favourite whisky. 'All those wedding presents must have come in handy too. You won't have to buy a glass or an ashtray for years.'

Morgan drew up a small chair to be nearer him and laughed. 'I think we also got twenty-seven decanters and eleven toast racks!'

'Swap them for something else!' the Duke announced crisply. 'That's what Lavinia and I did! Sneaked into Asprey's in Bond Street at dawn and swapped presents for something else. I seem to remember it was vases in our day. We must have been given over forty of the bloody things, not to mention six picnic hampers! When's Harry coming back?'

Morgan glanced at the gilt ormolu clock on the marble mantelpiece. 'Any time now. They usually close the gallery shortly after six, unless they have an important buyer. Before he gets back there is something I want to say . . .' She faltered and looked at him anxiously.

'Well, what is it, m'dear? No use being frightened of an old man like me. What's up?'

'It's – it's just that I want you to know that I really do love Harry, and I wasn't just after him for his title or anything.'

'Never thought you were.' He sounded emphatic. 'If anything, it seems to me, if you will forgive me saying so, that thanks to the extreme generosity of yourself and your family, Harry got the best of the bargain. Not much worth in an old title you know, and a crumbling ruin of a castle.'

'Yes, but your wife . . .' Morgan had learned to call the Duke Edgar; but having to refer to the old dragon as Lavinia was more than she could bring herself to do. 'She hates me! From the moment she first set eyes on me she disapproved of me. Frankly, I was amazed when you said she was joining us for a drink this evening.'

'You mustn't pay any attention to her, Morgan. She's a funny woman, but she's all right really. Strong willed and all that, you know, but then I like 'em with a bit of spirit.' The Duke's blue eyes twinkled as he took another sip of his whisky. 'Actually, she doesn't like many people. She's not even very keen on Harry; that's why I'm so glad he had the sense to marry you. He never got much affection as a child. Funny really, when you come to think of it, but Lavinia always seemed to favour my nephew Andrew Flanders. He's three years older than Harry, and they got on very well as children, but they're not so close now.'

Morgan remembered him at the wedding. Harry's tall, thin best man. They had hardly spoken, though he seemed nice enough.

'Isn't he your late brother's child?' she asked.

'Yes, my younger brother Angus. Killed in a plane crash when the boy was five. Tragedy really . . . not that he and I were close . . . never saw much of each other. He was always gadding about while I preferred to stay at Drumnadrochit. I had enough gadding about in Gallipoli during the war.'

'What about his wife, is she still alive?'

'He never married. Andrew was born on the wrong side of the blanket. I never knew, but I have a feeling his mother was one of those dancers at some club or other.'

Morgan's eyes widened in fascination and surprise. Even her family didn't have such interesting skeletons in their closet.

'And your brother brought the child up alone?'

'Well, he gave him a home, and there were always nannies and that sort of thing. When he went to Eton, either his guardian would have him in the holidays or we would. Poor little blighter! Seems to be doing all right these days, though.'

'Probably your wife was sorry for him.'

'I expect so, but I never thought it was quite the thing to put him before Harry all the time. Anyway, Morgan, don't you worry about a thing, Harry is happy. I've never seen the lad so happy, and I for one am delighted you've joined the family.'

Morgan jumped to her feet and planted a kiss on his weathered cheek. 'That's nice of you, thanks. I know we're going to be wonderfully happy. Harry is everything to me. Now that the house is finished I'm going to invite all his friends round and give dinner parties. It will be good for his business too, if we invite some of the top dealers and introduce them into society. I'm sure they'd like it.' She rose to refill their glasses, and then she asked, 'Now, how is Drumnadrochit coming along?'

The Duke slapped his thigh with glee. 'Capital m'dear, capital! I'm going up in a few days to see how the builders are getting on. Why don't you and Harry come too? See what they're doing to the old place, eh?'

'I don't think we can get away just yet. We've only been back a couple of weeks, and Harry says he has a lot of work to catch up on. It must be awfully cold up north too, isn't it?'

'Cold? No, not really, crisp and bracing, that's what I'd call it. Ah, Harry m'boy.' He rose rather shakily as Harry entered the room and the men shook hands.

They were talking about the improvements to Drumnadrochit when the newly appointed butler, Perkins, ushered the Duchess into the drawing room.

'Good evening, I'm so glad you could come. Edgar arrived a little while ago and he's already had the conducted tour, so you must allow me to show you round as soon as you've had a drink.'

The Duchess's cold reptilian eyes swept over her daughter-in-law's brown velvet suit, brown suede court shoes and gold and ruby earrings. Then, inclining her head, she went straight to Harry and allowed him to peck her on the cheek.

'Hullo, Ma. Can I get you some sherry?' It was her favourite aperitif.

'Thank you, Harry.' Stiffly she sat on the centre of the sofa in such a way that there was no room for anyone to sit beside her. 'You're looking well.'

'I'm blooming, we both are! Have you noticed Morgan's wonderful tan, doesn't she look great?'

'I've always heard sunbathing is very bad for the skin,' she observed as she took the fluted glass of sherry from Harry.

'Well,' asked the Duke, 'what do you think, Lavinia? They've made a jolly good job of this house, wouldn't you say? Bright and cheerful, eh?'

'I haven't really seen it yet,' she replied stiffly. 'I'm more interested in seeing what's going on at Drumnadrochit.' Her baleful eyes turned in Morgan's direction. 'I sincerely hope those builders of yours aren't going to do up the place too much. We don't want it to be showy or flashy.'

Morgan returned her look boldly. 'I'd hardly call mending the roof or putting in central heating flashy, would you?

Or cutting out the dry rot and woodworm, and adding a few more bathrooms?'

The Duchess dropped her gaze.

'Really, Ma,' exclaimed Harry crossly. 'What do you think we're going to do? Put a mirrored cocktail cabinet in the drawing room and turn the baronial hall into the Dorchester lobby?'

The Duke, after his third whisky, was greatly enjoying the conversation. 'The Dorchester lobby!' he chortled. 'I like that!'

'I want to make sure the place isn't spoiled,' the Duchess was saying stubbornly. 'It still belongs to your father and me, you know.'

Harry gave a sigh of annoyance. 'Of course it's going to be all right, it's only at the restoration stage as it is! If we do any redecorating –'

'Which we'll have to do,' said Morgan quietly.

'– we'll have someone like David Hicks. He does up all these big old places.'

'Humph,' Lavinia Lomond snorted. 'I don't see anything wrong with it the way it is. All we needed was some maintenance work, which we'd planned to do anyway.'

'*Yes, with Elizabeth Greenly's paltry little bit of capital,* thought Morgan. *I know how your mind works, you old bitch. You wanted a daughter-in-law who would dance to your tune. Not one who hired the composer and booked the band.* Aloud Morgan said sweetly, 'Can I show you round, so that you can see what we've done here? All the best ideas were Harry's actually. I had no idea he was so artistic.'

'I must say, neither had I,' responded the Duchess dryly.

Morgan forced her mother-in-law to look at every room, from the pretty top bedrooms – perfect for nurseries Harry had said – right down to the kitchen adjoining the little separate flat for Perkins and his wife.

'There's just the little garden to do now.' Morgan opened the French windows that led off the drawing room onto a large balustraded terrace. 'We've put in hundreds of spring bulbs, just to cheer it up for the time being, but I want to have the flowerbeds raised and have a little pool at the end – over there! – with a small fountain. That will leave room for some white Victorian wrought-iron garden furniture' – she waved her arms expansively – 'so that we can eat out here when it's hot.'

The Duchess didn't answer. Morgan suppressed a giggle. If the old bag disapproved of what she'd done to the London house – just wait until she knew what the plans were for Drumnadrochit.

10

'I'll come with you, next time you visit Zachary,' Greg assured Tiffany as they sat over their after-dinner coffee at Joe Allen's one night. 'It sure must be depressing on your own.'

'It is. Especially as he hardly talks. He's so uncommunicative these days. I end up feeling guilty that I'm enjoying a normal healthy life while he's stuck in that clinic.'

'Do you think the treatment's working?'

'It's hard to say, Greg. He's so changed, sort of morose and withdrawn. There's no question of him coming home yet, I'm afraid.'

Tiffany and Greg were dining together again, a habit they'd both dropped into during the past few weeks. She liked having Greg as a friend. There was something so relaxed and easy about him and she felt free to say anything without wondering if it was boring him. A friend, she had decided, was almost better than a lover. There was no worrying about whether they would spend the night together or not. Or spend the rest of their lives together, or not. She could just chat away, saying whatever came into her head, and know he'd always be there.

Tiffany hardly went out at all these days. Her life was all work, and she had to admit her designs had never been so good. The reviews for *Glitz*, she was sure, would be even better than for *Night Chill,* when they'd written about 'the clear-cut brilliance of the costumes by Tiffany Kalvin, who is sure to get an award one of these days'.

If only Hunt had been with her to share it all! She felt chilled and depressed and very alone. The empty hollow feeling inside her remained raw and aching, and she punished herself by scanning all the trade magazines for a mention of him or a photograph. Once she felt physically sick when she saw a picture of him at a film première, his arm round Joni – who looked vivacious and triumphant. Not long after his latest film for television, *Pentel Point*, had wrapped, she'd heard on the grapevine that he'd gone with his family to Montego Bay for a holiday.

Once or twice she'd called his number only to hang up the moment she'd heard his voice. Her unhappiness was deep and unresolved. She wondered if she'd ever stop thinking about him.

'... so shall we make it Saturday, Tiff?'

She was startled from her reverie and realized, guiltily, that Greg had been talking.

'Sorry, I was miles away. What did you say about Saturday?'

Greg grinned. 'I said shall we go and see Zachary on Saturday? We could drive out of town in the morning, have lunch somewhere on the way and see him in the afternoon.'

'That suits me fine.'

They looked at each other and smiled. We're in the same boat, said Tiffany to herself, but Greg is coping a helluva lot better than I am.

They arrived at the Moyes Clinic around three in the afternoon and found Zachary reading in the communal sitting room. He looked up eagerly when they entered. As soon as he saw who it was, Tiffany observed, a faint flicker of disappointment appeared in his eyes.

'Hi, Zac.' She greeted him with a kiss and took the chair opposite.

'Hi, Sis. Hi, Greg.' His voice sounded flat.

'You're looking good,' Greg said, as he pulled up a chair. 'Put on weight? The food must be good here.'

Zachary grimaced. 'The Plaza it isn't. I'm made to do fucking boring exercises.'

'How's it going, honey?' asked Tiffany.

'They're a bunch of bullies!'

Tiffany eyed Greg in desperation. This visit was going to be even stickier than they feared.

'Made any friends?' asked Greg conversationally.

Zachary shrugged. 'Some. They're okay, I suppose. At least their families visit them.' There was no mistaking the bitterness in his voice.

'I come to see you every week,' protested Tiffany.

'Yeah. And when did Mom and Dad come? Like never. They don't even write.' Zachary hung his head and his knuckles gleamed white as he clenched his fists.

'Well, you know how busy Daddy always is –' Tiffany stopped as Zachary's warning look dared her to continue.

'He just likes to make money because it protects him from the real world,' cried Zachary. 'He should stay here for a bit. This is the real world. Trouble is, he couldn't take it . . .' His voice drifted off disdainfully.

'I know, Zac, I know. The real trouble is I just don't think they know how to cope.'

'Maybe if Mom went shopping for a few less mink coats' – his voice had a dangerous edge to it – 'and Dad got off his ass and did an honest day's work, they'd be able to find time to care for their family!'

Tiffany was silent. Everything Zachary said was true.

'And does Morgan even write?' He was not going to leave it alone. He was going to go on chewing it over and over, extracting every thread of resentment and hatred and frustration, until there was nothing left. 'She's too fucking busy trying to be a lady to even remember we all exist.'

'That's not fair, Zac,' interjected Greg, who had been listening with close concentration. 'She's newly married, and I hear she's had a castle to do over –'

'Like I said,' Zachary sneered, 'too busy trying to be a frigging duchess. Anyway, you'll have to go now, I've got a session with my shrink in a minute.'

'On a Saturday?' cried Tiffany, bewildered. 'I didn't know you had sessions on the weekend. You never have before.'

'Nope?' Zachary was watching the door. 'Well, let me tell you, my sweet sister, this is not like the world out there, or hadn't you noticed?'

Stung, Tiffany rose and picked up her handbag. 'I'll come next week Zac, but I'll make it earlier.'

'I wouldn't bother. Now you'll have to scram, I can't be late.' Zachary was hovering near the door, agitated.

'Goodbye, honey.' She tried to keep the hurt out of her voice. 'Take care of yourself.' With Greg, she left the room and looked backwards at her brother for a minute. He was still waiting inside the door.

At that moment a young woman came teetering down the corridor, her high heels click-clicking on the polished floor. As Tiffany and Greg passed her they were vaguely aware of a crown of bushy hair, black at the roots and sandy-ash at the tips; of a generous mouth splashed scarlet with lipstick and a short tight dress of bright pink. A waft of cheap perfume lingered in her wake.

Morgan felt the sharp pain in her stomach again. It had started when she had awakened that morning, and now at breakfast it caught her with a low swift punch.

'Are you all right?' Harry was full of concern. 'Can I get you anything?'

'I'll be all right in a moment.' Morgan bent forward, feeling sick with the pain. A fine veil of sweat broke out on her forehead and upper lip and she knew she had gone very pale.

'Shall I ring for a doctor? We don't have one in London, but I could always –'

'No, it's all right. I think it's passing.' She closed her eyes and willed the pain to go away. Today of all days she could not be ill. They were giving their first big dinner party and she had a million things to see to. After a moment the pain subsided as quickly as it had begun.

'There!' she gave a wan smile. 'It's almost gone. I probably ate something last night that didn't agree with me. I'll take some Alka Seltzer in a minute.'

'Are you sure?' Harry hung over her nervously. 'Don't you think you'd better see a doctor? Maybe – maybe you're going to have a baby!'

Morgan shook her head. 'No, I know I'm not pregnant. Don't worry, honey. I'm really all right now.' She straightened up and drank her coffee. She wished he'd go to the gallery and leave her to go through her list of preparations for tonight. At last he finished his breakfast and rose with reluctance.

'Take it easy, darling. Perkins can do everything, and surely Mrs Perkins is doing all the cooking?'

'Yes, of course, everything's under control. I'll rest this afternoon.'

When he had gone she flew to the kitchen, pain forgotten in her excited anticipation. Rest this afternoon indeed! She was having a massage, a manicure, a pedicure, her eyelashes dyed and her hair done. She also had to pick up her dress from Zandra Rhodes.

In the kitchen Mrs Perkins was calmly at work. Morgan had chosen the menu with extreme care. They were starting with *terrine de saumon aux avocats,* followed by tender *contrefilet de boeuf,* with black pepper and a selection of lightly steamed vegetables, and whether it was done in Harry's circle or not, Morgan had decided they would serve a green salad with a wide variety of cheeses before the *bombe glacée Marnier*. Harry had already selected the wines and the brandy and port to follow. Everything had been delivered from Fortnum and Mason, including the Dom Pérignon to give the guests before dinner.

Next she went to the dining room, where Perkins was

arranging the right number of chairs round the large oval table.

'We'll use the Royal Doulton dinner service, Perkins, and the Waterford crystal, of course,' she commanded.

'Certainly, my lady. And the white napery?' Perkins was soft-spoken and very respectful. A faggot no doubt, thought Morgan, in spite of Mrs Perkins in the kitchen, but they always make the best menservants.

'Yes, the white napery, Perkins, and the gold flatwear, and of course the gold salt cellars.' Morgan gave one of her warm smiles. It was good to encourage these people, be nice to them; that way they stayed. 'Constance Spry are delivering the flower arrangements early this afternoon, so we'll have dark-red candles in the silver candlesticks – the Georgian ones tonight, not those dreadful modern ones we were given as a wedding present – so they will match the red roses in the centre of the table. See that the florists put the large arrangements in the hall, will you? And the two yellow and white arrangements in the drawing room. Oh, and Perkins, when you do the table napkins, just see that they are simply folded. I can't bear it when they are tricked out like water lilies or something.'

'Certainly, my lady.' He tried not to sound offended.

Perkins had worked in many large aristocratic households, but this was the first time anyone had even dreamed he would arrange the napkins in fancy shapes. He flicked a speck of dust fastidiously off the table, then stood with folded hands, in case there were any more instructions. Her ladyship certainly knew what she wanted for one so young.

'I'm going out now, Perkins, and I'll be out for lunch. I think that is all.'

'Very good, my lady.'

Morgan swept out of the dining room with her most gracious smile.

An hour later she left the house looking forward to the rest of the day.

By three o'clock Morgan had arrived at the beauty salon. She'd lunched in the Causerie at Claridge's with Lady Hobleigh, whom she'd befriended at a cocktail party the previous week, picked up her dress for the evening and was now looking forward to a session of pampering. There was nothing she adored more than clustering beauticians administering to her every need. Gaily she chose what colour nail-polish she'd like today, and decided to have her hair styled informally. It would make her appear more ingénue against the grand formality of their house.

As she was having her hair washed, the pain started again.

'Ah ... ah ...' she winced, screwing up her face and bending forward, her arms clasped round her stomach. *What the hell was wrong with her?*

'Is the water too hot?' cried the shampoo girl, aghast at how white Lady Blairmore had gone. Morgan shook her head. She was unable to speak. The manageress rushed over with a dry towel to mop up Morgan's shoulders, as her wet hair dripped around her face.

Gradually the pain subsided, and she accepted the glass of chilled water that was handed her. Shaken and pale, she sat back and submitted to her hair being finished. She really didn't feel at all well.

The first guests were Caroline and Neville Lloyd, old friends of Harry's whom Morgan hadn't met before. Caroline was as fine and brittle as Dresden china, with thin red lips and pointed features. Her eyes flicked sharply over Morgan's red-beaded chiffon dress and ruby and diamond necklace and earrings like a cash register. Neville, an ex-Grenadier Guards officer and now the head of outside operations for a large industrial company, rocked back and forth on his heels as he clutched his glass of champagne in a large beefy hand. He appraised Morgan with large stupid eyes. Hmmm. Harry had certainly landed a fine catch.

'Who else are you expecting?' Caroline asked in her high piercing voice.

Morgan shrugged with studied vagueness. 'Oh, you know the Southamptons, and the Mannerings –'

'The Duke and Duchess of Southampton?' Caroline's voice had practically risen an octave.

Morgan nodded, smiling. Caroline's obvious social climbing aspirations were showing. She wished she felt a bit better, so that she could give her a run for her money, but the pain kept coming and going in waves, making her feel slightly sick. *God, this would have to happen tonight,* she thought, *with all these important people coming, especially Prince and Princess Fritz of Luxembourg. They were so grand they hardly went anywhere.* 'We've also got a very interesting art connoisseur coming, Hans von Gruber, and his wife, and the Willesleys.'

'Henrietta and Charles Willesley?' piped Caroline. 'We met them at Ascot.' She swirled her glass airily and looked up at her husband. 'Remember Henrietta and Charles Willesley, darling? We met them on Gold Cup day.'

'Er – Oh, did we?' he replied, looking blank.

At that moment Perkins ushered in the Earl and Countess of Willesley who looked equally blankly at Caroline when they were introduced, so that she retired to her husband's side, defensive but unbeaten.

'My darlings,' Henrietta Willesley shrieked, 'I can't *tell* you what a boring party we've been to! I feel absolutely smashed. Well, my dear, there was *nothing* else to do but get pissed.' And with that she seized a glass of champagne from the silver tray Perkins was decorously holding.

Caroline watched the Willesleys with disapproval. Perhaps she didn't want to know them after all. The Duke and Duchess of Southampton when they arrived were also in high spirits, and began regaling the assembled company about a dinner party they'd been to the previous night. One of the lady guests had crawled on her hands and knees under the dining-room table and undone all the men's flies. Morgan and Henrietta laughed uproariously. Henrietta because she thought it was an *absolute* gas and Morgan because she knew that in Britain the higher the rank the worse the behaviour. And she wanted to belong. Not so Caroline. Never having really become a member of the aristocracy, she was totally horrified and shocked. And slightly worried too, because she knew she could never join in such ribaldry and still feel comfortable. Perhaps Neville had been right when he'd said she was middle class.

Morgan glanced round the room as Perkins quietly refilled everyone's glasses. Rosalie and Glen Winwood had arrived and were deep in conversation with Hans and Eva von Gruber about the Getty Museum. Caroline had latched herself onto Sir John Mannering and Neville Lloyd was giggling stupidly with Charles Willesley. Harry, the perfect host, moved round talking to everyone, introducing topics of conversation that he knew would be of mutual interest. Morgan felt quite proud of him. The house looked wonderful too. With deep satisfaction, she thought, *Now I've got everything. Every bloody thing I ever wanted. And nothing is going to spoil it.*

The Prince and Princess Fritz of Luxembourg made their entrance, a tall distinguished-looking couple in their fifties, the Prince with the carriage and bearing of hundreds of years of royal breeding, the Princess a regal and beautiful woman with snow-white hair drawn back into a black velvet bow to match her tight-fitting black velvet dress. Round her neck she wore the famous Luxembourg emeralds.

Morgan glided swiftly across the room to greet them, a dazzling figure in red. Suddenly her face seemed to break up, her eyes widened in bewilderment and a gasp sprang from her lips. She felt as if she was spinning down and down through a long black tunnel, and her feet were sinking into soft clay. Scarlet speckles swirled all round her.

The Prince and Princess stood stunned as Morgan crumpled and collapsed at their feet.

Ruth replaced the telephone receiver with shaking hands and sank slowly onto the sofa. Oh God, what was Joe going to say now? She sat gazing at the Chinese rug that adorned the living-room floor as if it might provide an answer. Then she rose again and went to the red lacquered cabinet where the drinks were kept. Even if it was only ten o'clock in the morning she sure could use a drink.

The Moyes Clinic had just informed her, in impersonal and professional terms, that Zachary had run away, having assaulted a male nurse who tried to detain him. No, they had no idea where he had gone. He had last been seen walking out of the clinic with a young woman, and when the nurse had asked him where he was going, Zachary had punched him in the face and knocked him out cold. Then, according to an eye-witness, Zachary and the girl had run off and been seen heading for the highway in a beat-up old Chevvy.

Ruth's head was in a spin. Taking another sip of vodka and tonic, she moved gingerly, as if any violent movement would make her body break up and fall apart. She tried to recall the details of her conversation with the director of the clinic but all she could remember was what *she'd* said. Did the doctor say they had suspected someone had been smuggling drugs to Zachary? When did he say this had all happened? Yesterday or this morning? But wasn't Zachary supposed to be in their care, and weren't they supposed to see that this sort of thing didn't happen? It was all such a shock. Oh, if only she could remember! Joe was going to be so angry at her foolishness. Shaking her head and spreading her hands Ruth spoke aloud, 'I don't know ... how am I supposed to cope ... it's all too much.' She sipped some more vodka and decided to ring Tiffany. She'd know what to do.

★

Tiffany, absorbed in working out how the scarlet and jet black costumes for the chorus would look good *and* allow them freedom of movement, tried to ignore the ringing of the telephone as it tore into her concentration. These outfits were going to be hell to make, and she'd have to set up a meeting with Dianne Giancana to see what could perhaps be elasticized.

The phone continued ringing. *Where* was everyone? Putting down her pencil impatiently she snatched up the phone.

'Yes, who is it?'

'Tiffany, is that you?'

Tiffany sighed deeply. This was the last bloody straw. What the hell did her mother want now?

'Are you there, Tiff?'

'Yes, I'm here.' Tiffany stifled a sigh and felt a pang of contrition. Ruth sounded really agitated. 'What's the matter, Mom?'

She listened intently as Ruth gave her a garbled version of the news about Zachary. Somehow she wasn't surprised.

Zachary had seemed in a funny mood the last time she and Greg had visited him, and he had been so anxious for them to leave. Something else came back to Tiffany also, that curious-looking girl they had passed in the corridor. Instinctively she knew there was some connection.

'Try not to worry, Mom,' she said. 'I'll see what I can do.'

'But what about your father?' wailed Ruth. 'What's he going to say? Should we ring the police?'

'Don't do or say anything for the moment,' Tiffany said firmly. 'There's a good chance Zachary might even be on his way home, or he might turn up here. I'm sure he'll be all right, so let's not say anything to Daddy, 'cause it's not going to help any! And I don't see the point in calling the police. He's not a child and he hasn't been kidnapped or anything. What the hell are the police going to do?'

'Don't swear, dear,' said her mother distractedly. 'All right, I'll say nothing to your father, but I am dreadfully worried. Suppose the press gets hold of this?'

'They won't. Now take it easy and I'll ring you when I have any news.'

'All right, dear.' Ruth put down the phone and, feeling slightly relieved, poured herself another vodka. After all Tiffany had told her to take it easy.

Tiffany spent the rest of the morning on the phone, frantically trying to get hold of anyone who might know something. The director of the clinic had little to add to what Ruth had already said, but the description of the girl Zachary had been seen with fitted her memory of the girl in the corridor that Saturday afternoon. She rang Greg and he promised to contact a private detective to help trace her.

'I'll sketch a fairly good likeness of her,' volunteered Tiffany. 'It won't be difficult because she was quite distinctive looking. She's probably from New York too, and she may even be the one who first got Zachary hooked! I wonder where he met her?'

'Probably in some bar or disco. We should start by searching in those sorts of places for him. Have you any idea where he used to go in the evenings?'

'No, he never said. I am scared, you know, Greg, although I pretended to Mom that I wasn't. You remember what a state I told you Zachary was in when he came to see me for that two thousand dollars. He could be in real danger.'

'I don't think so, Tiff. They won't hurt him while his family has money, you can bet your ass on that.'

Tiffany rang a few of Zachary's friends but each time she drew a blank. He hadn't been near the Horace Mann Day School either. She decided that if he hadn't turned up within a week the police had to be informed.

The waiting room of 24 Harley Street was dimly lit and

decorated in a depressing shade of cream. In the centre, on a walnut table, surrounded by chairs covered in maroon leather, were piled out-of-date copies of *Punch* and *Country Life.* Morgan figured that only in London would leading physicians and specialists work in a place like this. So shabby. So dingy. Not at all like the waiting rooms in New York, where it was all chrome and lucite and bright modern paintings. Twelve doctors shared this Georgian house. They must be making a fortune, Morgan decided. So why, she thought with irritation, couldn't they call in an interior designer.

'Lady Blairmore?' The secretary put her head round the door. 'Dr Tennant will see you now.'

The results of the tests she'd had done during the previous ten days had come, and this, she hoped, was her last appointment with Dr Alastair Tennant, the doctor Rosalie Winwood had called in the night Morgan had passed out with pain at her own dinner party.

After examining Morgan that night, Doctor Tennant had told her to stay in bed, and the next morning he had arranged for her to see a colleague of his who was an eminent gynaecologist. Doctor Tennant thought it likely she was suffering from an ovarian cyst.

The first test Morgan had was an ultrasound examination, and as the pains had completely stopped, she hoped she would be given a clean bill of health. If she'd had a cyst it must surely have burst and would be unlikely to recur. But then the gynaecologist asked her to come back. He wanted to carry out something he called a hysterosalpingogram examination. Morgan shrugged. These specialists were always so fussy. It wouldn't be anything serious because she was feeling so well again. Reluctantly, she agreed.

Now, unconcerned, she followed the secretary up the wide staircase to Dr Tennant's office. He was waiting for her in the doorway.

'Good afternoon, Lady Blairmore.'

'Good afternoon.'

He was a clean-shaven man in his forties, with a kind smile and compassionate eyes. Gesturing Morgan to sit in the large leather chair, he picked up a green folder and sat down behind the desk.

'Um ... ah, yes.' He scanned his notes and cast his eyes over a typed report. His white cuffs and collar gleamed against his dark suit, and Morgan admired his strong and capable hands.

'Is everything all right? ... I feel fine now.' For no reason her heart had started to thump.

Dr Tennant's eyes held hers as if he were sizing her up, then he smiled gently.

'Lady Blairmore, your general health is excellent. Heart, lungs, blood pressure are perfect, your weight is correct, in fact you are really a very fit young woman.'

'Yes?' Morgan leaned forward. She was sure he was holding something back and her heart was hammering harder than ever.

'But I am afraid I do have to tell you something that is very distressing,' he paused, still regarding her with speculative eyes. 'There is nothing I hate more than having to tell a healthy young woman such as yourself something like this, but I'm going to give it to you straight as I think you are a very strong and resilient person.'

Morgan felt the colour drain from her face, and it go stiff and cold.

'Have I got cancer?' Her voice was low and her eyes were wide and beseeching.

Dr Tennant blinked, startled.

'No, no – of course not!' he said urgently. 'Did you really think that was what I was going to tell you? I *am sorry*, I didn't mean to frighten you, I just wanted to prepare you ...'

Morgan slumped back in the large chair, still looking pinched, though a faint pink was coming back to her cheeks.

'If it's not cancer,' she whispered, 'anything will be good news by comparison.'

'Well ...' He looked down at the report again. 'You do have a serious gynaecological problem, I'm afraid, although it's not going to affect your general health.'

'So?' Morgan's eyes suddenly took on a suspicious look.

'As far as we can tell you probably had a very small cyst that burst by itself. That was when the pains stopped. We cannot confirm this because by the time you had the ultrasound examination it had already gone. But an unusual shaped uterus was spotted and that is why you were asked to go back and have a hysterosalpingogram examination. I'm afraid it showed your uterus to be markedly malformed. This is due to an extremely rare developmental abnormality. Do you understand?' He looked at her earnestly.

'I think so, but if I feel all right – and I don't get those awful pains again – does it matter?'

'I'm afraid it does, Lady Blairmore. It means you will never be able to have children. Let me try and explain. Sometimes people are born with certain organs missing altogether, or markedly malformed, like babies being born with a hole in their hearts, and no one knows why this happens. In your case you were born with a deformed womb. Now, this is something that never has and never will affect your general health. You have regular periods, don't you?'

Morgan nodded numbly.

'Quite. To all outward intents and purposes you are perfectly normal, and the only way you would have discovered this, if you had not taken this hysterosalpingogram test, is by the fact you would have eventually wondered why you had not got pregnant. You see, a deformed womb cannot carry a baby ...'

Morgan didn't hear the rest. Her mind spun in a jumble of conflicting realizations. Was she upset? Yes and no. How much had she really wanted children, anyway? Not desperately, but Harry did. My God, Harry did! Harry needed a son to continue the line. The Duke is dead. Long live the Duke. Without a son, the dukedom would become extinct. After three hundred years.

'Isn't there anything that can be done?'

Dr Tennant shook his head slowly but positively. 'You cannot re-create what nature has not provided in a situation like this, I'm afraid.' There was no way at all she could ever have a child.

'Now, Lady Blairmore,' he continued as he read her thoughts. 'Would you like me to tell your husband for you? Often in these situations it is easier if the doctor breaks the news, rather than the wife –'

'No!' Morgan spoke with sudden resolution and her eyes cleared. 'That will not be necessary, I'll tell my husband myself.' She rose and drew the mink coat around her. 'Thank you very much, Dr Tennant. You've been most kind.'

He escorted her to the door, and shook her hand warmly.

'If I can be of help at any time, Lady Blairmore, please do not hesitate to contact me.'

'Thank you.'

Morgan walked along the thickly carpeted corridor and vanished down the stairs towards the heavy door that led into Harley Street.

Dr Tennant returned to his office and found Miss Phillips, his personal secretary, placing a file on his desk for the next patient. She picked up the one marked BLAIRMORE, MORGAN (LADY) and tucked it under her arm.

'Jolly plucky little lady, that last one,' he observed gruffly as he sat down behind his desk. 'I had to give her some bad news and she took it very bravely.' He shook his head. 'Tragedy really, especially as her husband will want a son and heir.'

Miss Phillips gave a little smile as she left the room.

Riches

She was fifty-six and a virgin. But she got her kicks from reading her boss's case notes. This one sounded interesting.

11

Zachary carefully tapped the vein on the top of his instep until it rose blue and strong. Then he carefully slid the needle in and pressed the hypodermic slowly and steadily. Lying back he closed his eyes as the rush took effect. Wow! The high was worth every second of the low that would, in time, follow. The high was the only sensation to strive for, no matter what. He turned and looked at Smokey who was sleeping beside him. What a woman! What a goddamn fucking wonderful piece of ass. How she had managed to fix everything! He shook his head dizzily. He'd never know, but he was grateful. The way she'd got his parents' chef to give her the name of the clinic – and the way she'd sneaked drugs in to him, until that amazing day she'd picked him up in a rented car and they'd flown to Reno. It had been frigging sensational! What with all that dope she'd had at the bottom of her purse, his mind had been gloriously blown – spaced out – right through their wedding and the night that followed. What a trip, he giggled weakly, in every sense of the word. His cock still felt quite sore from the amount of humping they'd done. Now he had to get things sorted out, like the money his father had promised him, like finding somewhere better to live. He screwed up his eyes tightly and wondered how he was going to set about it. He didn't want to have to see his father. Perhaps money could be transferred or something? Oh fuck it, Smokey could take care of the details. She was good at that sort of thing. What about Tiff, though? He loved Tiff, perhaps he ought to get in touch with her – and have her meet Smokey. Hey, that was a great idea!

Zachary tried hard to concentrate. He'd fix something – like ring Tiff and say hi . . . then what would he say? Gazing vacantly into space, Zachary let his mind slip into neutral. He switched on the battered radio and loud rock music filled the tiny room.

Tiffany sat by herself in the fourth row of the darkened theatre, a clipboard on her knee. Every now and again she made feverish notes as she watched the technical rehearsal of *Glitz*, which was due to open at the St James Theater in a week.

For the past hour they had been working on act two, scene four. The set depicted a Versailles-style garden, very formal, with life-size grey stone statues arranged at various levels down a sweep of stone steps. In the foreground, an enchanting Fragonard-type couple cavorted on a swing made of flowers, and the lightness of their colourful costumes, and the gaiety with which they danced, stood out in brilliant contrast to the solidness of the background. The dance ended. The couple pranced into the wings, and the flowered swing rose into the flies. Tiffany leaned forward, watching intently, hoping to God the next bit was going to work as well as she had visualized. The music had now become mystical, and in the twilight of six blue spotlights, the statues gradually came to life, magically so. From hard unyielding stone one minute to a soft fluidity the next as the dancers drifted downstage. The costumes seemed to melt from hard granite to cloudy gauze as they moved against a now-darkened stage, lit only by a starry sky. The effect was incredible! One minute the figures were carved out of rock and the next they flowed like gentle liquid. The music crashed to a crescendo, the lights went up – and once more the 'statues' were back in position again, once more heavily solid and immobile.

Tiffany drew a long deep breath and ran a hand across her forehead. It had worked! It had actually worked! Her idea of making outer costumes, fixed to the stone steps, of fabric stiffened with plaster-of-Paris and painted grey had done the trick. She'd had quite a job persuading both the producer and dancers that it would be easy for them to slip into the hinged outer construction, so that only their heads, an arm here and there and the occasional leg had actually shown when they were in position. The rest had depended on the strength and hinging of these 'shells', and of course the lighting, so that they would become invisible when the dancers emerged from them in their real costumes. She caught the producer's eye and he was grinning broadly at her. Tiffany grinned back, feeling very good at that moment.

Next came Carla Tansley, the leading lady, in a dress for her big final number, a swirling mass of tulle appliquéd with thousands of tiny blue feathers. Tiffany was anxious to see how it looked under the lights and against the glossy set. She was also anxious to see what happened when Carla started whirling downstage in her energetic routine. If the dress started moulting she'd look like a cold chicken in a high wind. The costumes for the chorus in the flying angels sequence looked fine. So did the Lido scene. Tiffany had captured all the glamour and sparkle of Paris night life, and she'd even made the headdresses herself, from wire, gauze, glue and glittering stones. She glanced at her notes as the director went into a lengthy discussion with a sound engineer. Carla's white crêpe dress in act one, scene two looked flat. Maybe a huge necklace was the answer, and chunky diamanté bracelets on both wrists.

After thirteen hours of nerve-fraying repetition, the first run-through finally came to an end. It was ten o'clock at night and it was the moment when everyone doubted anyone's ability to do anything right. Nerves were twanging and egoes had become dented. Resentful chorus girls whispered that the choreographer was a 'sadistic old bitch', and the sound engineers cocked fingers at the director's backside muttering 'fuckin' faggot'. The leading man still ranted about wanting a pink spot – if Carla was having one why couldn't he? – and the air rang with 'sorry, darling' from those who had screamed abuse earlier.

Through a litter of paper cups and empty cigarette packs Tiffany made her way onstage. This is a truly crazy world, she thought, but I love every minute of it. She loved that backstage smell and the camaraderie, although it didn't always appear as such, but in a show this size, with its large cast, sixteen-piece orchestra and the numerous stage hands, they were all striving for just one thing, that the show should be right.

Tonight, though, everyone was tired and strung out. The first dress rehearsal was tomorrow. At least they'd all have had a hot meal and a night's sleep before then. It never ceased to amaze Tiffany how food and sleep restored everyone's sense of humour.

'You're wanted urgently at the stage door, Tiffany,' shouted one of the stage hands from the wings. 'They said it was a Mrs Kalvin.'

She glanced at her watch. Why on earth should her mother come to the stage door at ten-fifteen at night?

Gathering up her things Tiffany charged backstage and headed for the stage door. Eddie sat in his booth, lethargically chewing gum and looking at the baseball results. He was alone.

Bewildered, Tiffany glanced round the darkened stage door. A young woman in a bright pink dress, with back-combed hair, black at the roots and sandy at the tips, leaned against a far wall. Small insolent eyes looked Tiffany up and down and a heavily painted mouth smirked.

The fragmentary memory of the girl she'd seen at the clinic whirled through Tiffany's mind, and suddenly everything clicked into focus. A stifling silence hung in the air as the two women faced each other. Smokey was the first to speak.

'I'm Mrs Kalvin. Mrs Zachary Kalvin.' She stuck out her jutting breasts and spoke with the classy accent she'd been practising all evening. 'I think it's time we met up.' She flipped the stub of her cigarette onto the concrete flor, where she ground it out with her foot. She never took her eyes off Tiffany.

'You're married to my brother?' Tiffany's voice was a croak.

'Sure! Why shouldn't I be?' Smokey shifted her position against the wall and put her hand on her hip. 'I'm the only one who cares about him.'

'That's not true!' Swift anger brought flaming colour to Tiffany's cheeks and her eyes blazed. 'It's because we *do* care about him that we sent him to the clinic. I've been frantic with worry wondering where he was. We've – I've been trying to find you ... I knew it was you who made him leave!'

'You're fucking right I did, he was bloody miserable in that shit-hole.' Smokey forgot to use her classy voice. 'And let me tell you something. He's happy with me.'

'And back on drugs, I suppose,' Tiffany said sharply. 'Don't you know the doctor said he'd be dead in a couple of years if he went on like this?'

Smokey laughed mirthlessly. 'Jesus, you're a cube! And you bein' in the theatre too! Don't be such a fucking goody two-shoes! I bet you've tried it all and how!'

Tiffany took a deep breath, determined not to lose her temper. With care, this girl would lead her to Zachary.

'Where are you and Zachary living?' she asked lightly.

'At my place,' Smokey replied sullenly. 'That is until we get a nice apartment, like he's used to.'

'I'm sure.' Tiffany tried to keep the sarcasm out of her voice. 'Well, what can I do for you?'

'Zac said we should meet up, you being so thick with his family and all that. He's eighteen now and due for that money from his old man. And I thought mebbe ...'

Tiffany's eyes narrowed. She'd help Zachary, yes. She'd do anything in the world for her kid brother. But this was another whole ball game.

'Sure thing.' Tiffany smiled easily. 'When can I come visit you both? I haven't seen him since the last time I went to the clinic.'

Smokey thought for a moment, her plucked eyebrows contracting in a frown. 'Why do you want to know where we are?' she asked at last.

'How can I help you if I don't know where to contact you? And it's help you want, isn't it?'

Smokey nodded slowly. That was reasonable enough. Besides she quite liked Tiffany, not her type of course, but she seemed on the level.

'We're at 1105 21st Street at Ninth Avenue. Second floor rear.'

Tiffany copied the address down in her diary. 'Okay, I'll come tomorrow evening around eight. I'm working during the day.'

'Suit yourself,' Smokey shrugged. 'Beats me why a dame like you works at all, when you could live like a lady, like your sister I'm always reading about.'

'I like to work,' said Tiffany quietly as she put her diary back in her shoulder-bag. 'I'll have to go now, but I'll see you and Zac tomorrow. What's your name, by the way?'

'Smokey, I was Smokey O'Mally before I married your brother. And don't forget to bring some of the dough with you, we could sure use it right now. Took all my savings to spring Zachary and I don't intend to go on supporting him.' Then she was gone, her heels clicking as she left through the stage door and vanished into the dark and busy roar of night-time Broadway.

A weight of immeasurable sadness enveloped Tiffany as she stood alone in the street outside the theatre. She was struggling to equate Zachary the drug addict married to Smokey, and Zachary the sunny-natured happy-go-lucky teenager of a few summers back. What had gone wrong? Memories of him as a golden-haired baby came flooding back. Tiffany was six when he'd been born and she used to love to sneak into the nursery in the early mornings and peek into his cot, coaxing him to smile. Then there was Zachary as a five-year-old, kicking a ball on the beach at Southampton with his sturdy little brown legs, shrieking with excitement. And there was the Christmas when he was twelve when he'd been given his very own hi-fi for his room. She and Morgan had gone together to buy him some of his favourite records, and he'd driven the whole family mad by playing 'The Windmills of Your Mind' for three solid days.

Tears trickled down Tiffany's cheeks as she slowly made her way home. Her most recent memory of him was so different. That of an edgy, hostile young man, eaten up with bitterness against his family, waiting for a hooker to bring him another fix.

At that moment, Tiffany felt bitter too. Surely something could have been done to prevent this awful thing happening? Perhaps if their father hadn't been so ambitious for him; or if their mother had shown more interest and sympathy; or even if Morgan had been more friendly instead of always being wrapped up in her own pursuit of pleasure. Then Tiffany stopped in her tracks. She was being unfair. She was closest to Zachary, and yet she had let her absorption in work, and in Hunt, come first. Oh God, Tiffany thought, we're all guilty. We just got on with our own lives presuming Zachary was fine, without taking the trouble to find out what was going on in his head. A small sob escaped her lips. Oh, Zac! I love you so much and I feel so helpless. Please let me find a way to do something before it's too late.

Morgan walked slowly down Harley Street, oblivious of the rain. *You are never going to be able to have children. Never have children.* Unaware of cars and London taxis as they swished past, scuttering up muddy droplets, she walked steadily on until she came to Oxford Street. Her mind was in a turmoil. To be told at twenty-two you could never have children was bad enough, but it was devastating when you were married to a peer of the realm whose greatest desire was to have a son and heir. Her thoughts zigzagged disjointedly as she tried to grapple with the situation . . . and why had she insisted on telling Harry herself? It would have been much easier to have let Dr Tennant do it. Perhaps it was because part of her mind was refusing to accept the fact that she was barren. She had to come to terms with it herself first. Then she'd tell Harry. But not now. Not today. She tried to imagine Harry's reaction. Shock, of course, and deep deep disappointment, but she was sure he'd show love and compassion towards her. But then what? With unseeing eyes, Morgan walked along Oxford Street, jostled by the surging crowds of shoppers. Would she be made to feel guilty once the first flush of sympathy had worn off? Would Harry begin to feel their marriage had been a mistake and that he should have listened to his mother and married Lady Elizabeth? His blind adoration will begin to corrode and rust away as the bed begins to cool, which it always does in time, thought Morgan with rising panic. And then there would be no children, no son, to bear witness of their love. Harry would be without an heir. Morgan's legs were feeling shaky, as a sick fear clutched at her stomach. She'd have to sit down for a few minutes or she'd collapse. Hyde Park lay ahead, just beyond Marble Arch. Plunging through the heavy traffic amid furious tooting of horns, blind to the risks she was taking, she reached the park. It had stopped raining but a sharp wind scudded round her ankles as she sank thankfully onto one of the old iron benches.

She hadn't wanted children . . . yet. Probably, if she'd been asked this time last week if she ever really wanted children, she'd have had to be honest and answered 'No'. Children were noisy and messy. They meant loss of freedom and could cut down on your fun. There was also nine months of being fat and ugly, and then all that pain. Morgan was scared of pain. But marrying Harry inevitably meant that she would have to have children in due course. Harry was the last in line. He had no cousin to inherit because Andrew Flanders was illegitimate. If Harry did not have a son, there would be no Duke of Lomond after he died. No Marquess of Blairmore. After three hundred years the family tree would shrivel and die.

Morgan sat for a long time on the bench, the enormity of the situation filtering through her confused mind. She grew cold and stiff as the damp air seemed to penetrate her bones, and her eyes, green and sad, gazed vacantly across the park.

Perhaps Harry would eventually seek a divorce, thought Morgan, and marry some girl with broad hips and thick legs who could breed like a rabbit.

It was growing dark and the tall street lights in Park Lane were beginning to twinkle through the trees when Morgan finally rose to her feet. Feeling weary and chilled, she retraced her steps out of the park and stood looking for a taxi. But at least she had resolved what to do.

For the past hour a plan had been forming in her mind. A dangerous and foolhardy plan, but she was sure that with help she could bring it off. Something she had overheard many years ago, when she'd been barely eleven, could be just the lever she needed now to achieve what she wanted.

A son and heir for Harry.

Morgan let herself into the house and went straight to her room. Taking off her mink coat and damp shoes she ran a hot bath, liberally sprinkling the water with Taylor of London's jasmine bath oil. Finally she ordered Perkins to bring her a very large dry martini.

Relaxing in the heavily scented water and sipping her drink, she luxuriated in the sheer physical pleasure of feeling warm again, and very slightly heady. She'd missed luncheon because her fittings at Zandra Rhodes had taken longer than she expected and she hadn't wanted to be late for her Harley Street appointment.

At length, having topped up the bath with more hot water,

she got out and, wrapping herself in a large bath sheet, padded back into her dressing room to choose what she was going to wear for dinner tonight. They were dining with the Southamptons and she wanted to look her best.

An hour later, her make-up and hair perfect, she put on her jade-green silk jersey dinner dress, which clung to her body sensuously. Then she added her six strands of Mikimoto pearls, and pearl drop earrings. When Harry got back she was in the drawing room having her second martini.

'Hullo, my darling.' Harry always greeted her as if it was a wonderful surprise to find her there. 'Everything all right? How did you get on at the doctor's?'

'Fine, honey.' Morgan kissed him warmly. 'He said I was in wonderful shape.' Harry did not notice her hand shaking as she picked up her drink again.

'I could have told you that!' he quipped. 'I asked you how you got on, are you all right?'

'I'm fine . . . fully recovered. It was only a tiny cyst and he doesn't think I'll have any more. He said –' she paused to remember. 'Yes. He said, "Your health is excellent, heart, lungs, blood pressure, all normal." Oh, yes! and he said I was a very fit young woman!' Morgan's eyes dropped as she looked down at the olive in her drink. Then she looked up and smiled at Harry. 'So that was great, wasn't it?'

'Wonderful news, darling.' Looking pleased, Harry came and put his arms round her and held her close. 'I was worried about you, Morgan. Thank God there was nothing wrong.'

'Nothing wrong, Harry,' repeated Morgan, pressing herself closer to him as she rested her cheek against his.

The Duke and Duchess of Southampton lived in a charming house in Chelsea, overlooking the Thames. They were a middle-aged couple and to further his investments company they gave dinner parties regularly that were a mix of American clients, a few of their life-long friends, sometimes a member of the Royal Family, and a smattering of up-and-coming talent in the art world to liven things up a bit. As soon as Morgan entered the house with Harry that evening, she knew it was not home to the Southamptons, but an unlived-in showpiece arranged to impress. They gathered for drinks before dinner in what had originally been the adjoining stable, but which George Southampton, with considerable style, had transformed into what was now referred to as 'the gallery'. A couple of priceless Persian rugs lay on the polished floor, two jardinières filled with Boston ferns flanked a Louis XIV sofa, and the twenty or so spotlit paintings, mostly of the Duke's ancestors, hung on the white walls.

Accepting a glass of champagne from the Spanish manservant, Harry strode across to the far side of the gallery to look at the paintings.

'What a magnificent Canaletto,' he breathed.

'Great picture, isn't it?'

Harry and Morgan turned to find a large beaming man with a florid face standing behind them looking at the picture also. From his accent Morgan instantly guessed he was from the mid-west.

Harry nodded. 'It's in perfect condition too.'

'Hey, Bella,' he bellowed to his wife across the room, 'come and have a look at this.' He lowered his voice fractionally as she joined them. 'See this, honey? This here picture? Why don't we do the same with some of our best transparencies? Get 'em blown up to king-size like this, and then fix them on the wall with back lighting.' He turned to Harry for approval. 'It's a great photograph, isn't it!'

Lost for words, Harry stared back, then George Southampton came up and put his arm across the American's shoulder.

'Have you met each other?' he asked convivially. 'This is Jack Decker and his wife Bella – Lord and Lady Blairmore. My dear Jack, I'm glad you like my picture of Venice. I rather like it myself.' With an unseen wink at Harry he led the Deckers off to meet more people.

Morgan watched Harry from time to time during the evening and he was obviously happy and enjoying himself. What I am going to do is right, she thought.

It was after midnight when they got back, and as always the wine at dinner had made Harry amorous. Morgan tried to get undressed but he kept grabbing her, his eyes bloodshot and glazed, a good-natured grin on his face. Usually she found him tiresome when he was in this mood, but tonight she decided to take advantage of it.

'Harry, I want to ask you something.' She extricated herself gently.

'Ask away, love of my life' He made a deep mock bow, overbalanced and fell giggling in a heap on the bed.

'You know Tiffany has designed the costumes for *Glitz*?'

'*Glitz*?' He smiled back. 'Oh yes! Blitz the Glitz!'

'Fool!' She giggled too. 'Seriously, listen. It opens on Broadway in a few days' time and she rang today and begged me to fly over for opening night. It's the biggest thing she's ever done – it could put her in the running for an award – and well, I think I ought to go, just for a few days.'

Harry's expression was like that of a small boy who had been told he couldn't have a tree for Christmas.

'Darling, do you have to? I can't come with you, you know, because of the exhibition we're holding at the gallery.'

'That's what I thought, honey,' she said hastily, 'I wouldn't consider it, except that I know you'll be so busy I shall hardly see anything of you anyway. I'll only be gone for three or four days, five at the most. It would mean an awful lot to Tiffany, especially as she hasn't got Hunt any more.' She slipped into her Janet Reger black chiffon nightdress, so that her perfect body shimmered through the transparent folds.

'Well, I suppose if you have to.' Harry lay with a sulky expression on his pink face. 'But I wish you wouldn't. I'll be lonely.' Then he rolled off the bed and started tugging at his black bow tie.

'I'll be back before you know it.' Gaily she made for their adjoining bathroom. 'I'm just going to have a quick shower.'

'What – *now*?' He sounded cross. 'For God's sake, Morgan, come to bed.' Standing naked in the middle of the room he looked at her ardently.

'I will in a minute.' She turned back and led him by the hand to the bed. 'Lie down and gather your strength.' She gave him a playful push, so that he flopped backwards, trying to grab her breasts as he did so. 'You wouldn't want me to come to bed without brushing my teeth first would you, honey? Now lie there, I won't be long.' With a wicked smile she slid beyond his grasp and skipped coquettishly away, turning out the lights as she did so.

'Don't be long.' Harry lay in the darkness feeling slightly woozy but deliciously randy. He loved sex this way. He loved the floating sensation and slight sense of unreality. Thank goodness booze never affected his performance. Presently the bathroom light clicked off and he heard Morgan's bare feet pad across the thick carpet. Then she slid naked under the cool sheets beside him.

The darkness and the dizziness made him feel like a beautiful glowing pendulum as he rocked gently backwards and forwards inside her. When he quickened his pace to match hers, the shining hot pendulum swung to and fro, reaching a higher and higher pinnacle of pleasure with each forward swing. Morgan lay quietly beneath him, her arms round his neck, her legs enfolding his back.

As soon as it was over he rolled off with a loud sigh and instantly fell into a deep sleep.

Morgan lay awake for a long time, deep in thought. Tomorrow she would ring Tiffany and invite herself over for opening night. It would be such a nice surprise for her sister.

12

'*Wife?*' yelled Joe, rising from his desk with a violent movement. '*What* wife?'

'Smokey O'Mally.' Tiffany flipped a photocopy of the sketch she'd done for the private investigator onto his suede blotter.

Joe grabbed the foolscap paper and blanched.

'Jesus, I thought I'd got rid of her.' His voice was flat and grey.

'You know her?' Tiffany stared, dumbfounded.

Joe's colour returned and he started sweating again. 'That broad got two thousand dollars out of me. Said Zachary had made her pregnant.'

'When was this? Recently?'

Joe sat down heavily again and reached for his box of cigars.

'It was the day the press blew the story about Zachary's behaviour at our party. She just burst in here. I didn't know she was involved in drugs! She never mentioned drugs! I just thought Zachary had gotten her into trouble, so I gave her the money to fix it.' His voice trailed off wearily.

'Well, Daddy,' said Tiffany crisply. 'Your money didn't buy an abortion. It bought more drugs, a hired getaway car from the Moyes Clinic, airline tickets, a marriage certificate and a night of whoopie in some motel in Reno.'

'Jesus.' Joe sank his head onto his hands and for the first time Tiffany realized he was getting old. 'Jesus,' he repeated.

'I'm going to see Zac tonight, Daddy,' she said more gently. 'This girl has obviously got a hold over him but if I can find a chance to talk to him alone, maybe I can do something.'

'Don't give the bitch any money!' Joe looked up, showing a return of his old spirit.

'I'll play it by ear. The main thing at this stage is to appear to be on his side as far as Smokey is concerned. If he really loves her it is going to be more difficult to get him away from her.'

'Love, huh! What does the boy know about love! I just don't know what's the matter with him. You give a kid a good home, a good education, every opportunity, plus lotsa money – and what does he do? Gets himself frigging married to a whore and ends up a drug addict!'

'It isn't always enough,' said Tiffany softly as she rose to leave. 'I'm afraid Zac may be deeply disturbed.'

'How can anyone be disturbed coming from the sort of home *we* provided?' Joe looked genuinely baffled. 'Answer me that!'

'I wish I could, Daddy, but it's happening all the time.' Leaving his office she shut the door quietly behind her.

Smokey was alone when Tiffany finally found the dilapidated tenement that evening. She was reading a trashy magazine about pop stars and drinking from a can of 7-Up.

'May I sit down?' Tiffany gestured to the one chair in the room.

'Help yourself.'

Tiffany perched on the edge, afraid if she leaned back the pile of clothes draped over the back would tumble onto the floor.

'Where is Zachary?'

'Dunno.' Smokey eyed Tiffany's shoulder-bag greedily. 'Got a cig?'

'Sure.' Tiffany got out her pack of Marlboros and offered one to Smokey before lighting up her own. Then she dragged deeply as she looked round the room with growing distaste. Empty Coke cans and cookie wrappers lay on the floor beside the bed and the butts of several cigarettes floated in a half-filled plastic cup. There was a rancid smell of sweat mingled with sex.

'Have you lived here long?'

'A few months, but it's too small for us now. That's why we've gotta get a bigger place. I want an apartment near Central Park, with big rooms and a nice bathroom.'

I bet you do, thought Tiffany. Aloud she said, 'When do you think Zachary will be back?'

'Couldn't tell ya. Did you bring some dough?'

'I'd like to wait until Zachary gets back before I come to that.' There was a cutting edge to Tiffany's voice.

'Why don't you leave it with me? Look, lady, I am his wife so I've a right! What's his is mine.'

'It's not as simple as that.'

'Why? Do you need proof we're married? If that's what you want you can have it.' Smokey jerked open the drawer of the dilapidated bedside table and pulled out a document with triumph. 'See. A regular marriage certificate – between Zachary Joseph Kalvin and Kathleen Mary O'Mally, dated May 22nd – a week ago last Wednesday. What more do you want?'

'There are a lot of things to be gone into,' Tiffany hedged.

'Such as?' sneered Smokey. 'Look, I don't like this messing around. Give me the dough you've brought or there'll be trouble.'

'I don't think there will.' Tiffany regarded her coolly. 'I had a long talk with my father this morning. I told him I'd found Zachary. He wasn't interested. In fact he's completely disinherited him.'

She watched as Smokey's face contorted with anger. 'That fucking mean bastard,' she stormed. 'I mighta known! I should have gone myself, I knew it! I could have screwed him easily. Shit!'

'It wouldn't have done you any good if you had gone yourself.'

Smokey looked at Tiffany questioningly.

'No. He had enough of you last time!' cried Tiffany angrily.

The two women glared at each other. It wasn't going the way either of them had planned.

'My father didn't *have* to give Morgan and me a settlement when we were eighteen. He did it because he wanted to; he wanted us to have the sort of life he'd missed out on.' Tiffany paused, then looked squarely at Smokey. 'There's no way he's going to make over that sort of money to Zachary now. The doctors have said Zac will be dead within two years if he continues the way he's going. You can't blame my father; to give Zachary money now would be like signing his death certificate. He's not getting a cent.'

Smokey flung her cheap pink plastic purse across the room so that it hit the wall and spilled its contents onto the floor.

'That bragging little fuck-up!' she screamed. 'That god-damned fucking *virgin*! I mighta guessed he was full of crap! All he wanted was pussy and dope! Well he's not getting anything more from me.'

Tiffany rose to leave.

'Hey – where d'you think you're going?' Smokey jumped to her feet and ran over to the door, barring it. 'I want something for all I've done.'

Raising her eyebrows, Tiffany opened her bag and took out her billfold. 'What is your usual fee' – she glanced at her watch – 'for twenty minutes of your time? Probably not much – so here's fifty dollars, and I'm being generous.' She flung the crisp bills on the bed, and taking Smokey by surprise, pushed her away from the door roughly.

'Hey...!' Smokey yelled, but Tiffany was too quick. She wrenched open the door and ran down the stairs and into the street, the sound of Smokey's harsh voice still in her ears. Keeping close to the buildings, she ran along the sidewalk and turned the corner to where she'd left her car. Crouching low in the driver's seat she started the engine and eased the car forward. There was no sign of Smokey in pursuit. Tiffany drove the car a short way down Smokey's street, then parked on the opposite side, where she could see the entrance. It might be a long wait, but she was determined to sit there until she saw Zachary coming back. She wasn't even sure what she was going to do then, but a vague plan was forming at the back of her mind. There was only one snag. Suppose Zachary wouldn't listen to her?

Smokey picked up the dollar bills and put them in her purse, shaking with fury. How dumb she'd been keeping Tiffany's visit a secret from Zachary. If only she hadn't suggested he go and visit his friend, Mitch, he could have easily sorted out that goddamn sister of his! Made her see reason! Once again Smokey seethed at the way the rich always stuck together. Well, they weren't going to treat her like that. She was his wife and they were damn well going to show her the respect she deserved. She'd fix 'em!

'When will she be home?' demanded Morgan. She was calling from London, and it really was too bad of Tiffany to stay out all day and half the night without telling Gloria where she was.

'I don't rightly know, Miss Mor ... I mean Lady Blairmore.'

'Oh! Listen Gloria, give Tiffany a message ... will you do that for me?'

'Sure thing.'

'Tell her ... tell her I'm flying over for the opening night of her show, on the twentieth! Got that? And tell her I'll be staying in her apartment.'

'Here?' Gloria began to lose some of her cool.

'Yes, I'll be staying for several days and I'll arrive on the nineteenth. Do you understand what I'm saying, Gloria?'

'Sure, I understand.'

'Good. Now you'll give her that message. You won't forget?'

'I won't forget.' Gloria hung up. She was one heap glad she worked for Miss Tiffany and not her sister.

Tiffany got home half an hour later, stiff and tired. She'd spent the past four hours crouched in her car watching the activity in the rundown street, but there had been no sign of Zachary. Groups of black and Puerto Rican youths lolled in doorways and on the corner, silent and watchful. A drunk had come out of a building and clung swaying to a street light for a time. After a while Smokey had appeared, and after looking up and down the street for a minute, had crossed to the other side and vanished down a side alley. Tiffany was pretty certain she hadn't been spotted. Then several men with hooker-type girls had gone in and out of the building for the next hour or so, but Zachary had not appeared.

Eventually, and with a feeling of despair, Tiffany drove herself home.

On her message pad she found that Morgan had called three times, and there was also a note from Gloria, written in large child-like capitals. So Morgan was flying over for the opening. Opening night! Tiffany clapped her hand to her forehead and let out a gasp. She'd been so involved all evening, thinking about Zachary, that she'd quite forgotten about it! God! She still had so much work to do!

An early call from Greg the next morning awakened Tiffany.

'Hope I didn't wake you up, Tiff, but I have to leave for a meeting. I wanted to know how you got on last night with Zachary?'

Tiffany told him briefly what had happened.

'Shit! I wonder what we should do now?'

'Let's get the place watched. We have to get him away

from Smokey,' Tiffany declared. 'I have a hunch she hadn't told him I was coming last night. I suppose I should have watched longer, but I could hardly keep awake by midnight. But someone's got to grab him as he goes in or comes out, and I can't because I'm at the theatre all day – '

'I'll see what I can do.' He sounded reassuring.

'Thank you, Greg. Mind you, after I told Smokey there was no money for Zac, she just might be glad to be rid of him!'

'She might also be glad of a large settlement in return for agreeing to a quickie divorce,' Greg pointed out.

'Shit! I hadn't thought of that!'

'Cheer up, honey. I'll get the investigators to watch the place twenty-four hours a day. I'm tied up all morning but I'll dash over at lunchtime. If he's there, he may well agree to see me, and I'll take it from there.'

When Greg telephoned her again that evening he spoke briefly and his usually calm voice sounded worried.

'They've gone – left the building! I spoke to the woman who has the room next door to Smokey's, a real nosey type she was, and she said Zachary never got back last night, and this morning Smokey packed her bags and split, owing three weeks' rent.'

Tiffany gave a groan. They had been so close to Zachary and now they had lost him again. Perhaps it would have been wiser not to have blown her stack with Smokey.

'For Christ's sake ... what *is* this? Grand Central?'

Tiffany stumbled over a stack of Louis Vuitton luggage in the hall of her apartment.

'Morgan?' she yelled.

'In here.'

Tiffany rushed into her living room, where Morgan was tucking into a club sandwich and coffee, made for her by Gloria.

'I didn't know you were arriving so early?' Tiffany hugged her sister, spilling her coffee. 'I was stuck at rehearsals and I couldn't get away, then the traffic was awful. Anyhow, how are you?'

'You sound breathless! Why are you looking such a mess?' Morgan regarded Tiffany's white cotton track suit with amazement.

'I do a little something you've never encountered – work!' teased Tiffany. 'I've been flying round since dawn. I'm starving, can I have some of your sandwich?'

'Help yourself.' Morgan delicately dabbed the coffee stain on her pale yellow skirt. 'So, how's it all going?'

'You've heard about Zachary?'

'No.'

Tiffany told her what had been happening. 'I'm really worried. We've reported him missing and we've got a private investigator working on it, but he and Smokey have disappeared. They could be anywhere! I'm so scared for him.' A note of desperation crept into her voice. 'I'm glad you're here, Morgan. I could really do with some support in the family. Mom's gone into a decline and Daddy's raging ineffectively at everyone. Didn't Harry mind you coming over on your own?'

Morgan shrugged her beautiful shoulders. 'I thought it would be fun and Harry didn't mind, so here I am!'

'How is he?'

'Fabulous. Do you ever see anything of Hunt?'

Tiffany's face clouded and she paused for a moment before answering. 'No. He's gone back to his wife. I never see him.'

'I'm sorry, Tiff, I know how much he meant to you. Who's escorting you to the opening then? You can't turn up without a man on your arm?'

'I'm going with Greg. Now Morgan, don't look like that! Greg has been wonderfully supportive in the last few months, a real friend, and he's giving all his spare time helping me to find Zachary. I know you think he's a bore but I like him, and I don't know how I'd have kept my sanity without him.'

'Maybe you'd better marry him then!' There was a sharp edge to Morgan's voice.

'Don't be silly,' said Tiffany wearily. 'It's a purely platonic arrangement; he's a friend, nothing more.'

'Sounds a bit dull.' Morgan poured herself some more coffee.

'It isn't dull at all! Actually I think he's still fond of you. There are no other girls in his life.'

'Really?' Morgan sounded greatly mollified. 'Tell me, do Mom and Daddy know I'm over here? I didn't tell them.'

'Why the mystery? And why are you staying here? Not that I mind, but you'd be more comfortable at Mom and Daddy's. They've kept your room just as it was.'

'No mystery, Tiff. I just wanted to talk to you and I thought it would be easier and quieter here.' Morgan got up and wandered to the window and looked out. Manhattan was bathed in a golden glow as the sun set in the west; twinkling little lights were popping on in the towering skyscrapers and below, long snake-like lines of cars edged along the streets nose-to-tail. She was suddenly glad to be back.

Tiffany watched her anxiously.

'Is everything all right between you and Harry?' she asked suddenly.

'Sure.' Morgan turned back into the room, smiling. 'Harry and I are crazy about each other. I'm wonderfully happy you know. We've been entertaining quite a bit, now that the house is finished, and I can't tell you how lovely it looks; and Drumnadrochit will be finished in a month or so, so we can fly up to Scotland for weekends when the weather's good. It's so much fun being married!'

'It sounds like it!' remarked Tiffany with a touch of irony that was lost on Morgan.

'I want to do some shopping tomorrow. Come with me?'

Tiffany lay back on the sofa and stretched, reaching with her hands high above her head. 'No thanks,' she replied firmly. 'I shall be far too nervous tomorrow to do any shopping. All I want is for this opening to be over and then I can relax! And I can't stop thinking about Zac. I could kill that girl for getting drugs for him and springing him like that! She's the one, I bet, who got him hooked in the first place!'

Morgan lit a cigarette and inhaled slowly and thoughtfully, then she spoke. 'Honestly, Tiff, if it hadn't been her it would have been someone else, sooner or later. Zachary's always been weak. You have to admit that, and Mom and Dad haven't helped. They've spoiled him something rotten on the one hand, buying him anything he wanted, and they've pushed him too hard on the other hand, insisting he get good grades and end up in Quadrant. He never really had a chance.'

Tiffany stared at Morgan in surprise. It was the first time she had ever heard her make such a mature statement. 'You're quite right of course, and I'm afraid he hates them both right now. What really worries me is, does he feel he has a good enough reason to come off drugs? At the moment he probably feels, in a distorted sort of way, that he is his own man for the first time. They say that once you're hooked on something like heroin there's no substitute. Nothing again ever provides the same highs, I'm told, or gives the same sense of false confidence.'

'If you ask me,' Morgan helped herself to some more coffee, 'if he wants to commit suicide by inches in this way, that's his affair! You can't spend the rest of your life chasing round after him and paying off his debts.'

Shocked, Tiffany cried, 'But he's our brother! And he's only eighteen. We can't just abandon him!'

'He's also self-destructive,' said Morgan dismissively. 'He doesn't want to be helped. As you just said yourself, there is no substitute once you're hooked, so how is someone as weak as Zac going to get off it?'

'That's a terrible attitude to take, Morgan,' cried Tiffany springing to her feet. 'If it takes me all my time and every cent I've got I'm going to find Zac and see to it that he is cured.'

Morgan shrugged. 'You'll be wasting your time, believe me.'

The sisters faced each other squarely. Two pairs of almost identical green eyes sparked with anger. Then Tiffany turned and charged out of the room, a broken sob escaping from her lips.

Five minutes later she was in the shower, shaking all over, her tears mingling with the fast-spraying water. She felt like a violin string that an unseen hand was tuning tighter and tighter. She was afraid she would snap at any moment. She soaped her body in round massaging movements concentrating on her shoulders and the back of her neck. The warm water was soothing and little by little the tension reduced. When she stepped out of the shower, Morgan was sitting on her bed looking contrite.

'I'm sorry, Tiff,' she said immediately. 'I didn't mean us to quarrel on my first day back. You were right about Zac . . . and I'm really sorry to have upset you.'

Tiffany gave a weak smile. She couldn't help herself. Morgan suddenly looked like a little girl again, apologizing for some childish prank. It had always been like that between them.

'Forget it.' Tiffany wrapped herself in a white terrycloth robe. 'I'm sorry too. It's just that I'm terribly tired all of a sudden, and I couldn't help overreacting. What do you say to our going out for dinner? It's Gloria's night off and I don't feel like fixing us anything.'

Smiling again, as if they'd never had a cross word in their lives, Morgan bounced on the bed. 'Fabulous! Where shall we go? It seems like ages since I've been in New York! It would be really great to go out.'

'Then you choose. And while we're having dinner you can tell me what you want to talk to me about.'

'Oh, it will keep, honey,' replied Morgan lightly. 'I'm here for a few days, we'll talk when you've got tomorrow night over.'

'There really is nothing wrong between you and Harry, is there?' Tiffany asked anxiously. She remembered her feelings of foreboding at the wedding.

'I promise you.' Impulsively Morgan kissed Tiffany's damp cheek. 'Harry and I are blissfully happy! I think he's more in love with me than ever.'

It was the first night of *Glitz*. Tiffany had spent the day in an agony of nerves and now, as she applied her make-up at home, her hands trembled.

She had been backstage all day, checking every costume and giving the numerous dressers final instructions on how to get the performers not only into their costumes, but also out of them – and quickly. There would also be garments that would require washing or dry cleaning daily, and pressing nightly. The task was enormous, and as she passed from dressing room to dressing room, and down the long rails of costumes in wardrobe, seeing that wigs were on stands, shoes on rails and costumes properly hung, she wondered how on earth she and Dianne had got everything ready on time. Even the snake headdresses looked alarmingly realistic.

The entire cast was in early tonight, too jangled to stay away, and the atmosphere was one of tense bedlam. Unearthly wailing issued from some of the dressing rooms, as singers warmed up their voices; the director was still charging about, looking deeply harassed, giving final notes, and at the stage door the endless stream of telegrams, cards, bouquets and bottles of champagne threatened to swamp the little doorman. There was such a strong sense of comradeship, although everyone was suffering from first-night nerves, that Tiffany, as always, felt quite emotional. Everyone, from the stars to the stage hands, the musicians to the people on the lighting board, were intent on pulling together, and they seemed closer to Tiffany than her own family. She just prayed that her designs would do justice to this ambitious production. The show would either be a smash hit, or the critics would close it within a week, and Tiffany's work would play a big part in that make or break decision. At this moment she didn't know whether to cry or be sick. As is the custom before a first night, everyone in the company gave everyone else a good luck present. By mid afternoon, Tiffany had been deluged with bottles of champagne, perfume, ornaments, books, records, flowers and several pairs of fun earrings from the scene shifters. In return she had arranged to have a silver wine goblet for everyone, with their name, the date and *Glitz* engraved on the side.

Now, back at her apartment, there was only an hour left before Greg came to collect her and Morgan to escort them to the theatre. Ruth and Joe were going to meet them there.

This is the moment, Tiffany reflected, that I've been waiting for. It had finally paid off, all those years of studying, of tedious grind, of taking any job that came along no matter how small, of working until she was ready to drop. At last she was Costume Designer, with *Tiffany Kalvin* on every billboard, every fly-sheet, and in every programme, of the most lavish show to open on Broadway since the Ziegfeld Follies in the late 'twenties.

It was so exciting it was scary.

Morgan came into her room, fixing her long drop-diamond earrings. She was wearing a lilac georgette dress very much in the style of the 'twenties with a hem that fell into points and a bodice heavily embroidered with silver beads. A Zandra Rhodes special.

'Isn't this fun!' She did a little pirouette. 'It reminds me of when we were kids getting dressed up for a party. Say, I *do* like your dress.'

Tiffany had chosen a strapless evening dress in dramatic black taffeta, with a matching cape, made up of alternate layers of black ostrich feathers and taffeta frills.

'I feel terrible, I wish it was over,' confessed Tiffany. 'Where have I put my purse? I had it a minute ago. Oh God, where has it gone?' She jumped up from the dressing-table and started searching.

'Here, right in front of you!' Morgan pointed to the black silk Gucci purse on the bed. 'Why are you so nervous, Tiff? You've done your bit and now you can just sit back and enjoy the show! It's the people on stage who ought to be nervous.'

'You don't understand,' snapped Tiffany. 'A show is a team thing, whether you're the leading lady, or the guy who sweeps the stage between performances. If the critics hate my designs I'll be letting everyone down. It's terrifying.'

'I'll get you a drink,' Morgan said in a soothing voice. Privately she thought Tiffany was making a fuss over nothing. After all it was only a Broadway show, not a matter of life and death.

Within a hundred yards of the theatre Tiffany could feel the buzz. Energy was being almost visibly generated as CBS and NBC camera crews and press photographers mingled with the glamorous first-nighters.

Bewildered for a moment, she got an impression of long lines of shiny black limousines snaking up to the floodlit entrance, of satins and silks and sable wraps jostling on the sidewalk, of diamonds gleaming on smooth skin and of handsome men in immaculate tuxedos, and all the time the flash-bulbs kept popping.

As soon as she stepped out of the car she was mobbed, with photographers clamouring to get a picture and well-wishers trying to kiss her. By the time she had struggled to her seat in the centre aisle, where Joe and Ruth were already seated, she was trembling. This was the first time she had really been *recognized.* Sitting with Morgan on one side of her and Greg on the other, she clung onto his hand, her heart pounding.

Suddenly the sixteen-piece orchestra struck up the opening bars of the overture and the effect was electrifying. The tingle of anticipation from the audience was palpable, as velvety darkness swept over the auditorium. She could feel a thrill going through every single person as the terrific music swelled and rose to a crescendo. And she was a part of tonight. Everyone would see her designs, including her family, and maybe at last they would take her career seriously. Out of the corner of her eye she looked at Ruth and Joe, but they seemed no more excited than if it had been her graduation from Brearley. In fact less so. With a pang she suddenly wished Hunt could have been here tonight by her side, sitting where dear old Greg was sitting now. I think he would have been proud of me, she thought sadly.

The overture ended. The audience applauded wildly. There was a hush of expectation. Then slowly the curtain rose onto the dazzlingly spotlit stage.

Glitz had opened.

Harry was late arriving at the gallery in Dover Street. Most days he was there by half past nine, but with Morgan away he found it more difficult to get up in the mornings. Life seemed so flat without her. If it hadn't been for the exhibition of sporting prints they were staging, he'd like to have gone to New York too. He hated being left by himself.

Carefully angled spotlights hung from the gallery ceiling, shining down on framed prints of pink-coated huntsmen soaring over fences on satiny hunters. 'If you like that sort of thing,' he'd said to his partner the previous day when they'd supervised the hanging, 'we've got the best in the market.' Looking round now, he felt pleased. They usually stocked old masters but had decided to diversify on this occasion.

'Good morning, Sophie,' Harry greeted the receptionist with a friendly grin. Sophie was the sister of one of his friends and a good sport.

''Morning, Harry. We've got eighty-three people coming to the preview tonight, including the art critic from the *Guardian*. He rang after you'd left yesterday.' Sophie was pretty in a neat way. Every time she set eyes on Harry her heart fluttered and she wished she'd met him before he married Morgan.

'Good. Any other messages?'

'Yes, Harry.' She had a habit of pronouncing it 'Hurry'. Leaning forward over her desk she whispered in a confidential stage whisper, 'There's a young lady asking for you, over there in the alcove, she wouldn't give her name.'

Harry glanced over and at that moment the young woman came towards him. She was wearing a grey suit with a white silk blouse and her mouse-brown hair was pushed back from her face by a black velvet band.

'Elizabeth!' Startled, he took a couple of steps backwards. Intrigued, Sophie perched on the edge of her chair, watching as Harry blushed.

'Hullo, Harry,' Lady Elizabeth Greenly gave him a warm smile and moved closer. 'I was just passing and saw you had some sporting prints. I want to get Daddy a birthday present and it struck me that it would be just the thing!' She gave a high-pitched laugh as if she had said something very funny. Then her pellucid blue eyes wandered vaguely along the rows of pictures.

'Why of course!' cried Harry with forced joviality, as he flung out an arm in an expansive gesture. 'Help yourself.'

'Oh . . . I don't know' – she cocked her head on one side – 'I just can't make up my mind which one he'd like best. Which one do you think he'd like best, Harry? Could you help me choose?' She moved closer and looked up at him limpidly.

'Well, er.' Harry's eyes flickered nervously round the gallery and he moved away a couple of paces. 'I, er, I don't actually know too much about this sort of stuff, not my usual line you know. Er, why don't I get my partner, John Ingleby-Wright, to help you? Now he's an expert on sporting prints.'

Elizabeth slipped her arm through Harry's, and slightly and very gently leaned against him. 'Oh, you know the sort of thing I need. That one is nice, but is it terribly, terribly expensive?' She led Harry away from the reception area and down to the far end of the gallery, talking all the while in her soft clinging voice. Harry tried to signal Sophie to get John out of the stock room but she just smiled sweetly back, not understanding. His shirt was sticking to his back as he felt himself being submerged under Elizabeth's persuasive power.

At last she had made her choice and was writing out her cheque. Suddenly she said, 'Oh, I nearly forgot, silly me! I'm having some friends round for a late supper party tomorrow night. Why don't you come? There will be masses of people you know! Doodle and Biffie are coming, and so are Etta and Ropie. Oh! and Sossie and Quizzie. I've asked everyone for nine o'clock.'

'I'm afraid I can't,' said Harry, trying to sound firm. 'You see Morgan is away for a few days.'

Elizabeth looked at him with innocent eyes.

'Yes, I know she is, but you've still got to eat, haven't you? See you at nine then.' She was out through the gallery door before he had time to reply.

'An old friend of yours?' asked Sophie agog.

'Her family and my family are friends, sort of thing!' replied Harry in confusion as he fled to the safety of the stock room.

He was rather worried. Because in his heart of hearts he was sure he would find himself at Elizabeth's house at nine o'clock the next evening.

★

The rich velvet curtain of the St James Theater swished dramatically closed and the audience went wild. The applause and shouts of 'Bravo' swept over Tiffany like a roller-coaster and she felt her eyes brimming with emotion. The audience's reaction was overwhelming and there was enormous pride in her heart at being a part of *Glitz*. The show looked to be a smash hit. Greg was squeezing her hand and people all around were flashing her smiles of congratulation.

At last the cast took their final curtain call, but it seemed as if the audience didn't want to let them go and the clapping continued as the orchestra played a reprise of the show-stopping numbers.

Tiffany let out a long deep breath and suddenly realized her head and neck were aching from tension. As she walked up the crowded aisle she heard people praising the show and the loud voice of Virginia Graham from ABC radio exclaiming to her companion, 'Darling, I haven't enjoyed myself so much since my wedding night!'

Friends rushed forward to embrace Tiffany and she was quickly hemmed in, a radiant figure in her stark black dress and dramatic cape. Greg, trying to protect her from a barrage of flash-bulbs popping in her face, stood with his arm round her waist.

'Well done, Tiff!' he whispered.

'Did you like it?' Tiffany whispered, looking up at him and smiling.

Suddenly a hand was grabbing hers and a voice was saying, 'Fantastic, Tiffany! Congratulations!'

She looked up and felt the blood drain away from her face. Her heart started to thunder in her ears, and her breath caught in her throat. It was Hunt. Gasping, she stood paralyzed as he smiled down at her. She had never seen him look so attractive. His smile deepened.

'How are things, honey?' he asked softly.

'Fine...' she said automatically, but the words stuck in

her throat. All the months of searing pain and loneliness rushed to the surface, mingled with the knowledge that she loved him as much as ever. His eyes were looking penetratingly into hers, as if he were searching for something, and for a moment she thought she was going to faint.

Bending forward his lips brushed her cheek. 'I'll see you later, my love,' he murmured and then he was gone, vanished among the jostling crowds.

Tiffany turned to Greg, a look of shocked pain in her eyes.

'Let's get out of here, you could use a drink,' Greg said quickly, manoeuvring her into the street. The car was waiting and Ruth and Joe, with Morgan, were already seated in it. In a daze Tiffany climbed in, oblivious of Morgan's squeals of excitement and her parents' patronizing compliments. *I'll see you later*. What had Hunt meant? Was he also going on to the opening night party at Tavern on the Green? Suppose he had Joni with him – and he almost certainly would! For a moment she fervently wished she hadn't seen him again. Until that moment she had built a self-protecting shield around herself, and now it had burst wide open.

'Are you okay?' asked Morgan.

Tiffany braced herself and gave a wobbly smile. 'Yes, just tired. It's been a long night, and a helluva strain.'

'Yes, but you're famous now, the critics will rave about your costumes! You'll be a real celebrity by tomorrow!' retorted Morgan.

In the darkness of the car Greg squeezed Tiffany's hand sympathetically.

When they arrived at the party her eyes flashed nervously round the crowded room but there was no sign of Hunt. Seizing a glass of chilled champagne she drank it quickly then took another. People were crowding round her again and she was beginning to feel claustrophobic.

'Let's find somewhere to sit,' she begged Greg in desperation. 'I can't take much more of this.'

He found her a quiet corner and offered to get her some food.

'No thanks,' she shook her head. 'But I'd like another glass of champagne.' If people thought she was an antisocial alcoholic it was just too damn bad.

At midnight someone produced the first edition of the *New York Times*. And a great roar of jubilation went up from everyone connected with *Glitz*. The critic pronounced it 'Smashing . . . the best show to hit Broadway for a decade . . . original . . . lively . . . funny'. And there was a paragraph that said ' . . . outstanding costumes by Tiffany Kalvin . . . a brilliant young designer who is destined for the top.'

'There, didn't I tell you?' cried Morgan.

Tiffany sat smiling and wondered why she felt so hollow. She'd expected this moment to be so different. Then it suddenly struck her that the desperately unfulfilled blank she was feeling could never be satisfied by work alone. It just wasn't enough.

'Let's go,' she said in a choked voice.

'What, already? But I want to go dancing,' cried Morgan. 'It's much too early to go home! I'd never sleep.'

After some argument it was decided that the chauffeur would drop Ruth and Joe off first, and then Tiffany, before taking Morgan and Greg to the Le Club. There was a glimmer in Greg's eyes that worried Tiffany. If he still felt the same way about Morgan as she felt about Hunt he was about to get himself nicely burned. Greg caught her eye and raised his eyebrows questioningly.

'Okay with you, Tiff?'

'Okay with me, Greg. Go right ahead, but you're asking for trouble! You're playing with fire and it hurts,' she whispered in his ear.

When the car drew up at Tiffany's apartment she got out quickly. Suddenly she longed to be alone.

'Don't wait up. I've got a key,' shouted Morgan after her.

Tiffany got no further than the elevator when she sensed

someone coming up behind her. In panic, stories of muggings, rapes and murders flashed through her mind. Oh God, where was the night porter? He was supposed to be on duty until he was relieved at 6 a.m. Frantically she looked up at the elevator indicator. Christ! It was on the fourteenth floor! Stabbing the Down button, she realized it would be at least a minute before it reached the ground floor. And by then it would be too late. In a second she would be knifed or shot. It happened all the time in New York. Not daring to look round, she kept her finger on the Down button, paralyzed by fear. So this was it. On the night of her greatest triumph she was going to be assaulted or killed for the price of the diamonds in her ears. When a man's body pressed hard into her back, she knew the moment had come.

'I just had to see you, honey.'

Tiffany froze. That voice. Those hands. That whiff of familiar after-shave.

'*Hunt*!'

Slowly he turned her round to face him, and then she was in his arms and his mouth was devouring hers as if he had been starved for the taste and the touch and the smell of her for years.

'Let's go up,' he said huskily.

Tiffany got into the elevator as in a dream. Her legs trembled and her body felt as if it had been turned to molten lead. Leaning against his chest she buried her face in his neck as she whispered, 'Oh darling, I want you so much.'

As soon as they entered her bedroom Hunt started tearing his clothes off. He too was trembling and his eyes glittered almost feverishly.

'Quick, my darling,' he gasped. '*Quickly!*' Seizing her he flung her on the bed, his cock desperately seeking her welcoming wetness. Then with a thrust that seemed to pierce her very soul, he possessed her in a frenzy of pent-up longing.

★

Morgan strolled into the kitchen the next morning and found Tiffany sitting on the high stool by the counter drinking lemon tea. Spread before her were all the reviews of *Glitz*, in which everyone praised her for her sensational designs.

'God, I'm tired!' exclaimed Morgan, giving a loud yawn and stretching her arms above her head. 'We danced until nearly five this morning. I must be out of training. Pour some orange juice for me, will you, Tiff?'

In spite of her grumbling and yawning Morgan looked the picture of relaxed good health as she stood in a white satin robe, with matching slippers, trimmed with marabou feathers. Taking the stool opposite she added, 'I didn't disturb you when I got back, did I?'

Tiffany shook her head, avoiding her sister's eyes. 'No, you didn't disturb me. Some toast?'

'No thanks. Well, wasn't Greg in good form last night! I actually enjoyed myself.' Morgan proceeded to describe their evening but Tiffany wasn't listening. By five o'clock in the morning Hunt had left. This time it was really forever. He was moving permanently to Los Angeles to direct a new TV series. They wouldn't even bump into each other by chance now. He seemed remorseful about coming to her, and kept saying he shouldn't have done it.

'I'm hurting you, and myself, all over again,' he kept repeating, 'but I just couldn't stay away.'

Tiffany looked into his face, so beloved to her, and saw the pain in his eyes and the little lines of suffering round his mouth. She didn't mention Joni and neither did he. It was obvious he was sticking by her if only for the sake of Gus and Matt.

It wasn't until she heard the click of the door shutting after him that the tears came. Then she buried her face in the pillows and lay there, the damp spreading round her face, until dawn.

'. . . I don't know why you didn't come with us,' Morgan

was saying. 'It was awfully boring of you to just go home to bed!'

Tiffany got up and went to rinse her cup in the sink. 'I was dead beat,' she replied shortly. At that moment she decided she would not tell Morgan what had happened. Morgan would think she was a fool to have got embroiled with Hunt again.

'I've got some calls to make, see you later,' she said, heading for her studio.

'Oh, can't we talk? I really came over to talk to you about something, Tiff. Last night was just an excuse, but now that it's over I really need some of your time.'

'Well ... later. I've got to call up some people and then I want to take a shower and –'

'How about lunch, then?' persisted Morgan. 'I'll book a table at the Russian Tea Room for half past twelve.'

'Okay.' Shit! she thought as she left the kitchen. As if I didn't have enough on my mind. Knowing Morgan though, it was probably something easy like designing her a dress for the opening of Parliament or something to wear for Royal Ascot.

Tiffany stared with wide unbelieving eyes at Morgan. Her face had become as pale and translucent as wax and she stared fixedly in horror at Morgan, who had just dropped a series of bombshells in her lap, and had put forward a proposal that suspended disbelief.

'I – I can't!' she croaked, feeling physically sick.

'You can – and you must.' Morgan's tone was absolutely resolute.

'But you're crazy! It's sick and it's quite impossible.'

The sisters sat glaring at each other across the lunch table at the Russian Tea Room. Morgan had particularly asked for a corner table upstairs. She didn't want them to be overheard, and she also reckoned on Tiffany not making a scene in a public place. Now was the moment when she hoped she could bluff Tiffany and get her to agree to what she had in mind.

'I've told you what will happen if you don't! Daddy will be ruined, kaput! He'll probably get sent up for several years!' Morgan's voice was harsh and ruthless.

Tiffany shook her head in bewilderment, fear, and confusion. She knew what Morgan meant about Joe, and she wasn't exaggerating. But this scheme was horrific and evil. Suddenly she felt she didn't know Morgan at all.

'You couldn't – you surely couldn't do a thing like that,' she said at last, '*and* involve me too! It would ruin so many people's lives, Daddy's, Mom's, mine, everyone in Quadrant –'

'And Sig! Wouldn't you like that, Tiff, Sig ending his days in a cell?'

Tiffany closed her eyes at the mention of Sig Hoffman and a deep shudder of revulsion swept over her. She'd tried to blot out that summer, pretending it had happened to someone else. At times she'd almost succeeded, but now . . . Had she only been fourteen at the time . . .? Had that young girl really been her . . .? Morgan's words were making it all come back . . .

Tiffany, her long blonde hair tied back into a pony-tail, skipped up the sandy path from the beach and entered the cool white hall of Four Winds. Her wet swim-suit was clinging to her coldly, encrusted with sand. Sand rubbed between her bare toes and clung frostily to the fine golden hairs on her suntanned legs. The sun had burnt the tops of her shoulders, making them glow tenderly.

As she climbed the stairs to her room, she could still hear chatter and bursts of laughter coming from the grown-ups down on the beach below. Everyone had been swimming and now they were all coming out of the glittering sea to have a picnic. A champagne cork popped and she could hear a roar of approval from her father. Tiffany smiled to herself as she skipped into the bathroom. This was the best vacation they'd ever had. She, Morgan and Zachary were spending the whole of August in this, her favourite place in the whole world, and each weekend they were being joined by Mom and Dad, who usually brought some house guests with them. Sometimes their friends had children of her age and that was fun. This weekend they'd brought Daddy's partner, Sig Hoffman, and his wife. It was a pity they didn't have any kids.

Tiffany ripped off her sticky swimsuit and stepped under the shower. After the harshness of the noonday sun it was bliss to stand under the warm prickles of water. She soaped herself all over and stood watching the golden grains of sand swirl away down the outlet. Then she stepped out hurriedly and wrapped a pale blue towel round herself, sarong style, reflecting sadly as she did so that her breasts were still too small to hold it up properly. *When* was she going to grow nice-sized tits like her best friend at Brearley, Jackie Rosenberg?

On sudden impulse she clutched the towel round her slim body and went charging down the stairs to the television room. She simply *had* to find that wonderful new novel she'd started so she could take it to the beach with her. The idea of nestling in the soft dry sand after lunch with a good book, added perfection to a day already packed with joy. She picked up the book from where she'd left it on the window seat, but as she turned to rush up the stairs again, a large shadow loomed in the doorway, startling her.

'Uncle Sig?' She hitched up the front of the towel.

'That's right, my pet.' Sig, flushed and sweating, came forward, shutting the door behind him. He was wearing red bathing trunks and his red body was covered with long black hairs. 'I saw you coming back to the house,' he said. She wondered why his voice sounded so thick.

'Oh?'

'You're growing up fast, aren't you, baby.' He reached

out and laid a hand on her sunburnt shoulder. She winced slightly.

'Yeah ... well.' She gave an embarrassed giggle.

'So how about being nice to your Uncle Sig, then?' His hand had slipped down from her shoulder and was resting on her barely formed breast.

'I ...' Tiffany backed away, suddenly scared and confused. It had been *years* since she'd sat on Uncle Sig's lap while he bantered amicably with her father.

'You're growing into a beautiful girl, d'you know that? Oh, Jesus you're so beautiful ...'

She tried to cry out, terrified, but he pushed her onto the floor, holding her down, his mouth covering hers, stifling her scream. His great weight pressed her onto the hard floor so that her shoulder blades hurt and his pink, sausage-like fingers worked feverishly between her legs. And then ... and then ... Oh, dear Jesus, he was pushing his great rigid penis into her body. Oh, the excruciating pain ... she was being ripped open. He plunged fiercely into her, quicker and quicker, sweating ribs heaving, until he gave a final lunge as he came, and then stopped. He lay like a great dead object on top of her and she couldn't move.

Tiffany crawled cautiously to her knees, blood running down her thighs and her breath still coming in terrified gasps. Why did she feel so guilty, as if what had happened was all her fault? Sig was standing over her, struggling into his bathing trunks again. Then he picked up the towel off the floor and handed it to her.

'I'll look after the towel when you've cleaned yourself off,' he said shortly.

Naked and vulnerable, she dabbed at the terrible soreness.

'This is just between you and me – okay? You must never tell anyone.'

As if she would! The shame and horror of the last few minutes had banished the loveliness of the day forever, turning it into a nightmare of darkness and pain.

'D'you hear me, Tiffany? *No one* must know about this. If you tell, something dreadful will happen to your father.'

Tiffany gazed up at him, mute with fear and agony. Neither of them saw the shadow of a younger version of Tiffany fall across the window, as the listening figure crept along the verandah.

'Your father has been embezzling millions of dollars from the company.' Sig's eyes were glittering cold now, like a snake's. 'He's been my buddy for a long time, that's why I've covered up for him. But one word of this and I go straight to the FBI. And believe you me, kid, he'll pull forty years in the slammer when they find out. Okay? You understand what I'm saying?'

Oh, please God, make him go away. Make him leave me alone. Tiffany's breath caught in a sob, as she nodded.

'You promise?'

'Yes,' she said hoarsely.

As they stared at each other the shadow at the window flickered, faded, and was gone. There hadn't even been the sound of footsteps.

Sig grabbed the bloodstained towel from her and made for the guest room leaving her alone.

Bursts of happy laughter still came from the beach but the only sound that Tiffany heard was the sad cry of a seagull as it swooped fitfully around the silent house.

It seemed to be mourning her lost childhood with her.

Tiffany slowly opened her eyes and drew a long deep breath. 'I don't want anything to do with any of this, Morgan!' she cried vehemently. 'I can't! It's obscene!'

'Well, the ball is in your court, Tiff. Do this for me and Daddy will be safe. It's as simple as that! No one will ever know anything. Don't worry, I'll work out all the details. All it requires is for you to return to Britain with me when I fly home tomorrow, stay with Harry and me for as long as you have to, and then you can return here and carry on as usual. And Daddy will be safe. Remember that, Tiff.'

'Carry on as usual my ass!' cried Tiffany. 'You're underestimating a hell of a lot of things. I can't possibly go through with such an appalling scheme. It's immoral! And what about my work? Now that *Glitz* is obviously going to be a smash hit, I'll get masses of work –'

'You must do it! You've got no choice, have you? Unless you want Daddy to be arrested. I mean it, Tiff. If you don't do this for me, I'll spill the beans about the goings-on with Daddy and Quadrant.'

Tiffany looked at Morgan, shocked, and knew she was quite capable of carrying out her threat. Never before had she realized how utterly ruthless and calculating her sister was. She'd go to any lengths to get the things in life she wanted. And at anyone's expense.

In a turmoil that even pushed thoughts of Hunt, Zachary and her success with *Glitz* out of her mind, Tiffany left the restaurant in a dazed state. Only one thought was filling her mind. Whatever it takes, I must protect my father. *But this can't really be happening*, she thought as they hailed a yellow cab. *This can't be happening*, she thought as she looked at her sister's cool profile.

But as she found herself packing that night she realized it was.

As Morgan also packed that night for the return flight to England she smiled to herself.

I knew I could persuade her.

I knew I could bluff her into believing I'd tell the IRS about Daddy – as if I would! If all that ever got out we'd all be in the shit!

And then: *I knew I could count on Tiff.*

13

Smart in maroon livery and peaked cap, Duncan, the Blairmores' chauffeur, sat in their maroon Rolls Royce outside Terminal 3 at Heathrow Airport. It was early Friday morning. Concorde, with Morgan and Tiffany, would be landing in a few minutes and Duncan was glad he was early. It would never do to keep her ladyship waiting. In the short time he'd worked for them he'd realized two things: Lord Blairmore was considerate, kind, made sure he had time off for regular meals and would rather take a taxi home late at night than keep him hanging around until the early hours. Lady Blairmore, on the other hand, was selfish, demanding, rude at times, and wished him to be on standby day and night, and weekends too, in case she needed the car. That was the difference, he reflected after nearly forty years as a chauffeur, between real aristocrats and the *nouveau riche*. The latter had no idea how to behave towards servants. It must be fear, he thought. Fear that they would be caught out. He well remembered the words of his late mother, who had been a cook with the Duke and Duchess of MacIntyre in the old days. 'Them that are know them that aren't,' she used to say, 'and them that aren't know them that are.'

Duncan was a walking encyclopaedia on the varied and peculiar structures of class in Britain, and he fervently believed that there was a place for everyone as long as they knew what their place was.

At last he saw Morgan come through the swing doors, surrounded by airport officials and a flurry of porters and luggage. No doubt the personnel at Heathrow were giving her the VIP treatment. She looked immaculately elegant in a cream suit with a chocolate-brown silk shirt and accessories, but somehow she always reminded him of those orchids you could buy encapsulated in plastic. He got out of the car and went round to open the trunk, giving Morgan a slight salute as he did so. But his eyes were on Tiffany. Now there was a beautiful young woman. Pale and gentle, with eyes that had a heartbreaking vulnerability.

'How long will it take us to get into town?' demanded Morgan, arranging her sable boa and suede gloves on the seat beside her.

'I'm afraid the traffic's very heavy, m'lady. A lorry has overturned at the Hogarth Roundabout and it's causing a lot of congestion.'

'Oh God, what a drag. Just when I'm in a hurry too! Can't you take another route?' She frowned and tapped her foot.

'It wouldn't help, I'm afraid. All routes into central London are affected, especially at this time in the morning. It's the rush hour, m'lady.' He edged the car forward as he joined the long stream of traffic, creeping bumper to bumper.

Morgan sighed in a loud theatrical way and glanced at her watch. 'Get me Lord Blairmore on the phone,' she snapped.

Tiffany stared out of the window with bleak eyes, saying nothing. Her normally sensuous mouth was pulled into a grim line, her hands were locked tensely together in her lap.

Duncan was speaking into the car telephone as he guided the car slowly along. 'I'm afraid, m'lady,' he said over his shoulder, 'that his lordship isn't at the gallery this morning. He's gone straight to Christie's and they're not expecting him back for a couple of hours. Shall I leave a message, m'lady?'

Morgan's eyes sparked with annoyance. 'Oh, for God's sake! I told him I was coming home this morning. Tell the gallery to get him to call me the instant he returns. I want to tell him we're going to Scotland later today.'

'Scotland?' cried Tiffany speaking for the first time. She

turned to Morgan in astonishment.

'Well, why not? Duncan, you'll have to take us back to Heathrow later today.'

'Very well, m'lady.' At least it meant he'd have the weekend off. Seeing a gap in the traffic he put his foot down and the car swept silently forward.

'What's the idea?' demanded Tiffany as soon as they were alone in the house. 'Why the hell are we suddenly going to Scotland? That wasn't part of the plan.'

'I've decided it will be easier,' replied Morgan with confidence, as she flipped through the pile of letters that had been placed on her desk in the study. 'Invitations – invitations – what's this?' She ripped open a white envelope and drew out a folded sheet of white paper. 'Oh . . . yes.' She stuffed it quickly into a little secret drawer, hidden in the rosewood panelling. It certainly wouldn't do to let Harry know the name of her gynaecologist. She must remember to pay his bill.

Tiffany went upstairs to have a bath and change while Morgan went through the rest of her mail, made a few phone calls and had a word with Perkins and his wife. When Tiffany came downstairs again Morgan's good humour was restored.

'It's all fixed! I've got hold of Harry at last and he thinks it's a great idea to go up to Drumnadrochit,' she cried. 'I'd already checked the Lomonds are spending this weekend and the next in London, so there will just be the three of us. Harry wants to see how the redecorating is going anyway, so isn't that perfect? Hey, let's have a drink!' She rang the bell for Perkins.

Tiffany sank heavily into one of the deep leather chairs and gazed unseeing through the French windows at the little paved garden. The summer had gone and even the autumn seemed to be ending. The little garden had given up the struggle of being bright with flowers and glossy green leaves and was surrendering to the inevitable arrival of winter. She heard Morgan instructing Perkins to bring them champagne, inform Duncan he was to take them to Heathrow at three o'clock, and get Ruby (her new personal maid) to pack her cases.

'Certainly, m'lady.' Perkins's face remained scrupulously expressionless and he withdrew silently from the room.

'Cheer up, for heaven's sake!' cried Morgan catching sight of Tiffany's expression. 'It's not the end of the world. We'll be at the castle in time for dinner tonight, and tomorrow we can show you round. Then, as soon as it's over, you can leave for New York right away if you're so damn keen to get back.'

'But that isn't where it ends, is it?' said Tiffany in a tight voice. The sisters looked at each other. They both knew it was only the beginning.

By nine o'clock that night Morgan and Tiffany, with Harry, were seated at the long mahogany table in the candlelit dining room of Drumnadrochit Castle. The cut crystal and silver reflected on the mirror-like surface and the only splash of colour was an arrangement of deep-pink velvety roses in the centre. They'd arrived earlier in the evening and Morgan was in high spirits. Drumnadrochit was gradually becoming the sort of ancestral home of her dreams, and she was sweeping Harry along with her in a great wave of enthusiasm.

Gone was the decaying dinginess along with the dusty stags' heads hanging on the walls. The cold stone flooring was hidden under rich rugs. Banished were the wood-burning boiler and the peat fires. The castle now glowed with fresh paint and polished brass and jewel-coloured velvet and brocade hangings. Restored paintings of generations of Lomonds now sprang to life, their tints vivid, their varnish shiny. Shields and swords had been polished until they glittered and the carved armorial bearings and family crest above the great fireplace in the hall had been repainted.

Morgan had also chosen soft lighting everywhere, gas fires that looked like real log fires, plants, mirrors, deep comfortable sofas and downy cushions and smart arrangements of art books on low modern coffee tables. It all contributed to making each room look as if it were just waiting to be photographed for *Town and Country*, which Morgan intended it should be. Best of all, she rejoiced, the castle was now warm. Everywhere. All kept at a perfect seventy-two degrees.

That first night Morgan saw to it that they ate well and drank magnificently. After all, it was to celebrate her homecoming, and Tiffany's first visit to the castle. Bollinger was served in the great hall before dinner, from fluted Waterford crystal glasses; and with their mousseline of trout she ordered a Louis Latour Macon-Lugny '81. With the venison they drank a fine Chateau Calon-Segur '71. More champagne appeared with the raspberry soufflé and there was a 1963 port with the Stilton. Tiffany also noticed a Napoleon brandy ready to be served with the coffee. Yet Morgan drank little herself. Chattering animatedly, she regaled Harry with an amusing account of the opening night of *Glitz*, omitting, Tiffany noticed, any mention of dancing at Le Club with Greg. Then she talked about Zachary and Smokey and how worried they were, and finally began to describe the trip her parents intended taking to Europe next spring. She was sparkling and at her wittiest, and Harry, watching her with adoring eyes, wondered if there was another girl in the whole world who was as fascinating and bewitching and beautiful. He just hoped with all his heart that she'd never find out that he'd spent a couple of evenings in Elizabeth's company, harmless though they had been. Morgan would never understand. He smiled to himself. His wonderful Morgan. How he had missed her! Especially at night! He glanced at his watch surreptitiously. It was after eleven. Soon they could go up to bed.

*

On the surface the next week passed by pleasantly and uneventfully. Harry and Morgan took Tiffany on trips and picnics and showed her all the local beauty spots. But Tiffany wanted to be alone. Morgan's company was jarring on her more and more, as she babbled on about the improvements at the castle and her spring wardrobe. *Had she no notion of how serious her plan was?*

Tiffany took to going for long walks alone, telling Harry that was her way of dreaming up designs for costumes. Under different circumstances she would have revelled in the remote tranquillity to be found in the Highlands. She would have loved the brooding splendour that hung like a backdrop behind the castle. And under different circumstances she would have found the peace restorative after the pressures of *Glitz*, but as she walked through forests of larch, oak, beech and pine trees, her mind remained in a turmoil. Should she actually go along with Morgan's plan, and so save her father from ruin? Or should she try, for the hundredth time, to persuade her sister that the whole idea was totally evil, and utterly unworkable.

These lovely walks always gave her a momentary glimpse of a saner, simpler, better world. But they never solved anything. She and Morgan remained locked in silent struggle.

Harry lay in the darkness of their room waiting for Morgan to finish her bath. He really wished she hadn't got into this habit of going off to the bathroom for ages, just when he felt sexy. He wanted her desperately. The drink was fast taking effect and he felt at the peak of that lovely woozy feeling he so enjoyed. Sex was much better when he felt this way – much better – he loved the floating sensation and the slight feeling of unreality. But if she didn't get a move on, he reflected, as he felt his hard erection, she might just be too late.

At last he heard her padding across the carpet in the dark,

smelt the familiar Joy she always wore, felt the soft sweetness of her naked body and the silk of her long hair brush his bare shoulder. Without opening his now heavy eyes he sought her mouth as he mounted her. Once again he was a hot - red hot - pendulum, swinging with heavy glowing thrusts into her silent body. A burst of sweet agony tore itself from his groin - and then a sigh of pure contentment as he rolled off. In thirty seconds he was soundly asleep.

A few minutes passed, then she slid silently out of the bed and crept back to the bathroom. Closing the door quietly behind her she turned on the light and reached for her robe. Her breathing was fast and her heart hammered in her breast. She made for the door on the far side that led to the corridor, wrapping her robe tightly round her as she did so.

'Wait.' A figure in a silk negligée rose from a chair in the corner. 'How did it go? Was everything okay? He didn't . . .?'

Morgan and Tiffany faced each other, the subdued lighting reflecting dimly on their faces from the pink marble walls.

Tiffany nodded grimly. 'Yes, he thought I was you.' She hung her head in silence for a moment and when she looked up her eyes had a tortured look and her lips trembled. 'But may God forgive you for this.' Turning she slipped into the corridor and hurried to her room. She did not notice the housekeeper, Mrs Monroe, standing in the shadows at the top of the stairs.

Tiffany crawled into her bed, turned off the light and lay there, numb with misery and self-disgust. What a terrible thing she had done. Her only consolation was that if she produced the child Morgan so desired her father would be safe forever. Tormented, her mind went over and over the horrible nightmare of the past ten days. The constant nagging and interrogation from her sister. The endless questions. Were her periods usually regular? When did she last have one? Was she off the Pill? Yes, Tiffany had answered wearily, she'd come off the Pill when she split from Hunt months ago. Taking a calendar, Morgan had then worked out, taking an average over a three-month period, when Tiffany was most likely to ovulate. Not content with that she had driven into Fort Augustus, bought a thermometer and had insisted on taking Tiffany's temperature every night and morning, anxiously waiting for the reading to drop. Oh God! Oh God! Tiffany rolled around in her bed, running her fingers through her long hair. It had made her feel like a laboratory specimen or an animal on a farm, people waiting for her to come on heat and be ready for fertilization. And then this evening Morgan had looked up from the thermometer in triumph, her eyes glittering.

'It's dropped a bit,' she exclaimed hopefully.

'Of course it's dropped, you fool! I've just had an iced drink, it would be bound to drop,' Tiffany replied angrily. 'My mouth *feels* cold.'

'I still think it's a sign. After all, according to my calculations, this is the right time,' Morgan persisted stubbornly. 'I say we should go ahead.'

And so tonight had been the fateful night. Tiffany buried her face in her pillows, tears of humiliation streaming down her cheeks. Her own sister was blackmailing her into being a surrogate mother! Oh, Daddy, Daddy, a child's voice cried inside her. I'm doing this for you. For you. And may God forgive me.

They were back in London and it was Monday morning. Harry had already left for the gallery, having kissed Morgan as if he couldn't bear to let go of her. Then he pecked Tiffany on the cheek and said something about it being a pity she couldn't stay longer.

'There! You see?' cried Morgan as soon as they were

alone. 'It couldn't have gone better . . . he doesn't suspect a thing! In fact,' she added, with a brittle laugh, 'I almost feel jealous! When he woke up the next morning he wanted to make love again because it had been so terrific the night before.'

Tiffany fixed her eyes on her coffee cup, unable to look at Morgan. 'You make me sick.'

'Oh, rubbish, Tiff! We *are* sisters, for God's sake.'

'I think that makes it worse.'

'Stop being so sickeningly dramatic. You're going back to New York today and in a couple of weeks you can have a test done to see if you're pregnant. You ought to be, God knows we tried hard enough to hit the right time in your cycle. In fact I'm sure you've conceived my baby! I just feel it in my bones.'

'You're a monster. A sick and crazy monster! I'd never have agreed if it hadn't been for . . .'

'Quite,' Morgan cut in swiftly. 'Daddy has to be protected. Don't worry, Tiff! It will work! We've gone over it a hundred times. Once you know you're pregnant, I'll wait about eight weeks before I announce I'm having a baby. When I'm supposedly seven months pregnant I'll fly over to the States on a visit, just as you're actually having the baby! Then I'll call Harry and say it's arrived prematurely. It couldn't be easier! After about a couple of weeks I'll fly back, baby and all!' Morgan told it as if it were a lovely fairy story she'd read somewhere. 'And Harry will have his heir – the next Duke of Lomond, after him,' she ended.

Tiffany dropped her head into her hands and gave a shudder. Oh God, how could Morgan be blackmailing her like this. *And they all lived happily ever after*. 'You're mad!' Her voice sounded muffled. 'Don't you see a million things could go wrong? Have you considered what will happen if Harry wants to come to the States with you? Have you any idea what being pregnant is like? How are you going to manage? Won't he want to come to prenatal classes with you? What about your figure? You'll *never* get away with it ... and anyway it might be a girl.'

'Keep your voice down, Perkins will hear you.' Morgan glared at her sister. 'This may be a far-fetched idea, but I've *got* to produce a child. Somehow, anyhow. It may not work this time, but if you blow the works then the repercussions will be far worse! All you're doing is being a surrogate mother. It happens all the time nowadays, it's no big deal! If it wasn't for the title it wouldn't matter. I could have told Harry and if he'd been desperate for children we could have arranged a surrogate mother, or we could have adopted. But if the child is to succeed to the title one day, it must *appear* to be legitimate. It's vital, don't you understand? I tell you one thing, if it gets out about Daddy it'll be worse for you than doing this.'

'But it never *need* get out!' cried Tiffany. 'I didn't even know you knew until the other day! I've sat on the secret of Daddy embezzling funds from Quadrant – for years now. How come, if you've known this so long, you wait until the information comes in handy for your own purposes? That's disgusting, Morgan. You didn't mind taking that dirty money when Daddy gave it to you by the handfuls, did you?'

She looked at Morgan and it struck her how she'd changed since she'd married. A hardness had crept round her eyes and the shape of her mouth. Ruthless ambition marked her expression. She'd achieved what she'd initially set out to achieve, but now she wanted more.

As if reading her thoughts, Morgan said softly, 'I have to do this. If Harry were to find out I could never have children – well, it would be the end of my marriage, Tiff. He's desperate for a son and heir. And I don't want to lose him. I care about him you know.'

'You care far more for yourself! You always have! You're only interested in hanging in there until Harry's father dies and you become a duchess!'

'Tiff, what sort of person do you think I am?' she cried. 'I only want a baby! Is that a crime? Hundreds and hundreds of women want babies and can't have them and they arrange surrogate mothers, or adopt! I'm in a desperate situation, Tiffany.' Tears suddenly filled her eyes and spilled down her cheeks and her mouth trembled. 'You *can't* let me down . . .' she sobbed. 'I'll lose Harry.'

They sat in silence, each deeply preoccupied with their own thoughts. At last Tiffany spoke.

'You didn't give me much choice, did you?'

Duncan drove Tiffany to the airport an hour later. Alone in the back of the Rolls, feeling sick and cold, her thoughts went back to that terrible summer at Southampton ten years before. That's when this had all started. She thought she'd been the only one who knew what had happened, the only one who'd heard what Sig Hoffman had said.

But Morgan had known.

And now the past would stay with her forever.

14

The Kalvins' Park Avenue duplex was empty and in darkness. Ruth and Joe had left town during the afternoon for Southampton, as they did every Friday. The deserted rooms were immaculate. Newspapers and magazines were neatly stacked on the coffee table in the study, the large bed in the master bedroom was as smooth and blank as a dead face, and in the living room each cushion had been plumped up and set at right angles on the sofas and chairs.

So abandoned was the atmosphere, that but for the half dozen magnificent floral arrangements that had been delivered late that afternoon after they had left, the place might not have been lived in for months. A cloud of fragrant mimosa stood on a pedestal in the window, a shower of tiny purple orchids trailed from the top of a bookcase, and a profusion of roses and lilies, sweet scented stock and gardenias, set in beautiful bouquets, adorned the side tables and Ruth's desk. The two delivery boys from the florist said there was no card to say who they were from. Eva, the new maid who let them in, thought this was very romantic. If Mrs Kalvin had a secret admirer he was certainly very rich.

In the staff quarters the TV blared loudly as the staff started to enjoy a weekend off. A few went home to stay with their families, but four remained to play cards, relax over their supper and enjoy a few bottles from the stocks of liquor Mr Kalvin kept for entertaining. By midnight they had all gone to bed, having first locked and bolted the front door. With the family away it had been a pleasant and undisturbed evening.

*

By ten o'clock the following morning the police had been summoned and the Kalvins recalled from Southampton.

A shifted chair, a table at the wrong angle and a crooked picture on the study wall prompted the precise major-domo to remove the landscape painting by Alessandro Magnasco, that concealed the wall safe. The safe had been opened. Six million dollars' worth of jewellery and an unspecified amount of cash had been taken. The police estimated the time of the robbery somewhere between six o'clock in the evening and midnight. But how had the intruders entered? They came to the brisk decision that it was an inside job. There was not a sign of forced entry, nothing else in the apartment had been touched, nothing else was missing. Whoever had done it knew exactly what they wanted. All the staff were recalled and questioned. Only Eva, the new maid, had anything of interest to say. She remembered opening the door in the late afternoon to two boys delivering flowers. No, she couldn't remember their faces because they were mostly hidden behind the great arrangements, but she did remember when she saw them out, after they had made three or four trips from their van, that only one guy seemed to leave, saying the other had gone down in the elevator. She had believed him.

The doorman wasn't very helpful either. He had felt unwell during the afternoon and evening and had spent most of his time in the washroom. The result, he feared, of an anonymous box of chocolates that had been left for him at lunchtime by one of the kind tenants in the building.

Ruth wept for her missing diamonds and emeralds and rubies, not to mention her pearls, and Joe nearly had a seizure when he realized that the few thousand dollars he always kept for day-to-day emergencies had gone too.

A few nights later Tiffany dined with her parents, a silent gloomy evening with Ruth withdrawn and Joe breaking into sudden bursts of expletives as if he could not contain the agony of his loss. Tiffany was quiet too. She had returned to New York a few days before and there was deep pain in her eyes.

'So – the police haven't got much to go on?' she asked at last.

'They don't know what the hell they're doing,' snapped Joe. 'No one saw the delivery van, no one left any fingerprints anywhere. They guess one of the delivery boys hid in the apartment and as soon as the staff were sitting on their fat asses drinking *my* liquor on *my* time, the robber helped himself, then just walked out through the front door, as cool as you please!' He tackled his soft shelled crabs vindictively, crushing them to pulp. He'd already sacked Eva, on the grounds that only a fool would take delivery of six damn great arrangements of flowers late on a Friday when the family had gone away without even checking who they were from?

If it was the last thing he did, he'd find out who had robbed him. That, he owed himself.

'It does seem strange,' remarked Tiffany listlessly. She was sorry for her mother about the jewellery, but it was insured, and Ruth, she knew, would hasten to replace it.

Ruth gave a little shudder, and remained silent. Ever since it happened she'd been having awful nightmares, terrified that Joe would come to realize in time that the burglary might all have been her fault. In her dreams he was yelling abuse at her, calling her dreadful names and saying she couldn't be trusted to do anything right.

'I'm surprised they didn't take anything else,' Tiffany observed.

'They knew exactly what they wanted. Unmarked bills and jewellery that could be broken up, the bastards! I just want to know *who* knew the safe combination apart from your mother and me!' cried Joe.

Ruth looked down and crumbled her bread roll with shaking fingers. How could she ever tell Joe that because her memory was so bad she had written it down years ago on a piece of paper she kept hidden under her smart blue stationery. And that piece of paper was now missing.

Morgan was feeling edgy. The only news from home had been about the robbery, since when, apparently, her mother had been unwell. There was still no news about Zachary, and most important of all not a word from Tiffany. She had returned to the States nearly three weeks ago. Surely she must know the results of a pregnancy test by now? Morgan clipped on her ruby and gold earrings and studied her reflection. She looked rather pale and tight round the eyes. What she badly needed was a break in the sun. How she hated the English climate. Even when the sun shone it was a grey sun. Perhaps she'd suggest to Harry that they go somewhere warm for a couple of weeks, if he could get away from the gallery. She ran her fingertips over her cheeks. Her tan had faded completely and she was beginning to look like any Englishwoman – ordinary. 'I'll start a course of sun-ray treatments tomorrow,' she resolved. At least her hair looked good, long and shimmering, falling to her shoulders in soft shades of gold.

When the phone rang she heard Perkins pick it up in the hall below. Going quietly to the top of the stairs she leant over the rail to hear who it was.

'I'll see if her ladyship's at home,' she heard him say.

'Yes, Perkins?' she called.

'It's her grace, m'lady, the Duchess of Lomond. Shall I say you're at home?'

Morgan made her way languidly down the stairs, pulling on her cream suede gloves. As she reached him she said in a loud voice, 'No. Tell the Duchess I am *not* at home and you don't know when I'll be back.' I hope the old bitch heard that, she thought, glancing at the receiver in Perkins's hand.

Duncan was waiting for her by the car and as soon as she

appeared he ushered her into the expensive-smelling cocoon of pale grey kid.

'I'm lunching at 84 Eaton Square,' Morgan reminded him. 'Will you pick me up at half past two. I want to go to Harrods to do some shopping.'

'Certainly, m'lady.'

A moment later the phone in the car rang. 'It's his lordship.' Duncan manoeuvred the Rolls gently into Knightsbridge and handed Morgan the receiver.

'Harry? Oh, hi, honey!'

'That was terribly rude of you, Morgan,' he exclaimed without preamble. 'My mother's just rung me up to say she heard you tell Perkins you were out.' He sounded fretful.

Trust that bitch to be such a fast worker. Aloud Morgan crooned, 'Oh, honey, I'm so sorry. I was just leaving the house and I am running late for a luncheon party. I'll ring her back later. What did she want?'

'To tell us to keep November 23rd free. It's Ma and Pa's thirtieth wedding anniversary and they've decided to give a party. It wouldn't have taken you a minute to have talked to her! Now she's in a foul mood and I'm getting the brunt of it.'

'I'm really sorry, darling. I'll ring her as soon as I get home.'

'Okay.' He sounded mollified. 'See you tonight, darling.'

'Yes, dear.'

Morgan handed the receiver back to Duncan and wondered what she'd wear for the party. It would need to be something stunning.

It was a typical English ladies' luncheon and Morgan knew from previous experience that there would be no ice in the drinks, the food would be pretentious and the conversation dire. She had never enjoyed the undiluted company of other women but it was important she accept as many invitations as possible at this stage in the game. As soon as everyone had met her and got her name firmly onto their guest lists, she would pick and choose and only go to the most exclusive parties, like the ones given by Prince and Princess Fritz of Luxembourg.

Morgan found only one of the women there interesting. She was an elegant woman in her forties, wearing a beautifully cut black suit. Her eyes had a sophisticated sparkle and her mouth an amused tilt at one corner.

'This is Lady St August,' enthused Mrs Snedley-James, the hostess, glad to have another titled lady at her party.

The two women looked at each other. An appraising smile flickered on Morgan's lips. When she got home she would look up the St August family in *Debrett's Peerage* to check if this attractive woman was the wife of a marquess, an earl, a baron, or merely a knight. If only the British system of titles were less complicated. In any case, she might be useful to make up the numbers at a dinner party.

Looking surreptitiously at her watch Morgan saw it was already half past one and they still hadn't sat down to luncheon. She surveyed the bevy of social matrons as they jabbered with excitement. This lot she could do without.

When they were only half way through the long drawn-out luncheon and the conversation had reached a new low in trivia, the hired butler announced that her car had arrived and she took the excuse to leave, amid a flutter of startled ladies.

'My dear, so *soon*?' Mrs Snedley-James looked ready to burst into tears. The star of the show was going. 'You *must* come again,' she babbled, rising and escorting Morgan to the front door. 'Or you and your husband must come to dinner one night. I know my husband would love to meet you both.'

'Thank you,' said Morgan gravely, 'but I don't think we have any free time for the next three months.'

Mrs Snedley-James's sweaty pink face fell with disappointment. Morgan's last glimpse of her was standing on the doorstep flapping the boatshaped neck of her floral dress to allow the cool air to circulate down her vast bosom.

An hour later, having slipped into Harrods to buy a dozen pairs of black silk stockings with rhinestone seams designed by Zandra Rhodes, Morgan walked up Montpelier Street to her house in the Square. Tired and frustrated that three hours had been wasted so drearily, she let herself in, and put her packages on the hall table. Then her heart gave a great lurch.

There was a message for her on the silver tray. All it said was, 'Miss Tiffany Kalvin telephoned from New York and would like you to return the call.'

Edgar and Lavinia Lomond decided to hold their anniversary party at Claridge's. Lavinia was inviting one hundred and fifty guests, all members of the British nobility, and the list was heavy with titles. It also included two middle-aged ladies who had been her bridesmaids, one now married to a cabinet minister and the other the wife of a distinguished admiral. And of course Edgar's nephew, Andrew Flanders. Lavinia wrote his name carefully on an embossed invitation card, and for a moment her grey eyes took on a look of softness. How she loved that boy, though he was no longer a boy. At twenty-nine Andrew was a successful stockbroker with a promising career. So far he had no particular girlfriend, but Lavinia was certain that when the time came for him to choose a wife, he would pick a girl of good birth and background. Educated. Intelligent. Sensible. Lavinia sighed fretfully.

What a tragedy, she thought, that it would be Harry and Morgan who would inherit the title and Drumnadrochit. The idea of Morgan becoming a duchess one day filled her with bitterness. Harry had been a fool to have been taken in by blatant sex and money. New money, too. Drawing herself up stiffly Lavinia Lomond sealed the envelope containing

Andrew's invitation and wished for the hundredth time that he was Edgar's heir.

'I say, old chap, are you coming shootin' at the weekend?'

'Is it the Quorn or the Belvoir you hunt with?'

'Damn'd good day – we bagged a hundred brace!'

The glittering ballroom at Claridge's hummed with animated conversation on the subjects so dear to the hearts of the aristocracy. Under the blazing chandeliers, magnificently dressed and bejewelled ladies and portly men in white tie and tails were taking their places at the round candlelit tables, making an effort to look as if they were enjoying themselves. But the men, sweating in starched wing collars, would have much preferred comfortable old tweeds, with either a gun or a fishing rod in their hands, and the ladies would have felt much more comfortable in riding habits, yelling savagely at their horses and dogs. Only Morgan looked as if she was truly at home in the flower-festooned and elegant ballroom. Not for her the biting winds and mud of the hunting field, or trudging for miles in search of fish or fowl. Her fine skin and smooth body came from beauty parlours not barren moors, and her white hands with their long scarlet-painted nails were testimony to the fact she preferred reading magazines to reining-in horseflesh. Smiling and shaking hands with her in-law's friends as Harry introduced her around, she stood out like an exquisite exotic orchid among a field of overblown and thorny roses.

Morgan, hearing snatches of conversation that she could hardly believe possible, wondered where her mother-in-law had seated Harry and herself. She had heard that Edgar and Lavinia would each host a table of various relatives, while close friends each hosted the other tables. She went over to the elegant brass easel where a seating plan had been pinned. It showed that Harry was hosting a table that included the Duke and Duchess of Southampton, Prince and Princess Fritz of Luxembourg and a few other of their friends. With mounting panic she scanned the list. She wasn't hosting a table at all! The old bitch had put her on a table hosted by the archbishop who had married the Lomonds – he must be eighty-five by now – a few other clergymen and their wives, and the president of one of of Lavinia's favourite charities. *Shit!* Morgan's cheeks flamed with fury. She looked round wildly for Harry. He had to do something! She couldn't be stuck at the worst table in the room, it was too humiliating. For the first time in her life, she was thankful her mother-in-law had decreed that there should be no press photographers. 'Vulgar and common!' Lavinia had declared. At least this public snub wouldn't be recorded by Nigel Dempster in tomorrow's *Daily Mail*!

At last she saw Harry, already seated. There was a buzz of expectant conversation round the ballroom as everyone settled down to enjoy the first course of *salade de homard en gelée ratafia*. The small orchestra was softly playing 'New York, New York' in the background. Champagne corks were popping discreetly and crystal glasses clinked.

It was then that Morgan decided to make her move. Alone and dignified, her dress a slither of dark-blue sequins, low-cut and slit almost to the thigh, she made her way slowly across the empty dance floor and stopped at Harry's table. Gesturing lightly to the orchestra to stop playing, she placed her hand on Harry's shoulder as she stood behind his chair. Startled, Harry looked up and the head waiter came forward anxiously to see if anything was wrong.

'There's something I want to say,' Morgan's voice was low and tight.

'What is it?' hissed Harry.

She silenced him with a look and a gentle squeeze of her hand. The orchestra stopped playing at a signal from the head waiter, who banged a silver spoon on a table for silence. Guests stopped talking and twisted in their chairs, wondering if it was a signal to toast the Lomonds' health.

Across the room, above the quivering heat-haze of the

candles, Morgan saw Edgar's face, pink and surprised, and Lavinia's, white and grim, her eyes blazing questioningly. The room was now silent. Morgan smiled and took a deep breath.

'As we are all here to celebrate a very happy occasion, namely the thirtieth wedding anniversary of my parents-in-law,' she began, 'I thought you might all like to know that there is another cause for celebration tonight.' Here she paused, and smiled radiantly, a shimmering sexy figure. 'I am very happy to tell you all – that Harry and I are expecting a baby.'

A glass shattered, splintering against silver and china as the Duchess sprang to her feet, knocking over a second glass as she did so.

'She's ... she's ...!' came a garbled stutter from the Duchess's throat but the rest was lost as a surge of applause and shouts of congratulations filled the air.

Harry jumped up and embraced Morgan rapturously, his face buried in her neck. Someone was grabbing her hand and someone else was kissing her cheek. She was instantly surrounded by a warm flood of affection as, laughing and blushing, she clung to Harry, the epitome and picture of delighted motherhood.

'Capital, m'boy! Splendid ... splendid!' chortled the Duke, slapping Harry frantically on the shoulder and pumping his hand up and down. 'The best anniversary present you could have given us, m'boy. Congratulations, Morgan, m'dear, you've made an old man very happy.' Misty-eyed with emotion he kissed his daughter-in-law and patted her hand.

Thank God it worked, thought Morgan, as the guests lifted their glasses to drink their health. Thank God Tiffany got pregnant. Now there's only another seven months to go and with any luck I'll be stepping off Concorde with a future Duke of Lomond in my arms.

★

Morgan got up very early the next morning. Now that the news was out she wanted to get on with the preparations for the coming baby.

'I'm going shopping this morning, honey,' she announced, as Harry ate his breakfast. 'I want to start doing over the top floor as a nursery suite, and there are all sorts of things I have to get for the baby.'

Harry laughed indulgently. 'It's not due until June, darling, we've got plenty of time.'

'I know, but I'm so excited I just have to get on with everything! Prams, and a cot, nursery furniture, clothes . . .' Morgan wasn't quite sure herself what was needed, but she determined to start finding out.

'All right, sweetheart, but don't go overdoing it. You ought to get some rest now, and surely you should be drinking a lot of milk!' He eyed her black coffee doubtfully.

'Oh, I will, don't worry. I'll have to get some maternity clothes too, I suppose. Will you still love me when I'm all fat and bulging?' Her smile was tender and teasing.

For an answer he kissed her lingeringly. 'You'll always be my wonderful, beautiful, fantastic Morgan,' he murmured between kisses. Then he echoed some of his father's words of the previous night. 'You've made me very happy.'

As soon as he had left for the gallery, Morgan bathed and chose a soft woollen dress in deep burgundy from amongst the long racks of clothes she kept in the room adjoining her bedroom. On shelves under the racks were dozens of pairs of shoes, and above more shelves for matching handbags and gloves. Putting on her sable coat and matching hat she set off for Harrods. Making her way to the book department she then proceeded to buy up every book she could find on pregnancy, motherhood, infant and child care. The information would prove vital. As far as Harry was concerned it would show she was a responsible young woman, prepared to take care of herself and the baby. Her next stop was *La Cigcognia* on Sloane Street. Here she bought a profusion of exquisite baby clothes, shawls, tiny quilts and a bassinet with a canopy trimmed with yards of white muslin, lace and clusters of tiny blue silk ribbons. Lastly she ordered a large pram, in dark blue, the Rolls Royce of prams, and left instructions to have the Lomond crest painted on the sides. Later she would order linen and pillow-cases for the baby, all embroidered with the family crest.

Morgan had enjoyed her morning. Having a baby was fun, and buying clothes for the baby was almost as much fun as buying clothes for herself.

Sitting in Vidal Sassoon an hour later, Morgan started glancing at the books. She found them quite interesting, though some bits were frightening and others were positively disgusting. The most encouraging paragraph she read stated that pregnancy didn't necessarily show until between the fourth and fifth months. That was great! She planned to start eating fattening foods in about three months' time, so she would put on weight in general, and then she could pad herself out with a small cushion pinned inside her tights! Pleased with how simple it was all going to be, she read the chapters on 'Common Symptoms'. Better have a few of those! Backache, tiredness, indigestion ... easy! Nausea, faintness ... well she was good at acting. It was obviously much easier to pretend to be pregnant than to pretend *not* to be, as Tiffany had to. All she had to do was sit tight for the next seven months and fake a gloriously, radiantly, happy picture of a mother-to-be.

15

Straightening up painfully, Tiffany reached for the tumbler on the bathroom shelf and filled it from the cold tap. The water made her feel a little better but a film of perspiration clung to her face and she still felt queasy. Catching sight of herself in the large mirror she was shocked to see how much she'd changed. Her once amazing green eyes were lost in dark, bruised-looking circles and her cheekbones stuck out prominently. Four months pregnant and she looked and felt like a wreck! Where was the glowing skin and shining hair, the radiance one was supposed to have? She shuffled back to her bedroom and lay down gingerly as a great wave of exhaustion swept over her, making the desire for sleep overpowering. One thing was certain. She'd have to get out of New York – fast. She would go to Vineland in southern New Jersey where no one would know her. She would vanish among the Italian immigrant community, under a false name. Her family and friends would be told she was touring the States on an extended sabbatical.

Huddling under the covers she started to cry until great shuddering sobs racked her body.

'Goddamn and blast you, Morgan,' she wept. 'Goddamn your goddamn ambition and goddamn you for making me do this.' She thought of how she would miss her life in New York, her work, the theatre, her friends, even her parents. And she also had to leave town still not knowing where Zachary was. Anger welled up in her throat as bitter as bile. Tiffany, who had always been gregarious, had already begun to dread the isolation and loneliness that was to come.

Ruth had upped her daily intake of Valium. It was four

months since the robbery but she couldn't rid herself of the feeling that she was somehow to blame. By leaving the combination of the safe written on a piece of paper in her desk, had she handed the jewellery and cash to the robbers on a plate? Feeling restless she decided to have another search. The police might say it was an inside job, but if she could only find that bit of paper she could start blaming someone else. Cursing herself for being such a fool, she opened the first drawer and started searching. Why hadn't she hidden it more carefully? Between the leaves of a certain book, or tucked in the frame of one of her children's photographs perhaps? She bit her lip and tried to breathe slowly. It was not in the first drawer. She started on the second, nervously shuffling through old letters, bank statements, some snapshots and a couple of out-of-date address books. Nothing. She opened the third and last drawer, which she had already gone through a dozen times, because this was where she was sure it had been. It contained a stock of her personalized stationery, a copy of her will, some share certificates Joe had given her and their passports. The combination was still missing. Idly and more tranquil now, thanks to the last couple of Valium, she flipped open the passports. It was amusing to look at all the immigration stamps and how they varied. Hong Kong, Tokyo, South Africa, Britain, France, Italy – they were all reminders of the business trips she'd made with Joe, and the wonderful places they'd visited. Suddenly she dropped her and Joe's passports onto her lap and started rummaging frantically through the drawer. She grabbed handfuls of expensive blue writing paper and envelopes, scattering them onto the silk Chinese carpet. Where had it gone? It was *always* kept with theirs, an elastic band holding the three of them together. As the implication dawned on Ruth, her face turned to waxy white and she felt faint. Zachary's passport was also missing.

At the end of November, the Lomonds invited eighteen

guests to stay at Drumnadrochit for the grouse shooting, or as Morgan referred to it, 'the slaughter on the moors'. Shooting started on the 'glorious twelfth' of August and between then and Christmas the rich nobility had their weekends booked and their Purdeys at the ready. Most weekends there were only eight or ten friends staying at the castle but on this particular occasion the Duke had decided that things needed livening up a bit and had instructed Harry and Morgan to 'bring up some bright young things from London'.

Morgan was excited at the prospect. She had managed to avoid most of the shooting parties but this would be different. It would be the first time their friends had seen Drumnadrochit in all its newly decorated splendour, and she flew up a couple of days before to make sure everything was ready. A few elderly statesmen and Tory politicians were usually among the Lomonds' guests, sometimes the First Sea Lord, a couple of retired generals, whom the Duke stoutly referred to as 'damn fine shots', plus a few people the Duchess regarded as 'her oldest friends'. Old being the operative word, thought Morgan as the Land Rover that had met her wound its way heavily along the glistening road to the castle. The worst part of all was that the dreary, tweedy and worthy wives came along as well. Thank God she and Harry had invited the Southamptons, the Willesleys and an amusing couple they'd recently met called Louise and Simon Bourdillon. The martinis would soon be mixed and then they'd have some fun.

Leaving her red fox coat on a carved oak chest in the hall, while McGillivery saw to her luggage, Morgan made her way to the library. It was one of her favourite rooms, with its magnificent view overlooking Loch Ness, seen from two windows cut into the curving towers of the castle. Furnished with cushioned seats and drum tables, piled high with leather and gilt bound books, objets d'art and tumbling arrangements of parrot tulips and cow parsley, Morgan liked to settle herself in one of these comfortable nooks. Today she planned to work on her arrangements for the house party, compiling lists of things she wanted done before the guests arrived, and ordering McGillivery to keep her supplied with hot fresh coffee. And maybe she'd write to Tiffany. She'd like Tiff to see her new heavy cream writing paper, with the family crest emblazoned in red in one corner.

In the doorway she stopped, startled. The Duchess was sitting at the long refectory table that stood in the middle of the room, a pile of books in front of her.

'Oh! I thought you were arriving on Friday with the others!' There was a note of dismay and annoyance in Morgan's voice.

'I was under the impression *you* were arriving on Friday with Harry.' The Duchess's voice matched hers in aggravation. The two women eyed each other with undisguised hostility.

'I have things to see to here ... arrangements to make, Harry is arriving on Friday afternoon,' snapped Morgan, striding over to the desk in the window and picking up a pad of paper with the air of a busy executive. Fuck! What was the old cow doing here, sneaking up to Drumnadrochit without saying a word?

'I can assure you we have been entertaining here long before your time, Morgan. This is still Edgar's and my home you know, and we don't need you to tell us what to do. Mrs Monroe knows exactly what is required, and so does McGillivery.' The Duchess's voice was as brittle as dried bracken and as icy as a rapier.

Ignoring her, Morgan started writing busily.

'What exactly are you doing, Morgan?'

'There are hundreds of things they'll never think of,' said Morgan airily. 'There must be matching soap and towels in all the bathrooms. They think soap begins and ends with Imperial Leather, and I want flowers and books and magazines, not to mention things like tissues and iced water in the bedrooms. Then there are perfumed pads from Floris to go on the electric light bulbs throughout the place, fresh pot-pourri to be arranged in bowls everywhere . . . liquor for making cocktails, and I've also brought up some new tapes for the stereo and some films in video to show after dinner.' She wished it didn't all sound so trivial.

'We play games after dinner,' announced the Duchess, her daughter-in-law's impudence rattling her deeply.

'*Games!*' An expression of genuine bewilderment coupled with horror crossed Morgan's face. 'Not games like the Royal Family play . . .! Charades . . . and the word game, and that sort of thing!'

'What else? It's a tradition in this country among the upper classes. Maybe you hadn't noticed. We *always* play games after dinner.'

'You won't catch Harry and me and our friends doing anything so childish! I'll get the video set up in here. God, it must be hell staying at Sandringham or Balmoral.'

'How fortunate then, that you're unlikely to be afforded that privilege.' With a scathing final glance the Duchess swept from the room, taking a pile of valuable-looking books with her.

Still smarting under the insult Morgan continued scribbling, reduced by now to making notes of which clothes she'd wear when. Inside she still raged. *Snobbish bitch, trying to make her feel like some schmuck from the Bronx! Had she no idea how fashionable and chic New York society was?*

'Oh, sorry, I thought Aunt Lavinia was in here. Hullo, Morgan, how are you?'

She looked up, startled again. It was Andrew Flanders.

'Oh . . . hi!' She looked at his face – so like Harry's but with an edge of coldness combined with a certain eagerness to be ingratiating that she found annoying. He reminded her of a rather nasty small boy who knew he was nasty but still desperately sought approval from his elders. He was glancing round the library in a searching way.

'Looking for something?'

'Er, well, er, some books ... Aunt Lavinia was going to look them out for me ... do you know where she is?' He seemed distinctly ill at ease.

'I've no idea, but she was carrying some books when I last saw her.'

'Oh good. I'll see if I can run her to earth.' With that he backed out of the library, while Morgan smiled to herself. She was amused at his unconscious simile between the Duchess and a fox. But what was Andrew doing up here? Morgan couldn't even remember his name being on the guest list for the weekend.

Luncheon was a silent affair. Andrew seemed nervous and the Duchess poker-faced. Occasionally he addressed a remark to his aunt in fawning tones and to Morgan's surprise she actually smiled, a gentle hovering smile. Edgar had been right, she *is* more fond of Andrew than her own son, Morgan thought, though God knows why. He had none of Harry's easy charm, or good looks or warmth. As soon as luncheon was over the Duchess rose, commanding, 'Andrew, come with me. There are some things I want you to go through with me.' Andrew followed, like an expectant terrier at her heels. He did not even give Morgan a backward glance.

As soon as she heard their receding footsteps, Morgan crept to the dining-room door and peered along the passage. To her surprise they were entering the pantry which was on the left, just before the kitchens. The Duchess seemed to be putting her fingers up to her mouth and Andrew was nodding silently. Then they vanished through the green baize door. What the hell were they up to?

That night Morgan ordered supper in her room. There was no way she was going to endure being ignored at dinner while Lavinia and Andrew engaged in some sort of secret sign language. Settling herself on the sofa with a stack of magazines, she was just getting into an amusing comedy on the television when there was a sharp knock on her door.

'Come in,' she called, thinking it was McGillivery with her supper tray. Instead she looked up to see the Duchess standing regally in the doorway, a plaid shawl clutched over her drab green dress, and a pair of old-fashioned shoes with marcasite buckles on her feet.

'We don't have trays in our rooms unless we are ill. This is not an hotel and I don't like the staff being overworked running all over the place looking after people.'

Morgan's mouth fell open, forming a perfect 'O'. This woman was treating her like a naughty schoolgirl, and she flushed with anger.

'Considering there are going to be nearly twenty people staying here over the weekend, who will certainly have to be properly looked after, I don't think one little supper on a tray is going to exactly exhaust them,' she retorted acidly. 'Anyway I'm tired. I *am* having a baby you know.'

'Ye–es.' The Duchess said the word slowly and heavily, her eyes fastened to Morgan's face.

'Well?'

'I know you're pregnant. You made a big enough spectacle of yourself announcing it at our party.'

'*So?*'

'I'm sure it would have added to the general interest if you'd let us in on the secret of who the father is.'

Blank astonishment swept across Morgan's face.

'What on earth are you talking about?'

The Duchess pursed her lips fastidiously and her eyes were like polished grey marbles. 'It's more than coincidental that the baby is expected nine months after you return from staying with your sister in New York, isn't it? Was it your ex-fiancé you went to see? You may be able to fool Harry, you know, but you can't fool me.'

Morgan jumped up from the sofa, spilling the magazines so they cascaded to the floor in a slithering heap.

'You're crazy!' she burst out. So great was her amazement, she floundered, searching for words. 'I broke up with Greg before I got engaged to Harry. What is this, some kind of joke? Why – why are you saying these nutty things?'

The Duchess turned and moved slowly towards the door. 'Why do you think? You won't be able to deceive Harry for ever, you know. Sooner or later he'll find out, and then what are you going to say?'

'Tell him yourself! Tell him what you've just said to me! He'll kill himself laughing!' Morgan yelled after her. Then she sank onto the sofa in a state of shock. This was the most incredible twist and her head was spinning. The irony of the situation was absurd, almost laughable, but Morgan didn't laugh.

The Duchess either suspected something or had some nasty little trick up her sleeve she would no doubt produce at a moment most advantageous to herself.

Morgan paced up and down her room, chain smoking; several times she went to the telephone to ring Harry, but then decided against it. Whatever her mother-in-law was up to, she mustn't play into her hands. Any suggestion that Morgan might have resumed her affair with Greg might sow the seeds of doubt in Harry's mind; after all he had frequently remarked that she was very attractive to men.

Now was not the time for Harry to start having doubts.

Harry arrived with his father late on Friday afternoon. As soon as Morgan heard the car in the drive she ran out and flung herself into his arms. He kissed her lovingly, that look of wonder he had whenever he saw her filling his eyes.

'Hi, honey! It's good to see you.' She hugged him closer. 'I missed you so.' *Hell*, she thought, *another day stuck in this place with your prick of a mother and that creepy Andrew, and I'd have been driven nuts!* Aloud she added, 'All the guests have arrived, why don't we have a drink before we go up and change for dinner?' Her look suggested the last thing she had on her mind was changing her clothes.

'Fine, let's do that.' His answering look said he couldn't wait to get to their room either.

At last, after greeting everyone, Harry grabbed Morgan's hand and propelled her towards the staircase. Had he ever seen her looking so enchanting? The mountain air had brought a glow to her cheeks and her green eyes sparkled like jewels. Giggling, she ran up the stairs beside him, her hand already reaching for his fly. As soon as they reached their room he pushed her onto the bed, wrapping his muscular legs around hers so tightly, and pressing his hardness against her so fiercely, that she gave a little cry of pain.

'Morgan . . . darling . . .' he moaned, releasing her just long enough to tear off his clothing. Then, almost with anguish, so great was his longing, he was inside her, frenziedly, wildly, almost deliriously. He gave a shudder and she instantly felt him throbbing, spent, replete. Morgan lay beneath him with quiet disappointment. For her it was over before it had begun; maybe they could try again later, maybe she should tell him she needed more time. As long as it wouldn't dent his male ego and hurt his feelings.

'That was wonderful, honey,' she breathed huskily, pretending to be short of breath. 'You really are fantastic . . . I've missed you so much.' At least the last part was true.

'I love you so much, my darling,' he whispered, kissing her neck and ears. 'You've no idea how much I love you . . . I'd die if anything went wrong.'

'Went wrong?' She stiffened slightly. 'What could go wrong? Why should anything go wrong?'

'No, of course it won't.' He held her closer. 'It's just that you're so wonderful, I sometimes get this dreadful feeling that I might lose you one day. I honestly don't know what I would do if that happened. I've never said this before, Morgan, but you've given me the happiness and security . . . and the love that I never really had as a child. Pa was always wonderful, but I didn't see much of him, what with going away to school and the rest, and my mother can't be described as the warmest person. When I met you I realized what I'd been missing and now that I know what real love is I suppose I'm afraid something will happen and it will all come to an end.'

It was the longest and most revealing statement he had ever made and Morgan suddenly felt very touched and deeply protective.

'Listen, honey.' She pulled away from him and propped herself up on one elbow so that she could look into his face. If his mother had already been trying to sow any seeds of doubt in Harry's mind, she was going to rip them out, now, once and for all. 'I will *never* let anything come between us, never; I love you with all my heart and soul and nothing can prevent me from feeling that way for the rest of my life. *You* have given me everything I ever wanted, darling, and you have made me terribly happy. Nothing and *no one* is going to take that away from us, do you understand?'

He nodded, smiling. He too had never heard Morgan speak so revealingly. In a renewed wave of love and longing, he started to make love to her again. Only this time he did it with slow tenderness, kissing her neck and voluptuous breasts before burying his face in the sweetness that lay between her legs. And only when she indicated that she was burning hot with desire and longing did he allow himself to be swept along by his passions, taking her with him until they were both crying out from the pleasure of it all.

When guests came down to breakfast each morning they were greeted by the skirl of the bagpipes, as the local piper played Scottish laments while marching to and fro on the terrace of the castle. The sound reached Morgan, still in her room, and she knew the day had begun. In a short while the men, led by the Duke and Harry, would set off for the moors,where the loaders waited with the long line of beaters, ready to put up scores of birds. Most of the women went out later, following the guns at a comfortable distance. Morgan found it a great turn-on to watch Harry, handsome in the kilt, striding through the rough heather, Angus and Mackie at his heels. There was something so masculine about the way he handled his gun as his eyes searched the sky for high birds.

As Morgan, warmly dressed in layers of wool and cashmere in a particularly pretty shade of moss green, followed him this morning, watching him pick off birds with grace and ease, her thoughts suddenly turned to Greg. How could she ever have thought him attractive? Greg would always be the plodding lawyer, dutiful to his clients, faithful to his friends, dependable, kind – and fearfully boring. She watched Harry bring down a bird as it wheeled overhead. Poor old Greg. If he'd been the bird he'd have scuttled away through the gorse by now, lying low until the danger had passed.

At lunchtime everyone gathered at the small hunting lodge on the estate, where the staff from the castle had arrived earlier, bringing with them warming soups, game pies, rich beef stews and a variety of fruit and cheese. Two long refectory tables were set with silver and glass, and soon everyone was seated. Morgan and Harry hosted one table with their younger friends, while the Duke and Duchess entertained at the other. It had been a good morning, and as the wine flowed, everyone was marvelling at the number of birds shot.

'I don't suppose anyone will ever beat the record bag of 2,929 grouse in one day, though!' Harry joked. 'That would be asking too much.'

Morgan's eyes widened. 'In one day? Where was that?'

'In Lancashire, actually. In 1915. The sixth Earl of Sefton and his guests shot 2,929 birds on the Glorious Twelfth. Imagine doing that nowadays!'

Everyone laughingly agreed. Employing gamekeepers

and breeding birds was an expensive luxury that not everyone could afford.

After luncheon, Harry urged her to go home and rest. There was to be a large dinner party at the castle that night, when a lot of neighbouring friends had been invited to join them and he feared she would be tired.

'All right, darling,' she replied meekly. It would suit her very well. She would plaster her face with moisturizer to counteract the harsh Scottish wind, do her hair and nails, and perhaps watch TV.

Alone in the castle she decided on impulse to go up to the top floor where Andrew slept. The perplexity that had been hovering at the back of her mind for a couple of days was starting to unravel, but she needed some sort of evidence.

Glancing round his room she observed that either Andrew was meticulously tidy or the maids had done a good job that morning. On one of the bedside tables a travelling clock ticked quietly beside a copy of *The Decline and Fall of the Roman Empire*. Andrew *was* a serious reader! His brushes and comb were arranged with regimental precision on the dressing table, beside a bottle of Chanel after-shave, a pair of cuff-links and a small bottle of pills. Morgan picked up the bottle and read the label. Vitamin B12. How boring. She opened a few drawers and found neat stacks of shirts, pants and socks. Then she went to the long fitted chest. The same neatness prevailed. Rows of ties, a rail of clothes, a line of polished shoes. Then something caught her eye and she bent to look closer. A dark-blue travelling bag had been pushed behind the shoes. Crouching down so as not to disturb anything she slid back the zip and gave a gasp of astonishment. Lying in the bag was an assortment of small but valuable pieces of silver, and under that some even more valuable leather-bound first editions. So that was what the Duchess had been clutching in the library! To one side were some little parcels wrapped in cotton wool and tissue paper. With shaking hands, Morgan unwrapped one and found it to be a Royal Chelsea figurine worth in excess of two thousand pounds. She counted six of these little parcels until she came to a heavy round package, also carefully wrapped. It contained a Clichy glass paperweight, embodying a bouquet of minute pansies, roses and a thistle, exquisitely worked in shades of pink, violet and purple glass. She remembered it had recently been valued for insurance purposes, along with some other trinkets from the castle, for fourteen thousand pounds.

Morgan sat back on her heels and let out a deep breath. Quite a little hoard! Worth probably in the region of fifty or sixty thousand pounds! Wait until she told Harry his mother was in collusion with his cousin to rob the castle of some of its treasures! Edgar had said that Andrew was her favourite but this was ridiculous! These items were not hers to give away. They were part of the estate, and not even Edgar or Harry had the power to break the family trust and do what they liked. She would tell Harry as soon as he got back, and the Duchess – Morgan bit her lip in vexation. And the Duchess would fly into a fury and say Morgan was a fine one to talk about honesty when she was having an affair and the baby might not even be his, and then, and then . . .! No, Morgan decided on a better tactic. Zipping up the travelling bag again she removed it from the cupboard, and leaving the room exactly as she had found it, made her way to her room. Two could play at these little games! Locking the bag in the closet where she kept her furs, she hid the key in a packet of cigarettes at the bottom of her lingerie drawer.

Tiffany shut the lock of her large Louis Vuitton case and looked round to see if she'd remembered everything. She'd only packed essentials for her 'sabbatical'. Her jewellery had gone into a safe deposit box in the bank and her furs into cold storage. Nothing remained but to say goodbye to Gloria and get into the car.

Familiar objects – her Victorian cut-crystal perfume

bottles – photographs of her family – the silver-framed mirror Hunt had given her, suddenly seemed very precious. With a pang she realized that already she felt homesick. She wouldn't see any of her treasures again for five months. Or any of her friends. And her father would probably never know that she was making this sacrifice for him. As far as Sig Hoffman was concerned though, she hoped he'd eventually rot in hell.

Faster, much faster than she was prepared for, she was driving through the Lincoln Tunnel, and New York slipped behind her as she headed for New Jersey. There was no going back now. The links had been cut, the past forever severed from the present. And nothing in the future would ever be quite the same again.

The weekend at Drumnadrochit had come to an end and Harry and Morgan stood in the drive with the Duke and Duchess, saying goodbye to the last of the guests.

'Fantastic time, darling,' drawled Henrietta Willesley. 'Too divine.'

Morgan kissed her and promised they would meet for lunch in London later on in the week.

'I must say it's all been most lively!' beamed one of the generals.

'I liked the video films at night . . . most entertaining,' said another.

'Wonderful to be so warm . . . I dread going back to my place,' remarked a cabinet minister.

Morgan caught the Duchess's eye at this point and had some difficulty in suppressing a giggle.

When Andrew came down the castle steps carrying a large battered case, Morgan inquired with an innocent smile, 'Got everything?'

His cheeks flushed angrily and he gave a nervous laugh.

'Yes thanks.' He kissed his aunt, shook hands with the Duke then turned his back on Morgan.

'Are you *sure* you've got everything?' she persisted. He merely nodded, his eyes flickering in the direction of the Duchess who was looking stonily ahead, her thin jaw clenching and unclenching.

He climbed into the Land Rover with the others, and with a skitter of flying gravel it swung away down the drive and vanished out of sight beyond the dense fir trees.

'Game, set and match, don't you think?' said Morgan evenly to her mother-in-law, as the Duke and Harry ambled off to throw sticks for the dogs.

'I'm sure I don't know what you're talking about,' retorted the Duchess, walking back into the castle, her shoulders hunched in suppressed fury.

Morgan's eyes narrowed. Before long Harry would have to know what was going on behind his back. She couldn't keep a permanent eye on the contents of Drumnadrochit.

16

Morgan woke slowly and languorously, then sat up in bed listening intently. The house was absolutely still. Glancing at her watch she saw it was after ten. Harry would certainly have left for the gallery more than an hour before, and the staff were obviously working quietly downstairs, so as not to disturb the new routine of her ladyship. She leaned back against the pure linen and lace pillows and rang for breakfast. This was the best part of making Harry sleep in the spare room. She could enjoy long undisturbed nights and stay in bed as long as she liked in the mornings. Harry hated it of course, but it was the only way of ensuring that he never saw her naked, or realized her stomach was as firm and flat as ever. It had been easier to persuade him than she had imagined. She just quoted 'Dr Snyder' as saying that now she was 'four months pregnant, she must stop having sex, as that could bring on a miscarriage'. She even added that her gynaecologist had told her to 'put her husband in the deep freeze for a while'! Harry, though disappointed, agreed that if that was what was required then it must be adhered to. To this Morgan added that she was now suffering from backaches, cramps and insomnia, and Dr Snyder had *insisted* that she have eight hours' undisturbed sleep a night.

'It's awful, isn't it, honey?' she said, her mouth turning down at the corners, 'but I think it is better I sleep alone . . . just for the moment. Anyway, with you beside me, I don't know how I could resist making love to you . . . it would be just too tempting.'

Harry emphatically agreed. To see Morgan walking

about, scantily clad, was enough to give him an erection; to lie beside her would be an agony.

Now that she was supposed to be nearly five months pregnant, she wore a small cushion pinned in the front. It was really effective. Under a heavy satin nightdress cut on Empire lines it was convincing to an inexperienced man like Harry. With her new wardrobe of maternity clothes, which she had told the shop assistants were for a friend, it fooled everyone.

Perkins knocked on her door a few minutes later and came in with her breakfast, exquisitely arranged on a silver tray, with a crisp white lawn tray cloth, and her favourite Sèvres breakfast service.

What would she do with her day? Meet someone for lunch? Go shopping? Go to a matinée? Morgan suddenly realized that she was bored. Bored stiff. And it annoyed her that the staff seemed to hover around all the time trying to get her to make up her mind as to what her plans were. It made her feel unnatural, as if she was forced to live a life according to their expectations. Duncan, for example, wanted to know *when* she would want the car, and *where* she'd want to be taken. And *when* she wanted to be collected again. In New York her parents' staff had been there to jump to it, when asked. If she decided to invite a dozen people back to the apartment for supper after the theatre, the staff hustled around and produced supper. It was simple. That was what staff were for. Here, they wanted to work to some damn schedule, knowing her every move, preparing days in advance if she wanted to entertain, and they wanted to know exactly when they were supposed to be on duty and when they could get off. Suddenly she decided she would give them a run for their money. Hoist them onto their toes and keep them there, never sure until the last minute if there would be six for luncheon and twelve for dinner, or if she and Harry would be out. The same with Duncan. If she wanted to be driven somewhere on Saturday afternoon or

Sunday morning – or in the middle of the night – it was his job to be on call.

At that moment the phone by her bed rang. It was Rosalie Winwood.

'Hi, Morgan. How's the little mother?' chirruped Rosalie. Without waiting for an answer she starting talking about the party she was giving the following week. Rosalie was quite neurotic about this party and was ringing Morgan up daily.

'So you see, I think it would be better if I served iced vodka with the blinis, don't you? On the other hand I could get the caviar served straight away. Oh, you'll never guess who rang me yesterday, Morgan! Henry. What dear? ... Kissinger of course! He hopes to be over here next week, just for a couple of nights, so I told him he just *had* to drop by! Now I want your advice about the flowers ...' Rosalie rambled on neither waiting for, nor expecting answers.

'It sounds like it's going to be a great party,' cut in Morgan, seizing the split second it took Rosalie to draw breath. 'I must go now, but we'll see you next Wednesday. Thanks for calling, Rosalie. Goodbye.' That, she thought as she replaced the receiver, quite limp with exhaustion, is what happens to women who don't have children.

Meanwhile, she gave the staff no orders until three o'clock that afternoon, when she announced there would be eight for dinner.

For the Winwoods' party Morgan had chosen a gold lamé dress with a crystal pleated skirt that fell from her bosom to the ground in wide graceful folds, not hiding, but gently and in a discreet way proclaiming her state of pregnancy. More crystal pleating framed her golden tanned shoulders, setting off to perfection the antique pink topaz and gold necklace and earrings that had belonged to Harry's grandmother. Her hair was swept up into an elegant chignon.

'You're looking angelic, darling,' cried Harry as she came down the stairs. 'Are you going to be warm enough though?

Don't you need a shawl or a wrap or something?'

'A *shawl*!' She regarded him with mock horror. 'I'd rather die from pneumonia than ruin the whole effect! Come on, let's go.'

'All right, darling, just so long as you're warm enough.' He put his arms round her and tried to pull her close.

'Hey ... be careful!' she exclaimed. 'You'll crush my dress, not to mention the baby!'

His face fell but he made an effort to look cheerful.

'Sorry, darling, it's just that ... Oh God! I can't tell you how frustrating it is having you around and not being able to touch you.'

Morgan recognized the petulance in his voice that was always there when he couldn't get what he wanted.

'What about me?' she challenged, suddenly blazing. 'Don't you think I feel frustrated too?' Their eyes met and held for a moment, locked in hostility. Then she spoke more softly. 'Never mind, honey, it won't last forever. We don't want to risk losing the baby, do we? And Dr Snyder said it was something to do with my hormones, my not being able to bear being touched. He says it happens to a lot of women, but as soon as they've had the baby, they're fine again.'

Harry immediately relented and looked at her tenderly.

'I'm sorry, sweetheart. I know it's not your fault and I'm not blaming you. If I didn't love you so much it wouldn't matter.'

Morgan smiled at him radiantly. Poor old Harry. He was probably driven to wanking in the bathroom these days. She stepped closer and looked up at him. 'I tell you what, honey, when we get back from this party I'll ...' The rest she whispered in his ear in case Perkins was hovering about.

'Darling ...' He looked at her in worship, trying to control himself even now at the thought of what she would do later – providing he didn't touch her. If she wanted to tie his hands to the bedpost he wouldn't object. In fact it could make it all the more exciting.

★

Several dozen guests had already arrived at Cumberland Terrace by the time they got there, and Rosalie was rushing around making introductions in a voice that was bordering on hysteria. Morgan sighed inwardly. There was a terrible sameness about all the parties she and Harry went to. Same faces, same flowers, same food and drink, same hired staff. Suddenly she made up her mind. As soon as the baby was born she'd come back from America and give a party that was different. She would ask Lady Elizabeth Anson of Party Planners to dream up a fantastic night, with incredible decor; perhaps with a circus theme or a mardi gras. That would be fun! She'd stun London with a party the likes of which they would never have attended before. Money would be no object. Perhaps she could even get a member of the Royal Family to attend! With a feeling of exhilaration, Morgan proceeded to mingle graciously with the Winwoods' guests, tedious though it was.

Harry was taken off by Glen Winwood to meet some Americans who were interested in buying paintings and it was some time later in the evening when she heard his voice just behind her exclaim, 'Of course I remember you! How are you? Morgan will be delighted to know you're here. I wonder where she's got to?' Harry was glancing round the crowded room, searching for her eagerly.

Teasingly she ran her fingers down his back and said laughingly, 'Looking for me, honey?'

A second later she realized her dreadful mistake. Going scarlet in the face and obviously shaken she heard Harry say, 'Here's Dr Alastair Tennant, darling! Isn't it a nice surprise, but I'd forgotten of course that Rosalie called him to our house when you were taken ill.'

The Harley Street doctor, who had pronounced her totally barren eight months before, was regarding her swollen stomach with undisguised perplexity.

'Of course!' Morgan collected herself and extended her hand. 'How nice to see you again! Will you excuse us?' She slipped her arm through Harry's and hugged him to her side. 'There's someone I want my husband to meet.'

As she dragged Harry away she was aware of Dr Tennant's eyes following them across the room.

Early next morning Morgan was on the phone to Rosalie.

'I didn't know you were inviting Alastair Tennant last night,' she said coldly, having first thanked her hostess for a lovely evening.

'Who, dear? Oh, Alastair Tennant, but of course! He's a darling! He's become a great friend of ours. He arranged for my hysterectomy, you know. I suppose he's looking after you and the baby?'

'No, he's not.'

'He isn't? Why not, dear? I thought you were still going to him? He looked after you very well when you had that cyst, didn't he? . . . I remember you saying you liked him. What happened?'

'Nothing happened, Rosalie,' Morgan's tone was short. 'I just realized I didn't like him that much after all. He's too old. I want someone younger with more modern methods and ideas on childbirth!'

'I think that's a pity, Morgan. *Everyone* goes to him.' Rosalie was of the firm opinion that if one didn't go to the 'in' hairdresser, or the 'in' dress designer, or the 'in' doctor, one was most definitely 'out' oneself. 'Who do you go to now?'

'A Dr Snyder ... he's an American gynaecologist and excellent. Are you going to the première tonight?'

'Première ...what première?' Rosalie sounded as confused by the change of topic as Morgan had intended. 'Oh, the *première*! Yes, I'm in the receiving line to meet the Duchess of Gloucester, I think . . . because Glen gave a large donation to help the, help the, well, whichever charity it is tonight! Are you and Harry going?'

Morgan could hear the clanking of Rosalie's gilt bracelets as she fiddled with the phone.

'I suppose so. I hear the film's lousy but the party afterwards might be fun. See you then.' Morgan hung up, her brow creased in a furrow of anxiety. Somehow she would have to make sure they didn't run into Dr Tennant again. As it was, Harry had been curious by the way she had dragged him off.

'What's the matter?' he whispered. 'Why don't you want to talk to him?'

'It's embarrassing, Harry, as I've gone to another doctor for the baby. I'm not sure it's ethical either, but I like Dr Snyder much more. Anyway, Dr Tennant isn't a gynaecologist.'

Harry shrugged. 'Okay, darling, as long as you're happy, but I do think you were rather rude.'

'Well, I'll chat with him later and apologize.' She squeezed his arm and gave him one of her ravishing smiles.

She was thankful to see Dr Tennant leave the party shortly afterwards.

The morning after the Winwoods' party Dr Alastair Tennant sat at his desk, a puzzled frown on his face. He never forgot his patients, even the ones he only saw for their six-month check-ups, and he prided himself on the fact that he never forgot their case histories. Finally he could stand it no longer.

'Miss Phillips,' he called to the adjoining room, 'will you please bring me Lady Blairmore's file.'

A minute later the spinsterish figure of Miss Phillips came in, carrying the pale-blue file. 'She hasn't got an appointment today, has she?' she asked fussily.

'No. I just want to check on something.' He took the file from her and opened it.

Miss Phillips stood uncertainly for a moment, a tall

lumpish figure, wearing a sludgy green cardigan over her brown dress.

'That will be all,' the doctor said, without looking up. With a faint shrug Miss Phillips turned and stumped back into her tiny office. If Dr Tennant wanted to look up someone's case history, why hadn't he asked her? She could remember every detail of his patients' illnesses, especially the ones that referred to their sexual organs. She could have reminded him about Lady Blairmore in a second. Malformed uterus. She could never have children.

Every week Morgan telephoned Tiffany at the secret number she had given her in Vineland. The baby was due in about two and a half months, and it worried Morgan that Tiffany didn't seem to be well. She was still suffering bouts of nausea and at one time she had actually lost weight. Her high blood pressure also caused concern, and the doctor at the local maternity hospital had warned her to take it easy.

'But is the baby all right?' Morgan asked, speaking from the private line in her bedroom, when she was sure the servants were out of the way.

'Yes, all the tests were fine as far as the baby is concerned.' Tiffany's voice had a quiet resigned note of despair in it. She hoped the baby *was* all right, but from the moment she knew herself to be pregnant she had determined to distance herself emotionally from the child. That was what surrogate motherhood was all about. It wasn't hers. It would never be hers. Having it would be about as emotional as having a tooth out.

'And what was the result of the test to find out whether it is a boy or a girl?' Morgan had to steel herself to ask the question.

'I don't know,' replied Tiffany dully.

'You don't know? ... Christ, couldn't you find out?'

'I don't want to find out.' Tiffany sounded stubborn.

'But it's vital!'

'Exactly, vital to you! And what if it's a girl? Are you going to throw her back at me and say cancel the delivery? A girl isn't what you ordered? No, Morgan, there is no way I'm going to find out in advance because having put me through all this, you're going to have to be grateful for what you damn well get, boy or girl.'

'For God's sake, Tiff, cool it! I'll take the baby whatever it is.'

'Well, that's real big of you!' shouted Tiffany, gripping the phone so tightly that the bones showed through the pale skin of her hands. 'Real generous! I hope you are enjoying this pregnancy because I can tell you I'm as sore as hell about it! And after this, we're finished! I never want to see you again. I'm fresh out of sisters.' She was crying hysterically now and Morgan was scared. If Tiffany went on like this she could harm the baby.

'Honey, don't be like that! I didn't know you'd feel ill . . . and things . . .' stammered Morgan. 'It's pretty much hell for me too, having to pretend all the time. I just meant it would be . . . well, all *worth* it if it is a boy.'

'Worth it for you, yes! What about everyone else? How is Harry going to feel if he finds out you've . . . we've . . . duped him? What happens if I ever get married and have to tell my husband I've already had a child? Have you thought of that? Am I going to have to say it died? And who was the father anyway? I'm going to be strung up with lies for the rest of my life to protect you . . .' she sobbed.

'You seem to forget you're doing this to protect Daddy.' Suddenly Morgan's voice was icy. It hit Tiffany's heated state of mind like a bucket of water quenching a fire.

The sisters hung up.

The strain was telling on both of them.

Three nights later the persistent ring of the phone woke Morgan from a deep sleep. She lay there for a few seconds trying to work out what time it was. She turned on the light.

Three o'clock in the morning. Her mind sprang into action ... Tiffany!

'Yes?' She snapped out the word, her brain reeling with apprehension.

'Morgan, is that you?'

It wasn't Tiffany's voice. Maybe that meant she was in hospital? Perhaps the baby had arrived prematurely? Oh, dear God, that would be a bore, or perhaps the baby had died ...

'Yes, it's Morgan.' She was shaking all over.

'Could you get Harry – immediately! This is Lavinia Lomond.' Her voice sounded strange.

'Sure,' said Morgan uncertainly. 'I'll get him.' She slid out of bed and, throwing a large lacy wrap over her nightdress, made her way to the spare room.

'Harry.' She tapped his shoulder urgently as he lay asleep. 'Harry, wake up, it's not morning yet but you must wake up. Your mother's on the phone. For goodness' sake, wake up.'

Groaning, he stumbled out of bed and allowed Morgan to propel him in the direction of their room.

'Ma?' he said groggily, picking up the phone.

'Where were you?' demanded the Duchess. 'I've been hanging on – '

'Sorry, Ma, I was sleeping in the spare room, Morgan had to come and fetch me.'

Morgan made a little grimace as she got into bed again, carefully arranging the folds of her wrap over her stomach. The Duchess would be sure to make something of *that*.

Then Harry was letting out a cry of anguish as he slumped on the bed, running one hand frantically across the top of his head.

'No ... Oh no!' he was moaning. 'Oh Christ ... Oh *no*!' He was rocking himself backwards and forwards. 'When did it happen?'

Alarmed, Morgan leaned forward trying to catch what the Duchess was saying, but Harry had the phone clamped to his ear. It was his shocked face and loose gaping mouth that made her realize something was terribly wrong.

'I'll come round right away,' she heard him say as he woodenly hung up the phone.

'What's happened, Harry?'

He turned to her, his eyes brimming with tears and his face bleached to a sickly white.

'My father's just died . . . a few minutes ago, from a heart attack. Ma said it was very sudden. He . . . he was dead by the time the ambulance arrived.' His voice broke and there was a note of disbelief in his tone.

'Honey . . . I'm so sorry . . .' Even as she reached to put her arms round him Morgan felt a confusion of conflicting emotions. The Duke had been a very nice man. She had genuinely liked him. Been fond of him even. And he'd always made her feel she had a friend in the enemy camp. It was because of him that there hadn't been open warfare between herself and the Duchess. The Duke, that warm, friendly, twinkling, kind old man was dead. But *she* was now the Duchess of Lomond.

Cradling Harry's head she soothed him as if consoling a child.

Presently Harry went to dress, then left for his mother's house, insisting that Morgan stay in bed and try and get some sleep.

'You've had a great shock too, darling,' he reminded her, now completely in control of himself. 'You must rest. An upset like this isn't good for you and the baby. I'll be back later, but try and sleep now.' With that he kissed her and slipped out of the room.

For a moment Morgan felt positively guilty lying there in her comfortable bed, shamming pregnancy, while Harry had to go out into the freezing cold, on an errand of great sadness. Then she consoled herself with the thought that she was doing her utmost to provide him with an heir. After all, it wasn't her fault she was barren, and she did make him a wonderful wife. In fact she was an asset – and would be even more so in the future, now that he had succeeded his father.

During the next few days the whole operation of death and burial occupied Harry and his mother. The first thing that had to be conducted was a post mortem, as the Duke had died suddenly in his own home. It revealed, as had been thought, that he had died from a massive coronary. The death certificate had to be signed and dealt with, relatives and friends informed, announcements drafted for the newspapers, and all the funeral arrangements made. There were also the Duke's personal papers to be sorted out and his will read. Harry rushed about looking tired and harassed, spending a lot of his time with trustees and lawyers. The Duchess remained in her Belgravia house enduring the ordeal with dignity and formality. She wore black dresses and suits that were green with age and no jewellery except her worn gold wedding ring on her claw-like hand. Words of condolence were received with gravity and letters of sympathy replied to by return mail. It was not the thing to do, to reveal one's private grief to the world.

While Morgan accepted this was the way people behaved in England she privately doubted if the Duchess had even shed a tear in private. It was hard to imagine. More tight-lipped than ever, the Duchess absorbed herself in the funeral arrangements, and completely ignored her daughter-in-law.

But the Duchess had something to worry about, though she was too proud to even bring up the subject to Harry. It concerned the finer points of Edgar's will.

Harry was the undisputed heir, not only to the title, but to the land, property, and possessions owned by the Lomond family. But had the Duke thought to provide for his wife, separately, during her lifetime? She wanted to keep on the large house in Belgravia, and she wanted a good income to live on. She could imagine no worse humiliation than having to rely on Harry – and Morgan! – for everything she needed.

After several sleepless nights she rang up the trustees and demanded to know what arrangements Edgar had made for her. They refused to tell her, adding that even Harry wouldn't be seeing the will until after the funeral. Lavinia ground her teeth and fretted more.

It was bad enough being a dowager duchess – they were always relegated to the sidelines and their social standing was apt to evaporate as the new Duchess stepped eagerly into the ermine robes and coronet – but that the new Duchess was Morgan brought bile to her throat. She was being *forced* to abdicate her position, and she regretted more bitterly than ever that Harry had not married Lady Elizabeth Greenly. Now there was a young woman who would have shown apologetic embarrassment at even *trying* to assume the role that had belonged to her mother-in-law! Lavinia tossed and turned in the vast double bed that she would now have to sleep in alone forever, and wished with all her heart that a way to get rid of Morgan could be found. *And* that bastard she was carrying. It was time, she raged inwardly, that Harry was made to realize the truth about that girl.

Morgan had assumed the funeral would be held in London, but with some alarm she realized that plans were being made for it to take place in the small kirk in the grounds of Drumnadrochit Castle. The Duke had apparently made a wish that he should be buried alongside his ancestors in the family vault. It was a bleak spot. Morgan remembered Harry showing her the ancient little church set in a gale-swept graveyard, heavily shadowed by the branches of dark fir trees. *Damn*! Having decided she would wear a black velvet coat with black mink collar and cuffs, and a chic little hat with a veil, she'd now have to wear dreary black cashmere and no jewellery. What a way to make her debut as a duchess!

Hundreds of letters started to arrive as soon as the

announcement appeared in the papers, most of them addressed to Harry, from relatives she had never heard of and friends she had never met. Feeling slightly left out of things by this drawing together of people who were part of Harry's life before she knew him, she offered to answer them for him.

'Thanks, darling . . . are you sure? I would be most awfully grateful. It's a damn depressing job, though,' he said wearily.

'Anything I can do to help, honey, just say the word,' she replied softly. No sweat. She was just longing to start signing 'Morgan Lomond' on everything anyway.

After the funeral, at which Morgan shed becoming tears, the congregation went back to the castle for a buffet luncheon. It was a subdued affair with all the tenants on the estate reminiscing about the 'good old days' when Edgar Lomond, always a popular man, had strode the hills, young, virile and charming. He had cared about them all and a birth or a death in their families had brought him to their side at once with offers of help. Women in shabby black and rough-hewn men in their Sunday best, wearing black arm-bands, wept openly, declaring they would never forget the 'grand old Duke'. In the same breath they were anxious to reassure that their devotion and loyalty would now go to 'the fine young master ... God bless 'im', and wasn't it wonderful that there was a 'wee bairn' on the way?

Smiling gently and sweetly, Morgan assured them she shared their sentiments, absolutely, and was only momentarily taken aback when one of the farmer's wives crowed, 'Och, I can see it's a wee boy you'll be havin' by the way you're carryin' him so high, your grace.' Her husband nudged her violently, thinking she was being overly familiar, but it gave Morgan time to collect herself and say fervently, 'I do hope so.' She did indeed.

When everyone left, Morgan went up to her room to rest. The strain had been enormous and she wondered if perhaps she wouldn't leave for New York earlier than planned. Even if it meant sitting around until the baby was born.

The day after the funeral something happened that made flight imperative.

'I've been thinking,' began Harry as they strolled along the banks of Loch Ness, 'that we should base ourselves here until after the baby is born.'

Morgan stopped dead, her heart pounding and danger bells clanging as if an alarm system had been triggered in her head.

'S – Stay here?'

Harry nodded, his hands deep in the pockets of his cavalry-twill trousers. 'It's traditional that all babies in the family are born at Drumnadrochit. I was, and so was my father and his father before him. Now that Pa's died I feel very bound by that tradition. Anyway, what's wrong with your having the baby up here?'

'You may be bound by tradition, Harry – but I'm certainly not when it comes to something like giving birth,' she said quickly, as mounting panic overtook her. 'You forget I'm an American and we wouldn't dream of having a baby *anywhere* but in a fully equipped hospital with a top obstetrician in attendance – especially a first baby. I couldn't possibly have it here with some old crone of a midwife and the local doctor – what are you thinking of?'

'You, darling . . . and the baby.' Harry looked at her with loving and anxious eyes. 'Dr Murdoch came to the funeral yesterday – he's attended my mother and father for years, but I don't think you've actually met him – and when he heard you were having a baby in a few months' time he looked quite surprised! Said something about your being too thin. I'd like to have him check you over, darling.'

Morgan sat down suddenly on a large rock, and concentrated her eyes on a fishing boat moored some hundred yards away on the loch.

'Harry, I thought we agreed that I should go home to the States so that the baby can have dual nationality. It's a vitally important factor.'

'I know that's what we decided, Morgan, but things have changed somehow, now that Pa's died. I feel more deeply about this place now that it is mine, and I do want to follow the tradition of having all heirs born here. Can't you understand that?' Harry was suddenly looking pink and sulky.

'Not when it comes to something as important as the child having dual nationality, Harry! You're being childish. I intend to stick to the original plan, which we both agreed to some time ago. I shall fly to the States when I'm about seven months pregnant – it's supposed to be the safest time to travel. Then just before it's due, you can come over and join me.'

It was the plan they had agreed to. When Morgan had first suggested it, Harry had thought it was very sensible.

'But I want it born here now, Morgan!' he cried.

She rose from the rock and began walking slowly back along the beach, towards the castle.

'Morgan,' he shouted after her, 'I said I wanted you to have the baby here! It's you who are being childish.' With long strides he caught up with her. 'I can fly up every weekend to be with you, and then when the baby is due I can come up in a matter of hours, and be with you when it's born. Wouldn't that be better? This means an awful lot to me, you know' – his voice was pleading – 'and I would like Dr Murdoch to check you over.'

'I'm going home,' she repeated stubbornly, 'and you can't stop me. You're being awfully selfish, Harry. Can't you see that I'd rather have the baby in a modern hospital – with all my family round me? I'm not going to be stuck here on my own.' Anger and fear made her voice rise querulously.

'I'll be here with you, Morgan.'

She glanced over her shoulder at Harry, who was petulantly kicking stones into the loch.

Without another word she walked hurriedly back to the castle.

She would have to act now – and fast – and at all costs get him to agree that she must stick to the original plan. That night she told Harry she was returning to London the next day. In order to pacify her, because he didn't want her to get upset in her condition, Harry agreed to accompany her.

17

'Tiffany Kalvin Turns Down Chance to Design Costumes for Hollywood's New TV Series' ran the headlines in *Variety*. 'Tiffany Kalvin, who is touring the States for a six-month sabbatical, declined to say why she had turned down the opportunity of working on *Street Echoes*, the sensational multimillion-dollar TV series set to wipe *Dallas* and *Dynasty* off the small screen,' the article announced. It went on to say who had been cast for the exotic roles and ended with, 'Hunt Kellerman is directing thirteen of the first twenty-four episodes.'

'Fuck it!' With an animal cry of frustrated rage, Tiffany hurled the paper across her small living room. To have seen it in print made it much worse. The chance she had been longing for – and she'd had to turn it down! That was the last time she'd pay any attention to the messages Gloria gave her when she called home. If only she hadn't rung the Los Angeles number. If only she hadn't found out what it was she had to refuse. From now on she didn't want to know.

Lying back on the sofa she felt the baby kicking, reminding her of the new life she was carrying. Hate filled every cell of her body at that moment. She hated Morgan for forcing her to go through with this and Harry for being so drunk and dumb that he didn't even know if he was making love to his wife or someone else. She hated Sig for starting this whole thing so many years ago, and she hated her father for getting himself into a position where one leak about his business activities would land him in the state penitentiary. She hated her mother for being so weak and she hated this baby for coming between her and the career she had worked so hard for. Most of all she hated herself.

Rising heavily, she shuffled into the little kitchen and grabbed a bottle of milk from the refrigerator. Later she'd go and get some bread and fruit from the supermarket and maybe stop in and see her neighbour in the apartment below, who knew her as Tasha Kidder. She was a nice woman, her neighbour. Widowed with two kids and no money. For some it was tough. Suddenly Tiffany felt deeply ashamed. She still had everything, really. A career she could go back to, money in abundance, though she was living simply at the moment so as not to draw attention to herself, a beautiful home in New York, clothes, jewels. What right had she to curse fate when the poor girl below had no prospects other than to hope she could continue to scrabble together a life for herself and her children. 'I've been spoiled,' Tiffany said to herself, as she sipped a glass of milk. 'As spoiled as Morgan or Zachary.' She patted her stomach and as if in response the baby kicked back, a soft prodding movement. 'Poor baby.' Tears filled her eyes. 'I don't hate you ... but I daren't love you either. That would be really fatal.'

Changing into a cool flowing cotton dress and some flat sandals, Tiffany pinned her hair up loosely, and left the apartment to do her shopping. She had grown to like Vineland and it had proved to be the perfect place for her to stay. No one knew her here, and although she was using an assumed name, she felt free to go anywhere without fear of being recognized. She bought some simple provisions, a newspaper and a couple of fashion magazines. *Variety* she could do without. Then she walked for a while, idly and slowly, enjoying the morning sun. For the sake of the baby she tried to keep her mind in a relaxed state of limbo – she should never have got into such a fury this morning – she would try and forget about yesterday and avoid thinking about tomorrow. Concentrate on little things, observe the people about her, let the minute take care of itself. Suddenly she saw a flower shop, its window a riot of color.

Extravagantly, she went in and bought a great armful. She could give some to Bette, her neighbour. Then it struck her forcibly – what did a woman who had hardly enough to eat want with a great bunch of flowers? On impulse Tiffany entered a small supermarket and bought steaks, a large chicken, salads, a load of fruit and a bottle of wine. By now she was carrying so much she hailed a cab to take her home. Feeling more cheerful she decided she'd ring her mother when she got back. Ruth liked her to check in occasionally. Each time Tiffany pretended to be in a different state and while it exercised her imagination and improved her geography it had also made her a talented liar. Hullo, Mom, yes, Kansas City is lovely! Mm! It's good to be in Detroit! I'm heading for Las Vegas next!

When she got back she tapped on Bette's door. 'Hi, Bette ... are you in? It's me ... Tasha.'

'Hi.' Bette, a slender, pale woman in her early thirties, flung open the door, glad of adult company. 'Come in, I was just going to make some coffee.'

Tiffany staggered into the shabby sitting room and eased her parcels onto the plastic-topped table.

'Here,' said Tiffany laughing. 'I think I went a little crazy this morning, everything looked so good in the shops, but as soon as I got outside I realized that practically *all* food makes me feel queasy these days, so maybe you and the kids can use it, otherwise it goes into the trash can!'

Bette grinned. She wasn't fooled one bit, but she liked her neighbour's style.

'Boy, will the kids be pleased! Thanks, Tasha. Here, sit down and have a rest, I'll get that coffee.'

While Bette bustled about, her two small children played in a corner, constructing a highway from a series of cardboard boxes for their collection of chipped toy cars. Tiffany resolved that the next time she went shopping she would pick up some toys for them.

The women chatted for a while and then Tiffany went up

to her apartment, but as soon as she got in the phone started ringing, and she eyed the instrument with some trepidation. Only Morgan had her number.

'You're absolutely right, Morgan! The baby must have dual nationality,' shouted Joe. There was bad static on the line between London and New York, and he could hardly hear her.

'Harry wants me to have it over here,' Morgan was shouting back. 'Daddy? Daddy, can you do something for me?'

'Name it.'

'First, can you ring Harry and tell him the advantages of being born with dual nationality. But can you also tell him something else?'

'What's that?'

'Can you tell him . . . Oh God, this *is* a bad line . . . can you call me back?'

'Sure!'

When he got through again the line was as clear as if they'd been in adjoining houses.

'Oh, that's better! Now listen, Daddy, can you tell Harry that you've set up a special trust fund for all your future grandchildren, but there is a clause which says that they are only eligible if they are born in the States? You don't really have to set up a trust, just *say* that you have.'

Joe was impressed. It was good thinking, whether it was true or not. Trust Morgan to come up with something, and he could understand the girl wanting to be with her family at a time like this. A girl needed her mother.

'Sure,' he replied. 'It's a great idea. I might just set up a trust anyway. Leave it to me, Morgan, I'll ring Harry and talk some sense into him. Now, when is the baby due? You'll be staying with us of course.'

Morgan hesitated. Staying with her family was not part of her plan. She intended to book into the Algonquin, where she could at least relax in the privacy of her suite and drop the stressful act of pretending to be pregnant. She also had to be ready at a minute's notice to go to Tiffany in New Jersey.

'The baby's not due for at least three months,' she lied. 'I'll let you know when I'm coming over. But you will ring Harry today, won't you! He'll listen to you, Daddy, he won't listen to me. At the moment you can't imagine how obstinate he's being.'

'Don't worry about a thing, I'll call him right away.'

Morgan put down the phone, satisfied. It was as good as settled. All she had to do now was call Tiffany and tell her she was coming over sooner than expected.

'Pa's will makes it very clear what he wanted done,' Harry explained to his mother. The Duchess had returned to London and had invited Harry to luncheon to 'discuss business'. She had also invited Andrew Flanders.

'No one has explained exactly what it all means,' she snapped, 'at least, not to me.'

'It means that this house is to be sold and a smaller place, maybe a flat, is to be bought for you instead. The trustees will also be providing you with an income for life.'

If Harry had told his mother she was about to be ejected into outer space she could not have looked more aghast.

'Leave this house?' Her voice took on a querulous note. 'What do you mean – leave this house? I have no intention of leaving here! It's been my London home for over thirty years . . . and what would I do with everything?' She cast her eye round the dining room, at the paintings on the walls, the heavy silver pieces on the sideboard, the rich furniture.

'It will go to Drumnadrochit, except for what you want to keep for a place down here. It won't be sold, Ma,' Harry said, as if to reassure her. 'In fact it's entailed, so we couldn't sell it – or even give it away for that matter,' he added, looking pointedly at Andrew.

Morgan's tale of removing a case of valuable items from

Andrew's closet had been worrying him for some time now. How *dare* his mother think she could dispose of family things as she liked.

'I'm not going to leave! I should hate a common little flat ... with *neighbours*,' she cried.

'Ma, this house is too big for you, and too expensive to run, what with the taxes and everything.' Harry took a sip of white wine and wondered how quickly he could get away.

'Nonsense! Anyway I've asked Andrew to come and live here with me.' The Duchess nodded at Andrew knowingly, and on cue he smiled and gave a polite snicker. 'He'll help with the running of the place.'

Harry looked from one to the other, trying to quench the feeling of jealousy that was pricking at the back of his mind, and the uneasy suspicion he had that something was going on behind his back.

'It's not possible,' Harry said, a great weariness descending on him. 'The trustees have gone into everything in great detail. It's not only what Pa wanted *and* set out in his will, it is a question of money. A house this size costs a lot of money to run –'

'How could your father have done this to me?' the Duchess blazed. 'He promised me I would be looked after properly, that I would have nothing to worry about; now my hands seem to be completely tied.'

Harry felt anger rise within him. 'Pa *has* provided for you, and if Andrew chooses to leave his flat in Regents Park to live with you, that's his affair. This place has got to go! We'll find you a much more comfortable place to live in, with a maid to look after you –'

'While you and that wife of yours get everything?'

Her words left Harry hurt and floundering.

'Th – that's not fair! Morgan has got nothing to do with it! You seem to have forgotten that the cost of living has risen, and there's capital transfer tax as well – Christ knows how we're going to pay that! I just hope I don't have to ask

Morgan or her father for financial help, but I'll certainly have to sell some of the land in Scotland.'

'And Andrew is not mentioned in the will?'

This is the trouble – the cause of all her anger and bitterness, thought Harry. Her precious nephew did not figure in the will. Briefly he said, 'Andrew was provided for by his late father. Pa was anxious that nothing should go out of the family.'

'Andrew is family.'

'By "family" I mean children and grandchildren,' said Harry, rising to leave. 'I must get back to the gallery now, the exhibition opens the day after tomorrow and there's still a helluva lot to do.'

The Duchess rose too and her grey eyes pierced Harry's with deep malice. 'Family *does* mean children and grandchildren, Harry, legitimate ones.'

'Yes?' He looked at his mother, not comprehending. 'Of course it means legitimate children – so? I don't understand, Ma.'

'You rarely do, Harry – but ask Morgan! Ask her what she was really doing in New York last September, when she ostensibly flew over to see her sister! Ask her who else she saw! Ask her who is the father of the child she's having! She refused to tell me when I challenged her, but she might just be persuaded to tell you.'

Harry felt as if his head was exploding. The Duchess recognized fear as he stammered, 'What do you mean?' – and panic in his bewildered eyes.

'You're so naive, Harry.' Her voice was ice cold. 'You never could see what was under your nose. We all knew what she was like when you married her, and we all knew she'd make a fool of you one day! She only married you for your title and position, everyone knows that. She's nothing but a pushy brash American, with vulgarity written all over her. And you imagine the baby's yours? Ha!'

'I won't listen to this!' Harry was red in the face

and sweating profusely. Sick terror gripped his stomach although his brain was telling him that everything his mother said was a lie.

'You've always hated Morgan, though God knows why! Of *course* the baby's mine, there is no question of it. Morgan and I love each other! This is preposterous.' Breathless and blustering Harry slammed out of the room. They could hear him charging across the marble floor of the hall and out into the street.

'Well,' said the Duchess, sitting down again fully restored to good humour, 'he *is* in a state.'

Andrew nodded in agreement.

Companionably they finished the bottle of wine.

Harry ran down the stone steps of his mother's house and hurried across the mannered stateliness of Belgrave Square. His mother's words still filled his head. *And you imagine the baby's yours?* How she must hate Morgan to say something like that. What had got into her? Part of him wanted to go right back to Montpelier Square, this very minute, so that he could tell Morgan what his mother had said, but another part of him was filled by fear. Not so much fear that it might be true, but fear that it might put the idea into her head.

She was so beautiful, so utterly desirable and wonderful. There must be dozens of men around who wanted her. Maybe she would be tempted to want them? And what about this chap, Greg? Morgan had certainly been anxious to fly to New York. Perhaps Tiffany's show *had* just been an excuse?

In torment, Harry walked on, unable to decide what to do. Then it struck him – his mother was just trying to break up his marriage. Viewed in this light the whole idea of Morgan going to bed with Greg was ludicrous. *Of course* the baby was his! He knew Morgan better than his mother realized. He knew she was socially ambitious. And above all he knew she revelled in having a title. Therefore it was absurd to suppose she'd risk everything just for the sake of having a lover on the side.

By the time he reached Green Park he felt better. Commonsense had overtaken his original panic. He would damn well not let his mother come between him and Morgan, and he decided not to repeat to her what his mother had said.

Harry was adamant. 'I don't care what your father says,' he cried petulantly. 'All this business of a trust is just another excuse to buy us! I know your father, Morgan. He's utterly possessive and he wants his own way all the time. Ever since we got engaged he's been busy trying to buy us.'

'How dare you talk about Daddy like that!' Morgan stormed. 'It was out of the kindness of his heart that he gave us the money to restore Drumnadrochit and do up this house. What do you mean – *own* us?'

'He who pays the piper calls the tune,' quoted Harry who always talked in platitudes when cornered in an argument. '*Now* he says he'll give our child a trust fund *if* he's born in America! It's the most absurd thing I've ever heard! As for this nonsense about dual nationality –'

'How can you be so stupid, Harry! Everyone knows there are enormous advantages in having dual nationality. Christ, you're so insular! You think the world begins and ends with this ditzy little country –'

'I'm not going to argue about this any more, Morgan.' Harry rose with stiff dignity. 'It's been a tradition for generations in our family that the heirs should be born at Drumnadrochit, and that is where our child is going to be born. I don't intend to break with tradition just for the sake of money,' he added pompously.

'I don't care what you say!' Morgan had risen too, an angry flush turning her pale skin red. 'I'm going home.'

'You're doing nothing of the kind. You're staying here

and at the week's end we're going up to Scotland.' Arrogantly he strode out of the room, his head held high. A few minutes later she heard him stomp into the study. *Why are the weakest men always the most obstinate,* she fumed as she stormed up to her bedroom.

By ten o'clock the next morning, Morgan was giving the butler his instructions.

'Perkins, get Duncan to bring the car round at once,' she commanded. Her manner – he was to tell Harry later – was quite distraught. 'And start taking these cases down. I have to get to Heathrow within an hour. I'm flying to New York.'

'Yes, your grace.' Perkins was consumed with curiosity and hastened down to the kitchen to ask his wife if she had any idea what was up. Here he found Duncan, enjoying a cup of tea and a cigarette.

'Her grace,' he did not even try to disguise the sarcasm in his voice, 'wishes you to take her to Heathrow. She says she is catching a plane for America.' Perkins watched with pleasure the startled look on Duncan and Mrs Perkins's faces.

'Bloody 'ell!' cried Mrs Perkins. 'We got a dinner party tonight ... fillet of beef ... fresh asparagus ... a kiwi flan ... ask 'er what she wants doin' with that bloody lot!'

In the bedroom, Morgan was snapping shut the last of her cases. Thank God, she thought, Harry left early for the gallery this morning, or I'd really have had to travel light.

'Get these into the car,' she said as soon as Perkins tapped on her door. 'I haven't been able to get hold of the Duke on the phone, but I've written him a note. Please see he gets it as soon as he returns.' She handed him an envelope.

'Will you be gone for long, your grace?'

'It depends.' There was no way she was going to satisfy the old poof's nosiness. 'Here, this case has to go as well, and my jewel case. Take them down and I'll be ready in a minute. Oh, and Perkins ...'

'Yes, your grace.'

'If anyone rings, I don't care *who* it is, tell them I'm out and you don't know when I'll be back. Is that understood? The same applies to Duncan and the car phone. Now hurry, I haven't got time to waste.'

'May I ask what is to happen to your dinner guests tonight? Mrs Perkins is preparing –'

Morgan shook her head crossly. 'Ask the Duke when he gets back, Perkins, I've no idea.' She put on her sable hat, tucking her hair up so that it didn't show, and then she slipped on her coat. She glanced around her room making sure she had everything. A photograph of Harry on a side table caught her eye, a laughing shot of him taken in Scotland, looking very young and carefree. At his side were Angus and Mackie. It was her favourite picture of him, but it was too late to pack it now. What the hell – Harry would be here and waiting when she got back, as much in love with her as ever. Without a backward glance she strode out of the room and down the stairs to her waiting car.

'Flight 709 to New York is now boarding at Gate 18.'

Morgan picked up her lizard-skin handbag and jewel case and left the VIP lounge. The strain of the past few months was almost over. Soon England would be left behind and she'd be back home.

In first class, the stewardess welcomed her with a smile as she checked her name. Then she helped Morgan off with her full-length sable coat and offered her a pillow for her back.

'I'm fine,' Morgan smiled back as she carefully smoothed the skirt of her fine wool maternity dress. Her blonde hair fell to her shoulders in a tumble of silky waves as she removed her hat.

'Champagne, ma'am?' The stewardess hovered with a bottle of Dom Pérignon.

'Thank you.'

'Anything else I can get you, ma'am?'

'I'm fine, really.'

The stewardess cast a professional glance over Morgan. 'When is the baby due?'

'Not for ages yet. Don't worry. My doctor said it was all right for me to fly.' Morgan sipped her champagne. It was beautifully chilled.

The stewardess beamed with relief. She'd been with the airline since they'd started the New York route fourteen years ago, but a pregnant woman on a long flight still made her nervous.

'Great!' She topped up Morgan's glass. 'I must say you look wonderful.' Then she moved away to look after the other passengers.

Morgan suddenly found herself laughing quietly at the irony of the situation.

For a pregnant woman she certainly did look wonderful.

18

'I fucking scared her off, didn't I? She wouldn't dare work with you, after what I did to her! Lousy bitch!' Joni Kellerman was back on the booze in a big way.

'Tiffany wouldn't have known I was directing, when Magnima Films offered her the contract,' cried Hunt throwing down the copy of *Variety*. 'For God's sake . . . it's over between Tiffany and me! How often do I have to tell you, I haven't seen her in nearly a year! How much have you had to drink today, Joni?' he added.

'I don't have to be drunk to know you still have the hots for her. I bet it was you who got them to ask her in the first place.' Joni walked unsteadily over to the coffee table and fumbled with a pack of cigarettes. She had difficulty getting one out and finally tipped the pack upside down and shook it. A shower of cigarettes landed at her feet.

'You're disgusting. You sound like a broken record,' Hunt was yelling. 'You and your constant suspicions. She might as well be here, the way you keep – '

'That's what you'd like! Her working here in Los Angeles so you could go on screwing her day and night like you used to.' Joni was crying now, tears of rage and vodka storming her eyes and cascading down her cheeks in rivers of mascara.

Hunt walked to the far end of the living room, and with clenched jaws stared unseeing at the window. Why *had* Tiffany turned down the chance to work for Magnima? It didn't make sense. She would never let a personal matter come between her and the sort of offer she'd been waiting for. Something must be wrong. He was tempted to ring her up and just ask her outright – but if he were to hear her voice again . . . Christ, perhaps she'd been wise to refuse.

Joni was snivelling and pouring herself another drink. Hunt turned and looked at her, and through his disgust, felt a wrench of pity. What he saw was a frustrated no-talent would-be actress, her original prettiness shot to pieces with liquor, her mind blown. And he knew that his job, which caused him to spend his time mixing with beautiful and successful women, wasn't helping any.

'Joni,' he said, and there was gentleness in his voice. 'Wash your face. The boys will be back soon. Have you fixed something for them to eat?' At the moment maids were staying on average three days.

Sullenly she rose and left the room.

Hunt continued to prowl restlessly about the living room of their Spanish-style house in Benedict Canyon, his brows knotted and his mouth grim. This just couldn't go on. Gus and Matt were getting that pale anxious look they'd had in New York – that look of dread that said *I hope there's not going to be another fight.* How much more could they take? For the first time he began to wonder if it mightn't be better for them if he and Joni were divorced, providing he got custody. And yet he dreaded the idea of having to make the decision. When Joni first came out of the clinic he really had hoped they could start over. She had cared for the boys, kept the place clean and was thrilled when they moved to Los Angeles. Maybe she thought someone would 'discover' her there and make her a star. But within a few weeks she was back to demolishing two bottles of vodka a day and still raided the refrigerator at night. He glanced at his watch. The boys would be back any time now. He'd better go check the kitchen to see how things were going.

As he passed their bedroom he glanced through the open door. Joni was sprawled on the bed. In the crook of her arm, nestled like a baby, was a half-empty bottle. Removing it quietly, Hunt threw a cover over her and left the room, shutting the door behind him. She'd be dead to the world for hours.

The next morning Joni lay in bed beside him, her face bloated and her mouth open as she snored hoarsely. Hunt nudged her shoulder and for a few seconds the snoring stopped, then she heaved herself over onto her other side and the rhythmic noise continued. It was useless. He'd have to see to the boys, get them off to school and then rush to the studio, arriving late again.

During the morning Hunt rang several agencies in his efforts to get a housekeeper. He also wondered if he should engage some sort of nurse. Suppose Joni fell into the pool, or set fire to the house with her endless cigarettes? One agency promised to find him an older woman who would cook, clean, see to Gus and Matt and try to keep an eye on his 'sick wife'. He expressed appreciation and hung up. Then on impulse he dialled another number, one he knew by heart. As he waited for an answer he could feel his heart thumping in his chest.

'Hullo?'

'Gloria, this is Hunt Kellerman. Could I speak with Tiffany, please?' His throat suddenly contracted.

'Mr Kellerman, she ain't here.'

'When will she be in?'

'She's away, sir. Been away for a long time now – going on four or five months.'

'Four or five *months*,' cut in Hunt, staggered. 'Where did she go?'

'I don't rightly know, she's jest travellin', but she rings me every week to see how everything is,' said Gloria.

'Is she in Europe?'

'Naw, jest round the States, all over. She wasn't well so she went for a rest.'

'When will she be back, Gloria?'

'I dunno, Mr Kellerman – not for a while I guess.'

'Where was she speaking from the last time you heard from her?' Hunt was beginning to feel like an FBI agent.

'I dunno,' she repeated, placidly.

'You say she was ill. What was the matter with her?'

'She was jest real sick, Mr Kellerman, wouldn't eat or nothin'. Can I give her a message?'

Hunt hesitated a moment. 'No thanks, Gloria. Nice talking to you. Goodbye.' He replaced the receiver thoughtfully.

Would the ache in him that wanted Tiffany ever stop?

Perkins met Harry in the hall, an anxious smile on his pale face, a silver salver with an envelope on it in his hand. 'Her grace asked me to give you this.' Perkins held out the tray and inclined his head with deference.

'Really?' Puzzled, Harry picked up the envelope and opening it took out the sheet of crested paper. Intently he read the note.

Honey. Forgive me for this, but I feel so strongly that the baby should be born in the States, I am leaving for New York now. I know you will see I am right, and I don't want to upset Daddy. There seems to be a problem with Zachary too, so I have to be with my family, to see what I can do to help. Take care, my darling. I'll ring you as soon as I land. I love you. Morgan.

Harry went into the study, sank into one of the leather armchairs and started reading the letter again. So she'd gone! A great wave of desolation swept over him. She'd packed her bags ... just gone! Like that! *Oh, Morgan! Morgan! I love you. Why are you so wilful? So headstrong? I know what's best for us. But you wouldn't listen.* Harry sat, gazing wretchedly into space, wondering if there was any way he could persuade her to come back. He could fly over to join her, but business at the gallery was really frantic and it wouldn't be fair to John to rush off and leave him to cope alone.

'Is there anything I can get you, your grace?' asked Perkins, standing his respectful three feet away.

'Whisky and soda,' replied Harry with unusual curtness, as he started to read the letter a third time.

When Perkins brought him the drink, he cleared his throat and said tentatively, 'Forgive me, but her grace asked me to mention that you are expecting ten guests tonight. Will the dinner party be taking place as arranged?'

Startled, Harry looked up, his eyes confused and worried. 'What? A dinner party? Oh God, do you know who has been invited?'

'I'm afraid not. Mrs Perkins has done all the preparations and I was given to understand the guests were invited for eight o'clock. It's, er, humph' – he coughed in a genteel way – 'it's nearly seven now, your grace.'

Harry let out a loud groan. 'Hell, I suppose we'll just have to carry on then, Perkins.'

Relief flooded the butler's face. He'd rather have faced the Argentinians in the Falklands than Mrs Perkins's wrath in the kitchen.

At about the same time as Hunt was calling Tiffany's apartment, Morgan was landing at Kennedy. This time there was none of the usual furore that greeted her and no car to meet her. Quietly and discreetly she slipped into a waiting cab and told the driver to take her to the Algonquin. Only Tiffany knew of her arrival. In large dark glasses, her sable hat pulled down low on her forehead, she had slipped past officials who might think to give her a VIP welcome.

Peering out of the cab windows she felt as if she'd been away years. Everything looked so much smaller in some ways, and sort of strange. The cab was charging through the fast-moving traffic to the very heart of Manhattan, then speeding along East 57th Street, down Fifth Avenue, past Doubledays and Saks and several other of her favourite shops, until they turned west along 44th Street, and, passing the New York Yacht Club, came to a halt outside the Algonquin. A minute later she was standing on the pavement, looking up eagerly at the towering buildings and sniffing appreciatively the smells of her home town. Suddenly it was very good to be back.

The first thing she did when she was alone in her suite was to strip, padding and all, and as a delicious feeling of freedom swept over her, she decided to keep her arrival a secret even from her parents – for the time being anyway.

It was such *bliss* to walk around naked without fear of being seen. She ran a hand over her taut stomach and revelled in its flatness. Pregnancy, she decided, did not suit her. Then she ordered champagne, Beluga caviar and a dozen oysters. When room service arrived she had showered and was reclining on her bed in a black satin robe, watching television. She couldn't remember when she had last felt so relaxed.

She should ring Harry. She ought to call her parents. She must contact Tiffany. But right now she was going to revel in self-indulgence. The whole world could go fuck itself at this moment for all she cared.

'Harry? Honey, it's me.'

'*Morgan*, what in Christ's name is going on?'

'Didn't you get my note, honey?'

'Of course I got your note, but what the hell do you mean by going off like this?'

'I'm sorry, Harry.'

'*Where* are you? I've been calling your parents and they said they weren't even expecting you! I've been frantic.' He sounded flustered and upset. And if he'd rung her parents, now *she'd* have to call them.

'Oh, honey!' she managed a little catch in her voice. 'I feel *dreadful* at leaving you like that, but what else could I do? You don't seem to realize how vitally important it is for the baby to be born here. Dual nationality is *such* an asset – and how can you want to deprive your son of a million-dollar trust fund? It could mean all the difference between being able to keep on Drumnadrochit when he inherits it, or letting it go to the National Trust, or something. Surely you see that, Harry? You're not being reasonable.'

'Well, I suppose if you're there you had better stay, but you shouldn't have flown in your condition in the first place!' Harry sounded only slightly mollified.

'No harm's done, honey. I had a very good flight, and I came straight to the Algonquin to rest, before I called Mom and Daddy. I agree that I shouldn't have too much excitement at the moment, that's why I'm here. I can sleep as much as I like and really stay quiet. There's also the question of Zachary. I know the family want me to talk to him, help persuade him to go into a clinic.' Morgan didn't tell Harry that no one had heard or seen anything of Zachary for months, but she needed all the excuses she could think of for being in the States.

'Oh, well . . .' Harry still sounded depressed. 'I'm missing you dreadfully, darling. I'm hoping to get away from the gallery long before the baby's due. Oh, Morgan, I do so want to be with you when our child is born!'

Morgan's heart skipped a beat. Harry thought the baby was due in two months' time.

'Wonderful, Harry,' she crooned. 'Give me plenty of warning though, so that I can get my hair fixed. I'm not looking my most beautiful these days.'

'You always look beautiful, sweetheart. Now take care of yourself.'

'I will. And you too. I love you, honey.'

'I love you too, Morgan. I'll call you tomorrow.'

'I'll call you, Harry, I miss you so much.'

She ended the conversation with more endearments, and finally she heard Harry hang up. Relief spread over her in a great weary wave. How utterly thankful she would be when this nightmare was over, but first, she had better call her parents, and then Tiffany. And she'd better inquire about Zachary, just in case Harry asked her about him.

If Morgan had given no thought in the past to the powers of telepathy, she was soon to change her mind.

'You're looking very well, Morgan, and quite thin ... considering,' said Ruth eyeing her daughter with mild and disinterested eyes. 'When is it due?' she added politely.

'In a few weeks.' Morgan was vague. It was a bore having to put on the padding and maternity clothes again.

'Why didn't you let us know you were coming over so soon? You could have stayed here.'

'I just had to get away. Harry was going on and on about our going to Scotland, so I thought the sooner I flew over here the better. Nearer the time I'll come and stay with you, but for now the Algonquin is fine. I've got so many people to look up – so much to do. I had hoped to see Tiff, though, but you say you don't know where she is?' Morgan watched her mother closely. She clearly didn't suspect a thing.

Ruth was examining her newly manicured nails, and twisting the huge forty-carat diamond on her finger. 'I've no idea what she's doing. She's been behaving rather strangely for some time now. I don't know what's the matter with her. She just took off saying she needed a rest, although I'd have hardly thought touring the States would be much of a rest. Anyway, she rings me about once a week. Your father's mad at her though.'

'Why?' asked Morgan.

'He says she should be cashing in on her success after *Glitz*. Then one of his secretaries, whose boyfriend is an actor, told Joe that in some paper it had said Tiffany had turned down a marvellous offer. He was furious.'

'What sort of offer?'

'Um, er, let me see, oh yes! There's going to be some new soap opera on television. It's meant to be better than *Dynasty*, and apparently they asked Tiffany to do all the costumes. It was a wonderful opportunity, I can't think why she said no.'

Morgan's face hardened. 'She'll have plenty more opportunities.'

'Your father doesn't think so. He says that in that business it's out of sight, out of mind. I just hope that's not true, she used to be so ambitious.'

'I wouldn't worry,' said Morgan airily. 'A change of scenery is probably just what she needs. She'll come back in a few weeks now, really refreshed.'

Ruth looked up. 'But we don't know if she will be back in a few weeks or not. Has she told you?'

Realizing her slip Morgan shook her head and said hastily, 'No, of course not, but she can't stay away forever can she? Is there any news of Zachary?'

At that Ruth blanched and then a deep flush slowly crept up her neck. 'I – we – that is, no, we've heard nothing.'

'Oh well!' Morgan shrugged again. Life in the Kalvin family hadn't changed much. Ruth still veered between being apathetic or highly nervous, and no doubt Joe would come blustering home soon, as full of bullshit as ever. As if reading her thoughts Ruth said quickly, 'Don't mention Zachary in front of your father, Morgan! The whole thing makes him very uptight – and it's better not to mention Tiffany at the moment either – '

'Dear lord, what *can* I talk about?' cried Morgan.

'Your father works so hard, honey, he needs to relax in the evenings. He likes to go out and meet new people – but he's thrilled you're dining with us tonight. There are some very interesting people coming who are longing to meet you. They've all heard so much about you.'

'Really?'

Not noticing the tinge of sarcasm in Morgan's voice, Ruth proceeded to launch into a detailed description of the guests they were expecting. They sounded about as exciting as the old Duchess's friends. Except that this lot wouldn't have a single drop of blue blood between them.

'If Tiffany should ring at any time, Mother,' she said as

she gathered up her things, 'do get her to give me a ring at the Algonquin. I'd like to have a chat with her.'

'I will. Now you'll be back by eight o'clock, won't you?' Suddenly Ruth was the anxious hostess.

'Don't worry, I'll be back.'

'It was *killingly* funny, Tiff!' Morgan chortled into the phone back in her hotel bedroom. 'I told Mom that if she heard from you she was to tell you to give me a ring! It's marvellous! She doesn't suspect a *thing* and obviously neither does Daddy! Why should they? With me padded to the eyeballs, and wearing a great tent affair!' Morgan went off into more peals of laughter.

'What are you going to do until the baby arrives? You're over here much too soon.' Tiffany sounded strained.

'I don't know. Can't you have it induced or something? It's *got* to be born before Harry comes over.'

'They don't induce babies to fit in with people's social schedules, Morgan,' cried Tiffany. 'You'll just have to wait. There's no way I'm going to risk the baby's health, or mine for that matter, to please you!'

'I know,' retorted Morgan impatiently. 'I'm not asking you to, but I had to get away from Harry, because he was about to whisk me up to Scotland to have the baby there! Listen, Tiff, I'll come to Vineland when it's due and then as soon as it's born, I'll bring it back to New York with me and we'll stay with Mom for a few days. I'll get a nurse to look after him, and then we'll fly back to England. Let's hope it arrives early.'

'And what about me?' Tiffany asked quietly.

'How do you mean?'

'I have the baby, and when I'm strong enough, I go back to this rented place to collect my things – alone. Then I struggle back to New York and try to pick up the threads of my life – again alone! Sounds fun, doesn't it?'

'Go on a nice vacation or something! Honestly, you'd

think you were suffering from a terminal illness, and – and stop trying to make me feel guilty!'

'I should have thought you'd have been able to achieve that without any help from me! Anyway, I've been on a bloody vacation for the past five months. People will think I've opted out of life permanently.' Tiffany's voice broke. She was depressed and the future looked as bleak as the present. And to think she could have been in Los Angeles right now, working on *Street Echoes*, fulfilling her life's ambition.

'Well, I don't know!' said Morgan angrily. 'Let's get this thing over and done with and then we can sort something out. I'll talk to you later. Leave a message here if you suddenly go into hospital.' She hung up. Really there were times when Tiffany carried on like a prima donna.

Tiffany felt deeply shaken. Morgan had infuriated and hurt her but she was used to that by now. It was the knowledge that Hunt had rung her up and spoken to Gloria. It had busted wide open every one of her barely healed wounds, and she felt raw. The pain was back inside her, as sharp as the last time they had said goodbye. Why had he called? What had he wanted? Probably just to say hi, and ask her why the hell she'd turned down the TV offer, but still ...

Shutting her eyes as if to blot out the memory of his face, his voice, his body, the smell of his hair and the touch of his hands, she rocked herself gently to and fro.

In Los Angeles Hunt drove slowly from the studio of Magnima Films, dreading the evening that lay ahead. He and Joni were supposed to be going to the première of *Forever Tomorrow*. They were also expected to attend the large glitzy party afterwards. Half of Hollywood would be there – the half that mattered – and the press would be swarming like a plague of locusts. Whether or not Joni liked it he'd have to go. Alone if necessary. Now that he was directing *Street Echoes* it was important for him to be seen around. What worried him was that his frequent solo appearances were causing tongues to wag. His name had already been linked with a couple of starlets and he didn't like it. It happened all the time in this town of course, but he was an intensely private person.

Parking the car, he climbed the verandah steps of his house. No doubt Joni would already be dead drunk. At least the new housekeeper, who was a positive saint, would be looking after Gus and Matt.

As soon as he entered the house he felt something was different about the place. Bursts of merriment were coming from the kitchen – the boys were obviously having supper – the place looked cleaner, tidier and there were fresh flowers in the vases. Then he noticed the ashtrays were empty. Finally it hit him that there wasn't the usual litter of dirty glasses and empty bottles.

Joni appeared in the doorway and Hunt involuntarily gave a gasp. She was sober. And looking marvellous. Her hair had been beautifully styled and her face made up with care and skill. In an elegant black jersey halter-neck evening dress, with the gold earrings he had given her for her birthday, he had to admit she looked pretty terrific.

'Hi!' she greeted him with a smile. 'It's the première tonight, isn't it? What time do we have to leave?'

'Hey, you look great!' Hunt consulted his watch. 'In about a half hour, I suppose. I'll have a shower and get changed. You really look fabulous, Joni.' He meant it. The make-up carefully concealed the puffy bags under her eyes and she had chosen a dress that flattered her curves.

'Do I?' She gave a pleased little laugh. 'I did try. I went to the beauty parlour to get myself fixed. Then I bought this dress at Giorgio's – and I haven't had one drink today.' She sounded humble and her eyes shone with a film of tears she was trying hard to fight back. 'I can go to the première with you, can't I, Hunt?'

Hunt felt a wave of pity and compassion. Christ, she *had* made a great effort and although she'd be obliterated in one second flat by Bo Derek or Joan Collins tonight, he couldn't let her down.

'Sure you can, honey! And you really do look fantastic.'

As he showered he wondered why he felt slightly put out that Joni had made such an effort. He tried to suppress the feeling. If Joni was really going to beat the drink problem, they could give Gus and Matt the secure sort of home life they needed. He could dismiss all thoughts of divorce from his mind.

But could he dismiss all thoughts of Tiffany too?

19

Morgan stayed in New York for the next week. The thought of burying herself in Vineland for longer than necessary was tedious. She rang Tiffany every day to find out if anything was happening but beyond that she indulged herself with shopping, seeing the latest shows and movies and lying about in her suite at the Algonquin reading magazines and watching television.

Friends, she avoided. It was such a relief to get out of the padding and heavy maternity clothes, such a relief to abandon the 'pregnant' performance. For the first time since she'd been a teenager she took to going around New York wearing jeans (Gloria Vanderbuilt designed, of course), casual tops, large black sunglasses and her hair hidden by a bandana. That way *none* of her friends would recognize her!

Her only worry was Harry. He rang every day, sometimes twice a day, and all he did was to demand what she was doing, why she was still at the Algonquin, who was she seeing? In desperation, she told him she had Zachary staying with her, and she was talking him into going back into the clinic.

'Zachary won't go near Mom and Daddy,' she explained. 'They don't even know he's with me, and they mustn't know. I'm making great headway with him and if they found out he was here, it would blow everything.'

Frustrated and cross, Harry hung up.

The Kalvin family, he thought, were the most obstinate, wilful and maddening lot he'd ever come across. The result of having too much money, of course.

At about the same time as Tiffany in Vineland, and Morgan

in New York, were waiting for the baby to be born, and Harry was fretting in London, Zachary decided he'd had enough of Paris.

He'd been wandering around the capital cities of Europe for months now and the urge to keep moving was still with him. Or was it the urge to keep running, to escape from the horror of what he had left behind, to insulate himself from the anxiety over it by stronger and more frequent shots of anything he could lay his hands on.

The night he and Mitch, disguised as a florist's delivery boys, had successfully pulled off the raid on his parents' Park Avenue duplex, was the night Smokey had died, stabbed to death by a mugger in a downtown back alley at nine o'clock in the evening, on her way to join him at Mitch's place. The two incidents, the robbery and the murder, were inextricably interlocked in Zachary's mind. Waking or sleeping he associated the priceless heap of his mother's diamonds and emeralds and rubies with the lifeless body of Smokey.

Mitch had played Mr Cool. Zachary must take the cash and split. He could be in Europe in a few hours, before the fuzz even knew where to start looking for him, and before they realized he'd taken his passport as well.

Zachary was hesitant – in shock – but Mitch made up his mind for him. Anyway Mitch was delighted with the way things had turned out. He kept the rocks, which he would have no trouble disposing of over a period of time.

That would do him nicely.

From then on everything went so incredibly smoothly that later Zachary would wonder if the whole thing hadn't been some sort of diabolical LSD trip.

He flew to Rome, took a taxi from the airport to the centre of the city and checked into a small hotel near the Spanish Steps.

Exhausted, he slept for twenty-four hours, waking suddenly in a violent sweat. His stomach was being torn to shreds with pain and he was shaking violently. He'd been here before. If he didn't get a fix quickly, he'd go out of his mind. He rummaged frantically through his travelling bag – and then remembered he'd brought nothing with him. Mitch had forbidden him to travel with drugs.

'Go clean, man, or you'll blow it,' Mitch had commanded.

At least he had the cash. There hadn't been time to count it but there were twelve large bundles of bills held together with elastic bands, each bill worth a hundred dollars. There was probably a total of nearly thirty thousand dollars. Enough to last him a while anyway.

An hour later Zachary was back at his hotel with enough heroin to last him several days.

From Rome he went to Naples and revelled in the slum areas as if he had been a part of them all his life. Happy to have found his own level, he decided that never again would he become a victim of his father's ambition.

After Naples he travelled to Munich, Berlin, and finally ended up in Paris. Sometimes he took a plane, cleaning himself up beforehand and mingling with American tourists like any student on vacation. At other times he hitched a lift and slept wherever he could.

Everywhere he went, drugs were in plentiful supply and it never took him long to find a dealer.

In a zombie-like state, unaware of the passing of time, the changing seasons or the varied cultures of the countries he passed through, he hovered in limbo. The most important thing was to keep on a high. He dreamed a lot about Smokey and often woke to his own sobs. He was drifting into an abyss of self-destruction, and he welcomed it, because it brought oblivion from pain, oblivion from pressure.

Paris was exciting at first, but then one morning he got out of bed and decided he was bored. Remembering that Morgan now lived in London, he decided to pay her a surprise visit . . .

*

Tiffany was suffering from little jabs of backache. The first one started just after she got out of bed in the morning, and an hour later she had another. She checked her bag for the hospital, put a call through to Morgan, and then wondered if it wasn't a false alarm. She'd ask Bette's advice. With two children she would know.

'Take a couple of aspirins, honey,' Bette advised at once. 'If it's a false alarm you won't get another twinge, but if they continue – you could be a mother this time tomorrow!'

Tiffany tried to hide the sudden fear she felt, especially at being referred to as a mother. She *wasn't* a mother. She was only a goddamn incubator.

'Have a coffee. It will help you relax,' beamed Bette. 'You know, I feel quite envious of you. Having a baby is a wonderful feeling. And you know, when it comes to the point, you'll be so excited you won't feel any pain.' Her face was glowing with enthusiasm as she hugged her own children.

Looking totally unconvinced, Tiffany lowered herself into a chair and hoped that Morgan would arrive soon.

'You look tired, honey, put your feet up and drink this.'

'Thanks, Bette,' said Tiffany gratefully. 'I shall miss you when I get back to New York. You must come and visit me and bring Gerry and Linda.'

'I'd like that. I've never been to New York. Wouldn't the kids just love going up the Empire State Building! Wow! Hear that, kids? Tasha's going to invite us all to New York!'

'When?' they chorused in unison.

Tiffany laughed. 'As soon as I can manage it,' she told them. It would mean telling Bette who she really was, but that's all she would tell her. Bette would be allowed to think she'd had the baby adopted.

As the day progressed the pains began to form a regular pattern.

By five o'clock there was still no sign of Morgan.

At six o'clock Tiffany called a taxi to take her to the hospital.

As she alighted from the taxi at the hospital entrance with her one modest bag, a stretch limousine drew up and out sprang Morgan.

'Hi, Tiff!' she called gaily, then she told the driver to take her luggage on to the hotel where she'd booked a room.

Tiffany looked up, unable to believe her eyes.

Morgan, looking fresh and incredibly glamorous in a pale yellow silk suit and high-heeled matching shoes, came hurrying towards her. Pearls gleamed at her neck and ears, she was flushed with excitement, and from her arms hung large packages, all beautifully gift-wrapped.

'I thought you'd be having it by now!' she cried with a hint of reproach in her voice. 'What are you doing here?'

Tiffany gave her a long hard look. 'Fat lot you know about babies arriving! It might not come until tomorrow, and oh, Morgan, I'm getting scared. What on earth have you got there?' She eyed the parcels in astonishment.

Morgan's face fell in disappointment. She'd thought it was such a lovely idea to stop off at Bloomingdale's on her way to Vineland and get some things for Tiffany and the baby. She'd bought a transparent chiffon and lace nightdress in eau de nil, a marabou-feathered bed-jacket to match, slippers, a large bottle of Joy and a gorgeous red lipstick. For the baby there were a dozen fine lawn gowns, hand-embroidered round the neck in blue.

'Presents!' For a moment she looked lost and rejected. 'I – I thought they would cheer you up, Tiff, and here's a teddy for the baby.' She tried to thrust the toy into Tiffany's arms just as Tiffany froze with another sharp pain.

'Say, are you okay? You look awful! Here, let's get you into the hospital. Why on earth didn't you check in earlier? When you called me this morning, I thought it was imminent.'

Morgan strode ahead into the hospital, an incongruous

figure in the clinical surroundings.

Ten minutes later Tiffany was lying in a narrow cot, being examined by the doctor. The pains were escalating to an incredible severity. She tried to remember all she had been taught at the prenatal classes. Relax. Breathe deeply. Go with the pain, don't fight it. It wasn't proving as easy as it sounded.

It was the beginning of the longest night Tiffany had ever known.

In the waiting room along the corridor Morgan drank endless cups of coffee and flipped through the magazines she had brought for Tiffany. This, she decided, is what it must be like to be a father. From where she sat she could see the door of Room EO5 where Tiffany lay, and she wondered what was going on. Soon the baby would be born. Later she would ring Harry. Morgan had kept on her suite at the Algonquin, leaving instructions to say she was out if anyone called. Everything was under control.

Ignoring the no smoking sign, she took a cigarette out of her slim gold case and lit it. Her whole scheme had been brilliant. Her future was now practically assured. In a couple of weeks she'd be back with Harry and they could pick up the glittering threads of their lives that had been so disrupted by her 'pregnancy' and the old Duke's death.

At 2 a.m. Morgan regretted not having gone to her hotel for the night. She was hot and sticky and her silk suit clung to her back. The skirt was a disaster of creases. How much longer was this going to take?

Sudden noise and activity in the direction of Tiffany's room made her sit up abruptly. A nurse briskly ran down the corridor, in obvious search of someone, another entered the room hurriedly, pushing a big trolley. Two white-coated doctors came out of the room, had a hurried consultation, then one rushed off and the other walked swiftly back into Tiffany's room. Morgan could sense something was wrong.

Their faces had been grim and they'd looked tense.

Rising, she went in search of someone who could tell her what was happening.

This was obviously an emergency.

It was four o'clock on a Saturday afternoon and Knightsbridge was acquiring that faintly deserted air that descends on the more fashionable parts of London at the weekend. Shoppers were drifting away from the dozens of expensive boutiques and stores; residents had gone to the country; Harry even found a space for his Rolls in Montpelier Square when he came home from the gallery in the early afternoon.

From the outside the house had an empty air. When Morgan was at home she always kept all the lights on, and passersby could glimpse through the heavily curtained windows the glittering chandeliers, a section of a Gainsborough or a Kneller; a corner of a Dutch marquetry desk, a spotlit corner banked up with orchids.

Without Morgan, Harry reflected, everything seemed lifeless.

Letting himself in, he went straight to the study at the back of the house, overlooking the paved garden.

If only Morgan were here, Harry groaned to himself. She'd only been away ten days but it seemed like months, and the baby wasn't due for weeks. What was he going to do in all that time to keep himself from going crazy? Life without her was empty, boring, dull, the days interminably long and the nights lonely. He had never realized he would miss her so much.

Last evening he hadn't even been able to get to speak to her. The damn receptionist at the Algonquin had merely said, 'I'm sorry, the Duchess of Lomond is out. Have a nice day!'

Have a nice day indeed! He'd woken up with a demoralizing hangover, had a furious argument on the phone with his mother, lost badly at a game of squash with his partner

John, and now he was back in an empty house facing an empty afternoon and evening and this was only Saturday! What the hell was he going to do with himself tomorrow?

Misery descended on him like a great wet blanket. If only he could just catch a flight to New York and be with her, but business at the gallery was booming as a result of their exhibition of Old Masters and he was rushed off his feet. He flicked on the television and picked up *The Times*.

Harry barely heard the front door bell ring. When Perkins came into the study, announcing that there was someone to see his grace, Harry looked up startled.

'It's Lady Elizabeth Greenly,' said Perkins primly.

'Oh!' Harry said slowly, the sound conveying a range of inflections. Jumping to his feet he went into the hall where Elizabeth was waiting quietly.

Harry greeted her with his attractive crooked smile. 'Hullo, Elizabeth. What a lovely surprise! How are you?'

'Hullo, Harry, I hope you don't mind my dropping in like this, but I've been struggling round Harrods for the last two hours, trying to do some shopping, and I'm exhausted – and there isn't a taxi in sight!' Her blue eyes were limpid pools of innocence.

'It's nice to see you. You'll stay for tea, won't you?' Without waiting for an answer he turned to Perkins and said, 'Bring us tea in the study, in a little while, please.' Leading the way, Harry escorted Elizabeth to a deep leather sofa, relieving her of some of her parcels.

Harry felt relaxed with Elizabeth these days. After all, he assured himself, they had known each other for nearly twenty years and they were *meant* to be friends. Not lovers. Not married, but good solid friends. He was so glad she felt the same way.

'Have you been busy?' she asked.

Elizabeth had always taken an intelligent interest in his work and he was happy to regale her with an account of the pictures he'd bought and sold lately.

Later tea arrived and with subtle purpose Elizabeth took charge of the silver tray, with its crested silver teapot and Minton china.

Harry had never been any good on his own. Now he was thoroughly enjoying himself. The cucumber sandwiches and buttered crumpets were delicious, the chocolate cake, made by Mrs Perkins, even better. Perkins had lit a fire in the marble fireplace earlier and it crackled cheerily, making the study cosy. Elizabeth's company was soothing too – sort of undemanding.

'What are you doing this evening?' he asked impulsively.

Elizabeth opened her eyes wide as if she hadn't given the matter any thought.

'I don't know really. Mummy and Daddy are away for the weekend, so I'll probably have a quiet evening. There's a good film on television, I think.'

'Why don't we go and have a bite to eat? There are lots of quiet little restaurants round here so we needn't bother changing. What do you say? Then I can run you home ... with all your shopping ... afterwards.'

Elizabeth hung her head to one side like a bird listening, and considered the matter with gravity.

'Well ...'

'Come on, Elizabeth! We needn't be late, and as we're both at a loose end we might as well have dinner together.'

'All right,' she relented and gave him a sweet smile.

'Wonderful!' Greatly cheered, Harry added, 'I must call Morgan before we go out. What time will it be in New York now?' he consulted his watch. 'Lunchtime, I'll ring her in a minute. I want to find out how she is and I couldn't get hold of her last night.'

'Ah!' Elizabeth gave him a sympathetic look. 'She's been away nearly two weeks now, hasn't she? Do you get very lonely? I know I would!'

Harry smiled. What an understanding girl she was.

'Yes, it's a bit tough at times,' he admitted, shrugging. 'I've never been much good at amusing myself.'

'I know.' Again that gentle smile.

They talked until it began to grow dark outside and Montpelier Square became as quiet as a country village. In the study, the lamps, in their apricot silk shades, glowed warmly, and the fire had settled into embers.

Harry, sipping a gin and tonic, basked in the easy flow of relaxed conversation and felt more contented than he had for a long time.

Harry took Elizabeth to dine at Menage à Trois, a chic little restaurant in Beauchamp Place, regularly frequented by the Princess of Wales when she went shopping with her girlfriends. They gave their order, Elizabeth choosing 'Josephine's Delight', three eggshells filled with a mimosa-like filling topped with red and black caviar and finely chopped smoked salmon, while Harry settled for the terrine of duck. Then they both decided to have boned quail wrapped in a filo pastry parcel, topped with a sauce of wild mushrooms, and a bottle of *Côtes de Buzet.*

Harry, his tongue loosened by several drinks before dinner, confided to Elizabeth the problems he was having with his mother. He expressed his misgivings at her idea of having Andrew move in with her.

'Frankly, I'm surprised he wants to! He'll lose his freedom, his independence. She'll want him to go everywhere with her. It's a mad idea!' he continued, wound up by now.

'You're right, Harry,' purred Elizabeth soothingly. She laid a hand on his arm for a moment. 'As always!'

It was midnight when they rose to leave.

'I'd no idea it was so late! I'll drop you home,' Harry said as they walked up Beauchamp Place to where they had left his car. 'I'm glad I gave Duncan the weekend off. I hate keeping the poor chap hanging around until all hours.'

In the car a companionable silence fell between them. Five

minutes later they drove through Eaton Square to her home in Cliveden Place.

'Thank you for a lovely evening, Harry, I've enjoyed it so much.' She spoke almost wistfully.

'I've enjoyed it, too.' He leant forward to give her a brotherly kiss on the cheek, but at the last second she turned her face so that he found his lips on hers. They were soft and tender, like a small child's and she was pressing them gently against his. Her arm slipped round his neck and he smelled the fresh fragrance of her flowery perfume. For a moment he stayed still, but a shaft of fire penetrated his groin and pulling her closer, he kissed her deeply. She clung to him, all ardent, loving gratefulness. Oh God, he thought, passion rising unbearably in him now, it's been so long. It was so long since he had met with such sweet encouragement – so long since he had indulged his needs.

She said it for him.

'Let's go into the house, Harry.'

A mile away a taxi was drawing up to the Montpelier Square house and a tall blond young man was clambering out and fumbling with a handful of loose change.

His clothes were crumpled and shabby and a moth-eaten looking beard covered his chin like a skin blemish. With slightly yellowed eyes, made more pronounced by the jade-green of his irises, he gazed up at the tall Regency house. For a moment he stood there, swaying, as the taxi drew away, the noisy rattle of its engine the only sound in the square.

It was 3 a.m.

He rang the bell and waited. After five minutes he rang again and banged the brass dolphin door-knocker. Then he sat down on the white marble steps and fumbled in his travelling bag. His hands were shaking and although it was a chilly night a fine mist of sweat covered his face.

Eventually the door opened quietly and a startled Perkins, in a dark-blue woollen robe, stood surveying the huddled figure at his feet. He was just about to slam the door shut when he heard the young man speak.

'Morgan ... I've come to see Morgan.'

'I *beg* your pardon?'

'My sister Morgan. Doesn't she live here? I've come to see her.' Zachary rose slowly to his feet, towering over the butler.

'I'm afraid ...' Perkins was utterly taken aback. This tramp, this *vagrant*, obviously drunk ... and the young Duchess?

At that moment he heard the distinctive purr of the Rolls Royce and with intense relief saw the Duke drawing up outside the house.

'Is Morgan here or isn't she?' Zachary was demanding belligerently.

'If you'll just wait a moment, sir.'

Harry was coming up the steps looking flushed and none too steady on his feet either.

'Your grace ...'

'What's happening, Perkins?'

'Harry, I've just arrived from Paris, where's Morgan?'

As recognition of his brother-in-law dawned on Harry, a look of total bewilderment crossed his face.

'But –' he began.

'Aren't you going to ask me in? I'm pooped!' Zachary lurched into the hall and threw down his travelling bag.

'But Morgan's in America! You saw her ... she met you ...' confusion and too much wine were making Harry babble disjointedly. 'What on earth are you doing here?'

Zachary looked at him with over-bright eyes. 'I haven't seen Morgan since ... since you got engaged!' he cried, triumphant at having remembered. 'You know, when you came to New York to meet us all.'

Harry rubbed his face with his hands and wished he hadn't had so much to drink. This had been the most extraordinary night of his life and now it was taking on the quality of a nightmare. He'd fucked – for the first time – his ex-fiancée and oldest friend, and now here was Zachary standing in his hall at three in the morning, telling him he hadn't seen Morgan for eighteen months.

'You'd better come into the study,' he mumbled, avoiding Perkins's eye.

Again and again she felt as if an axe were splitting her in two. Sweat poured down her face and her mind spun in panic. *I can't stand any more. I'm going to die.* Another wave of agony tore through her and in a frenzy she had but one thought. *This isn't fair. It's not even my baby. I'm being killed for nothing.*

Tiffany heard a woman scream and realized it was her.

There were hands everywhere. Heavy hands that probed her stomach and between her legs – hands that adjusted her feet in high stirrups, and gripped her wrist – hands of torture that wouldn't leave her alone. And those voices that commanded her to *push now, come on, push – push!*

Suddenly she decided she'd had enough. She was going to give up. Nobody could be expected to suffer this much. Another rending, splitting pain and she took a deep breath and closed her eyes. Darkness enveloped her and she hoped she was dying.

'Are you a relative?' the nurse asked Morgan. It was 6 a.m. and this elegant-looking woman had been sitting in the waiting room all night.

'I'm her sister. I want to know what's happening.'

'I'll see if one of the doctors can have a word with you,' she said, and hurried away down the corridor, all scratchy starch and efficiency.

A few minutes later one of the doctors came out of Tiffany's room and walked brisky up to Morgan.

'You're Mrs Kidder's sister?' he asked without preamble.

'Kidder?' Stupidly Morgan looked at him for a moment,

and then quickly said, 'Oh yes! Tasha Kidder. I'm her sister.'

'Okay. We have a bit of a problem. The baby's lying badly in a breech position. Every time we straighten it, it slips cross-wise again, do you understand what I'm saying Mrs, er . . .'

'Lomond.'

'Mrs Lomond, we're going to make one more attempt and try and lift it out with forceps but . . . well, the baby's heart is weakening. If this doesn't work we're going to perform a Caesarean section.' He was blunt and eyed her without a flicker of warmth.

'Will it . . . be all right?' *Please God let the baby be all right.*

'As I said, it's showing signs of distress, and so is your sister. We'll keep you informed, Mrs Lomond.' He gave a quick nod and walked briskly away.

20

Sunday morning in London dawned chilly and misty. Harry, deeply disturbed by the happenings of the previous evening, leaped out of bed, then clutched his head as a deep, throbbing hangover hit him. He staggered to the bathroom and a few minutes later submerged himself in a very hot bath, a glass of noisily fizzing Alka Seltzer in his hand. Waves of embarrassment swept over him as he remembered making love to Elizabeth. What on earth had come over him? And supposing she misread his actions? Lying back in the soothing water, he closed his eyes in mortification. Elizabeth was the sort of girl who'd think a quick tumble meant undying love, and under the influence of a lot of liquor, he'd gone and given her the whole fucking works! Telling her he loved her and everything. Christ, what a fool!

Groaning aloud, he got out of the bath and wrapped himself in a huge terrycloth bath sheet. Then he rang for strong black coffee.

Zachary had also got up early. He needed a fix and he wanted to see Morgan. Nearly all the cash he'd got from his father's safe was gone. He'd have to ask his sister for a loan. When he heard Perkins take the tray of coffee into Harry's room, he slipped on his jeans and went into the hallway.

'Can I get you anything . . . sir?' Perkins asked, looking at him disdainfully.

'I'll have a Coke,' replied Zachary, ambling along to the master bedroom.

Harry had almost finished dressing.

'Good morning, Zac. Want some breakfast?' Harry replaced his crested ivory hairbrushes on top of the walnut chest, and picked up his gold cuff-links.

'Nope, I'm not hungry.' Zachary stared at the crystal chandelier hanging from the ceiling. He blinked his eyes at the brilliant glass droplets.

'When did you last eat?'

Zachary frowned in an effort to remember, then he shook his head, giving up the struggle. 'Dunno. Sometime . . . in Paris, I think, maybe yesterday. Nice place you got here.'

'Umm. You've lost a lot of weight.' Harry looked at Zachary and was shocked by what he saw. At six foot three, he couldn't have weighed more than nine and a half stone and his skin was stretched like a smooth parchment over the bones of his face.

'So you and Morgan met up the other day?' asked Harry conversationally. 'She's looking marvellous, in spite of being pregnant, isn't she?'

Zachary regarded him with blank eyes.

'Uh? I haven't seen Morgan. Didn't you ask me that last night?'

Harry looked at him gently and spoke as if to a child. 'You *have* seen her, Zac, remember? You and she have been together in New York. You were staying at the Algonquin.'

Zachary flopped onto the chaise-longue that stood at the foot of the bed and buried his head in his hands. There was a long silence. When he looked up he had the strained expression of someone who has been asked to recall a vague dream.

'No, Harry,' he said at last. 'I haven't even *been* in the States for nearly a year. I can't have met Morgan.'

Harry knew Zachary was telling the truth.

With a swift stride he picked up the bedside phone and started dialling the number of the Algonquin.

Sunday morning in Vineland dawned hot and humid.

Morgan sat huddled in a chair waiting for news. Dark circles like bruises lay under her eyes and she was stiff and aching. No one seemed to have been near her for ages. At one time she thought she'd heard a baby's faint cry, but it could have been the wail of a woman or even a piece of hospital equipment squeaking along the tiled floor.

If anything happened to the baby! The complications were too awful to think about. She'd have to tell Harry she had miscarried and then he'd blame her for not staying quietly in Scotland – and there'd still be no heir to the dukedom.

Everything depended on what was happening in room EO5 at that minute and she'd go crazy if she didn't find out soon.

'Are you all right?' asked a young nurse as she passed. She had obviously just come on duty because she looked fresh and bright. 'Can I get you anything?'

'Can you find out how my sister is, please?' Morgan asked desperately. 'She's in that room down the corridor, EO5, her name's – her name's Kidder. She's having a baby and – '

'I'll see what I can do. You look as if you could use a cup of coffee. Shall I get you one?'

'Thanks.'

Morgan watched as the nurse walked away. She felt sick with dread. Surely there'd be some news soon. At that moment the door of Tiffany's room was flung open, and after a pause, during which Morgan's heart nearly stopped with fear, the doctor who had spoken to her earlier came out. He walked towards her, slowly and wearily. His eyes were like bleary dark oysters in his pale face and his mouth was a tight straight line.

Falteringly, hardly able to control her rising panic, she took a few uncertain steps towards him.

'Yes . . .?'

'Mrs Lomond, I'm happy to tell you your sister is going to be all right. We were able to do a forceps delivery.'

'But the baby?' Morgan burst out. 'How is the baby?'

A flicker of surprise crossed the doctor's face and he gave her a strange look.

'The baby's fine.'

Morgan let out a long trembling breath. 'Thank God. Is it a boy?'

'Is that so important? What matters is they're both going to be fine, but they need to rest now. No visitors. It was a very long and very hard labour.' He started to walk away. Morgan stood, her eyes fastened desperately on his tired face. She opened her mouth wide but nothing came out. Then he turned, as an afterthought, and his last words were slung carelessly over his shoulder.

'It's a boy.'

Tiffany tried to turn onto her side but the movement made her wince. She felt as if a steam-roller had crushed the length of her body into the hard ground and then reversed back over her again.

'He's a beautiful little boy,' the nurse was saying encouragingly. 'Wouldn't you like to hold him?'

Tiffany turned her head away and closed her smarting eyes.

'No.'

'Oh! Perhaps when you've had a little rest –'

'No.'

'You will have to start feeding him in a little while –'

'*No!* Take him away.' She could no longer trust her voice. Anyway it was none of the damned nurse's business. Morgan could hold him. Morgan could give him a bottle.

'Take him away,' she repeated.

When she was alone she had to stuff the pillow into her mouth so that no one would hear her sobbing.

It was past noon. Back at the hotel in the town centre Morgan dozed fitfully on top of the bed. When the hospital had refused permission to let her see Tiffany and the baby until later in the day, she'd crept away, overcome with tiredness and a strange feeling of anticlimax. Now she dreamed the vivid dreams of shallow sleep.

She woke at two o'clock, greatly refreshed and with a growing sense of excitement. Getting up quickly she showered and changed. Coffee she could do without. She'd drunk enough in the night to cause a world shortage.

Outside in the street, the day had turned cooler and a soft breeze lightened the previously stifling air. Morgan got a cab. Ten minutes later she was at the hospital.

On the fifth floor all was peaceful and sunny. The dark drama of the night before might never have happened. Nurses wheeled a trolley down the corridor. A young mother in a frilly robe carried her baby carefully. Giggling could be heard coming from one of the rooms.

Morgan stopped outside room EO5 and knocked lightly, her stomach tight with excitement.

'Come in.'

She found Tiffany propped up against a mound of pillows, her face a tense mask of pain and misery, and very pale.

'Hi, Tiff! How are you feeling?' Morgan placed a large bunch of pink roses on the bed and looked round for signs of the baby.

'Lousy.'

'Oh, honey, I'm sorry. You really had me scared for a while, it seems that things went wrong. What happened?'

'I don't know. Anyway I'd rather not talk about it.'

'Gee, that's too bad. Where's the baby now?'

'In the nursery, I suppose, with the others.'

'I can't *wait* to see him, is he beautiful?'

'I – I o–only caught a glimpse of h–him . . .' Great racking sobs overwhelmed her again and tears coursed down her cheeks.

Morgan rushed over and put her arms round her. 'Hush, honey, it's all over now! You can go back home and forget all about it. I'm so grateful, Tiff, you know that, don't you? I expect you're just exhausted. Don't cry!'

'I . . . c – can't help it.' Tiffany covered her face with her hands and continued to weep.

Morgan stood uncertainly beside the bed. This was the last thing she'd expected. Tiffany should be so relieved it was all over. She could go back to her career now and the fun life she enjoyed in New York. What on earth was there to cry about?

'Why don't I ask them to bring the baby in here, so that we can look at him together?' she coaxed.

'No, I don't want to see him I tell you!' Tiffany made a supreme effort to check her tears. 'I *never* want to see him! He's yours . . . I've told the doctor you are adopting him, so the sooner you get the hell out of here and take the b – baby w – with you . . . the better.'

'But *why*?'

'Can't you understand anything? I love him already! He's really *mine* . . . and I'm having to let him g – go.'

Aghast, Morgan looked at her sister. Tiffany, who hadn't wanted a baby and had sworn she would never get emotionally involved, was breaking her heart.

Morgan slipped from the room and went in search of the nursery. At last she found it at the far end of the corridor. Seven babies in all lay snugly asleep in seven hospital bassinets. Which one was hers?

A nurse wearing a mask came up swiftly, saying with a trace of suspicion, 'Can I help you?'

'Yes, I've come to see my, er, sister's baby. He was born this morning.'

'Wait here a minute.' The nurse indicated that Morgan should stay in the corridor and after a moment she reappeared, carefully pushing the clear lucite cot.

Morgan looked down on the tiny form. His small pink face just showed above the blanket and his head was covered with a soft fuzz of dark hair. Tiny hands, the fingers spread star-shaped, moved jerkily.

'He's beautiful,' she breathed, awestruck. 'How much did he weigh?'

'Only five pounds, but he's in great shape.'

'That *is* small, don't premature babies usually weigh about that much?' Morgan asked, with wide-eyed innocence.

'Some do, most weigh less.'

'Thank you for letting me see him. I must say he's gorgeous.'

'Your sister's a lucky lady. He's a fine little boy.'

'Yes ... yes, thank you.' She watched as the baby was wheeled back into the nursery. My baby! she thought with pride. My baby, the young Marquess of Blairmore, son and heir of the Duke of Lomond.

What a pity the nurse couldn't be told.

'The Duchess of Lomond *must* be there! I've been ringing for two days now, and she would have left a message if she'd been going away. Try her room again,' demanded Harry.

'I'm sorry sir, she's not answering,' said the Algonquin telephone operator after a pause. 'Did you want to leave a message?'

'Yes. Tell her to ring her husband as soon as she returns.'

'Very well, sir. Have a nice day.'

Harry began to panic. Anything could happen to a woman alone in New York. Visions of mugging and rape filled his mind – or perhaps Morgan had collapsed in the street and been taken to some dreadful hospital where they didn't even realize *who* she was! He turned to Zachary who was sprawled on the sofa, absently watching television.

'Zac, have you any idea where she could be? Your parents have no idea, she left no message at the hotel. Do you know anyone in New York who might know where she is?' Harry sounded desperate.

'Nope.' There was a long pause. 'Why are you fussing? Morgan can look after herself. She'll be okay.'

'How can you be sure? Oh, I wish to hell I knew what was going on.' With a groan, Harry sank into a chair.

Zachary got to his feet slowly and looked at Harry.

'I need a boost,' he announced thickly. 'Want anything? A benny? Some smack? A quaalude or some angel dust?'

Harry stared at him as if he were speaking a different language. 'What are they?' he asked curiously.

'You don't know?' It was Zachary's turn to look astonished. 'Hang around, I'll get the stuff from my room. I go for free-basing right now.' He wandered out of the study and Harry heard him going upstairs.

The phone rang. Leaping to his feet Harry grabbed the receiver and heard with relief the faint transatlantic hiccup on the line.

'Hullo?' he shouted at the mouthpiece.

'Hi, honey!'

Thankfulness swept over him in a great wave as he recognized Morgan's voice. In the same second he felt deep anger.

'*Where* are you?' he cried fiercely. 'I've been frantic with worry. Why didn't you leave a message – or ring me?'

'I'm truly sorry, darling ... but ... well, I've been rather busy.'

He could tell by her voice she was teasing him and it infuriated him even more.

'What the hell have you been doing, Morgan?'

'I've been having a baby, honey. A beautiful little boy.' Morgan stressed the last word.

'*What!* But – you've had the baby?' Harry felt his legs trembling as he reached for a nearby chair and sank shakily onto it. 'Morgan ... I don't understand! It isn't due yet, what happened? Are you all right?' *Christ*, his mind reeled. *He had a son.*

'I'm fine, Harry. He arrived yesterday. It was all very

sudden but he's absolutely fabulous. He looks just like you and although he is a little bit premature the doctors are thrilled with him.'

'Jesus! I can't believe it! Are you really all right, darling? Was it terribly painful?'

'Worse, er, worse than I expected,' she said genuinely, 'but it's all over now, and I'm going to Mom and Daddy for a few days to rest, with a nurse for the baby. We should be home by next week. Isn't it exciting, darling?'

'Yes,' replied Harry slowly. His feeling of shock was beginning to subside and there was a lot more he wanted to ask her.

'Where did you have him? Doctor's Hospital?'

'Not exactly. I heard Tiffany was in New Jersey, so I popped over for a day to see her. No sooner had I arrived than the baby started!' Morgan explained and added hastily, 'It was perfect really, having Tiff with me –'

'I've been telling you not to go rushing around,' Harry cut in.

'The doctor said my travelling had nothing to do with it.'

'You should have stayed here.'

'But everything's okay.'

'That's not the point! If you had been resting quietly in Scotland, like I wanted –'

'Harry, don't be cross!' Morgan pleaded. 'Of course I wanted to be with you, but it just started for no particular reason. Don't worry! The baby is perfect, and I'm fine too – and I miss you, honey! I can't wait to get home.'

'Hell! I wish I could get away to be with you, but John's got to go to some auction sales up north this evening and I've got to look after the gallery all this week. Oh, why did this have to happen now?' He sounded petulant again.

'Never mind, sweetheart – we'll be back very soon, and then we can really celebrate!'

He gave a deep resigned sigh. 'I miss you like hell, Morgan, and I want to see the baby.'

'I'll be back before you know it, darling. And I'll call you every day.'

Suddenly he remembered something. 'Morgan, there's something I want to ask you, something important.'

'Yes?'

'Why did you tell me you were with Zachary?'

'How do you mean?' Her voice sounded wary.

'Zachary is here. In fact, he's just come into the room this moment.' Harry turned as Zachary entered carrying a plastic bag.

'Zachary!' Morgan cried. 'In England? I don't understand!'

'Neither do I,' said Harry quietly. 'He says he hasn't seen you for over a year, that he's been in Europe all this time.'

'Harry, you can't believe a word that boy says! He's probably so stoned he doesn't know his ass from his elbow. Let me speak to him.'

'Hang on.' Zachary was feverishly spilling the contents of the bag on the floor. 'It's Morgan, she wants to speak to you. She's calling from New Jersey, I think.'

'Okay.' Zachary took the receiver from Harry. 'Hi, Sis! How's things?'

Harry didn't listen to Zachary's side of the conversation. Lying on the carpet, amongst small plastic packages, vials, pills and capsules was Zachary's passport. Harry scooped it up and, going to the window, flipped through the pages.

Roma – April 1985
Napoli – May 1985
Deutschland – July 1985
Holland – November 1985
De Gaulle – France – January 1986
Heathrow – England – April 1986

All the places Zachary had said he'd been for the past year.

It was the proof he needed that Zachary was telling the truth.

So why was Morgan lying?

21

Harry was waiting at Heathrow as Morgan sailed through customs, the baby in her arms wrapped in a large white lacy shawl, a nurse by her side. Behind her trooped a bevy of airport officials, giving her the VIP treatment. At the rear came porters struggling with a trolley stacked high with crocodile-skin luggage.

As soon as she came through the barrier, photographers alerted by the public relations department of Quadrant Inc. surged forward, flash-bulbs popping. Harry got shoved aside in the rush.

Morgan had returned to London, the darling of the popular press. A pop star couldn't have had a greater welcome.

'Harry!' she cried in delight, when she could get to him, kissing him so her best side would show in the photographs. 'How wonderful to see you . . . and here is our son and heir.' Carefully she placed the baby, who had just woken up, into Harry's arms.

Harry gazed down at the little face with a feeling of wonder and pride. 'He's beautiful.'

'Isn't he just? Aren't you proud of us, honey?' She smiled up eagerly like a little girl showing off a new doll. 'He's so good too. He slept most of the way over.'

'We'd better get him home. My God!' Harry looked at her luggage, horrified. 'We can't get all that lot in the car! What on earth have you been buying?'

'Have it sent on,' said Morgan blithely. 'Come on, I can't wait to get home.'

They trooped in procession, rather like royalty, to the waiting Rolls.

As Duncan drove into London, Morgan, with Harry and the baby in the back, kept up a non-stop flow of excited chatter. She talked about having the baby and how nice the doctors and nurses had been. She talked about her parents and what a restful stay she'd had with them. She talked about friends and shows and shopping and fashion. Tiffany's name was never mentioned.

If Morgan had seemed animated in the car her energy assumed a superhuman quality when she got home. The first thing she did was to get the baby installed in the top-floor nursery suite. This comprised a day nursery, a night nursery, the nurse's room, and beyond a bathroom and tiny kitchen. Here Morgan gave instructions to the nurse, who was staying until the old-fashioned English nanny arrived the following week.

Then she went to her room, where she instructed one of the maids to do her unpacking. She also inspected the contents of her already bulging closets, put her jewellery in the wall safe, and called up Elizabeth Arden to book a facial, a manucure, a massage and a hair appointment for the following day. Finally she had a quick shower and changed into a beautiful new dress she'd bought in New York from Adolf. She looked round her room before going downstairs. Ah, yes. She must tell Perkins to change the flowers. She hated tulips.

'Everything all right?' Harry greeted her as she joined him in the study.

'Fine. The baby's being fed at the moment ... goodness, what a lot of mail!' Morgan sat down at her desk and picked up a large batch of letters. There were a lot of invitations, a lot of charity circulars – and an awful lot of bills.

'Aren't you feeding the baby yourself?' Harry asked. She could hear the touch of criticism in his voice. She looked sad. 'Unfortunately no. My milk never really came through and he was hungry all the time and crying. The doctor said he'd do much better on a formula,' she replied.

'What a pity,' he said quietly. 'Have you seen Zachary?'

'Is he still here?' Morgan paused as she opened an envelope.

Harry nodded. 'I'm terribly worried about him. I've tried to get him to see a doctor, I even found out about clinics over here, but he absolutely refuses. At the mention of help he just freaks out and says he doesn't want to give up drugs because there is no substitute.'

'They all say that,' said Morgan dismissively. 'I'll talk to him. Where is he now?'

'God knows. He was up and out before I left for Heathrow – no doubt buying more supplies. He tells me it's the easiest thing in the world to get drugs, uppers and downers, speed, heroin and cocaine, which he mixes with ether – he calls that "free basing". I can tell you I've learned more about drugs in the past ten days than I knew existed. He's only nineteen, but if he goes on like this, I tell you he will be dead in six months, if not sooner! *Something* has got to be done to help him.'

'What can we do?'

'You're his sister, talk to him. Tell him he *must* get treatment.'

'I think he should go back to the States,' said Morgan firmly.

'What good would that do? He ran away from the Moyes Clinic, and, if I may say so, your parents aren't the right people to handle him either. I can't find out what he's doing for money, but he's spending hundreds of pounds a week. Where's it coming from?'

Morgan looked thoughtful. 'I'll talk to him when he gets in.'

'Morgan, while we're on the subject of Zachary, why did you lie to me?' She looked up, a flicker of alarm crossing her face at the suddenly cold tone of Harry's voice.

'I don't know what you're talking about!' she flashed back.

'About meeting Zachary in the States. It wasn't true, was it?'

'I told you on the phone, half the time he hallucinates and doesn't know what the hell he's doing. Of course I met him in New York, but he's probably just forgotten.'

'He hasn't *been* in the States for over a year.' Harry's voice was dangerously quiet and his blue eyes bore into hers.

Morgan flushed and threw down a pile of invitations on her desk. 'Nonsense! Of course he's been in the States.'

'I've examined his passport. He's been in Europe since last April. So why did you lie to me, Morgan?'

'Harry!' Her beautiful face was starting to crumple and inside she felt a cold shaft of fear. Something had happened while she'd been away, and she sensed it wasn't only to do with Zachary. Harry seemed aloof, wary, as if he were wondering about her. For a second it crossed her mind that he might have been unfaithful but she dismissed the idea instantly. Harry was crazy about her. And in bed tonight she'd show him just how crazy she could be about him.

'Honey, why are we quarrelling?' she whimpered. 'I've been away so long and I've just come back – with our baby – and I thought you'd be pleased, and – and now you're giving me the third degree.' She looked at him with stricken green eyes.

'I'm not, I just want an explanation. I hate deceit and certain things just haven't added up lately.'

Morgan got up slowly and walked to the window. Below lay the paved garden, a riot of colour with spring flowers. When she turned back to look at Harry her cheeks were wet.

'You're right, honey. I haven't been levelling with you and I used Zachary as an excuse. I'm sorry, but I couldn't tell you before because it wasn't my secret to tell. I'm not supposed to tell anyone even now, but I know I can trust you. You see I had to protect someone else – I was *sworn* to secrecy – but I realize now how terribly unfair I was being to you. Please forgive me, I didn't mean ...' She broke down, sobbing.

Alarmed Harry rose and went towards her. He hated scenes and half wished he'd never said anything, but he had to dispel the nagging doubts in his mind. He had to press Morgan for the truth.

'What happened?' he said at last.

Slowly she turned from the window and looked at him.

'It was Tiffany. You know she's been taking a long sabbatical?' Harry nodded. 'The reason she left New York suddenly was because she was ill. Do you remember a letter from Daddy saying she looked dreadful and always seemed tired?' Harry nodded again.

'It seems,' Morgan continued, 'that she thought she had cancer. She was too frightened to see a doctor so she just ran off, away from everything and everybody, refusing to say what was the matter. Sometimes she rang me, but she never said what was wrong and then a few weeks ago she got worse. She started haemorrhaging and really panicked. That's when she rang me. She was going into hospital and she was terrified. I was sworn to secrecy, she just couldn't bear the idea of anyone knowing. She begged me to come to her. She didn't want to be alone when they told her. Poor Tiffany, she suffered so much.'

What an accomplished liar I've become, thought Morgan as she heard herself spinning this newly invented yarn. *So accomplished that if I say it often enough I will come to believe I really did give birth to the baby. I will come to believe Tiffany really was ill.* It had all been meant to be so simple, and now it had become a morass of lies and intrigue and never-ending deceptions. Each time she thought she was in the clear, something else came up that could only be answered by more lies.

'My God! That doesn't sound like Tiffany. How is she?' she heard Harry asking.

Morgan smiled, her eyes still moist. 'All right, thank God. It wasn't cancer, just some female problem and she had a small operation and now she's going to be fine. Then just as she was coming out of hospital I started having the baby – so it was her turn to hold my hand! So that's why I had to be so mysterious, Harry. I'm truly sorry to have upset you – and lied – but I was doing it for Tiff's sake.'

Harry was still looking at her strangely and she couldn't make out what he was thinking. *Please let this stop. I've had enough of lies.*

'Now I'm home we can be a real family, honey. You've no idea how much I've been longing for this minute, and now' – her voice caught in another sob – 'now you're being so nasty to me and –'

'I'm not, sweetheart! Come here.' He put his arms round her and pulled her close. 'I didn't mean to be angry. Forgive me. I was just so frantic with worry, your rushing off like that to New York, and everything. I'm sorry, darling. I love you so much, and I want you so much. It just scared the hell out of me ... in case I'd lost you.'

'I know, honey, I know.' Morgan kissed him deeply. 'I love you more than anything else in the world and no matter what happens I will never leave you again.' *And I mean it, Harry.*

They sat close together for a long time, their arms around each other, each immersed in their own thoughts.

Harry felt relaxed and happy. Morgan was home again, and their baby son, the first of many he hoped, was up in the nursery. The loneliness and the uncertainty of the past few weeks was over. They would live happily ever after – as long as Morgan never found out he'd been to bed with Elizabeth.

Morgan still felt edgy. She almost wondered if the whole thing had been worth it. All the lies! Oh God, who but Harry would have believed such fantastic fabrications! But what was done was done. She had somehow produced an heir for Harry, and all she could do now was to go forward.

'Have you thought of names for the baby?' she asked

suddenly. 'I had to put something on my passport for him so I chose David.'

'He'll also have to be christened Henry because it's a family name, and how about Edgar, after my Pa?'

'David Henry Edgar, Marquess of Blairmore. I think it sounds great. Let's have some champagne, Harry? Let's drink a toast to David Henry Edgar, and my homecoming – and one other thing too.'

'What's that?' Harry was nuzzling her neck.

Morgan took his face gently in her hands and looked lovingly into his eyes. 'How about drinking to the return of full conjugal rights?'

As he held her tightly to him she could feel his rising hardness.

Everything was going to be all right, she thought. So why did she still have this uneasy feeling?

22

Tiffany lay by the blue mosaic pool, her eyes shut. The sun stung her skin with tiny prickles of fire and the air felt solid with heat. She had been at Four Winds for three weeks now and it would soon be time to go back to New York. The family house in Southampton held such terrifying memories for her that she wondered why she'd returned here to convalesce. Was it to exorcize that sunny afternoon so many years ago? To come back and look around and say, *This is where it happened and I'm no longer afraid?* She *was* no longer afraid. She'd never be afraid again. Twice was enough. Twice the victim of someone else's desires.

Rising, she walked to the edge of the pool and did a perfect swan dive into the tepid water. As she swam her long brown limbs hardly caused a ripple. She rejoiced in her fitness and the blissful ease with which she could once again move. The baby had been born only a month ago yet her figure was back to its normal slimness, her waist trim, her stomach miraculously flat. But that very flatness shouted her loss, leaving her grief-stricken and empty. A part of her had been taken away and somehow, night and day, she had to force all thoughts of the baby out of her mind. She'd be back at work soon; her apartment needed redecorating; there were friends to catch up with; she concentrated fiercely on the future and tried to forget the recent past. But nothing had prepared her for the workings of her subconscious as she slept. Racked by nightmares, she awoke, night after night, shaking and sobbing. Her dreams were always the same. She'd lost her baby by dropping him, leaving him in Central Park, realizing he'd been abducted, or worse, finding him dead from starvation in his cot because she'd forgotten to feed him. Relentlessly, her phantom baby haunted her and refused to go away.

From the second he had been born a passionate love for him had developed in her. Her longing to hold him had been almost overwhelming.

'I don't want him,' she had gasped as the nurse had tried to thrust him into her arms. 'Take him away, I don't want him.'

Tiffany remembered now the pain she had felt, the aching hollow pain she was still feeling. She knew she would go on wanting him for the rest of her life.

The only thing that was going to help her get back to normal was to get into a regular busy routine and adhere to it strictly. So each morning she got up early, walked briskly to the deserted beach and swam vigorously for half an hour. Then she exercised on the sands before walking back to Four Winds. After a light luncheon she drove to Gin Lane and played tennis with friends at the club before going home to swim in the pool and sunbathe on the terrace.

The evenings were her favourite time. Theresa, the housekeeper, served supper on the verandah running along the back of the white slatted wood house, and here she watched the sun setting over the ocean, and, as darkness closed in, the tall cypress trees in the garden melt into the black sky.

'My, Mizz Tiffany, you're sure lookin' great!' declared Gloria, when Tiffany arrived back in New York the following week. 'You've got yourself a nice colour.'

'Thanks, Gloria, it's great to be back. How's everything? Any problems?'

'Nary a one. Plenty of messages for you, and mail. Mr Kellerman has rung several more times, but I didn't tell him anything 'bout you, like you said.'

Tiffany gave a brisk nod and smiled at Gloria. Dear loyal Gloria. Hunt had rung, had he? Her new resolve was to look forward, not back. Looking back could turn you into the wife of a guy named Lot.

Picking up her mail and message pad she went to her studio at the far end of her apartment. The moment she entered she felt as if she had been hit by a waft of cold air. The studio she had created with such loving care seemed hostile, rejecting her presence. Sketch-pads, paints, pencils and pens, lay on the shelves, untouched for months. Her drawing board and stool and the wooden easel in the corner stood blank and deserted. Her best costume designs, framed and hung round the white walls, glared down at her accusingly. Quickly, she shut the door and hurried into her living room.

Feeling like a stranger in her own home, Tiffany decided to unpack, go through her mail and do something normal like watch television. *That* was the same the world over and might bring back a sense of normality to the situation.

When the phone rang she stared at it. Let it ring. She wasn't able to cope with her own apartment yet, let alone the outside world.

'Hullo!' she said grabbing the receiver. *She'd been in hiding too long.*

It was the warm, deep-timbred voice of Greg.

'Greg!' she cried in delight. 'How are you ... how's everything?'

'Fine, honey, but how are you? I thought you'd disappeared behind the Iron Curtain, you've been gone months.'

'I know, I know, but I'm back now with a very upmarket Southampton tan.'

'Great! When can we meet? What are you doing tonight?'

'Nothing,' Tiffany replied without hesitation.

'Fantastic! Let's have dinner. I'll pick you up at eight, okay?'

'You've no idea how nice that will be,' Tiffany said sincerely.

*

Greg took Tiffany to Sardi's for dinner, thinking she would like to spend her first night among the people and in the atmosphere that had formed a backdrop to her life for so long. Tiffany realized as soon as they were shown to their table that it was a mistake. The crowded restaurant, the hubbub of animated voices and the heat jarred on her nerves. The waiters skimming and dodging about, balancing trays, made her edgy. She longed to be back in the quietness of her apartment with supper on a tray – alone.

Greg ordered for them both and chose the wine, while Tiffany sat silent and subdued, reluctant to look round the room and see who else was dining. It might be someone she knew.

'Tell me your news, Greg,' she asked at last, trying to make an effort. 'What have you been doing with yourself?'

Greg looked at her, wondering why she was so changed. The girl who was always so effervescent and animated now sat with a flat dead look in her eyes and a tentative smile.

'Life's pretty hectic,' he said, his expression wry. 'I've had several boring cases lately, mostly divorce and all the ensuing litigation, the usual stuff, but it doesn't leave much time for play!'

'No girlfriend?'

Greg shook his head. 'No. I take out quite a few girls but none of them inspire me.'

Tiffany looked into his mild eyes. 'Is it still Morgan?' she asked softly.

A shot of pain crossed his face for a split second and then was gone. If she hadn't known him so well it would have passed undetected.

'Maybe.' He cut into his steak firmly then said, 'So what's your next project, Tiff?' It was obvious he wanted to change the subject. No sweat, thought Tiffany. I don't want to talk about my sister either.

Conversation became an effort. For the first time she found herself unable to be natural with Greg. A great barrier of nearly six secret lost months was boxing her in and her excuse for going away to 'recharge her batteries' sounded as false as it felt.

At last they left Sardi's and Greg saw her back to her apartment, kissing her lightly on the cheek as he bade her good night.

'Thank you for a lovely evening, Greg,' she lied. 'I'll call you soon and you must come and have dinner one night.'

'I'd love to, Tiff. Take care – and see you soon.' Then he was gone with his warm smile and familiar little wave.

Tiffany closed the door and fixed the security chain. Then she wandered into this other person's apartment.

It was going to take a lot longer to pick up the threads of her life than she'd imagined.

The baby was crying. She bent over the cot, picked him up and held him close. Jerky sobs racked his tiny body and he buried his face against her shoulder. Rocking him gently she tried to soothe him with comforting noises but he went on crying. He was hungry. She knew because as soon as she'd heard him her breasts had begun to tingle and become tight, heavy with the milk she longed to give him. She turned him in her arms and undid the buttons of her blouse. The baby arched his back, yelling with frustration, arms flailing, face red. She pulled him closer, ready to put her nipple in his small mouth, but he wriggled. She tightened her grip but he twisted away and as she frantically tried to hold on to him he slithered beyond her grabbing hands – falling out of her hold – falling . . .

Tiffany awoke as a silent scream tore at her throat. Her breasts still prickled painfully.

It was 3 a.m.

She went to the bathroom and took a sleeping pill.

'She went off her rocker and had to be put in a clinic, surely you heard, Hunt?'

'Are you sure? It doesn't sound like –'

'Sure I'm sure! Runs in the family. Her brother was a loony and her –'

'Her brother had a drug problem,' Hunt interrupted. 'There was nothing wrong with Tiffany. Where did you hear this garbage – the hairdresser's I suppose?'

Hunt was angry. This wasn't the first time Joni had come home with a juicy tidbit about Tiffany, picked up during one of her forays into Hollywood.

Joni shrugged. '*Everyone*'s talking about it! It'll make the trades, you'll see. She's finished!' She dropped her terry robe and lay by the pool, her skimpy bikini top barely covering her large drooping breasts. 'You've got to admit, Hunt, she was always unstable –'

'*Crap!*' he roared. 'There's nothing unstable about Tiffany! Of all the people I know in showbiz she's the – '

'You just can't take off those rose-coloured glasses!' spat Joni. 'According to you, Tiffany's fucking perfect! Well, that fucking perfect broad has been put away, and high time if you ask me!'

She flopped onto her stomach and buried her face in her bright pink arms.

Hunt got up in disgust and walked back into the house.

Had Tiffany really had a breakdown? It seemed unlikely, knowing her as well as he did. Yet it would account for her sudden disappearance, turning down *Street Echoes,* and Gloria's unhelpfulness when he rang. He went to the bedroom and picked up the phone. If he was the cause of anything that might have happened to her he had to know.

'Hullo?'

Shit. It was Gloria's motherly voice again.

'Is Tiffany there?' His voice was a hoarse whisper in case Joni came back into the house.

'She's out right now. Who is that?'

'Hunt Kellerman. When will she be back?'

'I ain't sure. Shall I give her a message?'

Hunt was sweating profusely. 'Gloria ... is she okay? I mean, well, is she all right?'

'She's jus' great, Mr Kellerman!'

'Okay, thanks. I'll ring her back later.'

Quietly he replaced the receiver.

A second later a great vase of lilies came hurtling through the air, landing with a crash against the wall, a foot away from his head. Broken glass and smashed flowers and water exploded in his face.

'I mighta guessed you'd be checkin' on that fucking bitch!' Joni was screaming from the doorway.

Within a week of her return to New York, Tiffany had an offer of work. She was asked to design six costumes for an off-Broadway one-man show. Not exactly a spectacular production compared to *Glitz*, but she accepted it for the challenge it offered. Sam Earl, a brilliant young actor, had written and devised the show and it required four quick changes. He insisted they take no longer than twelve seconds each and three of them took place in act one.

Tiffany struggled with the intricate designs incorporating Velcro stitched along the seams so that the garments could be ripped off during a blackout, but it didn't work. The tearing sounds marred the effect and set everyone's teeth on edge. Next she tried using snaps but they had to be strong enough to hold the fabric together and they bulged at intervals and looked lumpy. Racking her brains one night in her studio, she suddenly gave a whoop of joy. She'd cracked it! During her studies she'd been particularly fascinated by Japanese Kabuki theatre and the amazing illusionary effect they achieved, and how a performer could do a quick change under bright spots, when one costume appeared to *melt* into another.

Working all night she arrived at rehearsals the next morning with two specially prepared costumes. Sam Earl was instructed to put on the first costume, and then the second on top. Intrigued, he wondered what Tiffany had up her sleeve.

'Ready?' she asked.

'Go ahead,' Sam replied. 'Surprise me!'

She did.

Standing behind him with a dresser she had primed, they pulled a series of black threads that held the seams of the top costume together. Six seconds later Sam stepped forward in the second costume.

'Fantastic, darling!' he cried in an awestruck voice. 'Hey, Tiff – that's really incredible!' He looked round at the first costume, now a neat little pile of fabric on the floor. 'That's great, how did you do it!'

'It's Eastern magic!' Tiffany laughed, pleased that it had worked so well. 'We'll do all the quick changes like that. The wardrobe mistress may not be too thrilled – it means tacking the costumes together again after every show – but if we put in markers it shouldn't take too long. I reckon we can cut the time of the quick changes by four or five seconds.'

Suddenly everyone clustered round her, patting her on the back and saying how brilliant she was.

When the show opened two weeks later the critics raved: 'There is no end to the talent and versatility of Tiffany Kalvin.'

But the morning her assistant, Maria Roth, breezed into the studio, looking as if all her Christmases had arrived at once, was the day Tiffany realized how deeply the loss of her baby had really bitten.

'I'm pregnant!' Maria cried, her eyes blazing with joy. 'Can you beat it? I'm actually gonna have a baby!'

Tiffany was consumed with unbearable jealousy. 'That's great,' she said politely, 'when is it due?'

'Oh not for ages. I'm only eight weeks gone but isn't it terrific? Bobby and I have been wanting a baby for ages. Say, if it's a girl I'm gonna call her Tiffany! How about that?'

Congratulating Maria, Tiffany hurried out of the studio and locked herself in the bathroom, the tears streaming down her face, shocked by the violence of her own feelings. At that moment she hated Maria as much as she envied her. Maria would be able to hold her baby and love it, and keep it forever. It wouldn't be taken from her and brought up in a far land. The desire to cuddle little David swept through her, making her feel sick with longing. Oh dear God, how could she have let Morgan take him?

More offers of work came in. Then, within a month, she was asked to design the costumes for a major new musical, *Gertie*. It was loosely based on the life of Gertrude Lawrence, and Tiffany could hardly believe her good fortune. *Gertie* was an even bigger production than *Glitz*, which was still playing to full houses. *Gertie* was everything Tiffany wanted at this moment. Especially as she'd had to turn down *Street Echoes*, which she noted was still top of the Neilsen ratings. *Gertie* would restore her confidence, keep her so busy she'd have no time to think of anything else, and put her once more on top of the heap.

Enthusiastically, she began researching the 'twenties, fascinated by the bias-cut clinging dresses, the dropped-collar coats edged with fur, the long ropes of pearls and the shoes with straps and buckles. More amazing was the tucking, pleating, piping and lace inserts that had gone into the making of the clothes of that period. And the fastenings! In an old photograph of Edwina Mountbatten in a pale blue crêpe dress, Tiffany counted *eighteen* tiny fabric-covered buttons, fastening each sleeve at the wrist, and *thirty-two* tiny buttons down the back! Miniature buttons she would do – for ornament – but it would damn well be a zipper or Velcro that would actually do the job!

There would be problems over finding the right fabrics, too. In these days of man-made fabrics where were they going to find satin-back silk crêpe? Or shantung? Or crêpe de Chine? Thank God she had been able to rehire Shirley and Maria.

Early each morning she started working in her studio, which had by now welcomed her back. She was surrounded by the glorious mess of sketch-pads and paints, reference books and swatches of fabric, and she hadn't felt so happy for a long time.

On the surface her colleagues in the theatre welcomed her back with open arms, but behind her back they gossiped and bitched and spoke of how she'd changed from a lively young woman to a sad-looking, depressed one. Some said she'd had her heart broken by Hunt Kellerman, others said she'd had a nervous breakdown and had been confined to a clinic. The majority said they'd thought she was different, but only a spoiled bitch with a billionaire father would let one success go to her head and take off on a luxury trip round the world, even if she *was* working again now.

Tiffany knew what they were saying and there was nothing she could do about it. She just had to get on with her work and in time prove them wrong.

She also began going out in the evenings again, mostly in a group, but it was a start. There were shows to see after her long absence, new restaurants to visit, exhibitions to view. Her nightmares about the baby became less frequent and she had managed to push memories of Hunt to the back of her mind, tucked away in a closed compartment where they couldn't hurt her.

Gradually she began to feel better. A new maturity touched her face and eyes, giving her a gentle knowing look, turning her into a woman of mystery. Best of all she felt strong, positive, in control of her life at last.

It was a good feeling. Nothing could touch her now.

Tiffany saw him in the elevator as she went up to a cocktail party in her parents' apartment. He was six feet four inches tall, blond, athletic-looking and incredibly handsome.

When he discovered they were both getting out at the same floor he gave her a delighted quirky smile and asked charmingly, 'Are you visiting Mr and Mrs Kalvin also?'

'Yes.' Tiffany returned his smile.

'Great. I'm Axel Krasner, by the way.'

'I'm Tiffany Kalvin.'

'You must be . . .'

'I'm their daughter.'

'Really?' He lingered over the word, his eyes sweeping her face with an appreciative intimacy.

Tiffany felt her cheeks grow hot and she suddenly felt very self-conscious.

Ruth greeted them with her usual vague smile, forgot Axel's name, then let them into the drawing room where everyone was drinking champagne.

It was the usual crowd. Businessmen from Wall Street, politicians from Washington, socialites from New York, and a few old friends from Southampton. Beside them, Tiffany reflected, Axel Krasner stood out like Sir Galahad at a gathering of geriatrics.

Several times during the evening Tiffany was aware of Axel's eyes on her as she acted out her role of dutiful daughter, talking to everyone and seeing that they had drinks. Once their eyes met and an unaccountable and almost forgotten feeling of excitement shot through her.

'Who's Axel Krasner?' she asked her mother when they had a moment on their own.

'I think he's a client of your father's. I've never met him before, but he seems quite nice.'

'What does he do?'

'I've no idea. Why don't you come and meet Nancy Lee-Wilkins? Her husband's the President of the Bellika Corporation and she's chairman of the Southampton Beach Ball.'

'I'll join you in a minute, I want to powder my nose,' Tiffany replied swiftly, edging herself out of the room.

A minute later a hand gripped her elbow and she found herself looking up into a pair of brilliant blue eyes.

'You're not leaving yet?' Axel was asking.

'I wish I could,' Tiffany replied honestly, 'but as the daughter of the house I'm supposed to make polite conversation to all the guests.'

'I'm a guest! You can make polite conversation to me. Can we have dinner together afterwards, Tiffany?'

Tiffany hesitated. It was so safe and secure inside the protective capsule she'd built around herself. Axel smelled of danger and excitement and sex. She made up her mind. If the capsule was that strong and protective she had nothing to fear. A little supper, some laughing banter – she'd be home by eleven.

'I'd like that,' she replied simply.

Suddenly it felt like being in the mainstream again.

Within a week they were lovers. Tiffany found Axel both experienced and imaginative in bed. He was also indefatigable. She loved his sense of humour, his ability to see the ridiculous side of every situation, and his dry mockery of everything that most people held in reverence. He spared nothing and no one, least of all himself, from his abrasive wit. Axel never took life seriously. He wouldn't let Tiffany get heavy about anything either, and soon he had her laughing at herself.

This, thought Tiffany, feeling as if she'd had a shot of adrenalin, *is the best thing that could have happened to me.*

During the weeks that followed, Tiffany discovered that Axel had hit the jackpot the year before when he'd opened the Axelance nightclub. Manhattan was ripe for a new nightclub, and he'd taken an old theatre on Madison and 47th Street, and with more instinct than experience managed to appoint the right manager, barmen, waiters, stewards, and most important of all, disc jockey. He'd hired a top designer to transform the theatre into a wonderland of black and silver with a fantastic laser show, and the crowds at his opening night had practically stopped the traffic. The success of Axelance was assured the next morning when the newspapers showed photographs of Andy Warhol, Grace Jones, Madonna and Calvin Klein, all in the party mood.

Within nine months Axel had paid back his investors. Now he was thinking of expanding the operation to San Francisco and Los Angeles, hence his being at Joe and Ruth's party. He hoped Quadrant Inc. would become backers.

Tiffany also found out he was thirty-four, had never been married, lived in a small apartment in Southgate Tower on 31st and 7th and that both his parents were dead.

So far so good. He obviously didn't want to talk about his past and Tiffany didn't probe. For the moment it was enough that she had a man of her own who could stay all night and every night.

23

Morgan awoke, instantly aware that something was wrong. Then she heard it. Thumping and crashing from somewhere in the house, below their bedroom. Beside her, Harry lay supine, snoring softly. With a swift movement she slid out of bed and ran onto the landing. Below her, the hall lights blazed. The noise was coming from the dining room.

A man's voice roared something she couldn't understand, glass shattered and a second later she heard it tinkling in the street outside – then there was an anguished shriek.

Tight-lipped with fury, Morgan strode back into the bedroom and snatched up her velvet robe.

'Harry,' she shouted, 'wake up, for God's sake. I need your help. Zachary's gone berserk again.'

As they reached the hall Perkins appeared, alarm etched on his sleepy face, ruffled grey hair sticking out in wisps all over his head.

'Help me, Perkins,' commanded Morgan curtly.

An appalling sight met their eyes as they entered the dining room.

Chairs and tables were knocked over, silver, dented and twisted, was scattered on the floor and valuable china lay smashed. Holding a carving knife Zachary was flinging himself around the room attempting to slash Lomond family portraits. He didn't even notice Morgan and Harry as they stood, aghast. Then he flung down the knife, scarring the mahogany dining table, and, seizing a silver candlestick, hurled it through the remaining window.

'Zachary!' screamed Morgan.

He spun round, his eyes blazing, while Harry snatched the knife off the table and flung it into the hall. Before they could stop Zachary, he leapt to the fireplace and started banging his head against the wall like a crazed creature. Blood was trickling down his cheek and there was blood on his hands.

'You – motha – fuckin' – bitch!' he was shrieking, punctuating each word with a self-inflicted blow. 'I – don't – want – to – die. You'll – never – get – me!'

Grabbing him by the arms, Harry and Perkins forcibly removed him from the wall and dragged him towards the door. Suddenly his legs buckled and he slipped out of their grasp, slumping on the floor and clawing at the rug. Then great painful sobs burst from him as he cried out in fear.

It was the third time in two weeks that Morgan had seen this Jekyll and Hyde switch in Zachary's personality. One minute he would be gentle and docile and dreamy, and then suddenly he resembled a wild caged animal, demented and deranged. It was the most frightening metamorphosis.

'Get him to his room,' Morgan said, shaken. 'Lock him in – and Perkins, remove any valuables first.'

Perkins looked at her wretchedly. 'Shall I call a doctor, your grace?'

'No, there's no point, he seems to be getting quieter. Harry, isn't there anything we can give him to knock him out completely for the rest of the night?'

Harry was helping Zachary to his feet. 'It's too dangerous, Morgan. We don't know what he's taken already.'

'You – filthy – lying – whore!' spat Zachary, but with no less venom than before. 'I – hate – you!'

Morgan turned sharply and walked out of the room, her cheeks flaming. That was it. Zachary couldn't possibly stay any longer. It was dangerous to have him in the house with the baby, and it was embarrassing in front of the servants. It undermined her authority. It would also be disastrous in society if it ever got out what kind of brother she had.

Tomorrow, she vowed, when he might be docile again,

she would take him to Heathrow, buy him a one-way ticket and put him on a plane for New York. He could no longer be her problem. And if, on landing, he got arrested for bringing drugs into the country, well! might it not be for the best? Zachary, locked away permanently where he couldn't harm himself or anyone else? An idea took shape. She hadn't forgotten either, that he'd been foolish enough, during one of his euphoric moods, to admit that he and Mitch had been responsible for cleaning out Joe's safe. Yes, thought Morgan, it would be much better for everyone if Zachary was put away.

Axel's tongue flicked over Tiffany's nipples until they became hard and erect. He continued gently down her body, across her stomach, coming at last, lingeringly, to the hot source of her pleasure. Tiffany moaned, arching her back. The exquisite agony was driving her crazy as he teased her with his tongue, denying her the ultimate release and keeping her aching on the very edge of fulfilment.

'Take me . . . give yourself to me . . .' she almost sobbed, as she turned her head from side to side on the pillow. The peak was so near – she wanted him so much.

'Now my darling – now.' His voice was choked and his breath was coming in gasps. With a swift movement he entered her, thrusting deeply, his eyes glazed and unseeing. Clinging together, consumed with mutual desire, as he plunged wildly, the sweat pouring from his body, his cries mingling with hers, until with a searing wrenching sweetness, they came together and lay throbbing, spent and sated.

'Will you marry me, darling?' Axel suddenly asked, as they lay together afterwards in the stillness of her room.

Tiffany looked at him, startled. This was the last thing she had expected. An exciting affair, yes. Companionship and laughter, yes. For as long as it lasted. Surely that was the name of the game these days. But marriage?

'Are you serious, Axel?'

He traced the line of her cheek and jaw with a long tanned finger and pulled her, gently this time, towards him.

'I'm very serious, my darling. We love each other. Isn't that a good enough reason for getting married?'

'We haven't known each other very long though. Marriage is an awfully big step.'

'So? I fell in love with you the moment I saw you, Tiff. I know that sounds corny, but I've never felt this way about a woman before. Besides, you're so good for me.'

'Good for you? How do you mean?'

Axel shrugged. 'Just good for me. You turn me on, in more ways than one. I actually like *talking* to you!'

Tiffany's laughter cut across his words. 'Don't you usually like talking to your girlfriends? After all, in a relationship one spends more time talking than actually making love. It's vital to be able to talk!'

'Exactly! You're a friend as well as a lover. It's easy to find sex, much harder to find a friend.'

Tiffany agreed. That's what had been so wonderful about her relationship with Hunt. They had been able to communicate on every level. Hunt. Swiftly she kissed Axel and said, 'I'm not sure yet, honey, that I want to get married at all. I love my independence and being free and . . . well, I just think it's too soon to start talking about marriage. Let's leave things as they are for the moment, huh?'

'Okay.' He sounded disappointed. 'I'm going to keep on asking you until you say, yes, though. You need someone to look after you, darling, someone to care for you.'

'I can look after myself, you'd be surprised!' she replied.

'I'm sure you can! But maybe I need someone to look after me.' His tone was bantering. 'Come here, we've talked enough! I want to fuck your brains out.' Axel slid his hands round her buttocks and pulled her towards him.

Tiffany wasn't arguing.

*

Joe Kalvin sat slumped at his desk on the twenty-ninth floor of Quadrant House, feeling sick to his stomach. Whichever way he looked at it Zachary was in for it, and unless Joe could pull all the strings he could lay hands on, the whole family were about to be utterly and irretrievably disgraced.

Someone – some nosy interfering goddamn son-of-a-bitch – and Joe would like to have throttled whoever it was – had gone and tipped off the airport police at JFK that Zachary was flying in from London with drugs in his possession. And the informant hadn't stopped there. They'd gone on to suggest Zachary be questioned about the robbery at the Kalvins' apartment the previous year when jewellery and an unspecified amount of cash had been stolen.

Despair, self-pity and a deep anger filled Joe. He had the terrible feeling he was losing his grip. Was it fair, he asked himself, that after nearly forty long years of hard work and planning he should be plagued this way? Hadn't he built up the company so that he could provide for his family and create a future for his son? Zachary should have been at Harvard now. In three years' time he would have been taking his place on the board of Quadrant. Eventually he would have become president.

'The fucking waste of it all,' Joe suddenly said aloud. He reached for the cedar-lined box on his desk and snatched out a cigar. For a moment he almost wished he'd never had a son. Or that his son was now dead. The boy had turned into a junkie and a common thief and was a misery to himself and everyone else.

Zachary was a problem that wouldn't go away.

With an effort Joe straightened his shoulders and lit the cigar. The problem would have to be made to go away. He glanced at his gold watch. It was nearly 8 a.m. In a few minutes Quadrant House would be throbbing with life as the business of the day began.

Grabbing his alligator-bound memo pad, Joe jotted down cryptic notes, so everything would be clear-cut in his head when he rang his lawyer, Abe Schwartz, the most powerful and influential attorney in New York. Joe bit into his cigar and swore softly. A few years ago everything would have been clear-cut in his head without making notes first.

Item One, he scribbled. *Get bail set.*

Item Two. Get all charges dropped re burglary.

(Shut Zachary's big mouth.)

(Insurance already paid up on jewellery.)

(Can't reveal amount of cash.)

Item Three. Put in plea of mental illness.

(Fix to get doctor's report. Moyes Clinic etc.)

Item Four. Find top security clinic.

Joe buzzed his intercom.

'Yes, Mr Kalvin?' It was the smooth voice of his secretary.

'Get me Abe Schwartz right away, and don't put through any calls until I tell you.'

'Very well, sir.'

'And get me some coffee.'

'Yes, Mr Kalvin.'

Joe stubbed out his soggy cigar and took off his jacket.

He had work to do.

Saving his family from shame.

24

Morgan planned David's christening with as much detailed care as Joe had planned her wedding eighteen months before. It was, after all, his debut into the exclusive world of the aristocracy and she wanted to mark the occasion properly.

Holy Trinity, a few minutes' walk from Montpelier Square, was booked for the ceremony six weeks hence and two hundred embossed invitations were being sent out. After the baptism there was going to be a traditional reception back at the house with champagne and a large white-iced cake, topped by the Lomond coat of arms in frosted sugar.

Morgan also arranged for the antique Limerick lace robe generations of Lomonds had been christened in to be sent down from Drumnadrochit Castle. Her outfit was being designed by Hardy Amies, couturier to the ladies of the Royal Family.

Morgan spent much of her time at her desk in the study, compiling lists and making appointments with various specialists in their different fields. Caterers came first, with sheaves of menus, designs for a marquee to cover the garden, specifications for buffets, tables, little gilt chairs and silver samovars. There were the number of catering staff to be decided upon, the hire of glasses, silver platters and containers of ice.

Then came the florist, John Plested, to whom Morgan had been recommended by the Duchess of Southampton.

'He's the best in London!' she declared dogmatically. 'If you want something special John is the only person to get to do it.'

Morgan did want something special – and more besides! She was planning a surprise for both Harry and their guests, and the only clue they had so far was an extra line printed along the bottom of the invitation card. *'Dinner. 8.30 p.m. Black Tie.'* She hoped her guests would think it was going to be a boring little buffet party. This party, however, was going to be something else! Already she could feel the glow of self-congratulation as she pictured the amazed faces of her guests.

'For the teatime reception,' Morgan told John Plested in clear tones, 'I want the house to be a bower of blue and white flowers. Everywhere! I want them round the front door and garlanding the front railings. I want flowers in all the reception rooms and in the marquee. I also want the cake, which will be standing on a round table in the window, wreathed in flowers, with cascades of white ribbons. I'm sure you know what I mean?' She gave John her most winning smile.

John did. He also wondered if the young Duchess had any idea how much it was going to cost.

But Morgan hadn't finished.

'Now, that is only the first part of the arrangements,' she continued. 'The guests are scheduled to leave around five-thirty. As the ceremony is at three o'clock we should be through by then. At eight-thirty everyone is returning, because I'm giving a ball that night.'

John nodded happily. He was used to this sort of thing. He frequently did the flowers for a wedding that was followed by a party at night. All that was required was perhaps to replace a few wilting blooms if it was a hot day, and spray the arrangements with water. Before he could say anything Morgan started talking again.

'The theme of the ball is a Night in the Jungle. I want the whole place completely transformed into a jungle setting, with banks of exotic plants, trailing orchids, cornucopias of fruit and lots and lots of stuffed animals. I mean like lions and tigers and monkeys and maybe a few real birds in bamboo cages or something! And we should have special lanterns of course – and maybe you could light some of the plants from behind? What do you think? It's a fantastic idea, isn't it? I can just see it now, it will be the party of the year!'

'We are talking about the same day?' John faltered, eyes goggling.

'Of course! There would be no point having it any other day! We are going to have a wonderful supper with things like passion fruit sorbets, and roasted wild boar. I'm also thinking of having a snake charmer to amuse the guests and a steel band for dancing.' Morgan suddenly noticed John looking at her strangely. 'Don't worry, Mr Plested, money is no object. I want my son to have a memorable christening.'

It might have been Joe Kalvin talking.

John swallowed several times. Then he started making rapid notes on his clipboard.

'It won't affect you, Mr Plested, but I'm going to have a video film made of the ceremony and the ball at night. Of course I'm planning to fly Norman Parkinson over from Tobago to take the formal photographs.'

Of course.

To Morgan, nothing constituted a problem. If you had the money, you got the best. Other people were being paid to sort it all out.

Armed with pages of notes John Plested departed. She didn't even notice his glazed expression as she turned to thoughts of suitable godparents.

Joe and Ruth Kalvin were of course flying over for the occasion and had decided to stay at Claridge's again. What really annoyed Morgan was Tiffany's refusal to attend. Surely her sister wanted to see David, now that he was an enchanting three-month-old baby? Had she no interest in him? Really, fumed Morgan, Tiffany could be quite exasperating at times. Nobody spoke about Zachary these days. He was out on bail and had been sent to a clinic in Maryland from which he would not be able to escape.

The biggest blow came to Morgan when the old Duchess informed Harry in lofty terms that she would not be attending because she and Andrew would be 'fishing in Scotland at that time'.

'Fishing my ass!' stormed Morgan when she heard. 'It's a deliberate insult. What on earth will people think?'

Harry looked perturbed. Not only would it look bad, it must also mean that his mother still believed the baby wasn't his.

'Well?' demanded Morgan. 'What are you going to do about it? She's got to attend, not that I particularly want her there, but if she took space in the personal column of *The Times* to announce how much she hates me, she couldn't be insulting me more!'

'I'll talk to her again, or maybe I'll talk to Andrew. He can usually get round her.'

'Huh!'

'I can't do more than that, Morgan. If she won't come, she won't come. We'll just have to make some excuse or something.'

'Nobody treats me like this!' Morgan's green eyes narrowed and quite suddenly it struck Harry that the kitten he had married had turned into a cat.

Then something happened that momentarily put everything else out of her mind. She received a cable from Joe. As always it was short and terse. Joe had so many people to inform of the sudden event that had taken place the previous day that he decided it would be quicker to get his secretary to inform everyone in the same fashion.

Ripping open the envelope Morgan gasped as she read:

PLEASED TO INFORM YOU THAT TIFFANY MARRIED AXEL KRASNER THIS MORNING STOP JOE KALVIN.

25

'How does it feel to be Mrs Axel Krasner?'

Tiffany looked up at Axel with shining eyes, and flung her arms round his neck.

It was the second day of their honeymoon at the Mark Hopkins Hotel.

'It's the most wonderful feeling in the world,' she replied kissing the deep cleft in his chin. 'I just wish I'd met you ten years ago!'

'And got me run in for child molesting?' He threw back his head and laughed and she could feel the laugh rumbling deep in his broad chest. She pressed closer to him.

'I'm so happy now, darling,' she said simply.

Axel gazed into her eyes tenderly. 'I'm glad. I'm happy too,' he replied. Then his arms tightened round her and he grinned. 'Hey, we didn't fly all the way to San Francisco for our honeymoon just to stand gazing at the Golden Gate, and do nothing but talk! Let's hit the sack, sweetheart, remember we can do it legally now!'

They missed dinner that night and very nearly breakfast the next morning.

During the ensuing week Tiffany realized she'd forgotten what happiness was. For the first time in what seemed like years she felt vibrantly alive, aware of every part of her body, seeing and feeling with a clarity she had never before experienced. Axel was hers for life and she couldn't believe her luck. She kept twisting the wide gold wedding ring he had given her, as if it was a symbol of her new-found security, and she revelled in the knowledge that whatever happened in the future she would have someone to share it with. No more solitary hours waiting for Hunt and wondering if he'd turn up at all, no pang of emptiness when he left to go back to his wife. No more contact with Morgan. No more nightmares about the baby. Tiffany blinked quickly, suppressing the threatening tears that always sprang to the surface when she thought about the baby. It was something she had to put to the back of her mind, especially as Axel had been so understanding when she'd told him she'd had a child that had been adopted. Tiffany never said who the father was, and he never asked. She never told him who had the baby now. It wasn't necessary. Axel had just listened quietly, nodding in agreement when she said her parents must never know. Then he had taken her in his arms and held her close. If she felt a pang of guilt at not having told him the whole story, she reminded herself that he had told her nothing about his past, and a man of thirty-four had to have a past. It was as if, by unspoken mutual agreement, they had both decided to forget everything that had happened to them before they met. Start with a clean slate and don't bring the hang-ups from previous relationships into this marriage, Tiffany decided.

Axel also asked her to become a partner in Axelance, and help him set up the new operations in San Francisco and Los Angeles. She would be in charge of the design concept while he looked after the business side. Thrilled, Tiffany offered to invest some of her own money in the new projects, as Joe had already agreed that Quadrant Inc. would be the main backers. On a strictly business arrangement, she insisted. Joe agreed. He respected Axel's business acumen and he liked the way he and Tiffany wanted independence. It was how he had started and he wished them luck.

Now in San Francisco, on the fourth day of their honeymoon, they set out to look for a good site for their second club, in the Fillmore district.

Almost immediately they found exactly what they were looking for, a disused cinema that lent itself perfectly for conversion into a large bar area with adjoining restaurant, and a dance floor big enough to accommodate twelve hundred people.

'Jesus!' exclaimed Axel, taking a notebook out of his breast pocket. 'If the price is right we're in business!' He started to jot down figures for conversion, refitting, and expected overheads. Then he worked out a nightly turnover based on a thousand people. The profit margin was much better than he thought.

'Say, Tiff! This is really terrific. Tiff? Where have you gone?' He looked round the gloomy interior with its rows of musty red velvet seats and abandoned air.

'Tiff!'

'Over here, honey.'

He found her wandering about the stage, behind the mouldering curtains. Her eyes were glowing.

'Listen, Axel,' she cried excitedly. 'I've come up with the most wonderful idea!'

'Let's have it then?' He looked at her quizzically. Tiffany's ideas always amused him, they sounded so far out but somehow they usually worked.

'Let's have a giant screen here, one that will fill the whole proscenium, and then with back projection, create amazing effects linked to the light show! Imagine if we had a film made of a journey through the galaxy as seen from a spaceship, so that people would really feel they were travelling in outer space. And we could have a rotating dance floor – or a moving one like those airport walks –'

'And waiters dressed as sputniks, I suppose?' Axel said, laughing. 'And the disc jockey . . . a little green man from Mars? Does the coffee come on flying saucers? Oh, Tiff, you're wonderful!' He wiped his eyes, then went off into another paroxysm of laughter.

Tiffany laughed too. 'It is an idea though, honey. We have to come up with something different, there's so much competition!'

Axel put his arm round her shoulders. 'Of course we do,

sweetheart!' He started to giggle again. 'We could have the bar staff hung up on wires, floating around in space-suits too, trying – trying to dispense drinks...' Overcome with laughter, he sank onto one of the cinema seats.

Axel spent the next few days trying to strike a deal with the owners, Meridian Film Distributors. They were glad to get rid of the place, and contracts were quickly exchanged. Axel got it for eighty thousand dollars less than he had expected to pay.

Tiffany set to work on the designs. It had become a working honeymoon, but she couldn't have been happier.

It definitely beat going solo every time.

Hunt could hardly believe his eyes. The newsprint seemed to blur as stabs of jealousy attacked him, crippling him with rage and misery.

Tiffany – *his* Tiffany – had gone and got herself married!

He read the piece in the *Los Angeles Times* again, more slowly this time, and a sick cramp clutched at his stomach.

If it had been an old friend like Greg, whom he knew she often saw – an old family friend – then he could have understood – perhaps. He'd have told himself she had married for companionship and security because she felt lonely. Especially if, as the gossips said, she'd had a nervous breakdown. But this Axel Krasner! Who the fuck was he? Hunt covered his face with his hands. He felt deeply betrayed. She hadn't even told him what she was going to do. Tiffany belonged to him. She was his love, his happiness, his life. Past tense. She had *been* his love and he'd been the one to split. She was free to do as she goddamn wanted. His thoughts raced back to the last time they'd been together. How could she have married someone else so soon? Hunt crashed his fist on the desk and uttered a silent oath. Always, but always, he thought, he'd had this deep inner conviction that he and Tiffany would end up together. Somehow. His eyes strayed to the script for the next episode of *Street*

Echoes. He'd been so sure Tiffany would follow him to Los Angeles. That offer from Magnima Films should have been irresistible to any young costume designer. But not to Tiffany, it seemed.

Slowly he picked up the script and tried to concentrate. But all he saw was Tiffany in the arms of another man.

An hour later he drove his new Isuse Impulse into the parking lot of a seedy bar in Pasadena where no one would know him. The day had become a wipe-out. He entered, and going to the bar, ordered a large whisky. He gulped it down, shuddering as he felt his toes curl. Bitterness was like bile in his mouth and misery hung round him like a vapour. He was determined to get drunk. It was all he could think of to soften the hard edge of pain that was like a spear in his heart. Swallowing the second whisky he ordered a third. With a blank expression, the barman set the glass down in front of him.

Some time later, he wasn't sure how much later, a vague thought began to insinuate itself into his mind. He tried to grab hold of it but it slid away again, then it came to him again and somehow this time he caught hold of it. He leaned across and grabbed the barman's arm.

'D'you know what?' he slurred. 'I know why my wife drinks so much!'

The barman looked at him, not answering.

'She drinks so much because . . .' The thought was slipping away from him again and he had to struggle to hold it. 'She drinks so much because . . . because . . . she's so fucking unhappy! Gimme another.'

When the drink arrived he was hit by a wave of self-pity that obliterated all thoughts of Joni. With a shaking hand he raised the glass and peered at the deep amber liquid. His jaw clenched and unclenched fiercely. He really wished he could find it in his heart to drink to Tiffany's happiness.

'So how's married life?' asked Joe when Tiffany and Axel

sat down to dine with them a few weeks later.

'Wonderful, Daddy,' cried Tiffany smiling radiantly.

'Sure is! Everyone should try it,' said Axel smiling at Tiffany. 'You and Ruth must be coming up to your thirtieth anniversary soon, aren't you? Well, I don't have to try and convert the converted, do I?' he laughed.

There was an uneasy silence in the Kalvin dining room.

'Not quite yet,' said Joe a little heavily. 'Another two years to go. I must say you're both looking very well. You've put on a bit of weight, Tiffany. It suits you! I never could stand skinny women. How's the San Francisco operation going, Axel?' Joe preferred to talk about nice safe subjects like business.

'We should be ready to open in three or four months,' Axel replied. 'We've seen the architect's drawings, and Tiffany has just finished the designs . . .'

While the men talked Ruth insisted on giving Tiffany a blow-by-blow account of David's christening. And what a sweet good baby he was. So pretty. Slept so well. Gaining weight. Tiffany wanted to scream.

'I must show you the photographs after dinner,' Ruth announced. 'He's the image of Morgan, a real green-eyed blond! Of course you and Zachary were like that too when you were babies. David certainly takes after my side of the family.' She lowered her voice so Joe would not hear the last part.

The agony of seeing the photographs of little David was almost more than Tiffany could endure. Her mother had been right about one thing. He was a very pretty baby and his toothless grin was enchanting. Her eyes filled with tears so the images became blurred but she could not fail to see the look of triumph on Morgan's face as she held David in her arms. Tiffany dug her nails into the palms of her hands, fighting the desire to cry out, But he's my baby! I want him! I conceived him and gave him life and he's mine! But Ruth kept chattering on, the proud grandmother, unaware of the salt she was rubbing into the wounds.

At last it was time to leave. Tiffany made the excuse that they had to drop in to Axelance on the way home to see that the new manager was coping.

'Let's go and see how things are anyway,' said Axel as they got into their car. 'Spot checks keep everyone on their toes.'

When they arrived, a long line had formed on the pavement behind the red velvet rope, jostling to get in. Inside was a heaving mass of humanity, writhing under the dazzling light show, oblivious to everything except the loud pounding music. The maitre d' showed them to a table on the gallery running down one side of the dance floor that was always kept for unexpected VIPs.

Tiffany, sipping the glass of champagne that had magically appeared before her, saw Axel talking to the manager. From his expression he looked pleased, but the music was so deafening she couldn't hear a word. She gave up trying and instead watched the dancers. They were all young, sweating heavily in their trendy gear, and utterly mesmerized by their surroundings. It wasn't, she decided, her idea of fun.

When Axel joined her at the table, she shouted, 'Do you realize these kids will be stone deaf as well as tone deaf by the time they're forty!'

'Sorry, I can't hear you!' he yelled back.

Tiffany shouted, 'Forget it!'

He couldn't quite catch that either.

The music blared on relentlessly. The lights revolved and flashed and the atmosphere was stifling. Tiffany could feel the sweat gathering in her cleavage and running down her back, and her head began to ache. When Axel rose, saying he was going to check the previous night's figures, Tiffany tugged at his arm, pointed to her watch and made signs that she wanted to go home. He nodded in agreement. Then they pushed and shoved their way out into the street. By comparison it seemed empty and silent.

Tiffany turned to Axel and grinned. 'I'm sorry, darling, I

think I must be getting old! That's my first encounter with what they call the generation gap.'

'Poor old lady of twenty-five!' he chided her, teasing. 'I know I'm too damned old for this sort of thing, but with a turnover of a million dollars a year I can't afford to be! Here are the car keys.'

'I'd rather take a taxi, darling. You keep the car to come home.'

As he hailed a yellow cab, it struck Tiffany for the umpteenth time that she had married an extraordinarily handsome man. Like an athlete he stood with his feet apart and there was a wonderful animal-like grace and looseness about his body that she found a terrific turn-on.

A minute later a cab drew up to the kerb.

'I'll wait up for you,' she promised as he kissed her lightly on the cheek.

Back at the apartment she had a glass of chilled fruit juice, a deep hot bubble bath and got into bed with the latest Harold Robbins novel.

It was after one when the phone rang. Tiffany looked at it suspiciously. Late calls only meant bad news. Maybe it was Morgan ringing, but it was a bit early for her. She still got the different time zones mixed but it would be six o'clock in the morning in London. Reluctantly Tiffany lifted the receiver.

'Yes!' she said crisply.

'It's me, honey.' It was Axel. She relaxed and settled back on the lacy pillows.

'Hi, darling. How's it going?'

'I'm sorry, Tiff, but something has come up. I'm still at the club and we've got a problem with one of the barmen. I think he's had his hand in the till. I'll have to stay here and sort it out. Don't wait up for me, darling, it might take a little while.'

'Okay. Sure there's nothing I can do to help?' Tiffany asked.

'Not a thing, dear. You go to sleep and I'll get back as soon as I can.'

'See you later then. 'Bye, honey.'

''Bye, Tiff.' He hung up.

Tiffany turned out the bedside lamp and lay on her side, missing the warmth of Axel's presence. She closed her eyes and was just beginning to drift off to sleep when something clicked in her head, making her throw back the bedclothes and sit bolt upright, her eyes wide and startled. Axel had said he was talking from the club. How come, then, there had been no loud pounding music, no voices, in fact no noise of any kind in the background?

Hunt found one in the living room. Then he found another on the kitchen table. The third one he found in the bedroom. Empty bottles of vodka. Within seconds he spotted all the old tell-tale signs. Dirty glasses dumped all around the place, deposited at random and forgotten.

Joni was drinking again.

Hunt strode out to the pool where Gus and Matt, on vacation, were splashing about with a big rubber ball, and shrieking with laughter. Joni lay, covered in oil, on a deckchair, a glass of clear liquid with a slice of lemon in it by her side.

'Hi, honey,' Joni murmured without looking up.

'Hi, there!' Hunt sat down on one end of a marble garden seat. 'What's that you're drinking?' he added pleasantly.

'Mineral water. It gets so hot out here.' She reached for the glass and took a long swallow. As she was about to put it down on the tiled deck again, Hunt reached out for it. 'Hey...!' she cried.

Hunt took a small swig and made a wry face. 'For Christ's sake! Just as I thought, it's neat vodka, Joni!'

'It has some mineral water in it,' she said sulkily as she smoothed the oil into her thighs.

'I thought you'd quit!' Hunt flushed with sudden anger. 'I

really thought that this time you'd given up liquor.'

'A little drink on a hot day doesn't do any harm,' she whined. 'You drink! Why last night I saw you drinking Scotch.'

'I'm not an alcoholic.'

Their eyes met. Then Joni was on her feet in an explosion of temper.

'You fucking hypocrite!' she yelled. *You're* not an alcoholic! Well, hot damn for you then, buster! I'm not an alcoholic either. I can stop any time I damn well want to, but *if* I want a drink, I'll have one. Gimme back that glass, Hunt!'

Calmly Hunt tipped the contents into the pool and then set the glass on the table. Joni made to grab his arm but he stepped back beyond her reach.

'Listen, Joni.' His voice was quiet and calm.

'Don't you Joni me, you louse.' She was weeping now. 'It's all right for you – you're at the studios all day, while I'm stuck here with those damned kids! It's not fair! I should be doing something with my life, not just sticking at home all the time. I've got talent, real talent, and looks! I could have been big box-office if it hadn't been for you! What have you ever done for me? I'll tell you what you've done for me, you son of a bitch, all you've ever done for me is to make me pregnant and then leave me at home to look after your fucking kids!'

The silence round the pool was oppresive. Gus and Matt watched them with pinched pale faces and staring eyes. Then Joni started to sob. Great broken drunken sobs.

'That's enough,' snapped Hunt, more to himself than to her. He went over and tried to lift her to her feet but she struggled and broke away.

'Leave me alone, asshole!' she was yelling.

Then she stumbled into the house. Hunt stood still, looking after her. Suddenly Matt's voice piped, 'What's the matter with Mom?'

'She drinks too much,' remarked Gus succinctly. 'She should go back to that clinic.'

Hunt turned to look at his sons. They were growing up a damned sight too fast for their own good. Especially Gus.

'Your Momma isn't well,' he said firmly. 'She has an illness and she can't help herself.'

'Like I said,' insisted Gus confidently. 'She oughta go back to that clinic, 'cause she sure isn't much good as a mother.'

Hunt stayed up late that night, slouched on the garden seat by the pool. The dark water reflected the poolside lights and the humid night air hung around him like damp silk. He felt calmer now. The boys had finally gone to sleep after a rough session of trying to settle them. Gus had rampaged all over the house, being rude and refusing to eat his supper, and Matt had burst into tears every time anyone spoke to him. Joni of course was out for the count on top of their bed.

Hunt lit another cigarette. Then he reached for his drink. His mind was made up. Tomorrow he'd start divorce proceedings. By his reckoning if Gus and Matt couldn't have a mother they could relate to they'd be better off with no mother at all. Any more rows like the one earlier in the evening and the boys would end up psychos. He closed his eyes as if to blot out the ugly scene and the things Joni had said. He knew it was mostly the vodka talking, but you couldn't expect the boys to realize that. He remembered how Joni used to boast that self-confidence was her middle name. It should have been self-destruction. Hunt searched his mind trying to remember some half-forgotten idea he'd had a few weeks back. It had to do with Joni. He nodded to himself as it came back to him. That was it. Joni must have a lot of pain inside her that had to be deadened with liquor. Was it his fault? Suddenly it came to him and for a moment he felt very old. The answer was clear. It was no more his and Joni's fault than it had been his parents' fault. Some people were just wrong for each other. And no matter how much they might care for each other, or how hard they might try, the basic chemistry could never work. It was just one of those things. He was who he was and Joni was who she was, and there wasn't a damned thing that was going to alter that.

He rose stiffly and stretched, then walked slowly round the pool. The irony of it all hit him like a visible blow. Just as he was about to be free Tiffany had got herself tied up.

26

Miss Eileen Phillips was fixty-six years old and a virgin. For the past twenty-three years she had been secretary to Alastair Tennant. Before that she had been in the clerical department of St Augustus's Hospital, a post she was happy to relinquish when the distinguished doctor offered her the job. The pay was better, the hours shorter and the conditions more salubrious. She took a small flat in the St Marylebone area because she could then enjoy a pleasant walk to work.

Miss Phillips, whose father had been a clergyman, had led a very sheltered life. The only time she had been invited out by a man was when she was twenty-three and he had taken her to a promenade concert at the Albert Hall. The young man had taken her directly home afterwards and had left her on the doorstep feeling hungry. Somehow she had imagined they'd be having supper somewhere afterwards. No one had ever invited her out since. Her experience of sex remained within the closely written case histories Dr Tennant compiled on his hundreds of patients. She pored, spectacles perched on her nose, over the 'interesting' symptoms and complaints of the patients he treated and such phrases as 'premature ejaculation' and 'introverted womb' became as much a part of her vocabulary as eggs and bacon.

Sometimes the reports went further: 'Tight foreskin, recommend circumcision' – 'unable to reach orgasm without masturbation' – 'tight vagina, intercourse painful' – 'prefers use of vibrator.' At these Miss Phillips would squirm in her seat, wondering at the strange hot sensation that flooded her groin which only a cold bath would relieve.

Life went on contentedly for Miss Phillips until the

morning she arrived at 24 Harley Street and knew as she entered and saw the face of the chief receptionist that something was wrong.

'I have bad news for you, I'm afraid,' she was told.

She braced herself. She couldn't have been given the sack because Dr Tennant would have told her himself. What on earth *was* it?

The receptionist didn't keep her in suspense.

'Doctor Tennant had a heart attack in the night. I'm afraid he's dead.'

Quietly Miss Phillips went up to her little office and systematically telephoned all his patients, cancelling their appointments and referring them to another doctor. Then she tidied her already meticulously tidy desk and stared around the office vacantly. More than anything she was going to miss the three filing cabinets that held the case histories. They were like old friends. Some of them she knew by heart. Finally she arranged the pens and pencils neatly in the tray on her desk, and putting on her coat and hat, walked out of the building without a backward glance.

Eileen Phillips was in no hurry to get another job, although her savings were getting low. Each morning she went out and bought just enough food for herself and her cat. In the afternoons she knitted, watched television or read a book from the library. She never bought newspapers because the TV news broadcasts told her all she wanted to know. She never bought magazines either, they were an extravagant waste of money.

That changed on the day she went into her local shop to buy a carton of milk. Her life was never to be quite the same again.

Stacks of newspapers lay along a low shelf just inside the entrance. She looked idly at them. Then a headline caught her eye. It denounced private medicine and extolled the virtues of the hard-working National Health Service doctors, who provided medical care, free of charge, to all those who needed it. She looked closer. Harley Street was mentioned several times. Taking twenty pence out of her purse she bought the paper, noticing it was the *Daily Sketch*, and tucking it under her arm, took it home to read.

The article talked about the scandal of the privileged rich being able to consult equally rich doctors in private practice, whose job it should really be to look after the poor and needy. It went on to give examples of private patients who were able to pay for immediate treatment while others on the National Health often had to wait months, sometimes even dying as they waited. 'This scandal must be stopped,' screeched the *Daily Sketch*. Why should the rich get the best treatment? Why should these greedy doctors profit from it?

Incensed, Eileen Phillips reached for her pad of writing paper and began to pen a letter criticizing the article in no uncertain terms. She cited her years of working for a private practitioner, and of the individual care and treatment of the patients. She wrote about the benefits of personal interest in patients, which could only happen in private practice. She then went on to mention the well-known patients her late boss had treated. Politicians, leaders of industry, film stars, socialites, company directors, pop stars . . . and she added that these people *needed* the swift treatment they required, regardless of money. With a feeling of deep self-righteousness, she wanted to put the record straight. Dr Tennant should be remembered for the wonderful service he had given to the rich community. Loyally, she thought he deserved nothing less.

Burning with indignation she finally covered eight pages in her small neat handwriting. Then she went out and posted her letter to the editor of the *Daily Sketch.*

Two days later she received a telephone call from a journalist who called himself Jeff Mackay. He said he was from the *Sketch* and that the editor had been so interested in her letter that he had asked Jeff to have a talk with her.

Flustered and flattered she agreed he could come and see her that afternoon.

A week later she had signed a contract for thirty thousand pounds to 'write' her memoirs, providing she agreed to name names – and give case histories. The 'interesting' ones. Jeff Mackay was to ghost the three-part serial and all she had to do was to sit with him for several days, talking into a tape recorder. It soon became clear she easily had enough material to fill a book. Riveting stuff, thought Jeff, as the piles of tapes mounted.

Out poured the names and dates of when famous patients had come to Dr Tennant's office with their complaints. She mentioned in detail their ailments too, from required abortions to social diseases, from the titled lady who had a bronze figurine of Napoleon wedged up her vagina to a well-known homosexual actor whose boyfriend had stuck an electric light bulb up his arse.

Twenty-three years of confidentiality was bursting its bank in a torrent of anecdotes. She was convinced that the articles would prove without doubt the need for private medicine, and the goodness of Dr Alastair Tennant.

'Then one of our patients was the Marchioness of Blairmore,' Miss Phillips was saying. Jeff pricked up his ears. That was another name he knew well. She was always in the press. Her husband had recently succeeded to his father's title, so that would make her a duchess now.

'Oh yes?' said Jeff conversationally, remembering the christening photographs that had appeared a few months back. 'Was that one of the famous society babies Alastair Tennant delivered?'

Eileen Phillips looked at him, a puzzled expression on her face. 'No, it was very sad, really. She was unable to have children. I remember the notes on her clearly. She had a malformed uterus, which was discovered during tests for a suspected ovarian cyst. She was barren. There was nothing Dr Tennant could do for her.'

Jeff Mackay was thoughtful for the rest of the afternoon. With instinct bred from years of working on Fleet Street he was catching the whiff of a scandal. He didn't know he was on the trail of a *cause célèbre.*

27

Morgan felt she was right on course for the first time since she'd married Harry.

The christening and the party afterwards had set the seal on her prowess as a leading hostess and now the rewards were coming in thick and fast.

Charities asked her to open their bazaars and be guest of honour at their functions. *Vogue* wanted to photograph her 'At Home' in a range of designer-made clothes. *House and Garden* magazine wanted to photograph Drumnadrochit Castle, with Harry and herself with the baby in the foreground. She was invited on a television talk show to discuss entertaining and *Tatler* Magazine asked if they could feature her in the outfits she had chosen for Royal Ascot. Already *Town and Country* and *Woman's Wear Daily* had run colour spreads on 'the stylish American duchess'.

Wherever she went and whatever she did, the media regarded her as a cross between a semi-royal and a pop star, and they loved her and the way she co-operated. But not as much as Morgan loved them. To be the centre of attention was like balm to her soul, and like adrenalin to an actress. She pored over her clippings, glowing with pleasure, and stuck them in large calf-bound albums.

Harry hated all the publicity. He said it was vulgar and cheap and it was bad form to show off. He had to admit however that business in the gallery was booming. Morgan attracted the rich international connoisseurs of art and Harry's turnover increased from three million dollars a year to seven. He just wished it could all be achieved in a much quieter way and that they didn't have to socialize so much. Every night they went to a dinner or a couple of cocktail parties, a reception or a ball. On the nights they were at home Morgan invited at least ten people to dinner.

'We're not seeing enough of David,' Harry complained one day when Morgan told him they were spending the weekend with Prince and Princess Fritz of Luxembourg at their Gloucestershire manor house. 'You, at least, should spend more time with him, Morgan.'

'Don't be silly, honey! I see him every morning and the rest of the time he's either sleeping or being pushed around the park by Nanny – or being fed or something,' she added lamely.

'Why don't *you* take him to the park, or even bathe him? A baby needs his mother you know. He'll grow up being more fond of his nanny than he is of you. I know I did! I'm sure if my mother had cared more for me when I was small we'd have a better relationship now. Anyway, I don't want to go away this weekend.'

'Harry' – there was a warning note in her voice – 'we have to go. This is an important weekend. You know who their neighbours are, don't you?'

Harry looked vague.

Morgan sighed in exasperation. 'Only half the Royal Family! Princess Anne and her husband and Prince and Princess Michael of Kent – they all live around there. David will be fine with Nanny. He's only four months old you know, too young to know whether we're here or not! If he were five or six years old it might be different, but it's crazy to stay in London all weekend when we could be at a country house party. Anyway, Nanny doesn't like his routine being disturbed.'

Harry shook his head. 'I think it's all wrong, and you're being terribly old fashioned! Nobody palms their children off on nannies these days. And it's not as if you had a job or anything.'

Stung, Morgan turned to look at him, a slow flush creeping up her cheeks. 'I *do* have a job! Look what's happening to the gallery since we started going around! In a year or two it will be internationally famous, a leading gallery, instead of the leisurely little back street outfit it was when I first met you.'

'I'd hardly call Duke Street "a little back street",' he said sarcastically. 'All the leading galleries are there.'

'Oh, you know what I mean. We're getting into the big time, now. Isn't that what you want?'

A dreamy look came into Harry's eyes and he didn't answer.

'Well, isn't it?'

Then he looked at her with a gentle smile, hoping she would understand.

'Not really, darling,' he replied. 'It's all right for the moment but I don't want to do it forever. You see I originally went into partnership with John because I had to have some sort of job. But I knew that when the day came that I succeeded Pa, I'd have the estates to run and have a lot more responsibility. What I really want to do is to become a silent partner in the gallery and live at Drumnadrochit. I want David brought up there too. It's a wonderful place for a child, Morgan, I don't think you've any idea how wonderful it is. He can have a pony and a dog of his own. I'll teach him to fish and shoot and swim in the loch. I want David to be brought up in the country, to learn the right values and to have the wonderful experience of running wild.'

Morgan looked at him aghast. If Harry had said he wanted David to be an astronaut she couldn't have been more horrified.

'You've got to be kidding!' she cried.

'No.' Harry looked at her innocently, something he was very good at when he wanted to pretend he didn't understand. 'I'm not kidding. I was brought up at Drumnadrochit, and the only time I ever came to London was in the school holidays, to go to the dentist or be fitted out for Eton or something. I never actually lived in London until I came down from Oxford.'

'You'll be burying the child alive if you make him spend all his time in Scotland,' Morgan cried hotly. 'He'll end up an unsophisticated boor!'

'Thank you very much!' Harry gave her his crooked smile.

'No, I mean it, darling! *You're* not a boor but times have changed. David must be taken to exhibitions and the theatre. He must go to dancing classes, and he must make some nice friends. Who the hell is he going to play with in Scotland?'

'The best times I ever had as a child were with Ben. His father was one of our crofters and they lived in a little cottage on the estate. We got up to some great larks, Ben and I, climbing trees, exploring caves, sometimes helping to herd the sheep and cattle. I remember he had a marvellous Collie dog called Rory.'

Morgan went over to the drinks tray and mixed herself a very dry martini. She needed it. Her plans for David included trips to Paris when he was older, and Rome, Florence and Venice. There would also be long holidays on Long Island and visits to New York and Washington, and always – wherever he went – the opportunity to meet influential people. A crofter's son indeed!

'Well, it's silly to argue about this now, my darling,' she said lightly, after she had swallowed her first martini in one gulp. 'David's only a few months old. There's masses of time to decide. Meanwhile I must go and change. Don't forget we're dining with the Nicholsons tonight. I believe the Prime Minister is going to be there.' Morgan poured herself another martini and left the room.

A few minutes later, as she was selecting what she would wear, she heard Harry slipping up to the nursery. It was half an hour before he reappeared.

*

All too soon for Morgan, the grouse-shooting season started again and Harry became as excited as a small boy. Especially at the prospect of taking his tiny son up to Scotland. As far as she was concerned weekends were long enough. She liked to fly up on Friday evening and fly back again Sunday night. Now she was to be stuck up there for several weeks. All she could do was to use it as an opportunity to entertain. Harry didn't object as long as the men were good shots.

Things had changed at Drumnadrochit since the previous year when the old Duke had been alive. For one thing the Dowager Duchess stayed away – this time she said she had heavy commitments in London. Andrew Flanders was not even asked.

Morgan, now in sole charge, decided to do it Her Way. The staff were instructed in a whole new routine. Breakfast in bed was to be suggested to those who would like it. All the women accepted with alacrity but none of the men. Luncheon at the hunting lodge was now to take the form of a barbecue, and be very informal. Dinner, on the other hand, was to be ultra-formal with all the silver and crystal on display, no less than five courses, and everyone changed into evening dress. Afterwards guests could dance in the hall, watch the latest movie in the library or drink and gossip in the drawing room. The only game played was to be Trivial Pursuit. Even more important to Morgan's tranquillity was the fact that the bagpipes would be played for only half an hour, during cocktail time in the evening. Never again was she going to allow the still of the morning to be shattered by the wailing shrillness of 'Over the Sea to Skye'.

She had also had the large storeroom next to the wine cellar converted into a sauna, complete with jacuzzi, wall-to-wall smoked mirrors and a bar.

Flowers and perfumed lights, soft music and the scent of pot-pourri arranged in great Chinese porcelain bowls, now permeated the rugged grey building. From the ramparts flew a flag bearing the Lomond arms, to show that the family was in residence.

To Morgan, Drumnadrochit Castle now resembled the comfortable palatial country seat of her dreams, where she could dispense lavish hospitality and impress her friends. Harry's old friends, when they were invited, went into shock but had to admit, in giggled whispered conversation when they were alone, that flashy and tasteless though it all was, it was great fun being pampered with such magnificent vulgarity.

The castle staff and the people in the village two miles away had something else to say. Especially when Joe and Ruth Kalvin flew over for a short visit.

Joe, in a loud checked suit, dropping cigar ash everywhere, revelled in every square metre, from the crenellated ramparts and turrets to the mullioned windows with their view of Loch Ness and the land beyond. He eyed the property with awe, wondering, admiring, touching and mentally adding up the assets. It might have cost him a fortune in the form of Morgan's dowry to put the crumbling old joint into shipshape order, but by God, it was a showplace now. This was real real estate.

Joe proceeded to take hundreds of photographs to show back home and insisted on having one taken of himself standing in front of the great fireplace in the hall beside the carved and gaudily painted Lomond coat of arms. He looked at it longingly. Maybe he would fix something like it for himself, to go in the Park Avenue duplex.

A few days after the Kalvins had returned to New York, Morgan was on her way to the jacuzzi one morning when Nanny stopped her in the corridor outside her room.

'May I have a word with you, your grace?' The nanny, a pleasant fresh-faced woman in her fifties, looked distinctly ill at ease.

'Yes, Nanny. Is there something wrong with David?'

'Oh no, he's fine. He's asleep in his pram outside.' She

smoothed her starched apron with nervous hands.

'Well?' Morgan's voice held a trace of impatience.

'Could we perhaps talk in private? I wouldn't want to be overheard,' whispered the nanny, glancing down to the hall below.

'Very well. Come into my room.' Morgan tightened the sash of her terrycloth robe and led the way back into her bedroom. She shut the door then turned and looked at the nanny. 'Well, what is it?'

'I – I don't really know how to say this, your grace . . . and I hope you won't think I'm talking out of turn, but . . . but . . .' she twisted her hands together in an agony of embarrassment and stared down at the carpet.

'For goodness sake, what's the matter?'

My God I hope she doesn't want to leave, Morgan thought in panic, *not with all the entertaining I'm doing.*

'It's – it's about the housekeeper, Mrs Monroe. I'm not one for telling tales, but I thought it my duty to tell you. Sh – she's been saying things.'

'What sort of things?'

'Nasty things, gossip. If I may say so I think she should be stopped. She's a very dangerous woman.'

'Nanny, tell me exactly what she has been saying. That I've made a lot of changes here? That it's not the same as it was in the old days? That I've spent a lot of money doing up the place? That sort of thing?'

'Well, that sort of thing. Spending a lot of money, yes. Wasting it, she said, but that isn't it. Sh-she's saying that the goings-on here are something dreadful! She says everyone who comes to stay is carrying on with everyone else. "A den of iniquity", she called it, and she even said . . .' Nanny's voice broke and a tear dashed off her rosy cheek.

'And what else?' Morgan's voice was tense and cold.

'She even said . . . you and your sister were sharing the Duke!' Nanny bobbed her head up and down unable to continue, while Morgan looked at her, her green eyes sharp with fear.

'She said that?'

'Yes, your grace, she said she was on the landing one night when your sister was staying and she – she saw ...' The nanny sank into a chair, unable to look at Morgan.

28

Three times now in the past ten days Axel hadn't got back to the apartment until three in the morning. Last night it had been nearly four. He'd crept in, undressed in the bathroom and slipped silently into bed beside Tiffany. Within a few seconds he'd been fast asleep. Tiffany turned away from him, miserable with disappointment and worry. Axelance seemed to be taking up all his time these days and she hated the nights he went out after dinner, leaving her to go to bed alone. Unloved. It was all too reminiscent of her time with Hunt.

An hour later she was still awake.

She got out of bed and, putting on her robe, walked silently along the corridor to her studio to have another look at her finished designs for *Gertie*. They looked good. Even at five o'clock in the morning they looked good. She was particularly pleased with the costumes she'd designed for Paula Grant, who was to play the part of Gertrude Lawrence. Picking up a pencil, Tiffany made a few adjustments to the sketches. Soon she was absorbed in her work.

By eight o'clock she was showered and dressed and having breakfast. A few minutes later Axel joined her, sleepy-looking and unshaven.

'Christ, I'm tired,' he groaned as he sat down on the chair opposite her. 'Thank God tomorrow's Sunday.'

'You were late last night,' Tiffany remarked as she poured his coffee.

'You can always come to the club with me, if you want to,' he replied defensively, as he reached for a fresh flaky croissant. 'But I thought you hated the noise?'

'I do hate the noise, because it makes conversation

impossible, but I hate being on my own more! Why do you have to stay so late? And you can deal with the business side during the day, can't you? So what's with all this night stuff?'

'Watch it, Tiff!' There was an edge to his voice. 'You're starting to sound like a wife!'

Tiffany looked at him, hurt in her eyes.

'I'm sorry, honey,' she said instantly. 'It's just that I don't see why it's necessary.'

'It's necessary all right! Let those assholes down there think I'm not watching them all the time and standards will slip. Give me some more coffee, will you?' He passed her his cup.

Silently, Tiffany poured out more coffee.

'You do see, don't you, Tiff?'

'What happens when we open in San Francisco and Los Angeles? Do you jet around taking in each club every third night?' She meant it as a joke. Instead of laughing Axel rose abruptly from the table and without a word stormed out of the room. A few minutes later she heard him in the shower.

Tiffany felt uneasy. It was unlike Axel to act this way. When they'd first been married he'd wanted her by his side all the time. That was why she'd become a partner in Axelance, to be involved, to help him make decisions, to plan the future operations.

Now he stayed out more and more, especially at night. She sat at the breakfast table trying to quell the frightened, insecure feeling she had.

The memory of that first night, when he'd said he was calling from the club and yet there hadn't been a sound in the background, kept coming back to her. The next time she'd been to the club she'd checked on where the phones were situated. One was in the entrance vestibule, another was behind the bar and the third was in the tiny office leading off the bar. She'd tried all three. The music had deafened her at every one.

Axel came back into the room, his hair damp, a dark blue towel wrapped round his hips. He bent over and kissed Tiffany.

'I'm sorry, honey,' he said briefly.

Tiffany caught his hand and pressed it to her cheek. It was such a strong hand and the lovely clean smell of soap still lingered on his skin.

'I didn't mean to make you angry, darling,' she said in a small voice. 'I love you so much, and I just miss you when you're not around.'

'Forget it, honey! The trouble is I'm not used to married life yet. I've been on my own for so long it's made me selfish. I don't seem to have learned anything about sharing and really being with someone all the time. That comes from too many casual relationships. I'm sorry, but you'll have to teach me,' he added earnestly, kissing the top of her head.

Tiffany rose and cupped his face lovingly in her hands. 'I have a lot to learn too. I've been basically living on my own since I was eighteen, that's probably why I'm over the top on the togetherness bit!'

'You've a right to be, Tiff, and I promise I'll try to work it so you either have no more lonely nights or I'll buy you some earplugs and drag you along with me! Hey, you could have rhinestone earplugs, with feathers sticking out! It could start a fad!'

Once again he was laughing and joking and Tiffany laughed too. He was so irresistibly funny and she liked it so much when he made her laugh.

The phone rang. Axel reached over and picked it up swiftly. Tiffany watched him as he spoke into it.

'Yes. She's here. Who is it?' he was asking. 'Hold on a moment.' Axel turned to her. 'It's for you. Someone called Jeff Mackay. Calling from London. Says he's on the *Daily Sketch*. Do you want to take it?'

Tiffany looked surprised. 'Yes, I'll take it,' she murmured, 'It's probably got something to do with *Gertie*. After all

Gertrude Lawrence was an English actress.'

Axel handed her the phone and left the room to get dressed.

Tiffany took a couple of seconds to compose her thoughts on the show then picked up the receiver.

'Hullo, this is Tiffany Kalvin-Krasner. Can I help you?'

Lunchtime, Saturday, in London. Tomorrow's *Sunday Sketch* was being put together. Jeff Mackay, sitting in his shirt sleeves, had exactly another two and a half hours in which to file his story. Absently, he lit another cigarette. As the smoke scorched his lungs a look of excitement settled on his face. This was page one stuff all right. He shuffled among the pile of clippings on his desk and looked at his notes again. Forty-three phone calls since yesterday morning and he'd got every fact verified. Not bloody bad, he admitted to himself. Thank God for his contacts in the States. Getting hold of the sister, Tiffany, had just about tied the whole thing up too.

Now he only had to make one more call.

He thumbed through his notes until he came to the telephone number for Drumnadrochit Castle.

Six hours later Jeff Mackay walked out of the newspaper offices and into Fleet Street. He made his way to El Vino.

Now he could afford to get drunk.

The banner headline ran: DUKE'S HEIR BORN OF SURROGATE MOTHER.

In sensational journalese, embellished with subtitles 'Scandal Rocks Society', 'Duke Deceived', 'Sisters Switched Places', the avid readers of the *Sunday Sketch* found something to shock and titillate them as they ate their breakfast.

Jeff's research had been thorough and inspired and his pursuit of the story carried out with relish.

Photographs of Morgan and the baby, Tiffany at the first night of *Glitz*, and one of Harry on the grouse moors filled page one.

Jeff had named names and quoted quotes. From all over the place.

Miss Eileen Phillips had let her imagination run riot as she described Morgan going 'very pale' when told she was barren. 'She was stricken! She had to produce an heir. It was a terrible blow.'

The doctor who delivered Tiffany of a baby in Vineland recalled 'the sister who sat up all night hoping it would be a boy'.

The night porter at the Algonquin had often seen Morgan going in and out just before the supposed birth. 'Naw,' he declared, 'there was nuttin' pregnant about that dame.'

Perkins said 'No comment' with monotonous regularity but Mrs Monroe, in contrast, had been happy to spill the beans all over the place. Jeff even got told a whole lot of information that wasn't relevant to the story, but he admitted it all made excellent background stuff.

Tiffany, caught unawares on the phone by Jeff Mackay, had fallen into the trap by saying in a stunned voice, 'How did you find out?' when he presented her with the full facts. Her first reaction had been to think it was some crazy stunt of Morgan's, but too late she realized she had been tricked. Her brain turned into a frozen block of panic and she stammered out enough to confirm to Jeff that his facts were correct.

When Jeff rang Morgan she tried to box cleverly. At first she denied everything. When he challenged her by saying Tiffany had admitted having the baby, Morgan let forth a string of expletives that shocked even Fleet Street-hardened Jeff.

'Where did you get hold of this story?' she shrieked into the phone.

When Jeff refused to reveal his sources she threatened to

bring an injunction against the *Sketch*, sue him personally, his editor, and the owner of the newspaper.

Jeff had foreseen this reaction.

He'd got the story passed by the legal department first and had delayed ringing Morgan until the last possible moment.

Even she realized she had run out of time.

The newspapers would be hitting the streets before she could do anything to stop it.

'How *could* you, you lousy bitch!' screeched Morgan into the phone, a few minutes after Jeff Mackay had rung her.

'Don't blame me! I got as big a shock as you did!' Tiffany yelled back. 'I haven't told a living soul what happened.'

'Do you realize you've ruined my life? When this story gets out I'm finished! Why the hell did you admit everything?'

'Listen, Morgan, *he* told *me* all the facts, everything down to the last detail. I didn't have to tell him anything. He *knew*!'

'But you went ahead and admitted it, didn't you? Didn't you realize he was setting a trap? All reporters do that when they want something confirmed. Jesus Christ, how could you have been such a damn fool!'

'He had enough evidence to print the story without even having to talk to me! That is if he can get it passed by the paper's legal department.'

'He already has,' said Morgan in despair.

'Then there's nothing we can do.'

'Oh my God, what am I going to do, Tiff? Help me. What am I going to do?' Morgan was shaking so much she could hardly hold the phone. 'I called a lawyer I know in London a few minutes ago but he said it was too late to take any action. What am I going to say to Harry?'

'Doesn't he know yet? Where is he?'

'He's out. Oh Jesus, I'm scared, this is just terrible! How could that reporter have found out?'

'Someone obviously tipped him off, probably someone with a grudge.' Tiffany didn't add 'against you'.

'It must have come from New York then, because absolutely nobody here *could* know. I always talked to you on my private line, I didn't confide in a soul. *You* must have told someone what was going on. You've got such strange friends, Tiff, and when they found out who I was, they must have sold the story.'

'Nobody I know *cares* who you are,' Tiffany replied grimly, 'and I didn't tell anyone either. Not Gloria, not my neighbour Bette in Vineland, absolutely no one. Oh, Morgan, I told you from the start it was a crazy idea.'

'Don't talk to me like that, you were in it too!' blazed Morgan, forgetting that it was she who had forced her sister to co-operate. She flung aside a nearby chair and it crashed to the floor. 'It's all right for you! You've nothing to lose, but I'm finished! What will people say, for God's sake? Oh, I could kill that rotten reporter. I'm going to sue, I'm going to make him wish he'd never been born! Why should I be victimized by some fucking guttersnipe like that?'

Tiffany was silent on the other end of the line.

'Tiff? Are you there – why don't you answer? What am I going to do?'

Tiffany spoke quietly and there was a lot of pain in her voice. 'You'll have to do what I've just done. Tell your husband the whole story and hope he stands by you.'

'Are you crazy? Your husband's a nobody, a jumped-up cowboy who runs a disco, what does it matter to him? Harry's a duke, a peer of the realm, we have a position to keep up and – Oh my God, I've just realized something!'

'What?'

'David won't be able to inherit now! Everyone will know he's a bastard!' Morgan started to sob with rage.

The receiver in her hand clicked. Tiffany had rung off.

'Goddamned bitch!' Morgan screamed, flinging the instrument onto the floor.

*

Tiffany put down the phone and threw herself into Axel's arms.

'That was *awful*!' she sobbed. 'All Morgan cares about is what's going to happen to her – and the fact that the baby can't inherit now.'

Axel held her close and stroked her hair. 'What *is* going to happen now, Tiff?'

Tiffany dried her tears with the back of her hand and looked unhappily at him. 'God knows! She hasn't even told Harry yet. She's threatening to sue the newspaper. How the hell did the reporter find out about everything? Morgan says it's going to be in the papers tomorrow. Oh, it's such a mess! I just hope it doesn't get into the press here, for your sake! It will kill Daddy too! Just imagine what he's going to say.'

'It's bound to get out, sweetheart. You're well known in this town and so is your father, and as for Morgan, you haven't been able to pick up a magazine for months without seeing her plastered all over it!'

'I wish I'd told you the truth before we married. I mean about Harry being the father,' Tiffany said regretfully. 'I feel awful about it now.'

'It's okay, honey. You obviously had your reasons for wanting to help your sister have a baby, and of course I can understand how upset you must be that your son, I mean, her son . . .' he broke off awkwardly.

'David,' Tiffany finished the sentence for him. Then she gave a wan smile. 'You're right. I never wanted David to find out when he grew up that I was his real mother. Think of what that could do to a child! And how is he going to feel when he's older and realizes that Morgan is really his aunt?'

As Tiffany grasped each new implication of the story getting out, her despair increased. 'After all this, how can I ever see him again? Or Harry for that matter? Do you know something, Axel? Two years ago we were an amazingly happy family, that is as families go. Zachary was at college and we thought he was doing fine. We all expected that one day he would join Quadrant, and now look at him! Locked up like a prisoner in a clinic he may never be well enough to leave. Morgan was engaged to Greg, and quite happy about it before she went on that trip to England. Then she got bitten by some fearful social climbing bug! Mom and Daddy were going along quite happily too! And I didn't think I had a secret in the world that mattered. And look at us now?' She flung out her hands in a gesture of helplessness.

'Cheer up,' Axel pulled her closer. 'Families have survived worse crises than this – and got over them. Zachary is having treatment. That at least is something. Morgan and Harry will just have to work things out for themselves. It can't be *your* problem, Tiff! You did something that was supposed to save their marriage, according to Morgan. It was a crazy scheme but you nearly pulled it off until this happened. There's nothing more you can do, sweetheart. You've got to ride out this storm, and it's not going to have the same devastating effect on you over here as it is on Morgan in London, where the whole surrogate scene is under fire! We're just going to have to carry on with our lives. And have you ever known a happier couple than us? Well, have you?' He grinned at her.

Tiffany hesitated for a moment. Not because she didn't entirely believe him, but because she still had one secret from Axel and it was preying on her mind. She hadn't told him Joe was an embezzler and that Morgan had blackmailed her into having the baby by threatening to expose their father. For a moment she was torn between loyalty to her husband and loyalty to her father, and she suddenly found herself wondering if she could really trust Axel! The thought appalled her. Why the hell was she doubting him? Yet, there at the back of her mind, an alarm bell was ringing. *I don't know who he meets and who he talks to during those long nights when he's at the club! And yet he's being so incredibly understanding.*

'Of course we're happy, darling!' *This is my husband, for*

God's sake. Then she rested her head on his shoulder and hoped that if she sat tight, the whole thing would blow over.
But she knew it was wishful thinking.

Morgan paced the library in a frenzy, trying to think clearly. Her first instinct was to say nothing. They were isolated at Drumnadrochit and besides that they never normally took the *Sunday Sketch*. There was even the possibility that the newspaper's legal department would change their minds after her threats and say the story was too libellous to print. She ran her hands through her tangled and dishevelled hair and wound it up into a knot on top of her head. It was unbelievable that just when everything was going so perfectly, this should happen! How could it have got out?
Then, as a thought struck her, she clamped her hand over her mouth to stifle a scream. What had the nanny said? *Mrs Monroe saw your sister coming out of Harry's room one night*. And Mrs Monroe always had the *Sunday Sketch* delivered to the servants' hall!
Morgan felt great waves of hysteria and panic washing over her. Going over to the drinks tray she poured herself a tumbler full of whisky. It tasted foul but she had to do something to get a grip on herself before Harry returned from fishing. She took long deep breaths. It didn't help. Her mind was still tearing round in demented circles and her heart was hammering in her rib cage.
What should she do about Mrs Monroe? Panic immobilized her, turning her legs to jelly and making her head swim. She wouldn't do, couldn't do anything now.
An hour later Harry pounded unceremoniously into their bedroom, flushed and windblown from being out on the loch all afternoon.
'I'm back, Morgan!' he cried, making her wince at the loudness of his voice, as she lay on their ornately carved four-poster bed.

'I'm just going to pop up and see David before he goes to sleep. Join me in the shower before dinner?'

Morgan shook her head, avoiding his eyes. 'I've got a headache. I think I'll go to bed early and skip dinner, darling. I'm very tired.'

Harry looked at her in surprise. 'Why are you tired? You haven't done anything today!'

'I'm exhausted because we've had so many people to stay, not to mention Mom and Daddy. Entertaining is an awful strain you know.'

He shrugged. 'You asked them, not me! Anyway I must go up to David. Has he been good today?'

'He's been fine.'

'Okay. See you later.' He was gone. And she hadn't been able to tell him. Paralyzed by fear she rolled onto her side and pressing her face into the pillow she started to cry.

She was finished.

And there wasn't a damned thing she could do about it.

Sunday morning. Fitful sunshine slanted through the narrow windows of Drumnadrochit Castle after a night of gales and torrential rain. Harry crossed the hall on his way to the dining room with Angus and Mackie scampering round his feet, their tails wagging and their mouths slavering with joy.

'Good boy! Down, down, Mackie! There's a good fellow! I'll take you out in a minute.' Harry ran his hand across Mackie's head and tugged gently at the silky ear.

At that moment the telephone rang.

'Hullo. Yes. Oh Ma! How are you?'

'Have you seen the *Sunday Sketch*?' Lavinia Lomond asked without preamble.

'No, we don't take it. Why?'

'I think you had better get it today, Harry.'

'What's up, Ma?' Harry had never heard his mother's voice shake like this before and she sounded peculiar.

In a trembling voice the Duchess read aloud to him the story on page one.

'What the –!' he kept blustering. This must be another of her inventive lies to discredit Morgan. But this was really diabolical! He must stop her.

'Mother,' he said coldly. 'That's not funny. First you said Morgan had a lover and now you're trying to say –'

'Get Mrs Monroe to show you her copy if you don't believe me!' she rapped back. 'She always gets it. I'm not making this up, I assure you, Harry. There's a photograph of you, and one of Morgan –'

'God, I'll sue them! How *dare* they print such filth! If they think they can get away with this sort of thing ... it's libellous!'

'Harry!' cut in the Duchess. 'Listen to me carefully, Harry. After what I have to tell you, you might not be so ready to sue.'

There was a pause. 'What is it?' Harry asked.

'Somehow, whoever wrote this disgusting article got the wrong end of the stick. He probably had his suspicions about Morgan, as indeed so did I. I knew all along that she would go to any lengths to get you and any lengths to keep you! But the newspaper has got hold of the wrong story.'

'*Of course* it's got the story wrong! It's farcical! How could Tiffany possibly be David's mother? How could they make up such lies?'

'Harry, this is going to come as a shock to you,' his mother was saying and Harry could suddenly feel tiny prickles of fear creeping up his neck and over his crown.

'Well?' His voice sounded weak.

'What they are saying about Tiffany being the baby's mother *may* be true, but that's only part of the story. They haven't found out the *real* truth behind this whole thing. Only I know that. Now listen, Harry.'

When the Duchess had finished talking, Harry replaced the

receiver and stared at it for a long moment. He felt numb and sick. But this time he knew his mother was telling the truth and it was the most devastating thing he had ever had to accept.

As the full impact exploded in his brain, he let out a wrenching cry and fled across the hall, out through the heavy doors, and into the drive where his Saab Turbo was parked.

Morgan was looking out of her bedroom window at that moment and saw him fling himself into the car. A second later the motor screamed and Harry shot off down the drive, the tyres throwing up waves of gravel.

So he knew.

Leaning her forehead against the cold windowpane a rush of fear swept over her leaving her weak. She was gripped in a mental and physical daze, unable to move, unable to think. She stood there for a long time. Then tightening the belt of her white satin robe she made her way falteringly downstairs, fighting the weight of inertia that had suddenly descended upon her.

The hall was deserted. On the carved chest under the window lay copies of the *Sunday Times, Sunday Telegraph* and *Observer*, neatly arranged as always, by McGillivery. In the dining room Harry's breakfast was untouched. Automatically she poured herself some coffee. It was dark and bitter. Then she rang for the butler.

McGillivery appeared immediately.

'Do you have – has the *Sunday Sketch* arrived for Mrs Monroe?'

McGillivery studied the rug intently. 'I believe it has, your grace.'

'Will you bring it to me?'

'Very well, your grace.' He turned to leave the room.

'McGillivery.'

The butler turned back, still not looking up.

'Has the Duke seen it?'

'Not to my knowledge.'

'Then why –?' She hesitated painfully.

'His grace received a telephone call before he went out. I'm afraid I don't know who –'

'That's all right. Thank you.'

When he returned a minute later his face was a study in pale gravity as he handed her the neatly folded newspaper on a small silver tray.

Morgan waited until he had left the dining room before opening it. Then she sank onto one of the carved dining chairs.

It took only a minute to take in page one.

It was even worse than she'd imagined.

Harry had only one thought and that was to get away. What his mother had told him was quite different from the story printed in the *Sketch*. But why had she never told him before? What had she hoped to gain by keeping it from him all these years? He pressed his foot down hard on the accelerator and the car seemed to explode forward, straining on the wet road.

Dripping trees and tawny bracken, bowed by last night's storm, flashed past. He took the mountain road that lay west of Drumnadrochit and urged the Saab on, faster and faster up the winding track until he reached the moors. The wild desolation that lay around him matched his mood. He opened the window a few inches and felt an icy blast of air hit his cheek that felt clean and fresh.

He began to make the descent on the other side of the mountain. It was a winding road with sharp bends and Harry took them at eighty miles an hour. At the bottom the road straightened out for three miles until it came to a forest thickly planted with fir trees. Harry, pressing his foot down until it was flat on the floor, was oblivious of the speedometer needle touching a hundred. Through the dark tunnel of trees he swept forward, the road rushing to meet him like a dull grey ribbon. Harry twisted the wheel as he began to take the right-hand bend that led to Glen Urquhart.

He just had time to glimpse the tree, torn down by the gale in the night and flung across the road, before he hit it.

Andrew Flanders put down the *Sunday Sketch* and looked at his aunt.

'You've rung Harry?'

'Yes,' replied the Duchess.

'What did he say? He must have been terribly shocked!' Andrew glanced at the headline again. 'Fancy Morgan going to those lengths to produce a baby! I say, it's quite a scandal isn't it?'

'It certainly is! That's what comes of Harry marrying that dreadful girl. I told you, didn't I, Andrew? I said from the moment I set eyes on her that she was a bad lot. But Harry wouldn't listen. She utterly bewitched him, just as he was getting engaged to Elizabeth Greenly too! He'll have to get rid of Morgan now.'

'Do you think he will? He's always been crazy about her, though I could never think why. She's always struck me as terribly hard and – sort of brazen.' Andrew sounded smug, as if he would never make such an unwise choice.

'That's because she's not *one of us*!' cried the Duchess. 'All that money and no background! What do you expect? She just wanted a title and thought she could buy one, helped by that dreadful little man, her father.'

'Then the baby's illegitimate, isn't he?' There was a gleam in Andrew's eye. 'He won't be able to inherit the title now. That will upset Morgan!'

'A lot of things are going to upset Morgan! Believe me I shall see to it that the baby inherits nothing. In fact, I'm going to make it my business to see that he is returned to America to be with his real mother.'

Andrew looked impressed. 'How are you going to manage that, Aunt Lavinia?'

The Duchess looked at him penetratingly. 'Leave it to me,' was all she would say.

'There is one thing that's amusing though, isn't there? You thought Morgan had a lover, but not only did she not have a lover, she didn't have a baby either, as far as we know! Who would believe it? I must say she carried it off very well, I would never have guessed,' Andrew chortled. 'What made you think it wasn't Harry's child, when in fact it *was* Harry's child but not Morgan's?'

Again the Duchess gave him a strange look. When she spoke there was a false note in her voice. 'Just a feeling. I never trusted Morgan.'

'I bet you never thought she'd go this far though! It's incredible.' Fascinated, Andrew picked up the *Sketch* again. 'Swapping with her sister in bed! And Harry never noticed!'

'Humph! Are you coming to church with me, Andrew?' The Duchess rose regally and walked to the door.

'Do you mind awfully if I don't, Aunt Lavinia?' He blushed with guilt. 'I promised to meet a chap at the Lansdowne Club for a game of squash and then we're going on to lunch afterwards.'

The Duchess smiled indulgently. 'That's all right. It will do you good to get a bit of exercise, you work so hard during the week. I'll see you for dinner tonight then?'

'Yes, of course.'

The Duchess went to her room to put on her hat. A few minutes later Andrew heard her leave the house. As if magnetized his eyes went back to the newspaper. Morgan's barren, he thought. Now there can never be a legal heir, that is unless Harry gets a divorce and marries someone else. Harry was only twenty-eight. He would be sure to marry again if he split from Morgan. But if they stayed together, Drumnadrochit Castle with all its treasures would have to go to the nearest living relative – himself! Suddenly it was very important that Morgan and Harry should stay together. And that the baby should be sent back to its mother in America.

Lady Elizabeth Greenly walked from her home in Cliveden Place to the newsagents on Sloane Square because they'd forgotten to deliver the *Sunday Times* that morning. When her father had to spend a weekend in London he said the only good thing about it was reading the newspapers. Elizabeth was just taking her money out of her purse when her eye caught a photograph of Harry on the cover of a trashy tabloid. She looked closer. There was also a photograph of Morgan and one of her sister, and the headline that ran across screamed DUCHESS DUPES DUKE.

Startled, she gazed at it for several seconds, before snatching it up.

As she walked home again she was so engrossed in what she read she was oblivious of everything else around her. It was the most incredible story and she could hardly believe her eyes. Surely Morgan had been really pregnant when she'd seen her last summer? And surely Harry couldn't have had sex with Tiffany without realizing it wasn't Morgan? Half of her felt it must be a pack of lies, a typical sensationalized so-called exposé of the rich and titled – the sort of thing the gutter press loved to write – but the other half of her couldn't deny that the thorough research done by the journalist meant that what was printed must be partly true. The reader was not spared. Every detail, dates, times and places were faithfully recorded. *What will Harry do now?* was her first thought.

Entering her house again, she handed the *Times* to her father, and took the *Sunday Sketch* to her room. She had to have time to think. Once more she read the article. Poor Harry! A wave of love for him filled her whole being and she put her hand to her heart, as if to quell its rapid beating. Of course this would end his marriage to that horrid common girl! Elizabeth smoothed the floral bed-cover with her pale neat hand and remembered – as if she could ever forget – the most wonderful night of her life. The night her dear, dear Harry, had made love to her, in this very bed, sweeping away her virginity with one rapturous plunge. How often had she relived that moment! And now . . . She jumped off the bed and went over to the long Victorian mirror. She patted her neat hair and smoothed the creases in her skirt. Tomorrow she'd go out and buy some pretty clothes at Laura Ashley's, then she'd drop in to Harry's gallery to ask his partner when he was expected back in London. After that? Well, a little sympathy, a listening ear, and some comforting and understanding words could work wonders.

Elizabeth smiled at her reflection. Her eyes were sparkling now, and there was a flushed rosiness in her cheeks. She'd let Harry slip through her fingers once before. This time she'd stick right in there, ready and waiting for the moment when he would most assuredly take another – and better, much better – wife.

Morgan sat at her dressing table waiting for Harry to return. The *Sketch* lay on the chair beside her. There was no way she could avoid a confrontation now, but what was she going to say? What new line of lies could she think up to get out of this situation? There weren't any. She would just have to tell him the truth. That she feared so much for her marriage when she discovered she was barren that she was prepared to go to *any* lengths to provide him with a son. He would have to believe her motives, he would have to say he understood and forgave, and that everything was going to be all right. He'd *have* to. Everyone had always forgiven her everything, ever since she'd been a child. Surely they always would?

The telephone on the bedside table rang.

McGillivery could answer it downstairs. She didn't want to speak to anyone. A few minutes later she heard urgent tapping on her door.

'Come in.'

McGillivery entered, his face paler than ever.

'I meant to tell you, McGillivery,' she began before he had a chance to speak, 'I am out, no matter who calls. Tell everyone I'm away and say you don't know how to contact either myself or the Duke.'

'It's the police, your grace.'

Morgan spun round. 'The police? What the hell do they want?'

'I'm afraid it's bad news. There's been an accident, your grace.' He looked near to tears.

Instantly she knew. The blood was draining away from her face, emptying her brain. She gripped the dressing-table. 'What's happened?'

'His grace's car has hit a fallen tree. They've taken him to the hospital at Fort Augustus.'

'He's not –' She couldn't say it. There was a buzzing in her ears and the room swam before her eyes.

'They didn't know the extent of his injuries, your grace, but a police car will be here in a few minutes to take you to the Fort Augustus Hospital,' McGillivery said wretchedly. 'Can I get you anything, your grace? Some brandy perhaps?'

'No.' Morgan ran to the closet, grabbed her coat and ran off down the stairs and into the hall. McGillivery watched her go. She might be a phoney, he thought, but she certainly isn't acting now.

Ten minutes later Morgan was being whisked in a police car along the road that lay on the west side of Loch Ness. With the siren wailing, they shot through the tiny village of Invermoriston, on to Portclair and Inchnacardoch, shattering the peace of a Sunday morning, alarming grazing sheep and frightening farmyard hens. In the back Morgan sat tense and pale, not talking. No one seemed to know how Harry was.

'The doctor will be coming to see you in a moment,' the young nurse assured Morgan. Morgan had been sitting in the reception room for what seemed like ten years. The strong smell of disinfectant was making her feel sick again and her legs wouldn't stop shaking.

'Can't you tell me anything?' she cried. *Christ, the girl's a fool.*

The nurse smiled sympathetically. 'The doctor in charge has all the information, he won't be long now.'

'How long will he be?' *I can't stand not knowing.*

At that moment a doctor in a white coat came up to her, a mask hanging under his chin. He smelled of antiseptic and talked in a broad Scottish accent.

'Would ye be the Duchess of Lomond?' he asked.

At last. 'How is my husband?' Morgan grabbed his arm.

The doctor looked at her evenly. 'He's in intensive care. I'm afraid he's suffered a wee bit of a blow to his head. He's got several broken ribs, but I dinna think there's any internal injuries. Ye canna talk to him, young lady, but you can have a peek if you've a mind to. Just for a minute, mind!'

'Why can't I talk to him?' *God, I need to talk to you, Harry!*

'He's in a coma, young lady.' His voice was heavy and stern.

'What does that mean?' *Oh God, Harry is going to die.*

'It means the next forty-eight hours are vury vury crucial, but dinna fret! I've got a top neurosurgeon comin' from Edinburgh in a couple of hours. We're doing everything we can to help your husband. Come wi' me and we'll have a wee look at him.' In a fatherly fashion the doctor guided Morgan along the narrow corridors to where Harry lay in a small room.

Nothing had prepared Morgan for the way he looked.

29

On Monday the story of the surrogate birth hit all the British newspapers, with the exception of *The Times* and the *Telegraph*. In New York *The Post* also carried a salacious version. This was to be picked up during the week by the *National Inquirer* and *People Magazine*. The intriguing scandal, involving a duke with a noble heritage and a beautiful rich New York socialite, was grist for any journalist's mill.

By Tuesday a whole new angle had developed and the sensation was verging on the point of overkill.

'DUKE IN COMA' screamed the headlines.

'SEVERE INJURIES AFTER CAR CRASH.'

'It is thought the Duke of Lomond may have attempted to take his own life by reckless driving when his car crashed into a tree on a lonely Scottish road. It followed the revelation that his barren wife had used her sister as a surrogate mother to produce an heir.'

'DISTRAUGHT DUCHESS KEEPS BEDSIDE VIGIL.'

'DUKE STILL IN COMA' ran a later edition.

'Tiffany Kalvin-Krasner, costume designer, refuses to comment,' wrote a frustrated journalist.

'Unaware of the raging drama surrounding his birth, six-month-old David played happily with his toys yesterday in the nursery of Drumnadrochit Castle. He is being cared for by his nurse,' gushed another writer.

Whichever way the newspapers wrote it, it made a damn good yarn.

Pockets of gossip all over Britain and in New York became inflamed and spread like ugly sores. In London, Morgan's and Harry's friends could talk of nothing else. Reactions veered from plain astonishment to malicious amusement. Cartoons appeared in the *Evening Standard, Mail* and *Express*, full of wicked wit and satire.

One showed Morgan sneaking Tiffany into a closet while Harry lay drunk in a four-poster bed, crying, 'Is it you, my darling?' Morgan was depicted as saying to Tiffany, 'I wonder which darling he means?'

Another cartoon showed Morgan, heavily pregnant, buying pillows in Harrods' bedding department. The caption read, 'I think I'll try this one for size.'

Harry had by now been transferred to Edinburgh, four hundred miles away, where the neurosurgeon had ordered a brain scan to see if there was any internal haemorrhaging in the brain. Morgan was informed there was not, but she could hardly bear to look at Harry, with his swollen and bruised face and eyes, a tube up his nose. They had shaved a part of his head, where the surgeon had stitched the deep gash. An intravenous drip containing glucose and vitamins was fixed to his arm.

Morgan averted her face and closed her eyes – it was all so *ugly*.

Outside the hospital the reporters and photographers hung around, hoping to get a shot of Morgan entering or leaving. She had booked into a nearby hotel, but spent every day by Harry's bedside. For once in her life she was not anxious to be photographed.

At Drumnadrochit Castle photographers climbed fences and trees, their telephoto lenses slung round their necks, hoping to get a shot of David in his pram. McGillivery locked all the doors and windows and forbade the staff to leave the castle, answer the phone, or even go near a window. Drumnadrochit was in a state of siege.

More newspaper men flocked to Montpelier Square and tried to set up camp on the doorstep. They found themselves foiled by Perkins, who had taken the same precautionary measures as McGillivery.

The Dowager Duchess of Lomond, with Andrew Flanders, slipped out of the back entrance of her home and was driven down to Devon, to stay with trustworthy old friends.

As far as the British press were concerned the Lomond family had closed ranks and pulled down the blinds. So the press wrote column inches of fiction because no one would give them the hard facts.

In New York, Tiffany was forced to disconnect her telephone and stay in her apartment. Advance bookings for *Gertie* reached a record high, thanks to the publicity surrounding the costume designer.

Axelance had lines stretching round the block. Everyone hoped Tiffany might turn up with her husband and they were dying to know what she was *really* like. Axel increased the price of drinks, allowed more people in than fire regulations stipulated and doubled the profits on each night's take.

The press also surged to the Kalvins' Park Avenue apartment and to Quadrant Inc. on Wall Street but Joe had left town.

Tiffany had phoned her parents on the Saturday after the reporter from the *Sketch* had rung her, and had told them what to expect. It was the biggest shock they'd ever had. Joe and Ruth left immediately in their Cessna Citation jet for Southampton, where they holed up at Four Winds, guarded by four security men from Quadrant.

Joe needed time to think. And he only liked the press when they were on his side.

'I still can't believe it! *Where* did you say Tiffany had this baby?' Ruth asked Joe as they soaked up the sun by the pool. It was Wednesday afternoon and vodka and Valium were adding to her vagueness by the minute. She was having a hard time absorbing all the facts.

'What the hell does that matter, for God's sake!' snapped Joe. 'The fact is that for some fucking stupid reason she agreed to have a baby for Morgan. *Harry's* baby! And that dumb fuck didn't even notice it wasn't his wife in bed with him!' In disgust Joe spat out a bit of cigar leaf. 'Why didn't she come to me? I could have fixed something – *anything* – that would have been better than all this embarrassment.'

'What are you going to do now?'

Joe rose from his deckchair and patted his pale fat stomach. His ulcer was giving him hell. 'I'm flying back to New York tomorrow and after I've talked to Tiffany I'm going to issue a press statement. It's damn stupid our staying out here, hiding like criminals.'

'But what can you say to the press, Joe? You can't deny what's happened,' said Ruth mildly.

'Leave it to me. This thing has got to be handled carefully – like we make out we knew all along that Tiffany was the surrogate mother – and that includes Harry too! You'd better stay here, Ruth. And don't talk to *anyone!* Not anyone! I know you, you could never keep a secret.'

Ruth looked at Joe with her faded green eyes and marvelled at his vain stupidity. She might *look* stupid and she knew she got confused at times, but Joe never gave her credit for anything. There were a lot of things she'd kept hidden from him over the years, like her dress bills and the money she'd given Zachary. Joe didn't even realize her nails were false and her hair dyed! Not be able to keep a secret, indeed! It was Joe who was stupid, not her. His head was a money machine and she could swear his eyes sometimes bore the imprint of dollar signs. Other than that he never noticed anything.

'I'm going to the club after dinner,' Axel announced as he and Tiffany sat in the living room of their apartment having an early evening drink.

'Again?' she tried to keep the dryness out of her voice.

'We're frantically busy,' he cried defensively. 'The place is swarming from the minute it opens until practically dawn.

Come on, Tiff. I do have work to do.'

'Yes, I know,' she said quietly. 'I'm sorry, honey, it's just so awful being cooped up here all the time. It's getting me down. And you're never home. Why, I've hardly seen you since Saturday. Ever since this nightmare started.'

'You must understand how important it is to consolidate the club, Tiff. Especially as business is going through the ceiling at the moment. I've got a helluva lot of work to do, and don't forget we're supposed to be opening up in San Francisco in a month, or had you forgotten?' Angrily he got up and poured some whisky into his glass. 'Where's your sense of independence gone, for God's sake?'

Tiffany looked at him, stung by his words. Something wasn't right in their marriage but for the life of her she couldn't put her finger on what it was. Of course she understood he had to work. She respected him for it and she backed him and encouraged him all the way. In a few years they might own a whole string of Axelances, in London, Paris, Amsterdam. And of course she understood he had to go to the club some nights. But this was something else, and in her bones she knew it had nothing to do with the club. Axel had definitely changed. A restless quality had crept into his manner, a pent-up, frustrated straining at an invisible leash. Yet he constantly told her how much he loved her and needed her. They still made love quite often, though not as often as at the beginning, but that, Tiffany supposed, was married life. Of one thing she was almost certain. There wasn't another woman. To her self-disgust, she'd even looked through his pockets for any clues, and smelled his shirts and jackets for any trace of perfume or make-up. She found nothing.

'Have you heard how Harry is?' Axel asked suddenly.

'Daddy rang the hospital in Scotland this afternoon but there's no change. He's still in a coma.'

'Poor devil! He must have been driving like a bat out of hell. I suppose you haven't talked to Morgan again?'

Tiffany shook her head and took a sip of her drink. 'We've nothing to say to each other.'

'I suppose not.'

They lapsed into silence. An uneasy silence, like two strangers who had nothing in common. Try as she might to be bright and chatty, it was obvious Axel just wanted to have dinner and split. His only response was the odd polite remark.

At last he was gone. Out of the apartment in a flash and off to the club. Feeling like someone who had got ready for a party only to be told it had been cancelled, Tiffany settled herself with coffee, cigarettes and a new novel on the living-room sofa. But the words danced up and down before her eyes, and having read two pages, she put the book down and stared up at the ceiling. Axel was forgotten for the moment. Her thoughts kept turning to David, the baby she had never intended to love, the baby who was an inextricable part of her life. For nine long painful months she had carried the child, firmly resolved to reject him physically and mentally as soon as he entered the world. And then she had heard him cry, and every cell of her being had revolted at the idea of giving him up. Now, all the publicity surrounding his birth had opened up that deep well of pain in her heart. With an overwhelming sense of loss, Tiffany suddenly started to cry. She cried for herself, and she cried for the baby who, for the rest of his life, would be remembered as the child whose birth had caused a scandal.

And she cried because once again she seemed to be so awfully alone.

Street Echoes had reached number one in the Neilsen ratings for the past month. Hunt Kellerman was riding on a roller-coaster of success and *Hollywood Reporter* and *Variety* hailed him as a director of outstanding ability.

At last he was getting where he wanted. He had a say in the story-lining, chose the script writers, and made his views on casting very clear. The series was scheduled to last at least two more seasons , and Magnima Films were holding an option on his contract for a further series.

He liked the bucks. He liked the success and he enjoyed the challenge. His professional life was exciting, fulfilling and was everything he'd ever wanted.

So why the fuck is my personal life as flat as stale beer? he asked himself, as he drove to the studio one morning in his car. He added up the bonus points in his head. Gus and Matt were happy, doing well at school, and loved Betsy, the middle-aged housekeeper who mothered them and smothered them with hugs and kisses and home-baked cookies. Manuel, the house boy, drove them to and from school and played soccer with them on the lawn behind the rose garden whenever his duties would permit. Joni and he had finally split. She'd gone to dry out in a clinic and she had finally agreed to a divorce on the condition that her settlement included half of everything he owned and was large enough to allow her to return to New York to do her own thing – namely pursue her acting career. Hunt wished her luck.

Then he added up the minus points. There was really only one but it filled his mind day and night and like a growing monster was beginning to overshadow everything else. He was utterly lonely. No matter how many girls he took out or how many parties he went to, or even how hard he worked, loneliness was eating into him like a cancer. And at the centre of his loneliness was a longing for Tiffany. There was a painful constriction in his chest every time he thought of her.

When he arrived at the studio he found all hell had broken loose. The star of the show was in a rage because the actor cast to play her son was thirty-two. It didn't matter that he looked twenty-five.

'It will make me seem so *old*!' she raged. 'You'll have to replace him with someone around nineteen.'

There was silence.

Hunt didn't want to be the one to tell her that not only was she old enough to have a son of thirty-two, but she looked it.

'Hey, read this!' cried one of the script writers, coming up to join Hunt and the hostile actress as they glared at each other. '*What* a story!' He was holding *People Magazine*. 'I wonder if we couldn't adapt it a bit and introduce it in the next series. It's way out – fucking wild! Listen!'

'Let me see.' Hunt reached for the journal.

'Look, Hunt! It's about this young English duke who had to have an heir but his wife couldn't have any children so – Hey, what's the matter?'

Hunt was reading the story and his face had suddenly gone grey.

It had been four days since the accident and Harry still lay in a coma. Morgan continued to spend her days by his side, but even her entreated cries of, 'Harry! Harry, it's me, Morgan! Can you hear me, darling?' brought no response.

Morgan had never felt so sick with fear in her life. Everyone was against her now, her own family, her friends, the press. And she could only guess at Harry's reaction when he came round. Not for a moment did she let it cross her mind that he wouldn't come round. The truth was she needed him. She needed his love and his admiration, she craved his praise and support. All her life she'd had someone to lean on and for the past couple of years it had been Harry. Without him, she would rank as nothing in England. He provided the very foundation and structure of her life and she was only someone because she was his wife. He had to get better. Their marriage had to go on.

She leaned forward and looked at his swollen and discoloured face. His eyes did not even flicker as he lay in a world beyond her reach.

'Harry,' she begged, her tears splashing onto his pale-blue pyjamas. 'Harry! Can you hear me?'

Somehow she had to make him understand how much she needed him.

Lady Elizabeth Greenly rang Harry's partner, John Ingleby-Wright each morning as soon as he arrived at the gallery. John was the only person she could ask. The hospital in Edinburgh refused to give her any information because she wasn't a blood relative and no one answered the phones at either Drumnadrochit Castle or Montpelier Square. Elizabeth was distraught and she didn't care who knew it. Harry was the only love of her life, and she was sure he was going to die.

'I'm afraid I've no further news,' John told her sympathetically on the fifth morning. 'There's been no change in Harry's condition.' He had just spoken to Morgan but he didn't want Elizabeth to know that the prognosis was bad. She seemed so pathetically distraught, but then so did Morgan, whom he'd always regarded as rather a tough cookie.

'I've sent him some flowers,' Elizabeth was saying, 'though I don't suppose he realizes . . .' Her voice caught in a little sob.

'He'll know all about it when he recovers consciousness,' John said placatingly. 'Morgan says people have been wonderfully kind, and she's keeping all the cards and messages to show him when he's better.'

I should be there with him, cried an agonized voice in Elizabeth's head. *It's me who should be with him now. Why does it have to be her? I've always loved him.* Aloud she said, 'Thanks, John, and you'll let me know if there's any further news?'

'I'll ring you right away, Elizabeth. Try not to worry, he's in excellent hands and they are doing everything they can for him.'

Tearfully she hung up. Then she made a vow to herself. If Harry gets better – *when* Harry gets better, she corrected herself, I shall do everything I can to win him back from Morgan. It made sense. He wouldn't want to go on being married to Morgan anyway, after what had happened. Apart from which, if it's heirs he wants, thought Elizabeth, I'll have as many children as he likes.

Andrew Flanders dreamily regarded the sweeping lawns of the Tregunthers' house in Devon, where he was staying with his aunt, and positively counted the hours. Any time now, he assured himself with growing confidence, they would hear that Harry had died, and then Drumnadrochit Castle would be his. He didn't see the baby as an obstacle to his ambitions. As his Aunt Lavinia said, David would be sent packing, back to the States to be with his American mother where he belonged. Morgan had conned them all but it seemed unlikely Harry would live to carry out his own vengeance. They would carry it out for him and it would be as if Morgan and David had never existed. And then he would realize his greatest wish. He would not inherit the title, of course, but that great, splendid ancient edifice, sitting squarely on the banks of Loch Ness would be his.

Andrew had never questioned his aunt's desire that he should inherit. It had certainly been Lavinia who had planted the idea in his head, even when he'd been a small boy. He could remember exactly when it had happened. He'd been five at the time, and he'd been out walking with her along the banks of Loch Ness. Suddenly she'd turned and looked back at the castle, proud and isolated, rising above even the tallest fir trees. 'It should go to you one day, you know, Andrew.' She gripped his hand tightly. 'You'd be the right person to have Drumnadrochit.'

Over the years he'd felt increasingly sure that she'd been right. He loved every stick and stone of the place, and his holidays there had been the happiest. If only his father had been the eldest son. If only his father had married his mother. If only . . . Gazing now at the soft Devon countryside, he recalled that his favourite fantasy when he'd been a little boy, had been that one fine day someone would tell him that it all belonged to him. All he wanted was to be grown up and be able to feel the castle in the Highlands belonged to him.

Now, nearly twenty-five years later, it might be about to happen.

30

It was Friday, six days after the accident, and Harry was still in a coma. His vital signs were stable but the neurosurgeon told Morgan that there was nothing they could do now except wait. Tense and despairing she continued to sit by his bed, trying to arouse him by talking to him and playing his favourite music.

To Tiffany in New York, it was the day when she was to know what it felt like to be a loser. Three things happened that were to leave her devastated.

Joe Kalvin was the first thing that happened. He burst into Tiffany's apartment shortly before nine o'clock in the morning, enveloped in a cloud of cigar smoke.

'We've got to talk,' he said crisply as he seated himself at her dining table, pushing aside the breakfast dishes.

'Coffee, Daddy?' she asked politely.

'No thanks. I'm releasing a press statement to the effect that you agreed to have your sister's baby on the grounds of compassion. You know the sort of thing – Here, look!' He thrust a draft in front of her. 'I'm saying that Morgan was suffering from a terrible depression because she couldn't have a child, so it was arranged that you would act as surrogate. You love your sister, you felt sorry for her. That's right, isn't it?'

'Are you asking me or telling me?' asked Tiffany drily.

'Why else would you do it? What we have to get across is that it's no big deal. People act as surrogate mothers all the time, and I add here – do you see? – that as a family we thought it was much better that you should be the child's mother rather than go to an agency. This keeps the whole thing in the family, and of course it was done with Harry's co-operation. Artificial insemination is almost a standard procedure in these cases nowadays. It's our word against that Monroe bitch – God, she's like Mrs Danvers in *Rebecca*, isn't she? – and I can guarantee ya we'd win this round.'

Tiffany looked at her father. He'd always had an inventive mind.

'Have you told Morgan what you're going to say?'

Joe consulted his watch. 'There's no use calling yet, it will be only four in the morning in England, but I'll put a call through to her in a couple of hours, I know she'll agree.'

'I'm sure she will,' Tiffany said quietly.

'Did you call her yesterday? Have you heard how Harry is?'

'I haven't spoken to Morgan since last Saturday – just before the shit hit the fan.'

Joe looked at her in astonishment. 'What's with you two?' he snapped. 'One minute you're hand in glove, arranging to have her baby, though God knows why, and the next you're not even talking! Now listen to me, Tiffany!'

Tiffany hid a secret smile. Joe was about to go into his Father Performance, acting stern and reproving and taking the line of don't-do-as-I-do-do-as-I-say.

'Yes, Daddy?'

'Why aren't you talking to Morgan? We can't have any more trouble in the family you know – and this is causing the most awful scandal – we've got to stick together, Tiffany.'

Stung, Tiffany turned away so that he would not see her brimming eyes. 'I did it to avoid a worse scandal.'

'What do you mean?'

'You don't think I went through nine months of sheer hell, having to turn down the best opportunity of work I've ever had, and gave away my baby just for *fun*, do you?' Her voice shook and her green eyes sparked dangerously.

'Then why the fuck did you do it?'

Shaking with rage she swung round to face him, her face

blazing. 'To protect *you* – that's why! And to protect Mom to a certain extent.'

'Protect me from what, for God's sake?' Joe roared. His eyes were like ice-blue chips.

'The FBI for starters! I've always known – that is since I've been about fourteen – that you were embezzling funds from Quadrant! I thought I was the only person who knew, but last year Morgan told me . . . My God! I can't bear this!' She covered her face with her hands.

'Go on.' Joe's voice was like cutting steel.

Tiffany took a deep breath and tried to continue. 'Morgan threatened . . . she said she'd report the whole thing to the FBI unless . . . unless I agreed to have a baby for her. I had no choice! I couldn't let that happen to you! You'd have been indicted and probably sent to prison for years.' She couldn't continue. Slumping forward onto the table, she buried her head in her arms.

Joe stared for a moment, then brought his fist crashing down on the table, making the cups jump in their saucers.

'Where the hell did you get a fucking screwball idea like that?' Agitatedly he ran the palm of his hand over his balding head. 'What sort of a goddam fool are you?'

Tiffany jumped to her feet knocking her chair over. 'Don't you call me a fool! Don't you dare say that to me! I did it to protect *you!*'

They glared at each other. Then Joe spoke.

'But it's not true!'

'What do you mean, it's not true? I *know* it's true!' Tiffany stood very still, her senses reeling. 'Someone told me.'

'Who?'

'I'd – I'd rather not say.'

'*Who*, Tiffany?!' Joe's eyes were blazing. In a moment, she thought, he'd have a stroke.

'Sig,' she said in a small voice.

'Sig? Why would Sig want to tell a bunch of lies like that? He'd be involving himself as well as me, it doesn't make sense!' Joe cried in bewilderment. 'You must have misunderstood.'

'I didn't misunderstand. I was fourteen at the time and what he said came over loud and clear. I've kept it to myself all these years. Then Morgan told me only last year she'd overheard everything. Oh, I don't understand what's happening!' she cried in bewilderment.

Joe was trying hard not to lose his temper. 'So you're telling me that one sunny day, for no particular reason, Sig just says casually, "Oh I thought you'd like to know that your father has been embezzling money from our clients!" You believed that crap?' he yelled, his face so red with anger that the veins stood out on his forehead. Abruptly he walked to the window, looked out with unseeing eyes, spun round and then walked back to her. There was a look of astounded but unmistakable hurt on his face. 'Are you telling me you actually believed that I was a *crook?*'

There was an awfulness about the way he was saying it, as if the words were tearing the guts from his body. 'And Morgan believed it *too?*' he added.

Tiffany closed her eyes. A sickening feeling was beginning to creep over her, leaving her cold and clammy.

'Well, Tiffany?'

She opened her eyes and looked at Joe and it was as if she were seeing him for the first time. Beneath the pompous, arrogant, pushy veneer there was a vulnerable little man, deeply hurt.

'Daddy!' she cried, aghast. 'But . . . Sig told me . . . I never thought . . .'

'Tiffany, I get the feeling you're not levelling with me. You're not telling me everything, are you? Something must have happened for Sig to spin you a bunch of lies like that. What's behind all this?'

There was a long painful pause as Tiffany tried to gather her strength together for the terrible story she had to tell.

'Something did happen at Four Winds, a long time ago.

And Sig threatened to expose you if I said anything about it,' she began.

'What happened at Four Winds?'

There was agony in Tiffany's face as she looked at her father.

Then she told him.

An hour later Joe stormed out of her apartment, ready to kill. 'Back to Park Avenue,' he told the chauffeur curtly. What he had to do could only be done in the privacy of his home. It would be some time before he could bear to set eyes on Sig Hoffman either. He decided not to go to Quadrant House today. Still seething with rage, he clambered out of the Lincoln and shot past the doorman into the building. The apparent slowness of the elevator incensed him further. At last he reached the quiet of his study, thankful that Ruth was out.

From one of the drawers of his desk he extracted a small address book marked 'Confidential'. It took him four seconds flat to find what he wanted. In another few seconds he had dialled the number on his private line.

'Krauss and Blumfeld, Private Investigators,' a voice answered.

'Gimme Hank Krauss,' Joe said, shortly.

There was a pause, a click and Hank Krauss was on the line.

'Hank? I want you to do something for me. Get your ass over here right away. And don't even tell your secretary where you're going.'

'A problem, Joe?' Hank and Joe were old buddies from way back. Joe could trust him.

'Yeah, probably a hell of a problem,' Joe said heavily.

'I'll be right over.' There was a click. Joe replaced the receiver and reached for a cigar. He puffed nervously and thoughtfully.

Maybe he had more than one score to settle with that son

of a bitch Sig Hoffman, before he was good and ready to crucify him with his own bare hands.

Joe had departed and Tiffany sat alone in her studio. Axel was out. He hardly ever seemed to be in these days and she felt drained by the morning's revelations. And ashamed too. All these years she had gone on believing what Sig had told her. How could she have been such a fool! She thought about Joe. He had looked so hurt. Funny, she'd never thought of him as vulnerable before. He'd always seemed so positive and self-assured, and he'd certainly ruled his family with a rod of iron. The memory of her father's shocked face haunted her, and the candid way he had told her the only bit of fiddling he'd ever done was a well-known tax dodge in connection with expenses. And Zachary had cleaned all that cash out when he'd raided the apartment safe. To witness him pleading his innocence to her had been both revealing and embarrassing – as if he'd suddenly appeared naked before her for the first time.

Sig, Joe told her, had carried out all the financial aspects of their deals. Joe got the business, talked future clients into letting Quadrant Inc. finance whatever project they had in mind, be it starting up a new business, doing a property deal or planning an industrial expansion, provided they could produce adequate security. From then on it was up to Sig to fix the rates of interest, depending on whether Quadrant used their own capital or borrowed from a bank, charging, in that case, a higher rate of interest to the client.

Joe had looked sad for a moment as he admitted that Sig had a better business brain than him.

'But,' he said, looking up with a slightly triumphant smile, 'Sig couldn't have done it without me! I've got the *chutzpa*!'

'Oh, Daddy.' Tiffany had reached out and touched his hand. 'How can I ever make up to you for all the years I thought . . . !' she faltered.

'You've suffered for it more than I have, Tiff, and don't

think I don't realize what you did to protect me, even if you were all wrong. Thank God we've got it out in the open now. When I think – ' He stopped short and then he and Tiffany both looked at each other. They had both had exactly the same thought at the same minute.

'Christ, I hope we're wrong,' Joe exclaimed, jumping to his feet, 'but after what you've just told me, anything's possible!'

'What will you do?' Tiffany saw before her the same old Joe, fiery, arrogant and very, very angry.

'Leave it to me,' was all he would say.

And now it was noon. She felt ravenously hungry. It was Gloria's day off, so she went into the kitchen to fix herself a snack. She'd have to think about what to cook Axel for dinner tonight – that was if he had time to come back.

The doorbell rang just as she had finished making herself a chicken salad. Thinking Joe might have thought of something and had decided to come back and tell her, she went to the door and opened it with a flourish.

Hunt was standing there, looking bronzed and lean, his dark eyes boring into Tiffany's.

'Oh!' she stepped back, shocked.

'Hello, Tiffany.' He said the words softly and gently. 'I'm in New York on business so I thought I'd look in to see how you are.'

Tiffany continued to stare at him, a blank expression on her face.

'Oh, yes. Great,' she mumbled, recovering herself. 'Come in.' Her heart was pounding so hard her chest felt constricted.

'How are you?' he asked, following her into the living room.

'Fine, absolutely wonderful. Can I get you a drink?'

'Yes, please.' Hunt eyed her up and down, taking in the slimness of her figure in black pants and a silk shirt, through which he could see her perfectly shaped breasts. 'I've been reading a lot about you lately. Been a bit busy, haven't you?' There was irony in his voice.

She looked at him defiantly. 'Yes, you could say that,' she replied coolly, handing him his drink.

'Why did you do it, Tiff?' He was searching her face now and he saw the blue shadows under her eyes and the way her lips were pressed together – something he remembered she always did when she was unhappy and under strain. 'Why did you have a baby for Morgan?'

'It's a very long story, Hunt. I'd really rather not talk about it.'

There was a moment's awkward silence then they both started to talk at the same time.

'How's Los Angeles –'

'I haven't seen –'

Hunt smiled and grabbed her shoulders. 'Oh God, darling, it's so good to see you again. Are you really all right?'

Gently Tiffany moved away, the feel of his hands still burning into her skin. 'The past week has been awful of course, what with all the stories in the newspapers and Harry having that terrible accident. He's still in a coma, you know.'

'I'm sorry to hear that, Tiff. Is he expected to live?'

Tiffany made a hopeless gesture with her hands. 'I don't think he's going to die, though that would be better than being a vegetable for the rest of his life, which depends on how long he's in a coma. We just have to wait and see.'

'I'm so sorry. Do you care for him, Tiffany?' Hunt looked at her with tortured eyes.

'I care about Harry as I would anyone who had nearly got killed in an accident.'

'I shouldn't have asked. Forgive me!' Restlessly he moved in his chair.

'It's just a very painful subject I'd rather not talk about.'

He nodded. 'I understand, Tiff. Are you busy?'

'I've just done the designs for *Gertie*. I think it's going to be a wonderful show. We open in about three weeks. And then I've got a lot of work designing Axelance II.'

'Ah, yes, the nightclubs. And how is your husband?' His voice sounded harsh although he had not meant it to.

Tiffany looked away, noting the harshness, but she was too proud to let Hunt see that all was not well with her marriage, that Axel had changed.

'Fabulous! Very busy of course,' she said with sudden cheerfulness. 'Axelance is doing record business here in New York, and then as soon as we've got the San Francisco one open, we're going to start up in Los Angeles.'

The minute she'd said it she wanted to bite her tongue. Los Angeles was Hunt's town now. Too close for comfort.

'Los Angeles?' he was saying. 'Oh, you'll love it and you'll get tons of work out there, with your talent. I've got a house in Benedict Canyon – Gus and Matt just love it.'

'How are they?'

'Great. Much happier in fact, now that Joni and I have split.'

A sharp pain seared through her heart making her catch her breath. 'Split?' she said with effort.

'Yes, the divorce will be final in a few weeks.' Hunt put down his empty glass and rose to go. 'Pity you couldn't have waited a bit longer, isn't it?' he said, with sudden bitterness. 'Well, I suppose that's the way the cookie crumbles! Anyway Tiff, I've got to be going, but it was nice seeing you again. Good luck with all your nightclubs.'

With long strides he had reached the door, while her mind screamed, *Why didn't you tell me you were going to get divorced! How can you be so cruel as to talk to me like this now! And they aren't my nightclubs, they belong to my husband! Husband! Husband!*

She managed to close the door behind him before her control snapped.

At three o'clock Tiffany decided to go out. Her concentration had been shot to pieces and it was impossible to work. She would go shopping, extravagant shopping like at Martha's or Henri Bendel. Disjointed thoughts kept flashing through her mind, driving her crazy.

Joe isn't a crook after all. Hunt is divorced and free. Sig is a lying bastard. And worse. *Morgan was just bluffing when she threatened to report Joe.* As if she would have done anything to jeopardize her own social position! And then again, *Hunt has got rid of Joni. Is Harry going to recover? If he doesn't, the baby will have no father. Only Morgan. What will become of my baby?*

In desperation she flung herself out of the apartment and made for West 57th Street.

An hour later she had bought enough crêpe de Chine and lace undies and nightdresses to see her through six honeymoons. She also bought some shoes, a cashmere sweater and four silk shirts. Then she browsed round Doubleday and bought four biographies. Lastly she wandered into Tiffany's, her troubled spirits calmed by now. There was one thing she and Morgan used to agree on. There was no balm to the soul so effective as a shopping spree.

In Tiffany's she decided to get a present for Joe, and something for Axel. After much indecisive wandering around, she ended up by buying them each a pair of gold cuff-links. Boring gifts, but her powers of originality weren't so hot today. She glanced at her watch. It was now six o'clock.

On impulse she decided to drop by her parents' home and give Joe his present in person. It would make a nice end to a day that had started so disastrously between them. But first she must put a call through to her own apartment. Axel sometimes came back around six before going out again. She called from a street box and it was her own voice that greeted her on their answering machine. She'd forgotten it was Gloria's day off.

'Hi, Axel. I've been shopping and now I'm going to see my

parents and maybe stay and have dinner if they ask me. Why don't you join us? Otherwise I'll be back around ten-thirty. I love you.' Tiffany replaced the receiver as the phone asked for more money.

'I'm afraid Mrs Kalvin is still on Long Island,' the butler told Tiffany when she arrived at the Park Avenue duplex fifteen minutes later. 'And we've just received a call from Mr Kalvin saying he is tied up on urgent business and won't be in for dinner.'

Tiffany tried to hide her feeling of deflation. For some reason she had really wanted to be with Joe this evening.

'Then I'll leave this for him,' she said, handing over the pale-blue Tiffany bag. 'Will you give Mr Kalvin my love and tell him I'll call him tomorrow.'

'Of course, Mrs Krasner.'

Tiffany walked slowly home. It wasn't going to be any fun spending the evening alone and she wished again that she could figure out what Axel did all the time.

As soon as she got into the hallway of her apartment she heard it. A familiar sound that froze her rigid. She glanced wildly towards the bedroom but it wasn't coming from there. With legs that felt as if they didn't belong to her, she edged towards the living room. There it was again! Louder this time. A wave of nausea rose in her throat and sick fear bathed her in sweat. She managed to push open the door and look into the room.

Lying half naked on the sofa was a young man she'd never seen before.

Axel was making love to him.

31

Her face was a blur, looming up large and close one minute and receding into a pale blob that hovered in the distance the next.

Then he heard her voice.

'Harry? It's me, honey, Morgan. You're going to be fine, Harry, everything's all right.'

He tried to focus his eyes but all he could see through the pain was a white shape surrounded by light golden hair. He tried to speak, but his tongue felt as if it was too big for his mouth. A great weariness was dragging him down into a warm black pit. For a moment he let himself slide, then he heard her voice again, calling him back.

'Don't try to talk, Harry. I'm here and everything's going to be all right. Just rest, darling, you're going to be okay.' He could feel her soft hand gripping his.

From a long way away he heard himself saying, 'What happened?' His voice sounded strange and gruff.

'You had an accident, but you're safe now.'

'How long have I been here?'

'Six days — since Sunday, when it happened. It's Friday now.'

With an effort he opened his eyes again and looked at her. Her face was clearer now and he vaguely thought how terrible she looked.

'Sunday?' he repeated. What had happened on Sunday? For a moment his mind clawed frantically back, trying to remember what it was, but just as he thought he'd got it, it slipped beyond his reach again. It was no use. Closing his eyes he drifted back to sleep.

When he awoke an hour later, Morgan was still sitting by his bed.

Harry turned his head gingerly and looked at her in perplexity.

'How long have you been here?' he asked.

Morgan gave him a warm smile. 'Every day since Sunday, darling.'

'Every –? Good Lord! I wish I could remember what happened.'

'You skidded in your car on the road to Glen Urquhart. They brought you here.'

'What was I doing in Glen Urquhart?'

'I don't know, Harry,' she said quietly. 'Anyway, it's all over now. Don't talk any more.'

Harry lay silent. He felt as if his life was a jigsaw puzzle that someone had snatched up and scattered all over the place, bit by bit. Somehow he had to find all those pieces and fit them together again.

'How's David?' he suddenly heard himself ask, and realized suddenly that whatever had happened last Sunday had something to do with David. He looked anxiously at Morgan.

'He's terrific! I think he'll be crawling soon – Harry! What's wrong?'

He was staring at her fixedly and there was anguish and horror in his eyes. 'I remember,' he said slowly.

'You saw the papers then? I can explain everything, Harry! Just as soon as you're better I'll –'

Harry silenced her by turning his head sharply away, a grimace of pain distorting his features. 'I didn't see the papers,' he said hoarsely, 'my mother rang me.'

'Oh, dearest, I'm so sorry. I wanted to tell you myself, to explain! I have so much to explain to you, but everything's going to be all right, it really is –'

'Go away,' he said weakly.

'But Harry!'

'Go away and leave me alone.' Harry shut his eyes again and his mouth was set in a hard line. 'Get out!'

During the following ten days Harry had a lot of time for thinking. Morgan still came to see him each day but he refused to discuss the matter of David's birth. Whenever Morgan brought it up, trying desperately to justify herself, he chilled her with a curt, 'We have nothing to discuss, Morgan.'

Then she tried to cajole him, tease him, flatter him; tried to recapture the affectionate bantering they had enjoyed in the past. She brought him little presents, snippets of gossip, books of amusing cartoons, tapes for his Sony Walkman. Everything that in the past had brought an appreciative tenderness to his eyes, and a gentle smile to his mouth. He did not respond. It seemed as if a cold steel wall separated them, making him aloof, disinterested, a stranger she could not get through to.

The doctors assured her he was merely suffering from shock. Give him time, they said. Don't push him, let him recover at his own pace. Just be patient and understanding. Everything would be all right once he was strong enough to go home.

Morgan hoped they were right.

The only person Morgan spoke to was Joe. She called him every day, ostensibly to tell him how Harry was progressing, but in reality to seek his love and approval once more. Joe seemed cagey and said little. He told her he had a lot on his mind and added that now Harry was out of danger she really needn't call him so often. Hurt and disappointed, she tried to contact Tiffany, who, according to Gloria, was away on a trip. Morgan felt utterly alone. No one wanted to have anything to do with her. Even invitations from her friends seemed to have stopped coming.

Harry, on the other hand, was deluged with cards, flowers and messages of good wishes. Friends whom he had known all his life sent cases of champagne or brandy, baskets of exotic fruit or chocolates from Charbonnel et Walker, and some sent large tins of Beluga caviar. From his mother he received a postcard with a picture of a church in Devon, where she was still staying, and a cryptic message, 'Glad to hear you are better. Very nice weather here. Lavinia Lomond.' There was nothing from Andrew Flanders.

Then one morning Harry received two dozen magnificent red roses. With them came a card that said, 'Darling Harry. I prayed for your recovery and thank God my prayers have been answered. Let us be together again soon. With my fondest love. Elizabeth.'

Harry hid the card in his bedside table and when Morgan arrived and asked who the roses were from, he said casually, 'Oh, a cousin of my father's. Jolly nice of her really, I haven't seen her for years.'

Morgan didn't stay long and he was glad. He had a lot to think about, a lot of adjusting to do. He also had to find out the truth about something of vital significance before he spoke to anyone.

Joe Kalvin's press statement had been met with some scepticism and given little prominence in the newspapers, but the story of surrogacy as a whole had unleashed a barrage of media interest in Britain, and both the BBC and ITN were devoting whole documentary programmes to the issue of surrogate motherhood. Feature writers wrote long articles on the moral, emotional and ethical aspects. Agencies who arranged surrogate births came under close examination. Questions were asked in the House of Commons, and there were demands for new legislation.

Morgan destroyed every cutting, every article, every reference to the subject. She prayed that by the time Harry came out of hospital the whole thing would have died a natural death, and the media would have found another story to scandalize and titillate.

She also dismissed Mrs Monroe with three months' severance pay, and engaged a cheerful young English housekeeper who had been widowed the previous year. McGillivery took to her at once, and so did the nanny. A more cheerful atmosphere now pervaded the servants' hall.

Morgan was more determined than ever to make a success of her marriage.

Tiffany sat alone in the semi-darkness of her parents' living room waiting for Joe to come home.

It was nearly midnight.

The staff had gone to bed and the only sound was the distant roar of New York's traffic coming through the open window. Occasionally the wailing of a police siren or the honking of an irate motorist pierced the air.

It was a warm and balmy night.

A night for lovers.

And still Tiffany sat, her eyes dry now, but the tears flowed on inside her, coursing down inside her chest in a constant torrent, washing over the pain in her heart.

It was after midnight when she heard Joe let himself in.

'Daddy?' her voice was hoarse.

'Tiffany?' he exclaimed in surprise, as he switched on the lights. 'What on earth are you doing here? Has Sig been in touch with you?'

'No, it's not Sig. I had to get away . . .' Her voice broke.

'Jesus, what's the matter? Hey, you'd better have a drink.'

Joe went to the Chinese lacquered cabinet and took out two glasses. Then he reached for the whisky. Tiffany had been on his mind all day.

'We haven't had a fight, Daddy. I just asked him to pack and get out. May I stay the night? I don't feel like going back until I'm sure he's gone.' Tiffany sipped the whisky and felt the fiery liquor scorch her cramped stomach.

'As serious as that? Yes, of course you can stay here, this is your home. But listen, Tiff' – Joe came over to the sofa on which she was sitting, and perched himself on one of the arms. His feet barely touched the floor – 'aren't you over-reacting a bit? I mean, what happened? Find him flirting with some chick at his club?'

Tiffany's face broke up and she could feel hysteria rising inside her. 'I caught him red-handed with a man!' she burst out. '*Now* tell me to stay cool! They were right there, in our living room . . .' She could see the scene again, Axel flushed and sweating, his eyes blazing with passion, the young man smiling. 'I just walked in, and there they were! He didn't think I'd be back so early . . . I'd left a message . . .' Her mouth opened wide and a silent scream swelled from her throat, tearing at her lungs, filling her eyes with anguish.

With a swift movement, Joe hopped off the arm of the sofa, put down his drink and then a moment later she was in his arms, clinging to him as she hadn't done since she'd been a little girl.

'Baby, baby, baby,' Joe was saying gruffly, as he cradled her head.

He hadn't called her Baby since she'd been a little girl.

After a sleepless night, for Tiffany and Joe had talked until the first faint cold light of dawn had crept over Manhattan, she showered and crept out of the Park Avenue apartment. She left Joe sleeping. He'd had enough to cope with during the past twenty-four hours.

Manhattan looked as jaded and sad as she felt. Grey and deserted in the clear morning air, it seemed to reject the pale watery sun, longing to recapture the hidden darkness of the night. Hailing a lone taxi, she rode the three blocks back to her apartment, planning what she would do next. A terrible feeling of failure swept through her. This was the third enormous mistake she'd made. Would she ever get it right? First Hunt, then little David, and now Axel. She'd never undergone analysis but perhaps now was the time. No doubt a shrink would tell her she really wanted to be unhappy, deep in the heart of her soul. Tiffany considered the thought. A shrink would add that because she had no self-regard, she subconsciously went for men who would always end up hurting her. But that was absurd, she reasoned. It might be true in the case of Hunt, but it certainly wasn't true in the case of Axel. He was a handsome masculine-looking man, with wit, intelligence and not a hint of gayness about him. She reckoned there was no way she could have known and yet she *should* have known. Was it that she didn't want to see it? Was she inflicting some form of self-punishment on herself because of what had happened so long ago? She shrugged and shook her head. It was too early to try and fathom the vagaries of the human mind.

As soon as she entered the apartment, she made for the kitchen. Gloria would have to know that she and Axel had split though she decided not to give out any details. It would be enough to say that she would, from now on, be living on her own. Again.

A noise in the bedroom made her jump and freeze. It was Axel's voice. With a feeling of overpowering dread she kicked open the door with her foot. Axel was sitting on the bed, still wet from the shower, a towel draped round his muscular body. He was talking to someone on the phone.

With a swift movement Tiffany turned and charged along the corridor to her studio. Once inside she sank onto the low leather chair. Her head was hammering and for a moment she wondered if she was going to faint. She ran a hand over her face. It was dripping with sweat. Why was Axel still here? she thought wildly. He was supposed to have left last night.

A moment later the door opened and he walked into the studio, wearing jeans, and round his neck a gold chain and medallion that gleamed against his tanned chest. For a moment he stood looking down at her. Then he spoke.

'Oh, Tiffany.' The 'oh' was drawn out like a long sigh. 'I couldn't leave until we talked.'

Tiffany felt her heart sinking. He was looking at her with such sorrow and compassion that it was all she could do not to break down again.

'What's happened – what you saw – doesn't mean I don't love you.' Axel spoke with difficulty. 'You must believe me, Tiff. I do love you, you're like a part of myself. I've never been as close to anyone as I am to you. You do believe me, don't you?'

Tiffany sat silent, unable to speak.

Axel paced nervously for a minute. 'This doesn't change how I feel about you. Last night meant nothing to me. I love you – as a man loves a woman.'

'You also love men,' she whispered, but there was no reproach in her voice. It was said as a sad matter of fact.

'I'm bisexual, yes. At first I thought I was gay, but then I began to look at women, to want them, and I started going to bed with girls. Then I met you. Oh, Tiff, honey. Does the other matter? I'll always love you, and nothing like last night will ever happen again. Christ, I could kill myself for bringing that guy back! It was only for a drink, then I found your message, and, well, it just seemed to happen!'

Tiffany looked up. He was so wonderful looking with his bronze body and brilliant pale-blue eyes. 'But there have been other men since we married, apart from last night, haven't there?' she asked in a choked voice.

There was a pause and then he said, reluctantly, 'Yes, there have, but it doesn't mean I love you any less. You must believe that! Sex is nothing! What counts is love and companionship, and friendship.' He dropped onto his knees before her and tried to cup her pale face in his hands, but she drew back as if he'd been about to strike her.

'Don't, Axel,' she pleaded. 'Please. I love you too, but we've got to split. There is no way I can spend the rest of my life wondering, sharing you, being lied to, not knowing... Why, in God's name, didn't you tell me?' she cried in sudden anger. 'I want a marriage where there's trust – and faithfulness! You can't expect me to share you with half the men in town!'

Axel dropped back onto his haunches, his hands hanging limply by his sides.

'Give me another chance, Tiff. We could work something out. I still want you and I still desire you. I love you, honey! And have you been unhappy with me? Has anyone ever made you laugh as much as I have? Have you ever had such a good time with anyone else?' His voice broke.

'That's true,' she replied gathering strength, 'but we don't stand a chance! If you *really* love someone you don't do *anything* to hurt them – and that goes for straight couples too. To love is to *give*, not make a pretence of giving while doing your own thing all the time. Why did you marry me, for God's sake?' There was bitterness in her voice now.

Axel sprang to his feet angrily. 'I married you because I love you and I need you. I need you desperately, Tiff. I've never been as happy in my entire life as I've been since I've known you.'

She thought of all those times Axel had made love to her, with unselfish gentleness and stormy passion. He was born for love-making. Suddenly she covered her face with her hands, the wrenching feeling inside her more than she could bear.

'Is it over then?' Axel asked dully.

'It *has* to be over! How can you ask? What peace of mind would I have wondering who you were going to screw next? I could no more stay with you than I could stay with a man who was always chasing after other women. For God's sake, I want a secure marriage. I want a husband I can trust. You'll never belong to just me! You never have.'

Axel faced her defiantly. 'Ask any straight married man you know just how often he's been unfaithful to his wife! Men are primarily hunters, Tiff. They need new conquests, but most of the time the wives never suspect a thing and the marriage goes happily on.'

'If I can't have the sort of marriage I believe in,' Tiffany said slowly, 'then I'll go solo for the rest of my life!'

'And then who's going to face a lonely old age! Aren't you being hypocritical? Weren't you the "other woman" in Hunt's life? What about his wife being deceived something rotten? Well?' he demanded, 'You can't have double standards, you know.'

'At least I was another *woman*!' she shot back.

'So that makes it all right, does it?'

'It doesn't make it all right but it makes it fairer! A woman can fight another woman – on her own terms. What chance has a woman got fighting her husband's relationship with another man? About as much chance as finding the Hope diamond in a box of Cracker Jacks! In any case, Hunt's marriage was on the rocks before I even met him. In fact, they're now getting a divorce.' Colour had returned to Tiffany's cheeks and she was thinking more clearly. 'It's no good, Axel. The quicker we split the better, for both of us.'

'Do you want out of the clubs too?'

'Yes, but don't worry, it won't affect you. Quadrant will continue to back you.'

He looked at her sharply. 'You don't for one minute imagine that money had anything to do with my marrying you?'

Tiffany managed to smile. 'No. I knew all along that Quadrant wanted to be backers. They would have gone ahead even if we'd never met. What will you do now? Where will you live?'

'In a jet I imagine, flipping from New York to San Francisco to Los Angeles and back again, in ever decreasing circles.' His sense of black humour was back. He gave her his quirky smile. 'Would you have stayed married to me if you hadn't come back last night and seen what was happening?'

Tiffany looked straight at him, and there was a faint quirky smile on her lips too. 'I'd have found out sooner or later,' she replied, 'and I always did have to have the whole cake.'

He walked quickly out of the studio and a few minutes later she heard him in the bedroom, getting his suitcases out of the closet.

Her marriage was over.

The day before Harry was allowed to come home from hospital Morgan busied herself, making sure that everything would be to his liking. The doctors had said he was to take it easy, have rests in the afternoon and early nights, and Morgan was determined that his convalescence would be so comfortable and happy that he would never want it to end. Like a second honeymoon. There would be no frantic socializing or friends to stay; his favourite foods would be on the menu and gentle entertainment would be laid on in the form of video films. She bought a selection of new books that would interest him, several jigsaw puzzles and Harrods sent up a crate of games. She was going to ask him to teach her how to play chess.

McGillivery was detailed to see that the little boat was ready to go out at a minute's notice and that Harry's fishing rods and flies were in order. Fishing was such a peaceful sport and would be good for him.

Nanny was asked to bring David down for breakfast and luncheon each day and she had some of his toys and a playpen set up in the library. Bath times, she announced cheerfully, would, in future, be a family affair. She would bathe David while Harry helped.

The staff at Drumnadrochit Castle eyed each other with astonishment. It seemed the leopard really could change its spots. In a gentle and slightly subdued manner, Morgan gave her orders to the servants, made sure they had time off, and was undemanding. Gone were the days when there were twenty house guests rampaging all over the place wanting trays in their rooms and breakfast in the grand hall at two o'clock in the morning after a night of dancing.

Morgan only bought one thing for herself in preparation for Harry's return. A pale pink crêpe de Chine and lace nightgown and negligée. The night before, she washed her hair and brushed it until it hung in a cloud of gold about her shoulders. The colour had returned to her face and the tight look of strain had dissolved. She had never looked more beautiful. Yet her green eyes flickered anxiously. Harry hadn't said a word about Tiffany being David's real mother. They would have to talk about it soon – or would they? Perhaps, like so many Englishmen she had met, Harry would bury the subject deep within himself and refuse to discuss it. Harry had always hated confrontations. Maybe he was determined to put his head in the sand again. If that was the case, and she went on nurturing the marriage, things could get back to normal. In future, she thought with determination, I will consider what Harry wants first. They could cut out all those endless rounds of dinners and receptions and cocktail parties in London that so bored him. She would take a more practical interest in the gallery, and if Harry really did want to come and live in Scotland in due course she would have to go along with it. If the honeymoon was over, the real marriage was just about to begin.

Harry sat in the large leather chair in the library and irritably flicked through *The Times*. He felt bored. He'd been home a week now, and although he felt much stronger, the headaches still persisted. And he also had something on his mind. Soon he would have to talk to Morgan. He wished he wasn't such a coward. Morgan had been cosseting him and caring for him all week and that made it more difficult. She, too, seemed reluctant to bring up the subject. And everywhere he went, there was David. In his highchair at breakfast, back again at luncheon time, or playing in a corner of the library, while Morgan hung over him, shaking rattles and making cooing noises. So far Harry had said he was too tired to watch bathtime.

David's presence was casting a shadow over him, and the situation had to be resolved, and quickly, if he wasn't to go out of his mind.

While in hospital Harry had managed to secure, in secrecy, some back copies of the newspapers, by bribing a cleaning woman. That Morgan should have gone to such lengths to provide an heir was incredible. That Tiffany should have gone along with it was extraordinary.

Harry also felt a fool. The thought of how the sisters must have laughed at him behind his back made his face burn. Imagine not even realizing he was in bed with the wrong woman!

But it was Morgan's behaviour that was amazing him now. She was acting as if nothing had happened! Of course he had to remember that she was a brilliant actress. He recalled the months of her 'pregnancy' and how convincing she had been! His face burned deeper. And all that time she'd made him sleep in the spare room because she was afraid sex would bring on a miscarriage! Yet here she was, flitting round the castle, merry and beautiful as ever, laughing and joking and acting brighter than the evening star!

Only once had Harry seen her look crestfallen and on the verge of tears. That had been on his first night home when he'd announced he'd be sleeping in the guest wing. But she had quickly recovered herself and said of course she realized he must have undisturbed sleep until he was better.

Then she had personally arranged flowers, a basket of fruit and a jug of iced water in his room.

It was, thought Harry, her role as Perfect Wife and Perfect Mother. He wondered how long it would last. He rose slowly from his chair and went to gaze out of the window. The sun was shining brightly now, and the wind had pushed the grey storm clouds away to the east. A perfect rainbow arched over Loch Ness, its vivid colours shimmering against the misty blues and purples of the distant mountains.

He had to talk to Morgan. In spite of everything he owed her that.

With a heavy heart and dragging feet he left the library and crossed the hall to the drawing room, where he found her sticking some recent snapshots of David into an album.

She looked up brightly as he entered. 'Hi, honey! Come and see this lovely picture of David. Look! He's holding that blue rabbit he loves so much!'

Harry shut the door behind him and came over to her. Then he sat down opposite her.

'We have to talk, Morgan,' he said tensely.

'Of course, darling.' Her hands began to shake as she sorted through the snapshots. She tried to keep her voice steady. 'I'm ready to talk whenever you are. I thought you wanted to wait until you were stronger.'

'I'm as strong now as I'll ever be.'

Morgan looked up sharply. She had never heard Harry sound so weary and resigned before. 'Harry,' she began tremulously, 'I haven't had a chance to tell you before how terribly sorry I am for what I did! I'm deeply ashamed, too. It was just that I wanted to make you happy, and I didn't want you to be disappointed in me. I love you so much and I was so scared that you'd stop loving me if you knew I could never have children. Do you understand what I'm trying to say?' She paused, looking at him searchingly, hoping to find some flicker of understanding, compassion, even love, in his eyes. But Harry was watching her with a distant look and there was something stiff and forbidding in the way he was sitting.

'I'm so sorry, darling.' Morgan's voice broke. 'I'd never have done it if I hadn't known how important it was to you to have an heir. You've no idea how terrible I feel now. Please say you forgive me, Harry, I need you... I love you...' Tears were rolling down her cheeks.

'Don't go on, Morgan,' he said with an effort, tearing his eyes from her woebegone face. 'All that is really only of academic interest now.'

Morgan dabbed at the front of her sweater, where her tears had fallen. It was a pathetic gesture. 'How do you mean?' she asked, her voice choked. Then she rose from her chair and dropped on her knees in front of him, laying a small hand on his knee. 'Do you mean we can – go on as before? Oh, it would be so wonderful if we could! I promise you we'll have a better life! No more parties every night, and if you want to give up the house in London, I'm perfectly happy to live here. There's no reason why we can't be happy again, is there? After all, you love David and he is your son even if he isn't mine. Oh Harry, say we can be happy again. Please!'

The distant, tortured look never left Harry's face. Then he rose abruptly, almost pushing her aside, as he strode to the open window. The rainbow had vanished. Instead thick turbulent clouds had gathered, blotting out the landscape. Everything was grim and grey again. He turned and looked at Morgan, still sitting huddled on the floor.

'Everything has changed, Morgan,' he said and there was a deep melancholy in his voice. Then he stopped. He had planned to tell her something that altered the whole situation, but somehow he couldn't.

He walked out of the library and closed the door behind him.

It was too soon. Too painful to talk about yet. It would have to wait.

32

Joe left the offices of Krauss and Blumfeld on 39th and Lexington and hailed a passing cab.

It was the second cab he'd taken in twenty-eight years. The first had been earlier that day. His investigations into Sig Hoffman's activities had to be carried out in the utmost secrecy. If Sig were to realize what was going on he'd cover his tracks quicker than a scalded cat.

'I'm bringing in two, maybe three independent accountants to go through everything,' Hank Krauss had told Joe. 'And you're going to have to fix it for us to get into the accounting department of Quadrant at night, when no one's there. That's the only way we're going to get to the bottom of this.'

'How long will it take?'

'Could be three, four nights! We've come up with two interestings things, meanwhile.' Hank riffled through his notes. 'The first is that Sig Hoffman is a heavy gambler. Did you know that?'

Joe looked at him in blank astonishment. 'I'd no idea! What is it, horses?'

'No, roulette. He's been seen on several occasions during the past few years losing as much as a hundred thousand dollars on the single spin of a wheel.'

'He doesn't have that kind of money to throw around!'

'He hasn't, but Quadrant has! The second thing we've come up with is that your chief accountant, Lee Schraub, was involved in some very shady deals on the stock market a few years ago. Now Sig Hoffman is either blackmailing him into cooking the books or they're splitting the rake-off from Quadrant.'

'But wouldn't Kohn and Rohner, our company accountants, have spotted something? For Christ's sake, you're talking big bucks!'

'By the time Kohn and Rohner do the auditing, you can be sure a lot of creative accounting has gone into the books,' said Hank calmly. 'What we have to do now is find out *how* Sig is operating, helped as I think by Lee Schraub. My own bet is that he's also running an offshore company, which means he is defrauding the IRS too. If all this can be proved, I'm telling you, Joe, he's in for a bumpy ride.'

'He deserves it all,' said Joe coldly, 'in spades.'

'Sure, but I've never seen you out for blood like this before, Joe. Not even the time one of your clients made off with three million dollars because their so-called security didn't exist!'

'I've got personal reasons for wanting to pin all I can on Sig,' Joe snapped. 'You just get all the proof needed to have him charged with embezzlement. I'll look after the rest.'

Hank shrugged. It was obvious Joe wasn't going to say any more.

Now, speeding down the FDR Drive on his way to Wall Street, Joe felt sick and betrayed. After nearly thirty years of friendship Joe realized he had never really known Sig at all. When had it all started? Joe thought back to the days when they'd first met at CCNY. Could he really be such a bad judge of character that he had thought Sig was on the level from the start?

Up until last week Joe would have trusted Sig with his life and everything he had.

It just went to show how fucking wrong you could be.

As Hunt caught the early evening flight back to Los Angeles, he was filled with dull rage.

Seeing Tiffany again had hurt more than he thought and now he wished he'd never made the trip. What was the point in breaking open old wounds?

Ordering a bourbon he settled back in his seat and tried to concentrate on the script for the next episode of *Street Echoes.*

Damn that woman! Tiffany had looked more lovely and desirable than ever, and now she was Mrs disco doll Krasner, married to some jerk who ran a would-be string of nightclubs! Why hadn't she waited for him, for Christ's sake? *Why didn't you let her know you were finally getting a divorce?* whispered a tiny part of his mind.

Hunt ordered a second bourbon and tucked the script down the side of his seat.

Memories of a thousand nights they'd spent together crammed into his mind – and memories of a thousand mornings too. Tiffany had always been particularly seductive in the mornings, rosy and bright-eyed and tender. She had always smelled sweet too, kind of musky and exciting. And then he recalled how she had been when he aroused her, all softness and wetness, drowning him in ecstasy, her nipples hard and her hips swaying as he pumped his very being into her. She had driven him crazy.

He ordered another bourbon and abandoned all thoughts of the script.

How could she have agreed to be the mother of Harry's baby? *How could she?* After all they had meant to each other it should have been his seed that had grown inside her. *His* child she had borne. How often had she cried out as she neared her climax, 'Fill me darling, fill me with all of you!'

Bitterness gouged great lumps out of his heart. How dare she smile brightly and tell him her husband was 'fabulous'!

Hunt ordered a fourth bourbon and lay back in his seat and closed his eyes. There would never be anyone like Tiffany again. She was his ideal woman, beautiful, intelligent, passionate and loving. He had explored the depths of her body, her mind and soul and there wasn't a part of her he didn't love. They'd been made for each other and now she had rushed off and married a comparative stranger.

Drunkenly, he hoped she'd be as unhappy as hell. It would serve her right for not waiting for him.

An uneasy sort of truce had settled between Morgan and Harry. They didn't fight, they never quarrelled. In fact, they were scrupulously polite to each other most of the time. If other people were present they even seemed to be on friendly terms. But it was as if they were walking on a cloud of delicate bubbles that the slightest jar would burst, dropping them on the rocks below.

When Harry was pronounced fit to return to London he made two things clear. First, he would sleep in the spare bedroom in future and second, he wished to see as little of David as possible.

The strain quickly told on Morgan. She veered from bewilderment to depression, was unable to sleep, lost her appetite and spent her days in a sort of limbo waiting for something to break. She wasn't sure what, but she knew she couldn't endure much more of this cold war.

She did, however, stick to the promises she had made. There was no more rushing every night from a cocktail party to a reception, from there to a dinner, then ending up at a ball or Annabel's. She'd also stopped giving lavish dinner parties every week and consulted Harry if they were invited away for the weekend before accepting.

This quieter life was not as difficult to achieve as she had imagined because so many of their so-called friends, people she'd got to know since her marriage, seemed to have dropped them.

Where once there had been a stack of expensive-looking envelopes on the silver tray in the hall each morning, each containing a thick white card bearing an invitation in copper-plate printing, now all she got were gimmicky invitations to the opening of a new restaurant or a hair-dressing salon. The invitations from the highest in the land had gushed in before, but now the tap was turned off.

A few people telephoned to invite them to drinks or supper but they were from the tacky end of society Morgan had been avoiding ever since she'd landed in London.

It was with growing horror that she realized that those whom she had regarded as friends now shunned her, while those she had never really had any use for merely invited her as Exhibit A to liven up their gossipy gatherings.

Morgan became more and more isolated as the weeks passed, the idleness and boredom driving her to have her face and hair done several times a week, buy a lot more clothes, lounge around the house flipping through magazines and plan the redecoration of some of the rooms. There was the occasional luncheon with Rosalie Winwood, but that relationship had changed too. She and Harry seemed to have been struck off the Winwoods' official guest list, because Rosalie always chose some discreet little Chelsea restaurant where they would be unlikely to be recognized.

Loneliness was something she had never had to cope with before and the public humiliation added to her sense of defeat. When she asked friends like the Duchess of Southampton to dinner she was met with polite evasion and pathetic excuses.

'I'm awfully sorry, Morgan,' was the line they all gave her, 'but we seem to have got ourselves tied up for practically *months* ahead. Life is just too hectic, isn't it, my dear?'

For Morgan it wasn't hectic at all. The pages of her diary were completely blank.

'Yes,' she would reply, 'we've got so much on too.' *If we had any less on, we'd be dead!* she thought.

Sometimes, fighting back the tears, she would go through her address book. It was incredible that in a few short months her position had shifted from someone who was asked everywhere and had hundreds of friends to someone who couldn't even rake up eight guests for dinner.

In spite of her attempts in Scotland to get to know David better, she also realized her maternal instincts were nonexistent. She had to admit he was a pretty baby with a sunny nature, but she had no desire to hold him or play with him or even see him. Anyway, he preferred the company of his nanny and bawled loudly if she left him. Maybe things would improve when he grew older and she could relate to him more. In the meantime Harry had made it clear that he wished to see as little of the child as possible.

At one point Morgan contemplated going back to New York for a while, but then changed her mind. Tiffany refused to speak to her, and Joe, once he knew Harry had recovered, had told her in no uncertain terms what he thought of her. That only left Ruth and Zachary. Ruth would never dare do anything to upset Joe and Zachary was still undergoing treatment in a clinic. He'd always hated her anyway.

As she tried to put on a brave face, she saw her world crumbling away. Time was the only thing she had on her side now. People forgot the worst scandal eventually. She was also young and her beauty had a certain poignancy now that it had lacked before. The lines of her cheekbones were more acute, her green eyes had more depth. Of one thing she was determined. Somehow, no matter how long it took, she would win back Harry's love. He'd been so crazy about her once, surely he could be made to feel the same way again? She knew now that crêpe de Chine nighties and a spray of Joy were not the answer.

She would have to think of something else.

Harry was soon strong enough to go back to the gallery, and he threw himself into work as if by doing so he could erase the emptiness of his marriage. Business was booming, and in his absence John had opened up another outlet for exporting pictures to America.

In a fever of activity, Harry installed two experienced restorers in premises near the gallery. So many American, Lebanese and Arab customers, he realized, wouldn't look at a picture unless the colours were brilliant and the varnish glossy. Rather like Morgan, he thought, who hated anything unless it looked new and bright.

He'd started a new routine that kept him from having to go home in the evenings until the last possible moment. It had begun when Elizabeth called him up at the gallery a few days after he'd returned to work.

'Elizabeth!' he had cried in delight. 'It's great hearing from you! How are you?'

'Oh, I'm fine, but how are you, Harry? Are you really better?'

'I think so. I still get the occasional headache but it could be worse.'

'It could have been a great deal worse.' Her voice was serious. 'I haven't seen you for such ages, why don't you drop in for a drink on your way home?'

For a moment Harry hesitated. What if Morgan found out? There was one thing he didn't feel strong enough for at the moment and that was a fight. At least Morgan was being polite and pleasant, and that was something. But then he thought, oh hell! Elizabeth's only an old friend. So where's the harm? He didn't plan to go to bed with her again, that had just been a drunken spur-of-the-moment madness so there could be no harm in seeing her for a drink.

'I'd love to,' he replied. 'By the way, I never thanked you for the flowers. It was very sweet of you.'

'It was the least I could do. I just wished I could have made myself more useful. It was awful being stuck here with you so ill and so far away.'

'It wasn't much fun!' he said drily. 'Anyway I'll see you this evening – about six?'

'That would be perfect,' she said. And she meant it.

It was the beginning of what was to become a regular habit, although at first Harry didn't realize it. He told Morgan he was out on a valuation and she seemed to accept that.

Once a week, then twice a week, he would drop in to see

Elizabeth on the way home from the gallery. Soon it was three times a week. He liked the peace and tranquillity of her home, and the air of casual confidence in its decor. The furniture and curtains had the slightly faded and grubby splendour so dear to the hearts of the old English aristocracy. The Aubusson tapestry rugs were so worn in places that the wooden floor showed through and the rooms were painted the original eau-de-nil Elizabeth's parents had chosen when they had married thirty-three years before.

Sitting with Elizabeth in the 'den', the little room that led off the hall opposite the drawing room, Harry felt content. This was like a private sitting room, with deep chintz-covered sofa and chairs, book-lined walls, television, and a profusion of newspapers, magazines and unfinished needlework. The mantelpiece was smothered with family snapshots, a Christmas card left over from the previous year and several framed photographs, all signed, of members of the Royal Family.

The house made a statement and it was one Harry approved of. A statement that said, *We arrived, hundreds of years ago. We don't have to show off.* Harry found himself comparing it to his own home. Morgan would never realize when she *had* arrived. With these thoughts, Harry basked in the comfort of Elizabeth's company more and more.

For Tiffany, this was the most negative period of her life. In a numbed sort of way she felt she was treading water, afraid of drowning, yet afraid of moving in any direction.

When her lawyer wrote and told her that her divorce from Axel would become final in a few weeks, she filed the letter methodically in her desk and felt nothing. Not even a pang. Her marriage had been a terrible mistake and Axel had probably caught her on the rebound from Hunt. She would never let such a thing happen again. She filed her lawyer's letter under *Personal.*

When she heard she'd been nominated for a Tony for her

designs for *Gertie*, she'd filed that letter too. Under *Business*. It was nice to have been chosen for an award but she doubted she'd win.

Joe kept her fully informed on Hank Krauss's investigations into Sig's activities and she listened with polite interest. Not that she cared a damn what happened to Sig.

If Greg telephoned to ask her out she gently declined. Making small-talk required too much effort.

When Ruth suggested they lunch together or go shopping, Tiffany always had too much work to do.

The days merged into weeks and they all had the same indistinctiveness about them. Grey and flat. Her senses seemed to have been sealed off from life, and she was thankful she had lost the power to feel. She could even think of Morgan with cool detachment. As for the baby, well, he had never been meant to be hers in the first place. *You don't hurt if you don't feel*, she told herself, and was glad.

The sky could explode and she doubted if she'd even blink.

It wasn't to last for long.

The week of Royal Ascot had arrived. Morgan had chosen her clothes for the four days' racing with extreme care. Some instinct told her to keep an elegant low profile rather than wear her usual style of eye-catching glamour. On the first day, the Tuesday, she had decided to wear a simple navy-blue dress with a pleated skirt and a long-sleeved jacket. For the Wednesday she chose a hawthorn-red silk shift, which would go well with her rubies. The next day was 'Ladies' Day' when the race for the Gold Cup would be run and for this she planned to go all in white. A white silk suit, belted with a wide white kid belt. Friday was not so important. On Friday she would wear a caramel linen skirt and a matching three-quarter-length coat with black collar and cuffs. The staffs at Ungaro and Valentino had been courteous and respectful when she had gone for her fittings, affording her the only bit of pleasure she had known in the past few weeks. Freddie Fox had made her exquisite hats to go with each dress and her shoes had been specially dyed to match by Rayne. At least she would look good, but for once it was poor consolation. She was dreading every moment of the week. Her fear of being cold-shouldered was acute. Harry, on the other hand, was unusually cheerful. He enjoyed drinking champagne, watching the races and seeing all his old friends. In that order. So had Morgan, the previous year, and she'd also enjoyed the opportunity of showing off her beautiful clothes and getting her photograph taken for all the journals and newspapers. Last year she'd made page one for four days running. She didn't need to be told that this year it would be different and if she was photographed the caption would make unpleasant reading.

At noon, Duncan dropped them off at the magnificent gold and black wrought-iron gates that led into the Royal Enclosure. In the past Morgan had loved the whole occasion so much, but now as she and Harry walked across the unsaddling enclosure, they were not even talking. They strolled on, Harry raising his top hat to several ladies he knew, and Morgan smiling politely, until they came to one of the bars in the forecourt, which was already packed with people sitting at little white tables, under royal blue and white striped umbrellas. Around them were sounds of affectionate greetings, popping of corks and bursts of laughter. As soon as they entered the bar an elderly couple rushed up and greeted Harry, asking him if he had quite recovered from his car crash. Soon they were all drinking Bollinger, and Harry was surrounded by more friends, enquiring how he was. Imperceptibly, Morgan felt herself being excluded from the circle, pushed to the very outside edges and ignored. It struck her forcibly that no matter what Harry did – even if it was something disgraceful – he would always be accepted, because he *belonged*. He was one of *them*.

'I'm backing Leading Star in the third race,' the elderly lady was saying.

'Rubbish, m'dear!' snorted her husband jovially. 'It's one of the Queen's horses – they never win!' Everyone laughed.

'I see old Charlie has got a runner today, in the first race! Know what its chances are?' Harry asked.

'Hopeless on the flat, old boy! My money's going on The Surrogate, hear she's a really fast runner!'

There was a second's stunned silence then one of the ladies in the group cut in with, 'I just *must* back Deception! Isn't it a wonderful name? Such pretty colours too, apricot and lime.' A second later she too turned scarlet and swiftly took a gulp of her champagne.

Fighting back the tears Morgan said, 'Excuse me – I must go and powder my nose.'

'Okay!' replied Harry lightly. 'Meet you back here and we'll keep some champagne for you.' She wasn't sure as she glanced at him whether he looked upset or was merely trying to keep a straight face.

Morgan slipped into the ladies' cloakroom and quickly repaired her make-up, angry with herself for being so vulnerable. They hadn't meant to be cruel. They were just stupid insensitive English upper-class *cunts*, the sort who always blurted out something asinine before they thought.

As she left the cloakroom she bumped into an interior designer she'd met at several cocktail parties. He was sporting a pink shirt, pink silk handkerchief in his breast pocket and pink kid gloves with his pearl-grey morning suit.

'Hullo!' he said. 'And how's the busy little mother? Any more sisters hidden in the closet for Harry?' He threw back his head, screaming with laughter. 'How is the little nipper by the way? I suppose he'll have to call you Aunty now!' Morgan stiffened, shot him a look of loathing and snapping, 'No, he's saving that name for you,' she stalked off to the bar to find Harry. She would get him to take her home. Now. She would leave England. Forever.

Harry was nowhere to be seen. The bar was almost deserted as everyone had gone to watch the arrival of the Royal Family. For a moment she stood uncertainly, then went round to the front of the grandstand. The sloping lawns were filled now by thousands of people. She'd never find Harry in this lot.

Going back to the bar she ordered herself a large vodka and tonic and sat at an empty table in the forecourt. It looked more dignified than rushing around searching for a missing husband, she decided, and the drink helped quell the rising feeling of panic at the ostracism she knew was now her lot.

The first race started. She could hear the roar of approval as the favourite crossed the finish line. People came flocking back for drinks before the next race. Still there was no sign of Harry. Pale-faced and desperate, she tried to pretend she was merely waiting for someone.

The second race started. It was one and a quarter miles and was longer than the first race. Once again the crowds roared. This time a rank outsider won amidst furious cheering. Once again everyone came jostling back to the bar. She couldn't possibly be *still* waiting, so she rose and with assumed nonchalance made her way back to the lawns. Then she saw him. In a hideous moment of déja vu she realized that this was exactly where she had come in.

Harry was standing on the Queen's private lawn just in front of the Royal Box, where the Queen, the Queen Mother and Prince Charles sat watching the proceedings. He was smiling and talking to the girl beside him, and then he slipped his hand under her elbow in a gesture of loving possessiveness.

Morgan didn't have to see the girl's face to know it was Elizabeth.

Joe was the first to receive the news.

There would be more phone calls, more searches and

more wondering, but it would all be in vain. No one could do anything now. Except wait.

Absent-mindedly he reached across his desk for a cigar, lit it, and then sank back in his deep-buttoned leather chair.

For some reason he couldn't fathom, all he could think about, even at this moment, was his own youth. All those years ago when he'd lived with his parents and brothers in the Bronx and the desperate need for money had become an obsession. For food, for clothes, and later for girls. He'd even had to walk to CCNY sometimes for lack of a few cents for his subway ticket.

Joe looked around the opulent room. Well, he had it all now. The magnificent panelling, two Cézannes and a Dégas, a George III mahogany table, a pair of bronze equestrian groups by Frederick William MacMonnies and some very rare Regency library chairs. And this was only the office. The Park Avenue duplex was crammed with works of art and the ocean-front house at Southampton filled with antiques.

Sitting now, in his Savile Row suit and handmade lizard-skin shoes, it hit him with tremendous force that he'd been a hell of a lot happier when he'd started out than he was now. That was the trouble with youth. You didn't appreciate it when you had it. By the time you'd striven to get everything you wanted you were old like flat champagne. Too old to enjoy life in the same way. The fun was in the getting there, not the being there.

He eyed the array of telephones on his desk, wondering who to call first. Ruth? No, spare Ruth for a while. She'd only start popping Valium and there was nothing she could do anyway. Tiffany? God, poor Tiffany. As if she hadn't gone through enough already. But it had to be done, sooner or later. And right now he needed her.

Gloria answered the phone.

'I'll go get her right away, Mr Kalvin,' she said respectfully.

He waited nervously. Tiffany would probably be philosophical at first and say they must never give up hope, but Joe knew better. In this sort of situation there was no such thing as hope.

Tiffany was on the line. 'Hi, Daddy!'

'Hi, Tiff.'

'What's wrong?'

'How do you know anything's wrong?'

'I can tell by your voice. Is it Sig? Have they found out more?'

'It's not Sig, it's Zachary. The clinic have just rung to say he's split. Escaped early this morning. They've no idea where he's gone.'

Zachary went straight to Mitch's place because in his mind it represented home more than anywhere else.

It had all started here, in this room, in this seedy tenement building, and it was here on the lumpy sofa that he and Smokey had spent their last night together. But there was no sofa now and the wobbly table and the clutter of empty beer cans and trashy journals and overflowing ashtrays had all gone.

Zachary stood staring around him and felt a deep sense of loss, of being cheated. Dirt lay thickly on the floor and a filthy fragment of cloth hung from a couple of nails, covering the broken window. On a wall an old torn poster of Elvis Presley hung like a flag at half mast. A pungent, rancid smell was the only sign Mitch had left to remind Zachary that his past, his present and his future lay within these four walls.

He lowered himself onto the floor and sat with legs outstretched, leaning his back against the peeling wall. He could hear Mitch's easy laugh echoing round the room and Smokey's whispered promises. But Mitch wasn't here any more. And Smokey wasn't here any more. Smokey wasn't anywhere any more. He looked up at the cracked ceiling and remembered that morning when he'd had his first trip. He'd been scared shitless – but not for long. Each trip had got better, had become a way of life, *was* life. And each trip took him higher and higher, so high even his father couldn't reach him.

He gazed around him, his eyes screwed up, as if focusing on something would help him to focus his mind. What day was it? Friday? Saturday? He'd jumped *that place* on Monday and ever since then the days and nights had merged. Who the fuck cared anyway! It was enough to have got away from that hell hole where they'd been depriving him of the only happiness he'd ever known. He had vague memories of hitching a lift on a truck, of stealing some woman's purse in a supermarket, of sleeping in the open one night, then more stealing, more travelling – but now he was safe. And he'd got hold of a fresh supply. Something to share with Mitch.

He groped in his canvas bag and carefully extracted the precious packet of heroin. Pure stuff, the dealer had assured him. One hundred per cent. With shaking hands he prepared for his trip to paradise.

The rush hit him fast, coursing round his body and striking his brain with an explosive force.

The last thing he saw was Smokey's face with her wide scarlet mouth. It seemed to be smiling at him, beckoning.

33

It was an achingly beautiful day when they buried Zachary. The sun, strong and bold, had risen into a perfect blue sky, not waiting for the living or the dead in its relentless upward climb. The trees in Valhalla Cemetery were motionless and not a blade of grass quivered. The only sound to be heard was the soft rumble of the funeral cars as they drove through Westchester, led by the hearse.

The Kalvin family had come to bury their only son and it seemed as if the world was holding its breath.

On the mahogany casket lay just one wreath of white flowers. The card read: 'To our beloved Zachary, who will always be in our hearts and in our minds. Mom, Daddy, Tiffany and Morgan.'

The cortège stopped and while the undertakers gently lifted the casket onto their shoulders, the doors of the first car opened slowly. Joe stepped out first, his shoulders bowed, his face fixed in an agony of grief. Ruth followed, a fragile figure in black, her pale gold hair gleaming dully under her heavy veil. Then Tiffany and Morgan climbed out and stood side by side, both dressed in black, both with their long hair coiled up under small black hats, both with ashen faces. They stood together uncertainly for a moment, their eyes fixed on the casket, which suddenly seemed pathetically small. They were both remembering the laughing blond boy who had once been their brother.

Friends were getting out of the other cars now, hovering nervously, unsure of what to do or say but catching each other's eyes, sharing the family's grief, remembering moments in their own lives when they had grieved.

Joe and Ruth moved forward, leading the way to the spot

where Zachary was to be buried. Others gathered round them, friends, business associates, people Joe didn't even recognize. Sig Hoffman and his wife stayed close. Joe didn't even see them. Staggering forward, his arm through Ruth's, he was blinded by the tears that gathered in his eyes. Ruth was composed, as if she didn't really know what was happening. There was a bewildered child-like look on her face. But behind her the tears streamed down Tiffany's cheeks and Morgan's loud sobs broke the stillness.

The service was simple. The minister spoke compassionately and lovingly of Zachary.

Everyone looked at the casket. A large bumblebee was hovering over the flowers that draped the lid, droning lazily in its quest for nectar. Tiffany watched as it circled once or twice, alighted on a bloom, then suddenly rose in the air and flew away. A free spirit. She hoped with all her heart that Zachary had flown away like that, a spirit freed from the addiction that had imprisoned his body and tortured his soul.

Beside her Joe was sinking to his knees, nearly dragging Ruth down with him. Tiffany put her hand on his shoulder and heard him say, 'Forgive me, Zac. Oh God, forgive me.'

It was the worst moment for her in the whole of that dreadful day. They all needed Zachary's forgiveness. From the moment he'd been the kid brother they'd all loved but taken for granted, to the time he was a troubled youth, afraid of the future.

Someone grabbed Tiffany's arm and turning she saw it was Morgan. Her face was distorted and swollen with naked grief. The rich-little-girl-lost look had gone. In its place was a woman struggling in her own private hell.

'Oh Tiff.' She rested her head against Tiffany's for a moment. 'I can't bear it.'

The funeral service drew to a close. The ground around the grave was now hidden by thousands of flowers woven into wreaths, sprays, crosses and bouquets. They came from the people who worked at Quadrant, the staff at Park Avenue and the house on Long Island. They came from the rich and the poor, from socialites and college friends of Zachary's. Harry had ordered a spray of lilies from London. Gloria had spent her week's pay on a cross of pink carnations. Greg's flowers bore a card saying, 'We all love you'.

Then Tiffany saw another spray of spring blossoms in shades of pink and gold. In handwriting she instantly recognized she read: 'To Zachary, who was like a kid brother. Hunt.'

But no one noticed the modest bunch of dahlias or the card that was tied to them which read, 'Give my love to Smokey. See ya pal, Mitch.'

'Can I talk with you, Tiff?' Morgan asked. 'I have to fly back to London tomorrow and we haven't much time and there's a lot to say.'

It was two days after Zachary's funeral and Tiffany was at her parents' home, where Morgan was staying.

'Sure. Isn't Daddy back yet?' Tiffany looked at her watch. It was half past six. Joe should have been home by now.

Morgan shook her head. 'He looked terrible when he left this morning. I told him not to go to the office but he wouldn't listen. Mom's been in bed all day, the doctor has given her another injection. They say she may have to be sedated for several days.'

'Poor Mother.' Tiffany sank onto the pale blue living-room sofa and closed her eyes. She ached all over and she couldn't remember ever having felt so tired.

'A drink?' Morgan walked with jerky steps to the bar cabinet, her hands fluttering nervously as she took a couple of glasses off the shelf.

'No thanks. Oh, I might have some mineral water.'

There was silence in the room. Morgan poured some

Perrier into a crystal tumbler and added a slice of lemon, then she mixed a strong martini for herself.

'What do you want to talk about?' Tiffany asked in a flat voice.

'Everything! I feel so dreadful. I don't know where to begin.' Morgan's eyes were lifeless and her hands shook. 'It's all such a mess, everything's a mess, and it's all my fault. I must have been crazy, Tiff, and I'm sorry I made you have the baby for me – and put you through so much. I was out of my mind when I found I couldn't have a child and felt I had to do *something*! Now it's all gone wrong and everyone hates me. Why did you let me force you, Tiff?'

'I don't know, now, but if you want to talk, we'll talk. You're not going to like what I've got to say, but I can't help that! You've got to realize, Morgan, that you'll always be in trouble if you go on combining the emotions of a spoiled child with the scheming bitchiness of a thwarted woman! Don't you think it's time you took responsibility for your actions, started to think what effect your ambitions and desires have on other people before you plunge in, feet first, messing about in other people's lives to get what you want?'

Morgan started to weep.

'Now don't start that!' Tiffany's voice was kind but firm. 'It just won't work for me any more. You know you're only crying for yourself,' she continued. 'You're not crying for Zachary, or Daddy or Mom – or me.'

'How do you know what I'm crying for?' Morgan sobbed. 'I'm probably the way I am because you've *always* interpreted my feelings *for* me! You've always said, "Oh you're only crying because . . ." *How* do you know what I'm crying about? They're my feelings, not yours,' she ended with certain logic.

'It's just that I know you so well,' said Tiffany gently. 'You're as transparent as glass! I know you're bereaved about Zac, don't think I don't. But in your heart of hearts you're more upset because you're not everyone's flavour of the month! What do you expect? You've just about screwed up the lives of everyone who ever loved you! It's incredible the harm you've done!'

'All I ever really wanted was Harry – and to be a duchess one day – and to live in a beautiful castle –'

'Don't we all, Morgan, don't we all – when we're little! The original Cinderella and the prince-on-a-white-horse syndrome! But most of us have to make our lives work without blackmailing Fairy Godmothers or hurting those who love us most. Life isn't a fairy-tale, Morgan. It's real, and you get one shot at getting it right.'

Morgan dabbed her eyes and the little-girl-lost look came back. 'But Mom and Daddy wanted those things for me too, you know they did! And it would have been the end of my marriage if I hadn't been able to produce an heir for Harry.'

'Did you give Harry a chance, or a choice? If he really loves you, would it have made any difference? He would have probably been very sympathetic. After all, it's not your fault that you can't have children! He didn't demand a certificate of fecundity, verified by a gynaecologist before he bestowed the family jewels on you. Maybe you could have adopted children.'

'You don't understand! It's not like that in England. These old noble families, like the Royal Family, look upon it as a terrible tragedy if there isn't an heir to succeed. It has to be a boy, too! Girls hardly ever inherit titles in England.'

'That *is* tragic!' Tiffany's voice was heavy with sarcasm. 'I'm not saying that everything that's happened has been your fault, but most of it is. I know Daddy was anxious for you to marry into an aristocratic family, and having married into one, you then found pressures being put on you that almost pulled you apart. But really, no one forced you to go to the lengths you did! Have you *any* idea – do you care? – what it was like for me? We were all three of us spoiled, Morgan. I know that. Do you? But we certainly weren't brought up to hurt and destroy other people.'

'Who's destroyed?' Morgan cried wildly. 'Oh, I don't know, I feel so confused! I know I've hurt you . . . I suppose you're right, I've hurt everyone, but let me tell you something. I've been hurt most of all! I'm desperately trying to hold my marriage together in the face of the most appalling humiliation –'

'Tell me. Do you love Harry?'

Morgan looked at Tiffany for a long moment and there was a sincerity in her eyes that Tiffany had never seen before.

'Yes, of course I love him now. In the beginning I suppose I *was* attracted to everything Harry had to offer. What girl wouldn't fall for a fantastically attractive man who also had a title, a leading position in society, everything I wanted! And I knew I'd be a credit to him too. I was so happy when we first got married! Harry was so easy and let me do anything I wanted and he thought everything I did was marvellous. I helped promote his gallery, you know. He's making a small fortune these days. And I did over Drumnadrochit and the house in London. Oh, Tiff, I did it so *well*, and it *was* so wonderful!' Morgan broke off as a shadow of anguish crossed her face. 'I'm praying it will be all right again, but I don't know if Harry will ever forgive me.'

Then she buried her face in her hands and started to sob again.

Tiffany put her arm round Morgan's shoulders and hugged her, feeling a sympathetic yet weary sort of resignation. It would always be like this, Morgan the wilful and rather pathetic child and herself in the role of an ever-forgiving mother.

At that moment Joe arrived, a grief-torn and exhausted figure, dragging his feet. In the past week he seemed to have aged ten years. He sank heavily into one of the deep chairs without speaking.

Gently, Tiffany pushed Morgan to one side. Morgan was young and resilient. In time, she would get over most things. Joe looked as if he couldn't take much more.

'Hi, Daddy. Can I get you something?' Tenderly Tiffany kissed his cheek.

Joe looked up at her, his eyes little hot spots of pain in his pale chubby face. 'I'll have a rye. Is your mother around?'

'She's in bed. The doctor has been again and given her an injection. Sleep is the best thing for her at the moment.'

'I wish I could sleep,' Joe remarked sadly. 'Nothing seems to work.'

'Shall I get something stronger sent round? You must get some sleep.'

'No thanks, Tiff. I'll be all right.' Joe sipped his rye gingerly, as if he was afraid it would sting his throat, then he let out a deep sigh. 'I wanted to talk to you girls tonight, especially since it seems Morgan has to hurry back to Britain on Friday. There are some things we have to get straightened out, because I don't know when we will all be together again.'

'I'm not going anywhere, Daddy!' Tiffany reached out and laid a comforting hand on his arm.

'Well, I *must* get back! I'm sorry, but I have to get back to Harry,' cried Morgan. She had dried her eyes and was applying face powder to cover up the pink blotches. It reminded Tiffany of a little girl experimenting with her mother's make-up.

'Be that as it may.' Joe seemed to have revived slightly, straightening his shoulders and looking at his daughters as they sat side by side, on the sofa opposite him.

He began with difficulty, as if he were having a problem finding the right words. 'I blame myself for Zachary's death. No, let me finish!' He raised his hand as Tiffany opened her mouth to interject. 'I do blame myself. It was something that should never have happened. I was too hard on him in some ways and too soft on him in others. Trouble is, I was usually too damn busy to even notice what was going on most of the time. I wanted the best for you all, everything I didn't have and always wanted when I was young. Neither of you have ever known what it's like to be broke, to pay regular visits to the pawn shop to buy food and pay the rent, stuffing your shoes with paper to keep your feet dry, and living in permanent fear of being washed up. All that happened to me and my brothers – and more. Well, you got it all. Everything. Whatever you wanted was yours. But money has to be used the right way and it seems to me that apart from you, Tiff, money has brought more heartbreak into this family than anything else. The point is, you two are all I've got left now.' Joe took a swift gulp of his drink to cover his emotions while Tiffany watched him anxiously. Morgan sat, looking scared.

'You, Tiffany, and you, Morgan, well, we've all got to see that there are no more tragedies. I know it's going to be hard but we've got to go on from here as a family.'

There was silence in the room. Morgan shuffled her feet nervously.

Joe turned to look at her. 'You've done some terrible things, Morgan. I can hardly believe that a child of mine would blackmail her sister, deceive her husband, lie, scheme – cause such terrible trouble. Oh God, where did I go wrong with you?' His voice was thick with despair.

The tears started to trickle down Morgan's cheeks.

'I suppose you know,' he demanded, 'that there wasn't a word of truth in what you overheard Sig tell Tiffany all those years ago? I've never done a criminal act in my life, but you were *both* ready to believe I had, weren't you?'

'You mean?' Morgan looked aghast.

'I mean that Sig was bluffing! He was the guilty one and very soon now I'll have enough evidence to bring charges. He'll get ten to fifteen years in the slammer! My best friend has been swindling the company for ten years and my own daughters believed it was me! There's just one difference though. You, Tiffany, were prepared to go through *anything* to protect me, as you thought, but *you*, Morgan, had no hesitation in using the information for your own purposes, to get what you wanted.'

'I'd *never* have told anyone, Daddy!' Morgan cried indignantly. 'Do you think I wanted the world to know my father was an embezzler, for God's sake?'

'But Tiffany wasn't to know that, was she? You scared the shit out of her! You actually made her believe that if she didn't agree to that surrogate mother bullshit you'd go stright to the FBI!'

Joe's old spark had returned. If he'd messed up his son's life, he sure as hell wasn't going to let it happen to his daughters.

'I'm sorry, Daddy, I really am.' A distraught sob escaped from Morgan's throat. 'What more can I say – or do? I'll never behave like that again and I'm truly sorry for what I did to you, Tiff. Will you all just stop being so hard on me! Please.'

Joe and Tiffany looked at each other. Morgan was Morgan. She'd probably never change. The child was set irretrievably in the mould of the woman. Morgan would always need protecting – from herself.

'Okay, okay,' Joe said gruffly. 'Now wipe your eyes and tell me what your plans are.'

'I'm going home to Harry.' She didn't dare tell her father that she thought her marriage was already over.

Not now.

Not yet.

Elizabeth smoothed Harry's hair back from his forehead and planted a gentle kiss on his temple.

'I love you,' she whispered, then laid her head on the pillow beside his.

'I love you too, darling,' Harry replied. They were the words she longed to hear but she wished he hadn't said them so fretfully, almost as if he were grumbling.

'Shall we go to Henley tomorrow?' Her voice was cajoling. 'They say the weather's going to be hot and sunny.'

'The Regatta's an awfully public place for us to be seen

together. All Pa's old friends from Eton and Oxford will be there. Christ, Leander will be positively crawling with people we know!'

'Leander's such a stuffy old club, but you're right,' she murmured reluctantly. 'What a pity! I always enjoy Henley. Perhaps we can drive into the country instead and have lunch somewhere.'

Harry smiled. Elizabeth was so sweet and undemanding, and he hated to disappoint her. 'That's a promise, darling. We'll find some old world pub and have a lovely luncheon.'

'Somewhere very discreet.' There wasn't a trace of bitterness in her voice. 'Where no one will know us. As long as we're together that's all that matters.'

'You haven't forgotten that Morgan will be home from Zachary's funeral in a couple of days, have you?'

Elizabeth stared up at her bedroom ceiling. 'I haven't forgotten.'

'I wish I knew what was going to happen.' Harry sounded fretful again. 'I really should have flown to New York with her, but somehow I just couldn't face it. Especially seeing Tiffany again. Anyway I had that bad headache that day and the doctor cautioned me against flying so I think Morgan understood, but still. It was an awful shock about Zach. Tragic really. He was basically a very nice chap.'

Elizabeth remained silent as she usually did when Harry was thinking aloud rather than talking to her. Then she reached out and ran her small hand down the length of his arm.

Harry turned his head on the pillow and pulled her closer.

'I made a bloody hash of things, didn't I? I should have married you in the first place. God, what a fool!'

'Never mind.' As usual, her voice was calm and soothing. 'Things will work out in time, you'll see, and meanwhile you're making me very happy, darling.'

'Am I? You and I were meant for each other, sweetheart. You make me happy too.'

They lay clasped together until the alarm on Harry's wristwatch buzzed loudly to signal it was time he went back to Montpelier Square for the rest of the night.

There was no point in giving the servants cause for gossip.

As soon as Morgan walked into the marble hall of the Montpelier Square house two days later, she sensed a distinct difference in the atmosphere. Warning bells screamed in her head. Something had been going on in her absence and she knew that something was Elizabeth.

Harry had been seeing her. She could see it in the way Perkins avoided her eye as he took charge of her luggage. She could smell it in the unused rooms. She could hear it in the deferential way the nanny asked her how she was.

'Bring me some coffee in the study, Perkins,' Morgan said tightly. The servants mustn't see how she felt.

'Certainly, your grace. I trust you had a comfortable flight?'

Morgan nodded. 'Are there any messages for me?'

'They are with your mail on your desk, your grace.'

'Thanks.'

'Is there anything else you require, your grace?'

'Ask Rose to unpack for me and then run my bath in about half an hour.'

'Very well, your grace. Will that be all?'

Leave me alone! a voice in her head shrieked. *Leave me alone and cut out that 'your grace' crap! I'm tired and scared and nobody cares a damn for me – least of all my bloody husband.*

Aloud she said, 'That will be all. Thank you, Perkins.'

The oppressive silence in the house told her that Harry had already left for the gallery although it was barely nine o'clock. The point was, had he come home last night at all?

In the study she picked up the stack of mail and sank into one of the deep chairs. Would there be an invitation from Buckingham Palace? Kensington Palace? 10 Downing

Street? Not bloody likely! Her depression increased as she ripped open bills, advertisements, charity leaflets, three brief letters of sympathy on Zachary's death and a reminder from her furriers that her furs should be in cold store for the summer by now. *That's all she fucking needed.* What was meant to be a roar of anger came out like a desperate whimper. Morgan threw the mail on the floor. London society and everyone in it could go fuck themselves!

Perkins came in with the coffee on a silver tray. He placed it on the low table in front of her. 'Will you be dining in tonight, your grace?' he inquired.

'Yes, we'll have dinner at eight-thirty.'

What was she going to do with the day? Have her hair done? See if Truslove and Hanson had any new novels in stock? Buy the new edition of *Vogue*? Have a rest? An enormous gulf of emptiness enveloped her. The rest of her life was going to be a purposeless desert of dressing up and having nothing to do and nowhere to go.

The nanny came bustling into the room, a healthy glow in her cheeks and David propped in the crook of her arm. 'Here's Mummy!' she exclaimed, using the special coaxing voice she always used when talking to David. 'Say hullo, Mummy! Tell her what a good boy you've been!'

David's bottom lip began to quiver as he stared at Morgan, his eyes wide and alarmed.

'Haven't we been a good boy?' Nanny continued in jolly tones. 'We didn't wake up once in the night, did we?'

'Hullo, honey!' Morgan said softly. 'I think you've grown even in the last few days.' She took his small hand in hers.

For answer, David's face crumpled, turned scarlet, and opening his mouth wide, he started to bellow.

Morgan turned swiftly away. It was too humiliating.

Even the child hated her.

It was six o'clock and Morgan poured out her second martini. Her hands were shaking so much she spilled some on the silver drinks tray. It had been a long day, during which she'd swung from acute boredom to moments of panicked frenzy. Supposing Harry stayed out all evening – or all night? She could picture the servants in the kitchen whispering and nodding their heads knowingly, while Nanny, up in the nursery, crooned, ''Bye, Baby Bunting, Daddy's gone ahunting.'

Morgan clenched her fists and fought the desire to scream. Harry *must* come home. She'd go mad if he didn't. In fact she'd do something else. She'd storm round to Elizabeth's house and demand to know what was going on.

Then she heard his key in the lock. For a second her heart stopped beating, then she took a quick swig of her martini, hurriedly put the glass back on the tray, and went into the hall.

'Hello, darling.' She was amazed how normal her voice sounded. She went towards him and slid her arms round his neck and lifted her face, waiting for his kiss.

Harry just stood there, his arms hanging by his sides, looking down at her. There was no emotion in his face at all.

Morgan pulled back stiffly and he could see the hurt in her eyes.

'How are you?' he asked.

'I'm okay.' She dropped her gaze, moved away and walked back into the drawing room, an erect proud figure in a simple black dress. *Oh God, Harry! Love me like you used to. Take me in your arms and hold me close. Please.* 'Can I fix you a drink?'

He nodded.

Morgan poured gin into a glass, added ice and topped it up with tonic water. 'There you are,' she said lightly.

Harry shuffled his feet and looked uncomfortable as a mixture of guilt and embarrassment flooded through him. He felt suddenly dreadful that while he'd been with Elizabeth, his wife had been going through the trauma of burying her only brother.

'You must have had a ghastly time,' he said lamely.

Morgan lit a cigarette nervously and inhaled until she felt the scorching in her lungs. 'Mom is absolutely shattered, and poor Daddy is blaming himself and feels awful.'

'Umm. I can imagine.'

A heavy silence blanketed the room, each searching his or her mind for something to say. Something safe.

'David looks well,' she said at last.

'Umm.'

'Been busy at the gallery?'

'Yes, very. We sold a Meninsky yesterday.'

'That's good news. And your headaches, any more while I was gone?'

'Oh no, thanks. I've been quite well. See many old friends in New York?'

'Everyone came to the funeral.'

'Oh yes! Of course.'

Another silence.

When Perkins announced dinner, he was quite overwhelmed by the way their graces turned to look at him – as if he were an old friend they'd been searching for, for years.

It was obvious, he reported to Mrs Perkins, that the Lomonds couldn't bear to be alone in each other's company any more.

Harry sat alone in the study until very late that night, listening to music and drinking. Both afforded him great solace. Morgan had long since gone to bed, a sad lonely figure, wishing him a dignified good night. He felt bad about Morgan. She'd behaved diabolically of course, and his mother had been right about one thing, she was an adventuress. No doubt about it. But was this the moment to ask for a divorce? She didn't look well, she'd lost weight and was drawn and anxious looking. There was also a desperate gleam in her eyes. Of course it had to be remembered that she was probably very upset about Zachary – and from facing Tiffany again.

Harry closed his eyes, listened to a passage of Beethoven he particularly liked and tried to get his thoughts in order. The thing was, could he *afford* to get rid of Morgan? How many million dollars had she and her family spent restoring Drumnadrochit Castle – not to mention this house? He glanced round the room at the specially built bookshelves, the Adam fireplace, the moulded ceiling and the heavy Italian silk curtains. It had all cost an absolute fortune and there was no way he could repay her.

Of course she could keep this house, but the castle had to stay in the family and that's where she had ploughed in most of the money. Would she demand a vast settlement? Most probably. She'd probably engage Marvin Mitchelson to take him to the cleaners. Would she relinquish the Lomond heirlooms that filled twelve jewel boxes? The diamond tiara and necklace, the pearls, the emerald, sapphire and ruby brooches and earrings and bracelets that he'd showered her with? Definitely not. Not without a fight. Divorce would mean months of litigation, claims and counterclaims, vicious acrimony and costly legal fees.

And yet he simply couldn't go on living with her. Everything about Morgan now jarred on his nerves, from her American accent to her covetous green eyes.

Miserably he poured himself another drink and cursed the day he'd been fool enough to fall in love with a pretty face and a pair of long legs that had no one inside.

He loved Elizabeth. It was as simple and as complicated as that. He'd loved her ever since the day her parents had brought her to stay at the castle when she'd been twelve and he'd been fifteen, and both families had taken it for granted that one day they would be married.

Then Morgan had come along, with her bewitching allure and a sex appeal that had scorched him and consumed him and had driven him demented. At one point, when she had first flown back to America, he would have given his soul to have possessed her.

Harry glanced up at the ceiling of the study. Above him she lay now, a silk-clad temptress, alone in her bed. And he felt no desire for her whatever. It was gone, evaporated as quickly as the morning dew when the sun rises. All he wanted was the gentle reassurance of Elizabeth's arms, the quiet way she acquiesced to his every wish and the undemanding warmth of her body.

And then there was David. What would he do about the child? That was the worst part of the whole dilemma.

Harry had had enough excitement to last him a lifetime. All he had to do now was get out of the bloody mess he was in. And it was going to be far from easy.

34

Tiffany clicked her last Louis Vuitton suitcase shut and, looking round her room, checked she'd got everything. She might be away for quite a while. Magnima Films had asked her to design the costumes for a new television series, *Connections*, a spin-off from the now highly successful *Street Echoes* and by this evening she would be in Hollywood.

It was, she reflected, like being given a second chance, and there were no doubts in her mind that she had Hunt to thank for it. He'd probably heard about her divorce from Axel and suggested to Magnima that they offer her this opportunity. If only she'd been able to get hold of him, but his line was either busy or his housekeeper said he was out. Desperate to talk to him, she reluctantly decided she would have to wait until she arrived. It would be time enough. At least she would probably see him tonight because she had been asked to dine with the producer of *Connections* and no doubt Hunt would be there to make the introductions, ease her into this new group of people with whom she would soon be working and perhaps...? Firmly she closed her mind to other possibilities. But she couldn't stop the trembling of her hands as she put the finishing touches to her make-up. In a few hours she'd be seeing him again.

There was a message waiting for her when she booked into the Beverly Wilshire later that day. Tearing open the envelope as soon as she was alone in her suite, she read the brief note, signed by Don Howze, the producer. It requested her to be in the bar of the hotel at seven o'clock, when she would also meet the director, Lou Vlasto, the executive director, Abe Gross, and the director of photography,

Isadore Gertz. There was no mention of anyone else. Suppressing a sharp stab of disappointment, Tiffany started to unpack, and very soon the sheer excitement of being in Los Angeles and of being given this wonderful chance to further her career took over. By the time she went to take her shower before changing for dinner, she was humming to herself.

She dressed with care, choosing a simple black dress, beautifully draped and belted with gold kid. With it she wore gold earrings and her collection of gold bangles. Studying herself in the long mirror she was pleased with the effect. It was glamorous but understated, and set off her long gold hair and softly tanned skin. Hunt liked her in black too and used to say to her, 'Men will always say you look pretty in pink, but they'll always be *looking* at the girl in black!' Smiling to herself she took the elevator down to the main lobby and a few minutes later entered the bar, all the time half expecting to run into Hunt.

Tiffany recognized the four men at once, Don Howze, Lou Vlasto, Abe Gross and Isadore Gertz. They were sitting round a small table drinking and talking intently. Four alert men in their thirties, bristling with drive, aggressively intent on proving their talents.

Introductions were made, the men's eyes sweeping over Tiffany with approval.

'What are you drinking?' Lou asked.

'I'll have a marguerita,' Tiffany replied, seating herself between him and Don.

The conversation was general for a while, but she knew she was being tested. Finally Don asked with a deceptively lazy smile, 'What do you know about the new series?'

'I know it centres around a powerful consortium, based in Miami,' she replied, thankful she'd done her research, 'and that apart from the intrigues surrounding various property deals, there is a strong human element in each episode, connected with the people who are buying or selling property, that deals with broken marriages, illness, corruption, a story within a story in fact. I've also heard there will be a lot about the company wives, their affairs, their boredom and their spending capacity when it comes to clothes! *That* bit I'm really looking forward to!'

Don turned and looked at her, undisguised surprise on his face. She figured he was really impressed.

'Right!' he said. 'You've got the basic concept absolutely! There's a cast of fifteen, a guest star in each episode, around twenty regular extras, chauffeurs, secretaries, servants, that sort of thing. Crowd scenes will run from fifty to a hundred and fifty. What we want to project is riches, success, power, glamour –'

'It must be better dressed than *Dallas*,' interjected Lou.

'But not as over the top as *Dynasty*,' Abe cut in. 'It has to be real classy and we want the women to be beautifully but believably dressed, not walking along the beach in diamonds or wearing mink in the tropics! D'you know what I mean?'

Tiffany smiled. She knew exactly what he meant.

They talked some more, another round of drinks appeared as if by magic and the conversation became technical. Tiffany listened with deep interest. Film-making was different to filming for television and both were worlds apart from the theatre. She had a lot to learn and she was determined to learn fast.

'Shall we go eat?' asked Lou at length. 'I've booked a table at a very nice Italian restaurant I think you'll like.'

'Fine,' she replied, and wondered for a wild moment if this was where Hunt came in? Perhaps he was waiting at the restaurant for them now? Her heart gave a little twist of excitement and giving Lou a ravishing smile she followed him to the waiting car.

The restaurant was packed, but as soon as they entered the manager showed them to the best table. Taking her seat, Tiffany counted only five place settings. It was evident this was where Hunt *didn't* come in.

'We liked your work on *Glitz*,' Lou was saying, 'and I hear you've been nominated for a Tony for *Gertie*?'

'Yes.'

'Isn't that great? As soon as I heard that, I said to our president, Elmer Winkler, we've just gotta get hold of that dame!' Lou laughed uproariously. Three double martinis were doing their work.

Tiffany nodded dumbly, unable to speak for a moment. So *that's* why she'd been picked! It had nothing to do with Hunt at all.

Dimly she heard the conversation going on around her as dinner progressed but one half of her mind was elsewhere. A feeling of deep disappointment and anti-climax enveloped her as she picked at her dinner. There she'd been, ever since she'd first heard about the job, visualizing Hunt eagerly awaiting her arrival, ready to offer her his love and encouragement and give her a hand in finding her feet in this strange frenetic city. In her heart she'd even hoped this might be a fresh start for them.

So much for daydreams.

Once more she'd have to go it alone.

Damn and blast Hunt Kellerman!

At three o'clock in the morning, five men in dark coats trooped silently out of Quadrant House into the wet darkness of Wall Street. Each carried a briefcase. None of them spoke. The first looked up and down, making sure they were not being watched, then all five walked swiftly to the car that was parked down the side of the block.

A minute later they had climbed in and with a squeal of rubber on wet surface the car sped away.

'Is that it?' Joe asked from the back seat.

'That's it,' Hank Krauss replied, as he drove the car along Maiden Lane and headed for Park Row.

Joe lit his cigar with trembling fingers as relief oozed out of his pores in a rush of sweat. 'For Chrissakes, I never want to go through that again,' he croaked.

For four nights now he'd had to creep back to Quadrant when he was sure everyone had gone home, and then, having negotiated a series of locks and alarm switches, let Hank and his assistant and the three independent accountants into the accounting department where, with blinds drawn and the lighting kept to a minimum in case they could be seen from the street, they proceeded to examine papers and share certificates and bank statements and invoices – everything they could find.

'We've got him by the short hairs!' Hank was saying laconically, as he took a right turn. 'We've got what we came for. I'll have a full report on your desk, Joe, within a couple of days.'

'His method was simple enough to make you weep – once we found it,' observed one of the accountants in a tired voice.

Joe looked at their grey faces and red-rimmed eyes, as they sat hunched in the car. Each one held his briefcase to his chest like a shield. He deeply envied and admired these men who could make sense out of columns and columns of figures. If he'd been that bright, Sig would never have got away with anything.

Back in his apartment Joe went straight to his study and poured himself a drink. It was now 3.45 a.m. Sleep was out of the question. He no longer even desired it because it brought nightmares of Zachary that startled him awake, his heart pounding, his whole being filled with misery. Awake he could concentrate on the matters in hand, and right now he had to decide about Sig. The law would deal with him as far as embezzlement went, but what about the other matter? He mustn't be allowed to get away with that.

Joe went to the window. Night had reached its lowest ebb and soon the great spires of Manhattan would be turning pink with the first creeping fingers of dawn.

First he would have to appoint a new vice-president to

take over from Sig, and he'd have to get rid of everyone in the accounting department and start over fresh. Then he started thinking about Zachary again, the son who had been meant to inherit everything. The son who now lay in a mahogany casket under the freshly turned soil. He leaned against the window, its cool glass pressed to his brow. For the first time in his life he longed for it to be all over for him too. His dumpy body sagged with tiredness and a despairing sadness came over him. How was it that once he'd thought the world was a wonderful place? It must have been a long time ago.

A soft touch on his shoulder made him jump and turning he found himself looking into the fragile but calm face of Ruth.

'Can't you sleep, Joe?' she asked him gently. 'Come to bed and I'll fix you a hot drink.'

'It's all right, Ruthie,' he mumbled, quickly dashing away the tears that had gathered in the corners of his eyes. 'I was just thinking, how would you feel if I gave it all up, Quadrant, everything, and we just lived quietly, maybe at Four Winds?'

Ruth's eyes widened. It was the first time she could ever remember him having consulted her about anything.

'I wouldn't mind at all, and I can understand just how you feel, but knowing you,' she smiled wisely, 'I think you only feel like this right now because you're tired and upset. Tomorrow you'll feel differently – but I'll do whatever you want.'

He looked at her steadily. He hadn't expected such an intelligent reply. She was right, of course he was exhausted and overwrought. All these damn nights at Quadrant House.

'Well, we'll see,' he said. 'Hadn't you better get back into bed and get some sleep now?'

'I've had enough sleep. It's all I seem to have done these past weeks. If you don't want to go to bed I'll make us some coffee. I could use a cup right now.'

She glided out of the room, a slender figure in her grey robe. Joe suddenly realized her presence had been comforting.

Tomorrow, or rather today now, he'd go round and see Hank and find out exactly what Sig had been up to. For Chrissakes, he told himself, he couldn't hang around for two whole days while someone typed out some great report that he probably wouldn't understand anyway.

Tiffany prowled around her hotel suite, unable to sleep. She'd got over her disappointment at finding Hunt had nothing to do with her getting *Connections* and now she was filled with deep anger. She'd been here a week and she hadn't heard a word from him. How dare he ignore her presence when they worked for the same company? He could at least have called her up or sent her a note. Grabbing a bottle of mineral water she decided to take a pill. She had an early start and she simply had to get some sleep.

The next few days passed in such a frenzy of work that when Tiffany got back at night she fell straight into bed, exhausted. Sometimes she even forgot to eat. Never before in her career had she been under such pressure or been forced to work at such speed. This wasn't like a theatre production where you killed yourself to have everything ready by the first preview, and by the time you got to the first night you could probably relax. This was like being involved in an unrelenting stream of first nights. It was never ending. She found herself designing everything from bikinis to ball gowns, from sportswear to lingerie. If she hadn't been so tired all the time she would have loved it, but she had to push herself through each day and she knew it wasn't entirely due to the workload. Something else was sapping her strength, a slow fuse of burning rage, coupled with a deep feeling of having been let down. To think she had been conceited enough to imagine Hunt had got her this job, because he wanted her to be near him again! How could she have been such a fool, and yet she remembered his acid remark the last time she had seen him, 'Pity you didn't hang on a bit longer.' Surely those were the words of a man still in love? Well, she'd been wrong. She'd been in Hollywood for *two* weeks now and still there was no word from him.

Meanwhile gossip about Hunt filtered back to Tiffany wherever she went. She heard he'd been taking a few girls out to dinner, but mostly he'd become a workaholic, totally absorbed in *Street Echoes*. Tales of his brilliant directing and tactful handling of the stars were apparently earning him the reputation of being one of Hollywood's most skilled directors. So bully for him! she thought.

She found herself torn between the dreadful and the wonderful prospect that sooner or later they were bound to run into each other. And she had no idea how she was going to handle that when it happened.

As far as other men were concerned, she adopted a bright professional and friendly manner. She wanted to make it clear that she was here to work and not to play. Abe Gross quickly spotted this and it bothered him. He was drawn to her but whenever he suggested they go and have a drink or supper together at the end of the day, she declined politely but firmly. It wasn't only Abe she was turning down either. Whoever asked her out got the same friendly smile, the slightly guarded look in her eyes and the tone that said you're very kind but I'm not interested.

'Have you got a boyfriend back in New York?' Abe asked her at last.

'No.' She turned away, and with a soft pencil defined the sleeve of a dress she was sketching.

'A husband then?'

'No.' Tiffany sounded a trifle impatient now.

'Then why are you so scared of men?' he asked.

Tiffany burst out laughing. 'God!' she exclaimed. 'Unless one has a full-time sex life around this place everyone thinks there's something wrong with you! Abe, it obviously hasn't occurred to you that I'm just not interested in any of the men I've met since I came here.'

Abe shrugged. 'So okay! But you remind me of my sister! She behaved just like you when her boyfriend ran off with someone else. I figured she was scared of getting hurt again because she wouldn't look at another man for nearly two years.'

'Well, I'm not your sister,' said Tiffany crisply, 'and the reason I'm not going out is because working on *Connections* is a marvellous chance for me to prove that I can design just as well for movies and television as I can for the stage. And that means conserving what energy I've got left at the end of the day, so no dates.'

'Pity,' Abe reflected sadly. 'You've got gorgeous legs!'

'They'll keep!' she said lightly and with a friendly smile she left the design studio.

But the next day he asked her out again. 'Come on, Tiff! Don't look upon it as a date, call it a break – and you sure deserve one of those!' he coaxed. 'Just a quick dinner between friends.'

'Okay,' she replied. Maybe if she had dinner with him just this once he would stop pestering her. There was also the possibility they'd go to a restaurant where they'd run into Hunt. The thought pleased her. She could just imagine Hunt's face if she strolled into *Ma Maison* with Abe Gross!

Abe, however, took her to a small Mexican restaurant, where he spent most of the evening trying to fumble her under the table. Tiffany's manner changed from jocularity to irritation and finally to anger.

'For God's sake, Abe!' she cried crossly, removing his hand from her thigh for the fourth time. 'Cut it out! I told you I wasn't interested and you promised me this would be a purely friendly evening.'

'But I'm crazy about you, babe!' Abe had been drinking heavily all evening and now his face was flushed and feverish looking. 'You turn me on like no dame has ever turned me on before. I can't sleep for thinking of you, I need you real bad, honey.'

Tiffany looked him straight in the eye. 'Well, I'm sorry about that, but I did warn you. I'm here to work, Abe, not play around. And now if you'll excuse me, I'm going to call a cab. I have to be at the studio by dawn.' No point being really rude to him, she thought, we've got to go on working together and she hated this sort of unpleasantness.

'I'll take you home, babe.' He grabbed her arm and she could feel the sweat of his hand through the silk of her sleeve.

'No, thanks! I'd feel safer walking!' Tiffany rose to her feet and walked firmly out of the restaurant.

Her treatment of Abe had exactly the opposite effect to the one she wanted. He continued to pursue her obsessively, because what Abe couldn't have, Abe wanted. Desperately. He thought about her all day, dreamed about her every night, and he kept sending her notes proclaiming his great love for her. The more she said No, the more he wanted her. When he had to fly to New York on business, he called her six times in two days, driving her frantic. It was on the return flight that weeks of frustration finally got to him, especially when he realized a blonde girl with limpid blue eyes was watching him from the opposite aisle seat. She gave him a smile and leaned towards him, her full breasts falling forward, exposing a deep cleavage. It flashed through Abe's mind that a man could get lost for days in a ravine like that.

'Have you got a light?' she lisped, a cigarette held between her chubby fingers. Her long scarlet talons looked like the stuck-on variety.

'Been to Los Angeles before?' she asked, after he lit her cigarette.

'I live there,' Abe replied shortly.

'Do-o-o you?' She drew out the 'do' with a long pointed inflection. 'I hear it's a fabulous place.'

'Depends what you're looking for.'

'I'm hoping to get into the movies, or television.' Her lisp was more pronounced than ever.

You would be. Like twenty thousand other hopefuls around the country. 'That's fascinating,' he said conversationally, his eyes still riveted on her cleavage.

'Are you in films?'

'God, no! I'm in the aviation business,' he said swiftly.

Her face perceptibly fell. 'Oh, well that must be interesting,' she said in a flat voice, while her eyes wandered fretfully around, looking at the other passengers. Surely *one* of them worked in the movies.

'I can give you an introduction though,' said Abe suddenly.

She turned the full force of her gaze onto him with renewed interest. 'You can?'

'Sure.' Abe rose from his seat and grabbed her hand. 'Come with me.'

'Where are we going?' she cried, rising. At that moment Abe noticed that her ass was even better than her tits. He led her down the aisle to the rear of the plane, then glancing round quickly to see that no one was looking, he dragged her into the lavatory and locked the door behind him.

'What the – ?' She looked alarmed.

'Like I said, I'm going to give you an introduction – to the Mile-High Club! You'll get nowhere in Los Angeles unless you're a member.' Abe's voice was warm and persuasive as he started to stroke her enormous breasts.

The girl with the lisp didn't even try to resist. In the movie business he might not be, but he was the sexiest man she'd ever laid eyes on.

'Slip off your dress, honey,' Abe was saying, 'let me look at you. Jesus, you've got the sort of body that drives a guy wild.'

'I have?' she simpered. 'There isn't much room in here, is there?'

'When two people are as close as us, who needs a lot of

room?' *Abe Gross, you're a class-one shit.*

She unhooked her bra and slipped off the tiniest lace G-string even he had ever seen.

'My, look at *you*!' she cried in awe. Abe was pressing his erection against her, and at the same time twisting her nipples between his fingers. Then he gripped her round the waist and lifted her onto the basin.

'O-o-o-h! It's cold!' she squealed.

'You'll soon be hot, honey, so hot you'll be burning up.'

Abe parted her legs and thrust himself hard up inside her. She was wet already. Her mouth was soft and wet too. Clinging to him, her legs wrapped round his hips, she moaned softly as he began to pump rhythmically inside her.

Then he could feel the pressure building up. His whole life was rushing to his groin, burning up his balls, setting fire to his cock. With an exquisitely agonizing surge the world exploded wildly, as he cried out, 'Tiffany! Oh Christ, Tiffany!'

'Isn't that the name of a jewellery shop?' asked the girl with the lisp as they made their way back to their seats.

It was bad luck for Abe that unknown to him, Tiffany's assistant, Rozita, happened to be on the same flight. Amid gales of laughter the following morning, she told Tiffany exactly what Abe had been up to.

When he came pounding into Tiffany's studio a little later, with a large bunch of red roses, she got enormous satisfaction by dumping them unceremoniously into the waste bin before turning to him and saying crisply, 'Well, fancy seeing you, Abe? I thought you'd have sprouted wings after graduating for the Mile-High Club yesterday!'

Abe avoided her from then on.

It was two weeks later, when she returned to the Beverly Wilshire, that she heard the phone ringing in her suite as soon as she opened the door. For a moment she hesitated.

She'd had a long day and now she wanted peace and quiet. On the other hand suppose it was Joe with some news about Sig? She hadn't heard from him for ages and it might be important.

Dashing across the sitting room she snatched up the receiver.

'Hullo?'

'Tiffany?'

Her heart dropped a beat, picked up with a choking lurch, then vibrated so hard in her chest she could hardly breathe.

'Yes,' she said faintly.

'Tiffany – it's Hunt.'

As if she didn't know. As if his voice and the way he said her name didn't bring back a thousand hammering memories. She sat down suddenly in a nearby chair, as her legs weakened.

'I've only just heard from Don Howze that you're on *Connections*,' he was saying. 'Why didn't you let me know? I had no idea you were in town!'

Tiffany took a deep breath and tried to clear her swimming head.

'There was no particular reason why you should know,' she said, amazed that her voice sounded so calm. 'Magnima Films suddenly offered me the series and I've been working flat out ever since.'

There was a silence on the line and then she heard him say, 'Are you all right, darling?' He sounded concerned.

'I'm fine.'

'Then why haven't you been in touch, for God's sake? Is your husband with you? He's opening a discotheque here, isn't he?'

So Hunt didn't know she was divorced! 'No, I'm not here with Axel,' she replied coolly.

'So when can I see you, Tiffany?'

'I don't really think you can. I'm working all the time. Anyway, I've heard you're pretty tied up yourself.' Tiffany almost winced at the bitchy way she'd said that.

'But – What's the matter, Tiff?' He sounded bewildered now. 'Why don't you want to see me? Is it Axel? Surely he wouldn't mind your meeting an old friend, would he?'

An old friend! That was the worst thing he could have said, she thought, deeply wounded. It makes us sound like pals from college days, or old colleagues, not lovers, not two people who had once dreamed of getting married.

'The choice is mine,' she cried angrily, 'Axel and I are divorced now anyway.'

There was a stunned silence on the line then she heard Hunt gasp, 'Divorced? For Christ's sake, that didn't last long, did it?'

'It's none of your goddamn business!' she retorted harshly. 'You went your way, and I went mine – remember?' Then she slammed down the receiver.

Trembling, she stared at the phone for a minute, horrified at the violence of her feelings. She could *kill* him right now. How dare he talk to her like that? And the calm way he had presumed he could walk right back into her life! Who did he think he was anyway? For a moment she was thankful he hadn't been instrumental in getting her *Connections*. This way she owed him nothing.

Joe bounded into the offices of Krauss and Blumfeld, his cheerfulness restored and his confidence high. Ruth had been right. He wasn't ready to retire yet. She had insisted he go to bed, after they had had a long and comforting talk, and she had given him one of her knockout pills. Then she'd left him to sleep. For eighteen hours. When he'd finally awakened he felt refreshed and ready to do battle with Sig.

Meanwhile he was anxious for Hank to tell him, simply and clearly, what had been going on.

Hank sat behind his cluttered desk, his ashtray overflowing, a cold cup of coffee half buried beneath papers.

'Can't you wait for the report, Joe?' he asked, running a

hand through his thinning hair. 'It'll all be in that and it's being typed now.'

'I want you to tell me yourself,' Joe said firmly. 'I have a few things to say to Sig before we blow the whistle on him, and I want to be sure of all my facts.'

'Okay,' Hank sighed. It was a complicated business and the accountants were far better qualified to explain it, but Joe was an old pal who liked to be given the personal treatment.

'Right,' he began. 'Now, when you have a client who wants to borrow money, no matter what for at this stage, Quadrant Inc. either lends him funds drawn from their own capital, or they borrow from a bank for the purpose. Okay?'

'Yes, providing we are satisfied that the client has sufficient security in bonds, property, whatever, to cover the loan.'

'Exactly. Now when you lend a client capital owned by Quadrant, you charge a set rate of interest, don't you?'

Joe nodded again. 'The only variance might be in how long the loan was required for.'

'Quite. Now, when Quadrant borrows money from a bank, they themselves incur interest charges, so they charge the client higher interest charges, and in that way make a profit from the deal.'

'I know, I know,' said Joe impatiently. When was Hank coming to the point?

'Now what Sig has been doing, to very carefully selected clients, ones he could really trust, is instead of charging them the higher rate of interest, he's just been charging them the flat bank rate.'

'So Quadrant made no profit! What was the point of that? I don't see –'

'The grateful client, Joe, who was perhaps being saved many thousands of dollars by not having to pay the higher rate, rewarded Sig with a nice cash kickback! Maybe Sig split a percentage of this with your chief accountant, or maybe Sig was blackmailing him, too. I think the latter is most likely because, as you know, we found Lee Schraub was involved in some shady stock-market deals. Sig couldn't have done it without him because all the invoices and records have been adjusted.'

Joe thought for a moment. 'Would Sig be getting large amounts in kickbacks, enough to make it worth his while?'

'That wasn't the only swindle he was operating! Sometimes a client would come along asking for financial backing, without having any security. He'd probably have tried a few banks before coming to Quadrant and been turned down. In that case, Sig agreed to lend him whatever amount he asked for, but Sig's condition was that there'd be an astronomically high rate of interest because of the risk factor. Of course Quadrant was only receiving the normal rate because Sig was skimming off the balance!' explained Hank.

Joe could see it all. And providing the chief accountant kept his mouth shut, no one was ever likely to miss the interest that didn't appear on anything. 'What if the client went bust . . . without security?' he demanded.

Hank shrugged. 'No doubt Sig would blame the client for producing forged documents as security. Sig is obviously a very shrewd and astute man, Joe, he mustn't be underestimated! I don't think he got into any serious trouble because he has an instinct for being able to smell success or failure a mile off!'

'That's probably why he came in with me, over thirty years ago,' remarked Joe dolefully. 'I was the one who got the business, made the contacts, inspired people to believe that by borrowing money from us, and making it work for them, they could wind up rich.'

'You were a good team, Joe, especially in the beginning. Sig is a wizard with figures and you are very charismatic.'

Joe gave a little flattered smile.

'If you ask me,' Hank continued, 'Sig has been skimming

off higher percentages and taking kickbacks for at least the last fifteen years, and salting the dough away in an off-shore company. Apart, that is, from what he used for his compulsive gambling.'

'What I don't understand is that I brought in the bulk of the business! There were some odd-balls of course, but the clients I brought in weren't looking for something crooked. Some were my friends. Would they go along with Sig, for God's sake?'

'You never know whether a man's crooked or not until you know his price,' said Hank quietly. 'I also think that Sig acquired a lot of clients himself, unknown to you. You see, no doubt his "favours" to clients, especially those with no security behind them, spread by word of mouth. Imagine a fellow owns a factory and he needs to borrow a million or two for expansion. His factory already has a mortgage. All other finance houses and bankers have turned him down, so what does he do? Comes to Sig, who says yes, okay, but the interest on a loan will be very high. Now, the client isn't to know that Quadrant Inc. isn't benefiting from the interest, is he? He says yes, fine, I can afford the interest. I agree that the clients who gave Sig a cash kickback in order to *save* themselves high interests were crooked! They knew the cash would wind up in Sig's back pocket – or on a roulette table! Do you understand what I'm saying, Joe?'

Joe nodded, and remained silent for a long moment. Then he asked softly, 'Reckon you know how much he's got away with?'

Hank looked at Joe sympathetically. 'Could be in the region of nearly thirty million dollars.'

'Jesus H. Christ.' Joe's voice was dangerously quiet.

Sig had embezzled thirty million dollars that by right belonged to Quadrant. And he'd also done something far, far worse.

'Send the report round to my home as soon as it's ready,' Joe cried suddenly, springing to his feet. 'But I intend to get a signed confession out of Sig before we hand him over.'

Hank looked at him blankly. 'How the hell do you propose to get that? He'll fight this tooth and nail, he's got everything to lose if he's found guilty.'

'He'll have more to lose if he tries to defend himself,' snapped Joe, as he strode out of Hank's office. 'Like his balls!'

Sig Hoffman's face was grey, a sickly grey, and his eyes had the flat look of a man facing inevitable defeat. His voice quavered. 'You're telling me that if I confess to these allegations' – he pointed a shaking hand to the Krauss and Blumfeld report – 'you'll not bring up . . .' His voice trailed off.

'That's right!' Joe said harshly. 'I'm not doing it to protect you, you bastard. Never think that for a moment! It's because, because . . . well anyway, if it wasn't for that I'd have the greatest pleasure in escorting you to the electric chair – personally!'

Sig's eyes came alive for a second, flashing with momentary terror. 'But you can't be executed for –'

'More's the pity.' Joe showed no mercy. 'You're scum. You're the lowest of the low, and if I had my way you *would* die for what you did.' He paused for a second to get control of himself, then continued, 'As far as swindling the company out of millions of dollars, well, I hope you get a good long sentence, but for what you did to Tiffany, I hope you never have a moment's peace of mind for the rest of your life.'

The police were waiting in the next office. They already had a copy of the report.

Now Joe rose to his feet and walking round from behind his desk, handed Sig a full typed confession, ready for signing.

Neither man spoke. In the silence of the room the only sound was the nervous scratching of Sig's gold pen. Over thirty years of building an empire together, of trust and of friendship, had ended.

Sig had signed it all away years ago.

The first bouquet of red roses had a card which said, 'Welcome to Hollywood, darling. Hunt.'

The second, which arrived the next day, bore the message, 'When can I see you? All my love, Hunt.'

From then on Tiffany received flowers each day and with each bouquet came notes in Hunt's handwriting of ever-increasing desperation: 'Forgive me if I hurt you,' 'Please darling, I must see you,' 'I love you, Tiffany.'

Then the phone calls started. When she got back to her hotel one night there were three messages to say he'd rung. Tiffany asked the switchboard to screen all her calls and check with her before putting anyone through.

The strain of having Hunt pursue her affected her deeply, opening up great areas of conflict within her mind that she couldn't resolve. A part of her cried out to see him, to be with him again, for reason told her there was nothing now to keep them apart. Then an angry voice in her head would cry, *How can you be such a fool! He only wants you because he can't have you! Hunt always went after the unattainable. That was probably why the affair lasted so long. He said he wanted to marry you but there was always Joni.*

Two days later she found Hunt waiting for her in the lobby of her hotel. As his tall lean figure rose from the depths of a chair and she saw his deeply tanned features she stopped dead, suddenly afraid.

The moment had come. She could avoid him no longer, and as he started walking towards her, something inside her, deep and aching, suddenly dissolved.

'Tiffany.' Hunt took both her hands in his and stood looking down at her. 'How much longer are you going to fight me?'

His directness threw her off balance and she looked back at him, almost fearfully.

'Let's talk. We'll go to the bar and have a drink.' With gentle authority he took her elbow, led her through to the bar and chose a table in the corner where they would be undisturbed.

As soon as he had ordered their drinks, he turned to her again and said quietly, 'What's all this about, Tiff?'

'*You* tell me.' Her voice quavered.

'Look, honey, I didn't know you were divorced from Axel. I didn't even know you were in Hollywood. When I heard you were here, I couldn't resist calling you. What's wrong with that? Why have you been avoiding me? We meant so much to each other and I can't believe it's all gone. Isn't it possible for us to get together again?'

Tiffany had gathered strength while he had been talking and now she managed to look him in the eye, although her pulse was still racing. 'Look at it from my point of view, Hunt. We split because for the sake of your sons you didn't want to divorce Joni. Okay. I understood. And I respected your feelings about not wanting your children to suffer from their parents divorcing, as you did. It hurt badly at the time but I accepted the situation. Not that I had much choice. When I met Axel I was free to do as I liked, and you've no idea what a wonderful feeling it was to be with a man who had no ties, a man who could stay with me all the time, a man who didn't have someone else to rush back to.'

Hunt stared at the ice in his drink.

'You see, Hunt, I had no idea that you were seriously considering splitting from Joni. You never told me. Looking back, I probably wouldn't have even gotten involved with Axel if I'd known. But there he was, in love with me and at the time I thought I was in love with him. And then, when my marriage to Axel ground to an end . . . well, what was I supposed to do? Come running back to you, knowing you'd built a whole new life for yourself in Los Angeles?'

Hunt flushed and took a swig of his drink. 'I know I should have told you about the divorce, but it all happened so quickly once the decision had been made. Then I read in *People Magazine* the sensationalized story of your being a surrogate mother for your sister! I'd hardly got over that when I found you'd married someone I'd never even heard of! Somewhere along the way I felt I'd lost you completely. I don't mind telling you it nearly devastated me. You remember that day I dropped in to see you in New York? There you were, being Mrs Housewife, rattling on about Captain Industry and his string of fabulous discotheques? God, I felt terrible.' Hunt shook his head from side to side and she could see the pain in his face.

'Captain Industry turned out to be bisexual,' Tiffany said drily.

'*No*! Oh God, darling, I'm sorry. What an awful blow. I should have kept more in touch, half of me wanted to go on seeing you, even when I'd decided to stay with Joni, and the other half of me felt I ought to keep away. To give you a chance to find someone else. I love you, Tiff. I've never stopped loving you. It's not too late to start over – is it?' *He's pleading,* Tiffany thought exultantly.

'Let's take it a step at a time,' she told him. 'A lot has happened to me since we were last together, and I've changed. I've become much more self-protective, and I'm more determined than ever to become *the* top costume designer in America.'

'You should, darling, you've got great talent. But don't you still care for me? I'll never stand in your way. Don't you want us to be together again, for keeps this time?'

'I've got to be sure, so sure,' she murmured, 'I feel I've been kicked in the teeth so often, I can't take the risk of it happening again.'

He took her hand and squeezed it. 'I can understand that, darling. But let me tell you something. I only stayed with Joni because of Gus and Matt, but it's you I've loved since the beginning, and we could have such a wonderful life together, darling. Think about it, Tiffany. It's what we always dreamed about, isn't it? You and I together – for always.'

For the first time she began to feel safe. She couldn't mistake the sincerity in his voice and the love in his eyes. 'Perhaps we can find a way of putting it all behind us, our splitting, Axel, my baby...' Suddenly her eyes brimmed and her throat contracted, catching her unawares.

'Do you miss him terribly?' Hunt asked softly.

'I try not to think about him but when I do...'

'How did it happen? How did Morgan talk you into it?'

'It's a long story.'

'If we're going to try and start over wouldn't it be better if we started with a clean slate? That is, if it's not too painful for you to talk about?'

'You're right.'

'I know you wouldn't have got involved in a deception like that without a very good reason and I figure Morgan was up to her usual manipulations. Am I right?'

A few minutes later Tiffany was telling Hunt the story of how Morgan, aged twelve then, had overheard Sig Hoffman telling her that their father was embezzling funds from Quadrant and that if it ever became known he would probably be sent to prison for life.

'The awful thing is that I believed Sig! And I went on believing all these years! Morgan never mentioned to me that she'd overheard all this until she wanted a baby. Then she threatened to expose Daddy unless I went along with her plan.' Tiffany gave a long sigh of despair. '*How* could I have been so naive? Morgan says now she was just bluffing, relying on my loyalty to Daddy. As I look back on the whole mess, I realize now that even Morgan knows better than to bite the hand that –'

'And your father was innocent?'

'Completely! The truth has all come out now. It's Sig

who's been embezzling, and for about the last ten or fifteen years.'

Hunt was looking at her penetratingly. 'Why should Sig make up lies like that in the first place?'

Tiffany took a nervous sip of her drink. 'It was the summer of '74,' she began in a low voice. 'We were all staying at the house on Long Island. I was fourteen . . .'

'And you never told anyone?' Hunt asked gently, when she'd finished speaking.

'No, no one. How could I? The only people who know I was raped are Joe and Morgan – and you.' Tiffany smiled wanly. It had been a great strain, having to relive that hideous experience.

'My poor darling. I can't bear to think what you went through. It's a wonder it didn't screw you up for life, as far as men and sex are concerned.'

She reached out and laid her hand on his arm. 'It nearly did. I felt so . . . dirty. So contaminated and so sort of, well, guilty, I suppose. It wasn't until I met you . . .'

'You mean –?'

'Yes, with you I was able to overcome my disgust and my fear. With you, I learned to love.' Tiffany looked deeply into his eyes.

'I think we can make it, don't you?' he asked tenderly.

'I want to. I really want to, Hunt. But I have to be so sure now. Don't rush me into anything. I need to feel that whatever we have could last a lifetime. I just can't let myself be hurt again.'

Hunt leaned forward and kissed her softly on the cheek. 'However long it takes, my love. I'll prove to you that you are all I've ever wanted, in spite of how stupidly I've behaved towards you.'

35

Harry couldn't get Elizabeth out of his mind. Thoughts of her tormented him by day, disrupting his concentration at the gallery, and at night, as he slept alone, he tossed and turned, his mind a frenzy of activity as he longed for the warmth and comfort of her body. She had become his *raison d'être,* his inspiration and his motivation in everything he did and he couldn't get through a day without her. She was like a drug for him, with her motherly concern about his well-being and her undemanding reassurance of her eternal love.

There was no pretending for Harry any more. His affair with Elizabeth had grown from a pleasant diversion into a demanding need. He loved her and he wanted her. All he had to do was ask her to marry him. It sounded so simple but . . . Dark clouds suddenly shrouded his thoughts, making his heart contract painfully. There was a possibility that she would turn him down.

Elizabeth loved him, undoubtedly, she wanted to marry him at this minute, yes. But would she, when he finally screwed up enough courage to tell her everything? He wondered. No doubt she'd be disappointed, but would that be enough to stop her wanting to marry him? Would it have stopped Morgan if she'd known? He doubted it, but then Morgan was so utterly different from Elizabeth.

Harry shut his eyes at the surge of agony within him. What he had to tell Elizabeth would put a lot of women off marrying him.

On impulse, his heart pounding, he reached for his office phone and dialled her number. They hadn't planned to see each other that evening but now he knew they must. He could no longer hold back the feelings that had been welling up inside him for so many months. He must tell her everything and hope that she loved him enough to agree to become his wife.

And then he'd have to talk to Morgan.

'When are you getting rid of that woman and the child?' demanded Lavinia Lomond. 'Really, Harry, you let things drift on so. And surely you want to marry Elizabeth?'

It was later the same afternoon and Harry sat slumped behind his desk in the gallery, regarding his mother with irritation.

'Yes, I do want to marry Elizabeth, but it's not as easy as all that,' he said. Elizabeth had told him earlier on the phone that her parents insisted she accompany them to a concert at St James's Palace, so they weren't going to be able to see each other until the next day. He had twenty-four hours to get through before they could talk and he felt twisted inside with frustration and uncertainty.

'Nonsense,' rejoined the old Duchess briskly. 'Just tell her to pack her bags and get out! I'll tell her for you if you like!'

'You'll do no such thing, Mother. Don't forget either, that Morgan and her family have spent a fortune restoring Drumnadrochit, and she did all the redecorating in Montpelier Square too! God knows what the lawyers are going to make of that. The whole thing could ruin me financially, apart from everything else.'

The Duchess narrowed her slate-grey eyes and lapsed into deep thought for a moment. Then she spoke. 'You're also going to need money to run Drumnadrochit once she's gone, aren't you, but there is a way round that, I think.'

Harry made a wry face and nodded knowingly. For once he felt very pleased with himself. He was a step ahead of her. 'Oh, I know all that!' he said airily. 'I'd more or less worked it out before I married Morgan, and then with her money it wasn't necessary, but do I really want to turn the castle into a hotel-cum-conference centre? The idea of hundreds of tourists wandering all over the place appals me. One would never have a moment's privacy.'

'You really are a fool, Harry.' The Duchess was scathing. '*An hotel*? My God, what a dreadful idea. You couldn't *possibly* fill Drumnadrochit with a lot of common people! Whatever will you think of next!'

Harry flushed uncomfortably. Why did she have this knack of making him feel like a stupid boy?

'Well, it's the only sound solution I can think of!' he retorted defiantly. 'Don't think I like the idea, and if Elizabeth marries me I don't suppose she'd be thrilled either, but I'm not going to make the mistake I made with Morgan, and that is letting Elizabeth be the moneybags! It was the greatest mistake I ever made, letting Morgan pay for everything.'

'I wasn't talking about Elizabeth's money. I was talking about Andrew's money.'

'Andrew's money?' Harry looked at his mother in astonishment. 'What's Andrew got to do with it?'

'Now listen to me, Harry, and try and be sensible. Andrew's father left him a great deal of money. Your uncle was a very rich man, you know. His mother, your grandmother, was a Fleming of Fleming's Shipbuilders. When she died she left all her money to Angus, because her eldest son, your father, was going to inherit Drumnadrochit and everything else. So you see –'

'So Andrew's loaded! Okay, I don't see how that's –'

'Share Drumnadrochit with Andrew,' she cried triumphantly. 'He's always looked upon it as his home, and he'd be very happy to pay the running costs! That way you and Elizabeth can share the place with him and you'll be able to manage without help from Elizabeth.'

'You must be mad!' Harry was aghast. 'We don't want Andrew living with us, and I don't suppose he'd like it either! What happens when he gets married? Oh, for God's sake, Mother, that is the most absurd idea I've ever heard.'

The Duchess set her thin lips in a tight line and the bones of her jawline jutted aggressively above the collar of her black coat.

'It is not absurd!' She spoke coldly. 'Andrew was virtually brought up at the castle and if *his* father had been the eldest son, instead of *your* father, then he would own it now, as well as having the title.'

'So what? That's like saying Prince Andrew or Prince Edward have a right to the throne, although they are younger than Prince Charles. This is all ridiculous, Mother, and it's your fault that Andrew feels he should have Drumnadrochit. From the time we were small children you kept giving him the impression that he had as much right to the place as I have. No wonder he's got such a chip on his shoulder now.'

'He hasn't got a chip on his shoulder! You've always been jealous of him, that's the trouble. Andrew is a kind and intelligent young man and he's much nicer to me than you are.'

'You bet he is!' Harry shouted, incensed. 'He knows which side his bread is buttered on, that's why! I haven't forgotten Morgan telling me how you were sneaking valuable stuff from the castle to him, first editions, silver, objets d'art. My God, of course he's nice to you, he's out for all he can get, the slimy bastard.'

'That is a cruel word to use in the circumstances, and very unfair. It's no fault of his that his parents weren't married,' cried the Duchess, rising with dignity. 'I think you're behaving very badly, Harry, especially as Andrew would be quite prepared to help you financially when you get rid of Morgan.'

'You've got Andrew on the brain!' Harry rose also and pushed his office chair back angrily. 'All I've heard, ever since I can remember, is Andrew, Andrew, Andrew. Well, I'm heartily sick of it. Christ, the man's only my first cousin!

The way you're going on you would think he was my brother!'

Lavinia walked to the door of Harry's office and opened it with a violent movement. Then she turned and looked back at Harry. Before she could speak he knew in that instant what she was going to say. The colour drained from his face and he sat down again.

'He *is* your brother, Harry,' she cried, 'and don't you ever forget it!'

Morgan strolled aimlessly down Bond Street indulging herself in an orgy of window shopping, feasting her eyes on the sumptuous displays. What would she buy today? The obligatory scarf from Hermès? A pretty crystal bonbonnière filled with chocolates at Charbonnel et Walker? Or some trinket from Aspreys. A little dress for herself at St Laurent or Valentino? Suddenly, boredom, like a deep physical sickness, stole over her. Nothing appealed. She had everything. And yet she had nothing. Nothing at all. She was lonely, isolated, and no one wanted her. Perhaps she would take a taxi to Knightsbridge and go into Harrods. At least it would pad out the day. Help pass the time.

Living so near Harrods, it had become like a shrine to her, a place from which she could derive comfort and consolation. To wander, dreamily, from department to department was like a balm to her soul, a drug to her senses. It was a fantasy world of exquisite luxury where she could indulge herself. Once inside, she let her eyes trail over jars of Beluga caviar, fancy boxes of handmade chocolates, flacons of perfume and diamonds as big as gulls' eggs.

Soaking up the atmosphere of the rich abundance and revelling in the lavish displays she began to feel better and proceeded to buy whatever caught her fancy.

The glittering rainbow facets of a crystal vase caught her eye. She bought it and galvanized by a sudden flow of energy went next to the flower department. Disappointed that they had no orchids in stock, she bought an expensive five-foot-high plant and had the salesgirl cut off the nine orchid blooms and wrap them up in paper for her.

'You can throw the rest away,' she said to the horrified girl.

Morgan also bought a white lace pillow, threaded with narrow blue ribbons, a gold kid evening bag because she liked the diamanté clasp, several fine gold bangles and a leather cigarette box that would look nice in the study.

Carrying her parcels home, she unpacked them lovingly. Placing the crystal vase, now filled with water, on the coffee table in the drawing room, she carefully arranged the large pale green orchids and stepped back to look at the effect. It really did look pretty. She put cigarettes in the new cigarette box, the pillow on her bed and the purse and bangles in her closet. Then she looked at her diamond watch. It was barely noon.

What the hell was she going to do with the rest of the day?

'What did your mother mean, Andrew's your brother?' Elizabeth was sitting with Harry in the drawing room of her parents' house the next evening and he had just blurted out Lavinia Lomond's amazing revelation.

Harry looked at her with dazed eyes. 'It's the strangest story you've ever heard. It answers a lot of things that have always puzzled me.'

'What happened? Was he your father's child? Born before he married your mother?' Her eyes were wide and limpid. 'That would explain everything, of course, why your mother feels Drumnadrochit should go to him, why she's resentful of your having everything. I suppose *she* looks upon you as the younger son, since Andrew's nearly three years older than you.'

'It's much more complicated than that!' exclaimed Harry.

The previous afternoon Harry had followed his mother out of the gallery and insisted on taking her home. She couldn't go around dropping bombshells like that without explaining what she meant, he told her, and insisted on knowing the whole story.

Reluctantly, for once she had spoken the words in anger she bitterly regretted them, Lavinia Lomond slowly told Harry what had happened. It was, he could see, very painful for her.

'So what happened, darling?' Elizabeth asked, leaning forward in her chair.

'It seems my mother and Uncle Angus were lovers, before she even met my father.'

'No! You mean ..?'

Harry nodded. 'Extraordinary as it sounds, to look at my mother now, she and Uncle Angus were having a roaring affair, it must have been 1949 or 1950. Anyway she wanted to marry him. She said yesterday he was the only man she'd ever loved, but he didn't want to marry her. He didn't want to marry anyone it seems. He always had far too good a time as a bachelor.'

'So?'

'When my mother found she was pregnant, and it was a terrible disgrace then, the whole thing was hushed up and she was packed off to Switzerland by her family to have the baby. She told me she couldn't bear the idea of an abortion. I have a feeling she hoped that once she'd had the baby Uncle Angus would marry her. Anyway, he didn't. Out of guilt I suppose, he arranged for Andrew to be brought back to England by a nurse and he gave him a home and educated him. He also left Andrew everything, which seems to have been quite a lot! Of course everyone was sworn to absolute secrecy. I suppose that's how the rumour that Andrew's mother was a chorus girl started. Imagine, it was my own prim and proper mother all the time!'

Elizabeth's mouth gaped wide. 'It's *amazing*,' she breathed.

'I know. And no one has ever found out! Even Andrew

doesn't know to this day. I don't know whether my mother will tell him now, but he must have thought it strange that for all these years she's made such a fuss over him. If she hadn't been so keen to push him forward now, and then lost her temper with me, I don't suppose anyone would ever have known. Her parents are dead, Uncle Angus died when Andrew was five and of course my father never suspected a thing.'

'She must be kicking herself now! How did she come to marry your father? Did she already know him through Angus?'

'Apparently not. They met at a hunt ball and he was attracted to her.' Harry shook his head wonderingly. 'I suppose she must have been pretty once, but I do find it hard to imagine that she had all these men running after her. It was awful yesterday, Elizabeth, when she was talking about it. Do you know what she said? She told me that she never loved Pa, but after what had happened she thought she was very lucky to get the chance of making such a good marriage. And there was another reason. She knew by marrying Pa she would be close to Uncle Angus and Andrew.' Harry's voice sank so low Elizabeth could hardly hear him. He would forgive his mother many things but never the fact that she had never loved his father.

'And so they married,' Elizabeth said gently, breaking into his thoughts.

'Yes.'

'I wonder what your uncle thought about it all!'

'God knows! I would think it must have been very embarrassing for him. Of course he wasn't to know he'd die when Andrew was so young. If he'd known he might have been quite glad that his son would have some sort of home life with Ma and Pa.'

'So what's going to happen now, Harry?'

'What can happen, darling? Andrew's still the illegitimate son of a younger brother, so he can't inherit the title. I suppose he and Ma will go on living together.'

'Harry,' Elizabeth began tentatively, 'have you told Morgan all this?'

Her question brought a smile to Harry's face. 'No!' he said succinctly. 'Wouldn't she just love it, though! Imagine her gloating. You're the only person I'm ever going to tell, darling, because I can trust you. If Morgan were to find out it would be around town in a day. She hates my mother, so she'd do anything for vengeance.'

Elizabeth looked pleased. Harry trusted her above all others and she knew she would never betray that trust.

Suddenly Harry's mind seemed to be on something else. Rising, he paced nervously round the room, picking up and putting down odd objects in an unthinking manner.

'May I have another drink, Elizabeth?' he asked abruptly.

'Of course, sweetheart.' Surprised at his sudden change in mood, she poured him another whisky and soda, carefully measuring the proportions exactly the way he liked.

Harry took the glass from her absently, then flopped back onto the sofa again. She waited in silence, watching him.

'Elizabeth,' he began.

'Yes, darling?'

'I have to talk to you.'

'Yes?' Her stomach muscles contracted and her heart started hammering. A moment earlier she'd thought for one wild moment that he was going to tell her he had decided to divorce Morgan and marry her, but now... She had a strange foreboding something unpleasant was going to happen. Harry was looking strained and seemed reluctant to say what he had to say.

'Yes?' she repeated, trying to keep her voice steady.

'I want you to do me a favour, darling, and don't say anything until I've finished speaking. I have something to ask you, but first, well, first I've something to tell you.'

36

His mouth was closing over hers and Tiffany could feel the warmth of his body as he held her close. Pressing herself against his hardness she undulated her hips, eager to take him and hold him inside her, never wanting to let him go. Now something sweet and deep and trembling started to sweep through her and she thrust herself harder against him. Then a great white heat came rolling up from the depths of her being, sending shudders through her, and she gasped and cried out.

Tiffany opened her eyes and found herself bathed in sweat and alone in the darkness. She was clutching her pillow and that too was damp. Shaken and still slightly breathless, she turned on the bedside lamp and looked round her room at the Beverly Wilshire. She really was alone, but the dream had been so vivid, so utterly real, that she could still feel her tender wetness and the hardness of her nipples.

God, how she missed Hunt when he wasn't with her. Ever since that evening when they'd met and talked late into the night they'd seen as much of each other as possible, but yesterday he'd had to fly back to New York for a couple of days on business.

She rolled onto her back and stared at the ceiling. He'd asked her to marry him several times and yet she was holding back from taking that final step. Something needed to happen, but she wasn't sure what, to prove to her irrevocably that he really loved her, and always would.

The weekends she had spent at his home in Benedict Canyon had been a great success. Gus and Matt seemed to accept her with typical childlike disinterest and she had been enchanted by them. Maybe, in time, they would help to take away the pain of losing her baby. That is, if she finally married Hunt. She decided to call him in the morning if only to hear his voice. Perhaps she *would* marry him soon, she thought, as renewed desire filled her. Life sure was hell without him.

Tiffany turned on her side, switched off the lamp and tried to sleep. But before she had time to call Hunt in the morning, she received a call from London that was to change everything.

In London, it had been a long, strange and terrible night for Morgan. Harry hadn't come home until nine o'clock and had refused dinner. Then he had followed Morgan into the study and in a stiff halting manner told her he wanted a divorce.

As she sat huddled in the big armchair, listening to the words she had so dreaded hearing, a terrible feeling of helplessness and impotence crept over her. Harry seemed to be droning on about incompatibilty and nobody's fault and clean breaks, while she felt herself spinning down and down into a cold pit of disaster. She had done everything in her power to prevent this, but still it was happening. A force she was unable to fight was squeezing her mercilessly out of a life she had created for herself, and there wasn't a damned thing she could do about it. Harry wanted out.

'You'll keep the house of course and all the contents,' he was saying, waving an expansive arm, 'and you can have the car. I'm afraid, though, you have no claim on Drumnadrochit.'

Morgan said nothing. Her mind had gone numb. She was only aware of her heart thudding thickly.

'I shall be living in Scotland,' Harry continued, 'and John will run the gallery for me. Er, what else?' He gave a nervous little cough and surreptitiously wiped his sweating hands on the seat of his trousers. *So far so good*, he thought. *Maybe this isn't going to cost me as much as I feared. Morgan seems to be taking it very quietly.*

On the other hand he hadn't told her everything.

'Now about David.' *This is it. The crunch.* 'I think he should go back to Tiffany.'

A flicker of surprise crossed Morgan's white face. 'Go back to Tiffany?' she repeated dully.

'Yes. He should be with his own mother. She'll give him a stable background and the sort of security a child needs. You're not really the maternal type, are you, Morgan?' It was not said as an accusation, but more as a matter of simple fact.

'Well, he's not my child.'

'Exactly. I'm fond of the boy, but he'll be much happier with his real mother. His grandparents are in America too. He will give Joe something to think about. It might help after losing Zachary.'

The life came rushing back to Morgan's face and her eyes suddenly blazed. 'Talk about being callous! You've always called me callous where the baby's concerned but you really take first prize! How can you talk about *giving* away your son? Is it because he's illegitimate? Is that it? Would he be an embarrassment to you?' Her voice rose hysterically. 'Or is it because you and Elizabeth don't want your future heirs contaminated by a half-American bastard?' Deep rasping sobs racked her slender body. 'David might not be my son, Harry, but he's yours and he's your responsibility. Tiffany probably doesn't even want him back. For God's sake, you're his father.'

Harry rose and shifted unhappily about the room, slamming his fist into the palm of his other hand. He seemed about to speak, then stopped, came back and sat down, and with a tremendous effort looked Morgan in the eye.

'That's where you're wrong, Morgan.'

Bewildered, she looked into his face and could not understand what she saw. 'Of course you're his father! What the hell are you talking about?'

There was an agonized look in his eyes. 'I'm not his father. I thought I was, right up to the time my mother phoned me in Scotland and read out the bit in the newspapers about Tiffany being a surrogate mother. All the time you were pregnant – or rather pretending to be – I thought I was the father. My mother kept trying to tell me you had a lover and it was *his* child but I couldn't believe that. I thought she was just trying to stir up trouble between us. I'm afraid the truth is that I didn't father David.'

Morgan clutched the arms of her chair. The room was reeling.

'Harry, *why* are you doing this?' she cried.

His tone was one of an adult patiently trying to explain something to a child. 'I'm trying to tell you David doesn't belong to *either* of us! That's why he must go back to your sister. I tried to tell you all this when I came out of hospital, but, well, I just couldn't.'

Morgan sprang up, raging. What sort of garbage was this ninny trying to pull off now?

'You're crazy!' she shrieked.

'I'm not crazy. Whoever Tiffany had the baby by, it certainly wasn't me.'

'*Of course* it was you! She went to bed with you! I arranged it. You and she – '

'I know.' He was still talking patiently. 'But that doesn't make me the father.'

'This is a trick! A dirty lousy trick! You're just trying to get rid of both of us so you can start over fresh with Elizabeth, you goddamn son of a bitch! How do you suppose Tiffany got pregnant then? By some fucking immaculate conception? David is your child and don't try and deny it.'

'Morgan,' Harry spoke her name gently, almost sadly. 'David can't be my child because I'm sterile.'

Morgan's mouth fell open and she stared at him with disbelieving eyes.

'*That* is what my mother told me on the phone – the day I had the car accident. I can never have an heir.' The pain in his voice was raw. 'As a youth I contracted mumps very badly. I remember the doctor mentioning something about orchitis, but I had no idea what it meant and at that age probably didn't care. Anyway my mother was apparently told it would make me sterile for life. She never told me and she didn't tell my father either. All these years I presumed I was absolutely normal. I'm afraid she was quite glad, you see, because if I don't have heirs Andrew will get Drumnadrochit when I'm gone.' He stopped abruptly, afraid she would make something of his mother's preference for his cousin.

But Morgan's expression of bewildered amazement and anger told him she was still trying to take in what he was saying. She had gone to all the trouble to conceal the fact that she was barren, only to be confronted with the news that all along Harry had been sterile. Clarity of thought came swiftly back to her. She regrouped her reactions. If Lavinia Lomond was running true to form this yarn was a load of shit. Harry must be made to see that between his mother and Elizabeth he was being persuaded to get rid of her – and now David – at all costs.

'Harry,' she said, suddenly calm, 'why should you believe your mother about this, any more than you believed her when she said I was having a baby by a lover? I don't swallow this story because it's all just too neat. In one fell swoop she gets rid of me and the baby, as if the last couple of years had never happened! God, you're such a fool to believe her.'

'For once you're wrong about my mother. When I was in hospital after the crash I told the doctor what she had said. He arranged for me to have a sperm count. The result quite definitely proved I'm sterile.'

Desperately Morgan looked round the room as if for inspiration. She must try to find a way to avert this disaster.

Everything, everyone, was going from her. She'd be alone. Isolated. Suddenly she asked, 'Have you told Elizabeth all this?'

For the first time that evening the faint ghost of Harry's quirky smile hovered round his mouth. He knew exactly what Morgan was thinking. 'Yes, I have told Elizabeth. I told her before I asked her to marry me. She was sad of course, sad for me mostly. The great thing about Elizabeth is that she truly loves me. And she asked nothing of me that I am unable to give her. We'll be getting married as soon as the divorce is through. It's no good, Morgan. It's all over.'

For a moment they looked at each other, like two pieces on a chess board that had reached checkmate. Neither spoke. Then, as the full realization of what Harry had said hit her, she flung herself down on the sofa, crying hysterically.

When the phone woke Tiffany in Los Angeles she wondered if it could be Hunt.

'Hullo?' she murmured sleepily.

'Tiffany! I've had a terrible job getting hold of you! I didn't have your number and Daddy had forgotten it.'

'Morgan?' Tiffany was wide awake. 'What's the matter with you? You sound terrible!'

'You've got to come over! Something has happened! I've got to get out of here! Why did you have to double-cross me, for God's sake?'

Tiffany sat up, stunned. 'What do you mean, double-cross you!'

'You've ruined my only chance of hanging on to Harry, and you've made me look a fool too! Why didn't you tell me you were already pregnant when you went to bed with him?' Morgan sobbed. 'Now he wants a divorce!'

'Hey, wait a minute!' Anger infused Tiffany's whole being. 'Let's get this straight. I wasn't pregnant when I came to England that time. Of course it's Harry's child.'

'It isn't! It isn't!' Morgan sounded quite distraught. 'Harry's just told me he's sterile. I know he's telling the truth. He wants a divorce so that he can marry that bitch, and he wants you to take David back. And where does that leave *me*?'

Tiffany licked her lips and said the undreamed-of words. through her. She didn't dare hope that it was true.

'Tiff? Answer me!'

Tiffany licked her lips and said the undreamed-of words. 'So I can have my baby back then?'

'Well, I suppose you'll have to! What would I do with him now? But Tiffany, you must have known you were pregnant! I don't believe you didn't know. Anyway, whose child *is* he, if he isn't Harry's? You'd split from Hunt months before this happened.'

Tiffany didn't answer. Her mind was racing. But the first thing she had to do was fly to England and get David back before Harry and Morgan changed their minds. If they did, they'd be in for the fight of their lives. Aloud she said, 'I'll leave right away, Morgan,' and she hung up the phone.

Tiffany first put through a call to Joe, then, as soon as she could, booked herself a seat on the first available flight to London. Then she sent a message to the studio saying she had been called away on urgent business but would be back within three days. It was lucky, she reflected, that she was ahead with her designs, and could leave everything to her assistant. Then she packed a small case of basic essentials and sat down and wrote a note to Hunt to be delivered to his home. He'd be back from New York tomorrow, and she wanted the letter to be waiting for him. This wasn't something she could explain over the phone.

The taxi drew up outside the elegant house in Montpelier Square, with its geranium-filled window boxes and bay trees on either side of the black front door. Tiffany got out and handed the driver a crisp twenty-pound note. The fare on the meter said fifteen.

'Thanks, luv,' he nodded, pleased when he realized she didn't want any change.

'Thank you.' Smiling, she ran up the white marble steps and pressed the brass bell.

The house was silent and had a curiously abandoned air. The heavy muslin drapes over the windows revealed nothing and gave the house a strange look of blindness.

After waiting a couple of minutes she rang again. She tried to stifle a feeling of mounting panic. Supposing they'd gone away – to Scotland or something – and taken David with them? Cursing herself for not having checked with Harry, she thumped the brass knocker loudly. Supposing this was all some ghastly trick of Morgan's?

At that moment the door swung open silently and Perkins, as impeccable as ever, stood looking down at her. He tried to disguise his surprise, although, as he reflected later, why he should feel surprise at *anything* that happened in this household, he didn't know.

'Ah, Miss Kalvin.'

'Is my sister home?' Tiffany blurted out, thankful to find the house occupied.

Perkins raised his eyebrows fractionally.

'I'm afraid not. Can I take a message, madam?'

For a moment Tiffany stood looking astounded, then she pushed past him into the deserted hall. She looked round anxiously as if searching for something. 'Is David here?'

'The young master is in the nursery, madam. With his nanny.'

'And you say, er, my sister isn't here?'

'I'm afraid not, madam.'

'Is the Duke around?'

'His grace may still be with her grace, madam. On the other hand he may already be at the gallery.'

'Where *is* Morgan?' She felt irritated by all this 'her

grace', 'his grace' shit. 'I've come over to collect David, but I'd like to see my sister first.'

Perkins coughed gently. 'I regret that is not possible, madam. The Duchess has been taken ill and was admitted to the King Edward VII Hospital. The Duke took her in himself.'

'Oh!' Tiffany's eyes opened wide and for a moment she looked anxious. 'Has she... did she...?' Pictures flashed through her mind of Morgan taking an overdose, slashing her wrists. 'What's the matter with her?'

'I've been told to inform everyone that the Duchess has gone into hospital for a period of rest,' he said primly.

'What does that mean?'

'The doctor thought she required rest and a, er, peaceful atmosphere for a little while.'

A nervous breakdown, thought Tiffany instantly. *The shock of all this has brought on a nervous breakdown. The highly polished performance has finally cracked.*

'Would you care to wait, madam? Perhaps I can get you some coffee.'

Tiffany looked straight into his unblinking grey eyes. 'I've just flown all the way from Los Angeles to collect my son,' she said firmly. 'First, I'd like a bath and a chance to freshen up. Then I'd like some coffee. And could you please get a message to the Duke that I am here and that I shall be flying back to America first thing in the morning with David.' She drew a deep breath. 'And now I'm going up to the nursery to see my son.'

37

'We will keep her under sedation for a few days,' the doctor at the hospital told Harry. It was the day after he had broken the news to Morgan. 'In a week or two she should be fine again. This type of breakdown, brought on by some specific event, is quite easy to cure. It is when someone has a breakdown for no apparent reason that we have a problem.'

Harry had briefly told the doctor what had happened. He had been scared to death, he added, at Morgan's condition. He had been unable to calm her. She had been almost suicidal.

'You did the right thing by bringing her here,' the doctor assured him, 'and in view of the circumstances I think it would be better if you did not visit her for a while. What she needs is plenty of rest and sleep and absolute quiet.' He was used to dealing with patients who collapsed from nervous exhaustion and mini-breakdowns. They were usually the rich, the idle, and in the case of women, the spoiled. A few days of pampering and a bottle of tranquillizers invariably did the trick.

Harry left the hospital feeling slightly relieved. Morgan's hysteria had really shaken him. She'd been completely out of control.

Twenty minutes later he was home again. Time for a quick shower and change of clothes before he went to the gallery. He must call Elizabeth also. Wonderful girl, Elizabeth. Always thinking of other people.

'Jesus Frigging Christ! This is getting stupider than *Dallas*!' snorted Joe, as he and Ruth sat having breakfast, discussing Tiffany's call. 'How come Tiffany didn't *know* she was already pregnant when she went to bed with Harry!' He slammed his coffee cup onto its saucer. 'It's not like her to play around either. Can you believe it, Ruth? She and Morgan go through all that rigmarole to produce a child and they end up getting the wrong father!' He made it sound like gross inefficiency.

Ruth was feeling frailer than usual. Joe had rumbled on until he had fallen asleep as dawn was breaking. His snoring had made sleep impossible for her. Now she was trying to come to grips with this newest piece of information.

'One thing will be nice, though,' she said placatingly, 'and that is having your first grandchild here in America. He'll be much better off with Tiffany than with Morgan, too. Do you remember, in Scotland last year, the child was always in the care of his nanny? He hardly ever saw his mother – I mean Morgan.'

Joe was silent. At the mention of Scotland he was wondering if he'd ever get back any of the dollars he'd sunk into Drumnadrochit. Morgan was a fool. He blamed her for this whole catastrophe. Why couldn't she have behaved herself like a real lady?

'Don't be too hard on Morgan,' Ruth said, as if she had been reading his thoughts. 'It can't have been easy for her either.'

'Listen, Ruth. I was pleased when she married Harry. Very pleased. But why wasn't she content just to be a member of the British aristocracy? It should have been enough. If she'd played her cards right she might have ended up, er, well, something like a Lady of the Queen's Bedchamber, or a Lady in Waiting! But oh, no. Not Morgan. She wanted to be more like a pop star or something – I ask you! Believe me, that's why Harry's leaving her. She's made a vulgar show of herself with all that bad publicity.'

Ruth buttered herself a slice of rye. It was not the moment to remind Joe that it had been him who'd turned Morgan's wedding into a media circus.

'She was always trying to run Harry's life,' he continued, 'making him go here and there, taking credit for the success of his gallery. I'm not a bit surprised he's had enough. Men don't like women who try to act clever, Ruth.'

'No, honey. Did Tiffany have anything else to say?'

'Only that she was flying to London today to fetch the baby. And doesn't that make you mad too? It's always Tiff who ends up zooming about the place at Morgan's beck and call.' He rose and picked up the *Wall Street Journal*, as usual.

'Joe?'

'Uh-huh?'

'It will be nice having David live over here though, won't it?' A delicate eager smile lit up her tired face.

Joe bent to peck her on the cheek. 'Sure. Who knows? Someday, maybe...' He let the words trail away.

'I've thought of that. But we won't make the same mistakes we made with Zachary, will we?'

'Tiffany wouldn't let us.' There was pride in his voice. 'But you never know! See you tonight, honey.'

'Yes, Joe.'

He bounced out of the room, his step lighter than it had been in a long time. David might not be the heir to the Duke of Lomond of Drumnadrochit Castle, but there was nothing to stop him being the heir to Quadrant Inc.

Harry stopped, startled, in the doorway of Morgan's bedroom and blinked with shock. There, sitting at the dressing table, brushing her long golden hair, was Morgan! She had her back to him and she was wearing a pink robe.

'Morgan!' he croaked.

The figure spun round, startled too. Then she stared at Harry for a long moment before smiling.

'Oh, Harry! You scared me.'

'*Tiffany*? Good Lord, I thought for a moment it was Morgan, but I didn't see how...' Harry suddenly blushed, remembering the last time they had met. 'You've heard she's in the King Edward VII?'

'Yes. How is she?'

'Overwrought, I'm afraid. I feel pretty bad about it all. I think finding out about David was the worst. She seemed to think he was some sort of link that might have kept us together. Anyway, you've come for him, I presume?'

'Yes, I have. I'm afraid I couldn't wait. I was also afraid you might change your mind and that I'd have to fight my way out of here with him.'

'It's only right you have him back, Tiffany. He is your child. He's a dear little boy too, and I shall miss him dreadfully.'

Tiffany beamed. 'I know. I've been up in the nursery for the past hour playing with him. I can't wait to take him back with me. I've asked Nanny to do his packing.'

'When are you off then?'

'I'm booked on a morning flight to Los Angeles.' She put down the silver-backed hairbrush and picked up her lipstick.

'You'd better spend the night here,' said Harry immediately. 'I'll be staying at Elizabeth's, and I'll get Duncan to run you to the airport in the morning.'

'Thanks, Harry. I'm very grateful and . . . I'd just like to say one thing, in case there's not another opportunity. I'm dreadfully sorry for all that's happened. Morgan and I must have caused you an awful lot of pain and embarrassment. I'm really sorry and I want to apologize.'

Harry stood looking at the young woman who sat so earnestly before him. She was so like Morgan in so many ways, and yet she was completely different. Her gentleness and sweetness were in complete contrast to Morgan's diamond-hard brilliance.

'Well . . .' He gave a nervous little cough. 'It's all over now, isn't it? I'm marrying Elizabeth, whom I should have married in the first place – and you've got your little son back. As for Morgan,' he gave a deep sigh, 'I'm afraid she's going to have to work out something for herself, but I think she's a real survivor.'

'She's that all right,' murmured Tiffany. 'The only problem is you're dealing with someone who has the emotions of a seven-year-old trapped in the body of an adult.'

'I had a sudden thought coming back here, Tiffany. Do you think it would be a good idea if she went back to the States for a bit when she comes out of hospital?'

'To get her away from London?' Tiffany considered the idea for a moment. 'Yes, I think you're right. She could always stay at Southampton. Maybe we should get an analyst for her.'

Harry smiled wanly. 'You Americans are very keen on that sort of thing, aren't you? We don't go in for it much over here.'

'I think she's going to need some help to get over this trauma. We can be supportive, as a family, but we're none of us professionals in this field. The divorce will be the final blow to her pride.'

'There's no other way, Tiffany. I have tried –'

'I'm not blaming you, Harry.'

'Can you tell me something?'

'What is it?'

'I never understood why you agreed to be a surrogate mother in the first place. Why did you let Morgan talk you into it?'

'It's a long story, Harry. A very long story. And water under the bridge now. I'm just so happy to be getting my son back.' Tiffany's face glowed with maternal pride.

'And the father?' Harry blushed again at the boldness of his question. 'Sorry, I didn't mean to pry.'

'That's all right Harry. That too is a very long story.'

She smiled at him and he knew she wasn't going to say any more.

At nine-thirty the next morning Tiffany stepped into the

waiting Rolls with David in her arms. Perkins and the nanny hovered anxiously, while Harry, returned early from Elizabeth's home, fussed over her.

'You're sure you're going to be all right, then?' he asked her for the third time.

Tiffany laughed as she held David close. 'I'll be fine! Nanny has told me exactly when to give David his meals and I've got everything here.' She indicated a plastic bag covered with teddy bears on the seat beside her.

'Good! Good!' Harry leaned into the car wistfully and ran a gentle hand over the baby's head. 'Take care Tiff, and the best of luck and everything.'

She thought she detected a sudden brightness in his eyes.

'Thank you for letting me have him,' she said impetuously.

'It's only right he should be with you. I knew he'd have to go back to you sooner or later. That's why, when I knew . . . Well, anyway, good luck.' Then he was gone. Back into the house without a backward glance.

Tiffany felt a lump in her throat as she looked down at the baby. Poor Harry. David had been the nearest he would ever get to having a child of his own.

That same morning a piece appeared in a popular London tabloid, accompanied by a photograph of Morgan and Harry taken on their wedding day. It speculated on the breakdown of the Lomonds' marriage and announced that the young Duchess of Lomond had been admitted to the King Edward VII Hospital for a period of rest, following a quarrel with her sister, costume designer Tiffany Kalvin, who had flown to London from Los Angeles to claim the child she had been surrogate mother to. It was understood, continued the story, that the Duke wished the child to remain in England.

As usual, the press had got it slightly wrong.

Morgan lay in the quiet atmosphere of her old-fashioned

room in the hospital, hovering between drug-induced sleep and the bottom of a deep pit from which she could not escape. Cold despair and apathy crept with slimy fingers over her inert body. Every now and then a wave of blackness hit her, pressing her down and down. It squeezed the tears from her eyes and the breath from her body. She was being held by tight imprisoning bands of wretchedness and all she longed for were the pills that brought oblivion for a few hours.

Memories of what she had lost flooded her mind. From being a dazzling young duchess with beauty, wealth and position she was once again just Morgan Kalvin with no background worth mentioning. What consolation were looks and money when the doors of a glittering world that had once been hers were now shut. Her marriage to Harry was over. So were the days of garden parties at Buckingham Palace, the opening of Parliament when she wore her scarlet velvet, ermine-trimmed robe, with the coronet of a duchess; Royal Ascot, Goodwood, polo at Windsor, the balls in Mayfair and the receptions in Belgravia. Gone. All gone. The list stretched into eternity. No longer would she be entertaining against the magnificent backdrop of Drumnadrochit Castle. The chic dinner parties at Montpelier Square were things of the past too.

An outsider now, ostracized by the aristocracy in the same way as they had ostracized the Duchess of Windsor, Morgan lay on her side, tears of defeat pouring silently down her cheeks. What was hurting most was the realization that she had brought it all on herself. If only she could go back. Far, far back. To when she'd been a little girl and everyone had loved and admired her and her parents had been so proud of her. Those days of her childhood seemed, in retrospect, to have been such a golden time. What had happened to the little girl who had been so happy?

Where had she gone?

*

'Sure she can come and stay with us.' Joe was talking on the phone to Harry. 'If she's that bad maybe we should get a nurse to keep an eye on her.'

'I don't think that will be necessary,' Harry replied. 'The doctors say she will soon be fine. She's not allowed any visitors, of course. Even Tiffany was discouraged from seeing her when she was here. But I'm told that an enforced rest and sleep will soon have her all right.'

'What Morgan needs is plenty of good food and a bit of sun, in my opinion,' said Joe crisply. 'A week or two at Four Winds or Palm Beach will do the trick. Where is Tiffany now?'

'I saw her off a few hours ago. She and David will be landing in Los Angeles sometime tomorrow.'

'Fine. Well, Harry, it looks like this is it!' Joe spoke gruffly.

'I'm afraid so. It's been an awful mess and I can't help blaming myself for a lot of it.'

'No one person is ever to blame in a situation like this. It's usually the result of combined efforts,' Joe replied succinctly.

A minute later they said goodbye.

Joe started to add up what the whole episode had cost him.

Lavinia Lomond was lunching with Elizabeth's parents, the Earl and Countess of FitzHammond, and as they toyed with their grilled Dover sole and petit pois, the conversation kept reverting to the thoughts uppermost in their minds.

'Harry says Morgan's returning to America as soon as she comes out of hospital,' the old Duchess informed them, laying down her George III silver fork. 'Then let's hope the vulgar stories in the newspapers will stop. I mean, my dear, did you see what they wrote in the *Daily Express* this morning? It really is quite dreadful.'

'Very distressing,' murmured Lady FitzHammond.

'It doesn't help that Morgan is such a beauty either!' interjected Lord FitzHammond. 'They wouldn't be half so interested if she looked like the back of a cab.'

The Duchess shot him a disapproving look.

'Elizabeth's so happy that it's all getting sorted out though,' cried Lady FitzHammond. 'I presume they will have to get married in a registry office but we can give a nice reception for them afterwards at the Naval and Military Club.'

The Duchess smiled in approval. 'Very appropriate, my dear. Especially after that last wedding! I really thought I'd die when I came out of St Margaret's and saw all those photographers – and even television cameras! *So* common! That dreadful father of hers turned the whole thing into a positive carnival!'

'Yes,' Lord FitzHammond nodded. 'We can't really blame Morgan for that. If you ask me, with parents like that, the girl really never had a chance.'

'Nonsense!' snapped the Duchess. 'She's had too many chances! She's the most spoiled, wilful young woman I've ever met, and it's high time that Harry came to his senses. He'll be a thousand times happier with your Elizabeth, she's such a nice little thing. And of course the right background. That's what's really important in a marriage. The right background.'

'You're right, Lavinia,' said Lady FitzHammond, although she was secretly fascinated by Morgan. Never in her life had she met a woman like her. Such daring! Such ruthless brilliance! Her poor little Elizabeth had never stood a chance once Morgan appeared on the scene. But now all that was over. Elizabeth was at last going to make a suitable marriage, though it was a pity they could never have children.

'Is Morgan really ill?'

'She's acting like a prima donna, that's all! Probably

thinks that if she feigns illness it will bring Harry running back. Thank God, he's no longer taken in by her, but I shall be glad when she's out of the country.' With satisfaction the Duchess sipped her white wine.

'And the, er, child?'

'He's already gone. I mean, it was an impossible situation having the little bastard around.' She put down her glass suddenly, her cheeks flushing. 'Not of course, that one must ever blame a child for being illegitimate, but, well, you know what I mean.'

Lord FitzHammond gave her a bland smile. 'Quite! Quite! Look how wonderful you've been to Andrew Flanders all these years, although he is a bastard. No one could say he's suffered! You've been as good to him as if you'd been his mother, instead of only his aunt-in-law. He's turned into a fine young man.'

In her confusion Lavinia Lomond knocked over her wine glass and a pool of clear liquid spread on the walnut surface of the table.

'Oh! How careless! I'm so sorry,' she cried.

'Not at all, my dear, please don't worry.'

The Earl mopped the table with his damask napkin. 'I knew his mother, you know,' he said calmly.

'You knew ..?' The Duchess's hand flew to the pearls at her throat. 'But she, I mean, I've always been told she was some chorus girl!'

'Oh, no. Nothing like that.' Suddenly the Earl found both women were staring at him. 'She was a debutante actually. Of course I was still up at Oxford when it happened but I saw her at a few parties though she never noticed me. Dashed pretty girl too! Good family.'

'Oh, Cedric! What happened? Who was she?' His wife leaned forward. 'Was she disgraced?'

'Not a bit of it! She went off to Switzerland and had the baby in secret and when it was all over she came back to London and made a brilliant marriage.'

'How too absolutely fascinating!' breathed Lady Fitz-Hammond.

Lavinia Lomond studiously examined the pattern of roses on her plate. Lord FitzHammond helped himself to a wedge of Stilton, and continued. 'The baby's father, Angus Flanders, behaved very decently considering what a rogue he was. He agreed to bring up the child and give it a home. That's right, isn't it, Lavinia? Old Angus provided for the child and Andrew used to spend his holidays with all of you at Drumnadrochit! Of course Angus should have married the girl but he never was the marrying type.'

'It's like something out of a novel!' His wife was entranced. 'But who was she, Cedric?'

'No names, no pack drill!' he replied.

Lady FitzHammond was desperate to know more.

'How on earth do you know all this, Cedric? Even Lavinia didn't know! You thought Andrew's mother was on the stage, or something, didn't you my dear?'

Lavinia nodded, not speaking.

The Earl shrugged his shoulders and looked jovial. 'Servants' hall gossip, m'dear. When the girl's parents knew she was pregnant they sacked all the staff and shut up the London house and went off to Switzerland. When it was over they engaged new staff. But my parents took on their old butler. If I remember rightly, his name was Scott. He was a chatty fellow and used to entertain me for hours in the pantry, telling me what life had been like in the great houses in the old days, not to mention what people got up to! That's when he told me this story.'

The Duchess dabbed her dry mouth with her napkin. There was silence in the room.

'Shall we have coffee in the drawing room?' asked Lord FitzHammond pleasantly.

Lavinia Lomond rose from the table, managing to avoid his eyes.

38

Pressing his foot down hard on the accelerator Hunt sped along the San Diego freeway. The lunchtime traffic was heavier than he'd expected and an anxious glance at the clock on the dashboard told him it was two-thirty. That meant he had exactly twenty-five minutes to get to the airport, park the car and go to the arrivals building.

Cursing softly, he swung the car out and tried to pass a long line of trucks. Ahead of him lay hundreds of cars, edging bumper to bumper, four abreast, crawling forward under a dusty sun. Revving the motor in frustration he plunged into the long line. There was no way he could be late. Tiffany's note was still in his pocket. It had merely said she had to leave town urgently for a couple of days, but could he meet her on Thursday. With thoroughness she'd added the flight number. From London. What the hell was she doing in London? There were parts of Tiffany that were still a mystery to him. And predictable she was not. Perhaps that was part of her fascination. Meanwhile he was longing to see her again and take her back to his house in Benedict Canyon. Gus and Matt were staying over for the night with friends, so they would have the place to themselves. He could hardly wait.

The stewardess's voice was clear and bell-like.

'We will be arriving at Los Angeles International Airport in fifteen minutes. Will you kindly fasten your seatbelts, see that your tray tables are in an upright position and extinguish all cigarettes.'

Fifteen minutes! A nervous yet thrilled trembling started in Tiffany's stomach and stretched to her toes. David was asleep in his travelling crib beside her, as he had been for most of the flight, but she was longing to get him home. Yet what home? If Hunt was horrified at the sight of her with David, whom he still supposed was Harry's child, it would be back to the Beverly Wilshire until she found an apartment. But if Hunt loved her enough to accept them both? This was the test of his love that she had been waiting for.

The plane was descending fast towards the runway and Tiffany swallowed to prevent her ears popping. In a moment they would be landing.

Did Hunt love her enough to accept David as well?

There was only one way to find out.

Tiffany saw him before he saw her, his dark curling hair and broad shoulders towering over all the other people. Hitching David, who had woken up in the customs building, higher into the crook of her arm, she pushed the trolley of luggage with her spare hand, wishing she didn't feel so crumpled and sticky.

Then Hunt caught sight of her. He grinned broadly, then a flicker of astonishment passed across his face.

'Tiff!' he yelled.

'Hi!' She steered the trolley in his direction. 'Thanks for coming to meet me.'

With searching eyes they faced each other for a long silent moment.

'*Well*!' he gasped. 'What have we here?' It was obvious he was trying to collect himself.

'This is my baby, Hunt. I've brought him back to live with me.' Tiffany's smile was calm, though her heart was hammering.

'To live with – Why, that's great, honey! Hi, little one.' For a moment he held David's small hand in his and smiled down at him. 'Here, let me take that case. Are you all right? I was a bit worried when I got your note.'

'I'm fine, a bit tired, though. I seem to have been flying for the past three days non-stop. At least that's what it feels like! But I'll be okay when I've had a chance to freshen up.'

'Let's get to the car. It's great to see you, honey, I've missed you.' Hunt put his arm protectively round her waist.

'Me, too,' she replied softly.

Expertly, Hunt loaded all David's things and her one small case into the trunk of his car. 'You'd better come back to my place, hadn't you?' he asked. 'It would be better for the baby than a hotel.'

'That would be great.' David started to whimper and she held him close. 'Do you mind if I get in the back, he's due for a bottle and I think he needs changing. He'll start to bawl in a minute otherwise.'

'Of course.' Hunt sounded happy, but his head was reeling and he was suffering from unaccountable jabs of jealousy. He had planned to have Tiffany to himself for the next twenty-four hours, most of which he'd hoped would be spent in bed, and now here she was in the back of his car, making cooing noises and wrestling with nappies.

He had, he thought wryly, known more romantic moments in his life.

Hunt's house was cantilevered out of the edge of Benedict Canyon, a white Spanish-style villa with little white domes on the roof that Tiffany had grown to love over the past few months. The cathedral ceilings and cool terracotta-tiled flooring that led out onto the patio and blue pool, surrounded by cypress and palm trees, seemed to her more rustic and natural than the studied chic and manicured grounds of 'Four Winds'. She loved the way ivy and sharp-smelling geraniums covered the grounds and the brilliance of the bougainvillea as it swarmed round the white arches.

Maybe this would be her home one day too. Or maybe not.

At last they were alone, David asleep in the guest room and the housekeeper and Manuel off for the night since Gus and Matt were staying over with friends. Showered and changed into one of Hunt's striped shirts, she curled up on one of the long sofas and watched while he poured champagne into two long fluted glasses.

'Welcome home, darling.'

'Thank you, Hunt. It's wonderful to be back.' Carefully she avoided using the term 'home'.

'Tell me about going to London. A bit unexpected wasn't it?'

'Yes. I'm sorry I couldn't get hold of you, you being in New York and all that, but I had to fly over and pick up David right away. I couldn't wait. I was mainly afraid someone would change their minds about letting me have him.' She leaned back against the silk cushions and smiled at him contentedly.

'Why have you got him back?' The question was blunt.

'Morgan and Harry are getting divorced and Harry's going to marry a girl he was practically engaged to before he met Morgan. Anyway, Harry thought David should come back to me, as I'm his real mother.'

'How strange he didn't want to keep David himself! Was he afraid Morgan would get custody? Didn't she mind letting him go?' Hunt asked, puzzled.

'Morgan didn't want David. She's ill anyway at the moment, with a sort of mini nervous breakdown. Harry honestly thought David would be better with me.'

'He probably will be, but I do find it strange, Tiff. Didn't Harry's future wife – what's her name? – want to have him?'

'This was Harry's decision. All I care about is having my baby back with me.'

'I can understand that. God, I'm thankful I've got Gus and Matt! I can understand how you feel. So does this mean you're going to give up work?'

Tiffany sipped the ice-cold champagne. 'I want to go on working, though I'll take it easy for a while when this series of *Connections* wraps. I have to get to know David.

Yesterday was the first time I'd even held him in my arms.' Her voice quavered. Hunt put his arm round her.

'You know you've got a home here, for both you and David. You only have to say the word, darling.'

Tiffany looked at him closely. His eyes were sincere and full of love. His smile was tender. Now she was almost sure.

'This does rather alter things though, doesn't it?' she said softly.

'In what way?'

'It was one thing your asking me to marry you when I was solo. You hadn't reckoned on my turning up on your doorstep with a baby, had you? How do you really feel about having David as part of your family? Will Gus and Matt accept the situation?'

Hunt put his arms round her and held her close. 'It makes no difference, Tiff. Nothing can make any difference now. I love you and everything that's yours. He should be with you, and I'm really glad you got him back.'

'You mean that, don't you?' She still searched his face to see if she could find a flicker of uncertainty. If there was she would go on doubting his love for the rest of her life. 'You're telling me that you'll never regret the fact that I've got a baby? That you'll never resent his presence?'

Hunt looked so wretched at her doubts that she felt a pang of guilt for torturing him this way.

'I promise you, darling, David will be like one of my own children. And Gus and Matt will be thrilled at having a little brother to play with. For Christ's sake, you've got to believe me, Tiff! I want both of you.' His voice croaked.

Tiffany relaxed as a great warm wave of happiness swept over her.

'Then it will be all right, won't it?' she said with a smile.

When Hunt kissed her, something inside her finally dissolved. The hard tight knot that had been building up in her stomach for years was gone.

But there was one more thing she had to say.

'I'm sorry for doubting your love, Hunt,' she began, 'and for not telling you before, but there is something you should know.'

He stared at her. Wasn't it only this morning that he had been wondering at her unpredictability? 'Well?'

She delivered it straight. 'David isn't Harry's child.'

Hunt seemed to stiffen and he shot her a questioning look.

'Do you remember the opening night of *Glitz*? When you turned up at my apartment afterwards?' she began.

He looked puzzled for a moment, remembering. Then he nodded, slowly, tenderly.

Tiffany put her arms round his neck and looked into his eyes. Her smile was trusting. Hunt had come through for her. He always would. At last she spoke.

'I didn't know, in fact I only realized it last week when I was told Harry was sterile, but on that night you and I started a baby. David is our child.'

39

Morgan, propped up in bed, in a pale-blue satin and lace bed-jacket, looked round her hospital room with amazement. It resembled a very expensive flower shop, with vases nudging each other on every available surface, and baskets, overflowing with roses and paeonies and tiger lilies, standing on the floor.

People cared! They actually cared enough to send all these sweet-smelling blooms. And there were the get well cards, too! She glanced idly through them. Some were from people she'd never heard of or couldn't remember, but it didn't matter. The point was they cared. Tears came to her eyes again. It was so nice to be loved.

Morgan had been in hospital for a week now and already she was beginning to rise up from the black pit that had swallowed her. At times she could even grab and hold on to moments that were filled with light and held a glimmer of hope. The doctor had told her she'd be well enough to leave in another ten days, providing she flew straight to her family in America and had a long vacation. The idea appealed to her. It would give her the chance to make friends with her family again, show them, perhaps, that she wasn't really the hard-boiled cookie they thought her to be.

Morgan had also come to the decision not to press Harry for a financial settlement. He had already offered her the house in Montpelier Square, which was worth in excess of half a million pounds, and the Rolls Royce. It was enough. And somehow, by not screwing him for all she could get, she began to feel better about herself. It was like a form of atonement, and what was money anyway? She was alone now, and some damned diamond tiara wasn't going to bring her happiness. Joe would probably be angry but it couldn't be helped. It had suddenly occurred to Morgan, during the long lonely days and nights in her hospital room, that it was *people* who counted! Why hadn't she thought of that before? She still had plenty of money in any case.

What she was short of right now was dreams.

And they couldn't be bought anyway.

Andrew Flanders wasn't sure whether he was pleased or horrified! Lavinia Lomond as a rich aunt was one thing – but as his *mother*? The shock settled on him like a hot prickly blanket, making him fidgety and uneasy. He found it almost impossible to accept the fact, and what was he supposed to do now? He'd made a point of worming his way into her favour, hoping to pick up all he could in the way of fancy little objets d'art, but now they'd be his anyway! Yet he couldn't exactly ditch her, just when she'd told him he was her son. Always highly acquisitive, although he had a large personal fortune, Andrew now reckoned he had it made. Especially when she added that Harry would never be able to have children. It meant that Drumnadrochit and everything that went with it would end up being his too! It was like his wildest dream coming true, and yet here he was, stuck with this domineering woman who wanted to run his life!

Finally, after much thought he came to three decisions.

First, he would move out and get a place of his own. He'd had enough of dancing attendance on her like some gigolo.

Second, he would join a health club and get himself fit. He was only three years older than Harry but he wasn't taking any chances. He *must* outlive his cousin.

Third, and this was the bit he was looking forward to most of all, he'd find himself a suitable wife and start a family. *He* needed heirs now!

The title might die out on Harry's death, but his beloved

Drumnadrochit Castle was good for another four hundred years, thanks to Morgan.

Without Sig Hoffman, Joe found himself working harder than ever, yet with renewed vigour. By the time his grandson was twenty-one, he vowed, Quadrant would be the leading finance house on Wall Street, a fitting legacy for David to inherit. He appointed a highly qualified accountant whose reputation was impeccable, to be the new financial adviser, and a highly sophisticated computer system was installed to guard against further loopholes in the system. The entire staff in the accounting department had also been replaced.

Never again would Joe risk Quadrant Inc. being put into disrepute.

Joe had another plan too. For all his sharpness he'd always played it legit and now he felt the need to make a final gesture to redeem the goodwill of Quadrant, which the scandal of Sig's imprisonment had pretty much dented.

Now was the moment, thought Joe, to pay back to society a little of what had been taken out.

He called his new financial adviser into his office one morning and briefly outlined his plan.

'I intend to start a charitable foundation to help drug addicts,' he announced. 'It will be called "The Quadrant Foundation" and it will be dedicated to the memory of my son, Zachary. These kids need help and I intend to see everything possible is done in terms of drug prevention, treatment and after-care. I want you to set the whole thing up for me and I want a press release issued to that effect. I'll get my wife to organize a benefit ball, and maybe in time we can set up a special clinic right here in New York. We'll need trustees, a committee and a medical advisory panel.' Joe paused for breath. 'Go to it. This foundation is top priority.'

When Joe was alone again he rose and went to look out of the office window. His beloved New York lay spread below him, ready to be conquered afresh.

Nothing would bring Zachary back now.

But at least it might help others; and it wouldn't hurt Quadrant's image either.

The Countess of FitzHammond had one big reservation about Elizabeth marrying Harry, and one evening as she and her husband were driving home from a dinner party, she decided she must voice her worries.

'Is it that they can't have children?' he asked sympathetically.

'No, it's not that, dear. I'm just so afraid that Lavinia is going to be bossy! She'll be running their lives if she has a chance, and that could wreck Elizabeth's happiness.'

'I wouldn't worry about it, m'dear. Elizabeth's just as tough as Morgan in her own way, you know. Remember how she kept Lavinia in her place? Morgan never stood for any nonsense.' The Earl chuckled at the memory of Morgan's dramatic announcement of being pregnant at the Lomonds' thirtieth anniversary party, and of how furious Lavinia had been when Morgan became the centre of attention.

'That's all very well, Cedric, but men never understand these things. Lavinia is a very domineering woman. She'll try and take over.'

The Earl permitted himself a silent laugh in the darkness of the Bentley. He had the power to put a stop to Lavinia's nonsense any time he wanted to. He patted his wife's plump hand.

'If there's any trouble, my dear,' he assured her, 'just leave her to me.'

Smoothing the soft folds of her long cream silk and lace wedding dress, Tiffany took a final look in the mirror. Cream flowers were woven into her blonde chignon and pearls gleamed at her throat, a present from Hunt. Then she picked up her bouquet of creamy flowers and held them close to her face. Looking back at her from the mirror was a young woman who looked happy and fulfilled. A woman who had come a long way.

Downstairs everyone was waiting for her in the flower-filled living room of Hunt's house, where in a few minutes the marriage ceremony would take place. Joe and Ruth were there with Morgan, a pale slim figure, much quieter and more subdued these days. And Greg, dear faithful Greg, with all their other friends from New York and Long Island and Hollywood.

Gloria gave a final adjustment to the train of Tiffany's dress, a broad grin spread across her usually placid face. Tiffany smiled back but there was a faraway look in her eyes. Hunt was waiting for her, too. With Gus and Matt, and little David. Her family.

Today the past could be forgotten.

Now there were only all the tomorrows to look forward to.